Arthur C Dresbach, Ada A. Dresbach

Young People's History of Illinois

From the Earliest Discoveries to the Present Time

Arthur C Dresbach, Ada A. Dresbach

Young People's History of Illinois
From the Earliest Discoveries to the Present Time

ISBN/EAN: 9783337326371

Printed in Europe, USA, Canada, Australia, Japan

Cover: Foto ©Andreas Hilbeck / pixelio.de

More available books at **www.hansebooks.com**

YOUNG PEOPLE'S
HISTORY OF ILLINOIS,

FROM THE EARLIEST DISCOVERIES TO THE PRESENT TIME,

CONTAINING, ALSO, A FULL DESCRIPTION OF THE

prehistoric mations,

TOGETHER WITH THEIR MANNERS AND CUSTOMS, AS WELL
AS THOSE OF THE

EARLY SETTLERS.

PRINCIPAL EVENTS, STORIES, AND BIOGRAPHIES, ARE ARRANGED IN
TOPIC FORM, FOR EASY REFERENCE, AND WRITTEN
TO INTEREST BOTH OLD AND YOUNG.

BY

ARTHUR C. DRESBACH,

ASSISTED BY HIS WIFE,

ADA A. DRESBACH.

CHICAGO:
HOME HISTORICAL SERIES.
1886.

PREFACE.

E purpose writing a brief history of Illinois that will cover a period of over two hundred years —from the first advent of Europeans among her primeval nations down to the present.

Of the prehistoric nations we shall recount the positive and theoretic knowledge of the origin, migrations and mode of living. We shall dwell upon the valuable discoveries made by the Jesuit missionaries. We shall follow the Kaskaskia, Cahokia and neighboring settlers through the early trials of wilderness life and note their mode of dwelling in friendly intercourse with the red men by whom they were surrounded. We shall treat the question, as to who were the rightful heirs—English or French —to Illinois soil, from a Western standpoint, allowing the reader to be the judge as to where the blame for the terrible butcheries, which we shall narrate in full, properly belong. In the Territorial Period we shall, of necessity, briefly sketch the history of Ohio, Indiana, Michigan and Wisconsin. In the State Period we shall arrange the history in Gubernatorial administrations, treating of the wars under sub-headings. Biographical sketches of Governors, discoverers and other distinguished individuals, together with thrilling and instructive stories somewhat distinct from a brief history, we shall insert at the last of periods or administrations.

We should be proud of our State and cherish her history. The world's experience is being our experience; yet who remains to tell the tale? We introduce this volume to fill a vacancy felt by the people in general and especially by the young whose storehouse of experience only goes back to the time when the great race had been run and the settlers began collecting the spoils of victory. The book itself, to the public, needs no introduction: suffice it to say, no other work similarly graded or arranged has yet been issued, that is within reach of the masses of the people; that contains statistics and narratives they desire, and that is easy of reference.

As to interest Illinois history is profoundly fascinating, unsurpassed even by the history of the United States of which she forms an important nucleus; yet, she has been robbed of justice by Eastern historians. When William Penn and followers were negotiating for satisfactory treaties with Indians in Pennsylvania, noble teachers were already instructing the primevals in their Western homes, and treaties for trade had been ratified. Before a white man trod the soil of Ohio or Kentucky, Illinois had a recorded history of one century. When the English began brooding over a plea to enter and explore lands west of the Alleghanies, five settlements of 150 families had been founded in the GARDEN OF AMERICA where schools, monasteries, churches and a valuable growing commerce had been established. When printing of books was in its infancy Illinois had published, to her credit, in London, England, a history that is often consulted and which may be seen in the State and the Chicago libraries.

In statesmanship Illinois has been unrivaled; in warfare her sons have been of the bravest; in biographical sketches her citizens have so caught the inspiration of active life that their sketches are of the most valuable. In every North American warfare, save local troubles, the heroic sons of Illinois were called upon for assistance, and in none have their efforts been paralleled by other States save in the American Revolution. Within her borders were found the noblest Indians ever met by Whites; also the most vicious whose bloody deeds stain the character of their race. Within her borders political questions have germinated—some have withered others taken root and flourished—while her politicians have often led those of the Nation. To Illinois history belongs the record of the growth and development of a world-renowned political division, whose industries are everywhere known and whose period of history extends through almost the entire period of United States history; to Illinois history belongs the record of a growth and development from the first invention to a rapid speed of the most complete net-work of railroads in the world; to Illinois history belongs the record of the marked rise of a great city—a city whose history is of the most tragical—her great conflagration, her political enthusiasm, her growing enterprise and her unhappy fate from the massacre at Fort Dearborn to the Anarchal riots; a city whose interests are gathering the wealthy, the enterprising and is gradually becoming the market center of the world.

Believing that there is a growing desire for a better knowledge of our State's history, that in the course of years its importance will require it in the curriculum of our common schools, that a home history is of the most consequence and that for the association of local events it is first necessary to understand and have access to a State history, we hope to give to the public, at a reasonable cost, a work filled with the most valuable statistics, at the same time simplified to interest even youth and so arranged as not to require the reading of volumes for the information sought.

In our researches we have carefully consulted over one hundred and twenty-five volumes in the Illinois State Library and the Chicago Public Library, while we have taken pains to be accurate in noting and comparing facts.　　**AUTHORS.**

CHICAGO, July 24, 1886.

CONTENTS

INTRODUCTION.

DISCOVERY PERIOD.

☞Appendix not indexed.

INTRODUCTION.

AMERICAN ABORIGINES.

HOW LONG AMERICA WAS SET-
TLED before the strange vessels, commanded by Columbus, hove in sight at
San Salvador, October 12, 1492, we are
unable to say. Probably it was inhabited
as early as the beginning of the Christian
era, and it is even possible that there were
people upon the continent long before
that period, though no records have yet
been found to prove positively that such
was the case.

The First Inhabitants of North
America built cities at least before the sixth century, A. D. These were after the pattern of Baby-
lon, Memphis and other admired cities of ancient
structure in the Old World. The buildings were
provided with towers, arches and pillars, while
the carving was neat and tasteful. What became
of this nation, or nations, is not known; they were
probably driven southward, and may have settled
in Peru where they began life anew; or, a conta-
gion or another nation may have destroyed them
entirely, leaving only a few ruins by which we can
gain but a faint idea of them.

The Second Race inhabiting North America, and perhaps the first of the present State of Illinois, was the Mound
Builders, a nation whose origin is as mysterious as its predeces-

sors, but whose positive existence has been distinctly marked by structures. Their peculiar works of art consist of mounds or embankments, distributed more numerously throughout the Valley of the Mississippi and Ohio rivers than in any other locality. Ohio alone contains 10,000 variously shaped figures of earth and stone, 1,500 of which are mounds. One in Adams County, of the same State, is almost one-half mile in length and represents a serpent, with mouth open, just uncoiling as if ready to make an attack. The design of the builders, generally, appears to have been to represent vicious animals. Most mounds are erected to a height of ten or twelve feet, upon the summit of which huge trees are now growing, demonstrating the theory of their antiquity and the habitation of the continent for many centuries.

Within a number of these mounds have been found human skeletons, also vases of earthenware, or copper, in elegant designs; pipe bowls decorated with images of human heads, resembling, possibly, people of that race—probably the owner; ornaments of great beauty to put upon the person; utensils to be used in and about the house; hatchets of stone and copper, mica, shell and obsidian. These must have been arranged as burial places for the dead, with whom were interred articles used by them and offerings made by friends. The embankments were doubtless thrown up as places of defense, often enclosing large areas which contain traces of ruined cities. One in Arkansas bounds just one square mile. Often mounds are arranged in symmetrical figures encompassing from twenty to fifty acres. Within some enclosures cisterns are found.

These people lived not as the savages found in Illinois but in settled communities, cultivating the soil. Their descendants, if any exist, are unknown for all traces of their identity have entirely disappeared.

Third Race.—The inhabitants found in America by Columbus and other early explorers were probably the third race which took the place of the first and second by gradually moving from the regions farther north and mingling with those already upon the soil; thus forming the distinction between those of the United States and those of Mexico. When Cortez, a Spanish adventurer, entered the latter country he found it inhabited by a semi-civilized people. Montezuma, **The Great King,** sat upon his throne in all the splendor of a European monarch, surrounded by his sportsmen and scholars. Feasts were given, at which the beautiful women assembled in their gayest costumes. The people believed in a future state and cited legends telling of a time when water covered all the land, but their ideas were crude, coinciding in but few instances with the barbarian beliefs of the Old World. Offering sacrifice was common among them as with the children of Israel in the time of Moses, but their cannibal characteristics led them to the sacrifice of human beings captured in war. After these victims had been offered upon the summit of a temple in sight of a multitude and the throbbing hearts hung before the god within, the flesh was devoured in sumptuous feasts where dancing and rejoicing were in order. When Cortez conquered this people he found them in possession of ornaments of the richest gold and precious stones which they said came from the northwest, no doubt referring to California; he also learned that the people once lived farther north. It therefore appears that tribes arrived in America at different times and came from the regions of Behring Strait.

Central America and Peru were likewise inhabited by people who built houses and lived in communities where business was carried on in the form of barter. In the latter country was the great empire of the Incas who worshiped the sun. The origin of this people is like that of all Pagan nations, all history being shrouded by traditions. The most common legend of their civilization is, that at one time all the world was in barbarism; the people worshiped almost everything they saw; made war a pastime; devoured the flesh of the captives, whom they preferred capturing alive. The sun, the great being that gave light to all the world, grew sad at such a spectacle, took compassion upon their degraded condition, united his children, Manco Capac and Mama Ocello Huaco, in marriage, and sent them to the earth to teach the people farming, weaving and other arts of peace. They gathered the natives together in assemblies who listened with a willing ear to messages from Heaven. As they congregated in great number the city of Cuzco was founded which grew to be very large. Children were instructed by parents and they in turn improved upon what they already knew; thus learned to make beautiful garments and raise large crops of maize.

When a ruler died his funeral was celebrated with great pomp and solemnity. The bowels were taken from the body and deposited in the temple of Tampu near Cuzco. With these his jewelry was buried and a numbar of his attendants and concubines, amounting if popular, to a thousand persons. A season of general mourning would then be observed all over the land, at times causing the weak minded to become insane.

The bodies of the Incas were embalmed with as much perfection as those of Egypt, and were taken to the Royal Sanctuary, where they were arranged in lines, seated upon golden chairs. The building was brilliantly illuminated by a great light to imitate the sun. Queens were on one side and kings on the other; each in an upright position with the head inclined forward and hands crossed upon the lap. Here a king could see his ancestors almost as if they were living. He regarded them as having certain living traits. On occasion of certain festivals these sacred bodies were taken from their sanctuary and removed to the public square of Cuzco where rich feasts were spread while gold, silver and diamonds were displayed in profusion. The dead were given the most prominent positions and were addressed as if living; after which they were again returned to their resting place with ceremony. When one of the nobility "was called home to the mansion of his father, the sun," his house and property were closed forever and were not inherited by his posterity, each having to start anew in life. This being the custom of the royal family other classes followed the practice.

Indians of the United States lived in a savage state. In place of stone houses tents were used to suit the shifting disposition of a lazy lord. These humble structures were made of bark, grass, maize and hides of animals, requiring no time, skill nor ingenuity in their mechanism. No roads nor bridges were constructed, for he followed the foot-paths of comrades or of animals. His sole ambition leading him upon the war path, or in search of game, he took no delight in tilling the soil and believed such work to be fit only for woman. Brutal to his wife he compelled her and his daughters to occupy the coldest and hardest beds while he, with all the majesty of a lord slept in state. Hence, while her lord roamed the wilds in sport or war, she, by the use of simple tools, cultivated her little field of maize. Laws, there were none; treaties were seldom kept, the sachem (chief) directing most of the plans of operation. Corresponding to Peruvian and Mexican priests were the "Medicine men," who dressed in costumes to represent hideous animals. These men were believed to have supernatural power, whose authority the other members of a tribe would not dare to disobey. These tribes believed in a Great Spirit that was all powerful and of a supreme existence. They feared a subordinate one, whose nature was evil doing to mankind. They believed the good spirit needed no prayer to induce him to watch over them, but that it was necessary to continually noticed the evil one. They looked forward to a future state where they could be happy with plenty of game and good fishing, besides they could dwell together in perfect peace.

Several tribes entertained the idea, that to enter the "happy hunting-grounds" they would be compelled to walk an edged tool over a deep abyss. If wicked they would fall into the regions of the Evil Spirit, where they would toil and be whipped by the master who knew all they had ever done. The soul, they believed, remained in the grave for a while after death: thus several tribes deposited food with the body at the time of burial and at stated intervals thereafter, until it was in an advanced state of decomposition. Dakota Indians enclosed their dead in skins and hung them in trees, and for the soul's subsistence during the supposed long journey to the future state, placed vessels of food by the aerial sepulchre.

The Indians of Illinois prided themselves in painting their faces and arms fantastically, wearing in the hair, feathers, and upon the person, ornaments. Endurance of torture without an indication of pain was a pastime amusement; they practiced dexterously the use of the bow and arrow; their tomahawks were made of stone and this sharpened weapon they used to cut the hair and flesh from the head. A natural thirst for blood and scalps seemed to be bred in several tribes that freqented Illinois soil. Often victims were scalped before dead. The

Kickapoos, Illinois, Miamis, Pottawatomies, Shawnees, Sacs and Foxes, and Winnebagoes all inhabited the present State of Illinois since its discovery. The Illinois composed five tribes—Kaskaskias, Cahokias, Tamaroas, Peorias and Metchegames, the latter living west of the Mississippi River.

THE ILLINOIS were the more peaceful and sympathetic. This nation was reduced by wars, generally by Iroquois of the East, Siouxs on the northwest or Kickapoos and Sacs and Foxes on the north, until, in 1800, they numbered but thirty able warriors. These took up a new home in Indian Territory in 1872, enumerating but forty in all.

MASCOTINE AND KICKAPOO are two names for the same tribe. A hostile disposition to the Whites manifested itself for 150 years. In 1612 Champlain found them near Saginaw Bay; in 1669, Allouez visited them near the mouth of Fox River. This tribe lost over a thousand able men in 1712, in attempting to reduce the fort at Detroit. Large villages stood at Danville and Bloomington, in Indiana near Logansport and Lafayette, also along the Embarras and Kaskaskia rivers. They were removed to reservations across the Mississippi soon after the War of 1812.

THE POTTAWATOMIES, Chippewas and Ottawas were originally one nation, but became widely separated in after years. The Indian signification for Pottawatomy is "we are building a fire." This tribe was first found by the French on an island in upper Lake Michigan and afterward between it and Green Bay. An early attachment was formed for the Whites, but later they became prejudiced against them and proved to be the main perpetrators of the horrible massacre at Fort Dearborn (Chicago). Pottawatomies were the last to leave for the West; those of Illinois departed in 1836.

THE SACS AND FOXES came from Canada where Black Hawk says his grandmother, Thunder, had been placed by the Great Spirit. After coming West this tribe carried on hostilities with other tribes until Governor Wm. H. Harrison put a stop to their ravages. In 1832 Black Hawk and his followers, two-thirds of the tribe, thought to regain their lands east of the Mississippi River, which they had sold, and declared war against the settlers. He was defeated, captured and punished.

THE MIAMIS formerly lived beyond the Mississippi River, but immigrated eastward as far as the center of Ohio. Becoming enraged at the French, about the middle of the eighteenth century, they ever after retained an enmity for that nationality. One tribe, that resided in Illinois, never faltered in their friendship to the Whites. The capital was at Ft. Wayne, Indiana.

THE WINNEBAGOES, noted for their bravery, fought desperately in the battle of Tippecanoe. They also threatened war against the Whites in 1827, and a portion joined Black Hawk in 1832, but the main body remained with their good chief, Nawcaw. They inhabited Illinois and by treaty at Fort Armstrong (Rock Island) they ceded all their lands in the State to the United States, September 15, 1832.

Indian Birthplace, as a race, will probably never be known. The strongest arguments offered by historians point to China as being the mother country. As America is nearer Asia than any other portion of the early settled globe, it is no mere supposition that its prehistoric nations came from that country. Chinese vessels sailed along the continent of Eastern Asia for thousands of miles beyond any settlements and it is within the bounds of reason to suppose that these vessels reached the opposite shores of Behring Strait, which is but twenty-eight miles wide and has several small island. Vessels may have coasted along these strange shores and the mariner found the climate pleasant, and fit for the residence of man. If such be true, the colonization fever may have brought a tribe to America. It is even more than probable that tribes arrived at different times as the indications are of three different races inhabiting the United States centuries apart. The first building houses, the second earthworks and the latter tents.

AMERICA DISCOVERED AND SETTLED BY EUROPEANS.

Mysteries.—One of the greatest mysteries to Europeans, at an early date, and especially to navigators, was the endless oceans surrounding the lands known to them. Curiosity being excited bold theories were advanced as to the limit of these mighty bodies of water. The numberless stories, often repeated, all tended to increase the dread of voyaging beyond known islands, lest vessels

might be carried by wind and wave so far that a return would
be impossible, or, a still worse calamity, be driven by storm over
an awful abyss beyond.   The imagination was not slow in the
mystified people, and they vaguely pictured regions of goblins
and hideous monsters.   A few bold seamen and an equipment
of vessels were needed to confirm or confute these ideas, for a
man had placed himself before the people ready to solve the
perplexing question; a man whose mind soared above the idea that
our earth had ends and sides.

Christopher Columbus not only believed the earth to
be round but offered to risk his life in defense of his theory.   He
said by sailing westward he could reach the eastern shores of Asia,
believing the Atlantic and Pacific oceans to be one broad expanse of water. His belief was both ridiculed and considered. As
he claimed that by sailing westward but a few leagues he could
reach land, a fleet was secretly sent out to test the short route to
Asia as he proposed, but it returned pronouncing the project a
failure.   Columbus could not yet willingly give up his theory
and with much difficulty persuaded the crown of Spain, Ferdi-
nand and Isabella, to furnish him an equipment of vessels and
men and set sail, reaching land October 12, 1492.   The voyage
proved his theory as to the shape of the earth but the discovery of
another continent was infinitely more glorious than his ambition
had pictured, hoping only to shorten the route to Eastern Asia.
Other vessels immediately hastened forward from Spain, also
from other nations.

Other Discoveries soon followed.   A great eagerness
prevailed in Europe to learn more about the New World and
to gain in it territory.   Many vessels began plowing the
broad Atlantic in search of suitable localities to trade with Indians and mine gold.   The exploration fever subsided with the
following results:

THE SPANIARDS had examined the coast along the Gulf of
Mexico on all sides: DeSoto had traversed the Southern
States, penetrating more than 200 miles inland; Cortez had
conquered Mexico and Pizarro Peru.   Settlements were made
in Florida and New Mexico before Illinois was discovered.

THE FRENCH sent out vessels also, which sailed farther north.

Cartier passed through the Gulf of St. Lawrence, up the river of the same name and visited a thriving Indian town upon the site of Montreal. In 1608 Champlain established a trading post at the present site of Quebec. This region, called New France, became rapidly settled.

THE ENGLISH explored the Atlantic coast of North America much of its length; hence claimed Virginia, a boundless territory reaching westward. Settlements were made by them near the Potomac River and in the New England and Middle States.

THE DUTCH also settled New York but gave up their territory in 1664, thus leaving the English, French and Spanish as claimants of North America.

Settlements had been made before the discovery of Illinois in Delaware, New Jersey, Connecticut, Massachusetts, Maryland, the Carolinas, New Hampshire, Virginia, New York, Rhode Island, Maine and Florida.

THE SUBJECT OF THIS WORK shall be our next topic, the history of which divides itself into four distinct periods; viz., Discovery Period, extending from 1670, the discovery by Perrot, to 1682, the settlement at Kaskaskia; Settlement Period, from 1682, the settlement of Kaskaskia, to 1787, when the Northwest Territory was organized; Territorial Period, from 1787, the organization of the Northwest Territory, to 1818, the admission of Illinois to the Union; State Period, from the admission of Illinois as a State to the present time.

STORY.

Montezuma and His People lived in Mexico. This race is known to have inhabited that region between 1200 and 1519 when the Spaniards arrived. This nation, known as Aztecs, was barbarous but in advance of the other tribes of North America. Hieroglyphics were used quite extensively, and by them they reckoned events accurately. They kept a calendar year and divided it into eighteen months of twenty days each, adding five days to the last to make out the 365. They cultivated the land, introduced maize and cotton; built roads, erected large monuments to the dead, and built temples and cities, their ruins remaining to this day, telling of the race that early inhabited that country.

They knew how to fuse metals, cut and polish the hardest stones, fabricate earthenware and weave garments. They believed in a supreme, invisible creator of all things, the ruler of the universe. Under this supreme being stood thirteen chiefs and 200 inferior divinities, all of whom they worshiped, setting apart a day for each god. The leading god, the Mexican Mars, was the more sacred, and to him were built temples in every town. These were their largest structures, were nicely furnished and contained rich ornaments of gold and precious stone.

Cortez, who was the first white to visit them, gives to the world the best account of Aztec life. He was a bad man. Coming from Spain in search of wealth, he learned that this people had golden idols, golden furniture, golden palaces and sparkling diamonds. Of these he wanted to rob them, pretending to be a friend. His army of a few hundred men was met by an army of as many hundred-thousand of the great Montezuma Empire, but he never failed to put it to flight.

When Cortez drew near the capital Montezuma decided to give up his empire, saying the time had now arrived, according to traditional prophecy, that the ruler from where the sun arose should come and claim his country. He therefore called his casiques together and said: "You have been faithful vassals of mine during the many years that I have sat upon the throne of my fathers. I now expect that you will show me this act of obedience by acknowledging the great king beyond the waters to be your lord also, and that you will pay tribute in the same manner as you have hitherto done me." Great tears were then flowing down his cheeks and his voice was choked with emotion. His nobles did not yield to his request, seeing that his heart was not in the decision, and it was not until three-fourths of the populace were killed, starved or subjected to pestilence by this murderous band of Spaniards that the country was subjugated. Thus the nation was lost forever.

When Montezuma admitted the Spaniards to the city and before the nobles began organizing for war they visited the temple where a sight met their eyes more sickening than their own barbarities. Upon a platform stood a large image with broad face, wide mouth and terrible eyes. He was covered with golden serpents; on his neck, fitting ornaments, were the faces of men wrought in silver and their hearts in gold. Close by were braziers and incense, and on these braziers hung three hearts of men who had been sacrificed the day before. The smell was like that of a lion's den. To supply offerings to this god, war was waged upon neighboring tribes and victims were captured rather than scalped, as was the practice of their Northern brothers.

Certain feast days were observed at which gayly dressed women assembled with all the dignity of a French court, the greater feast day being to the war god. Prisoners were provided with all the luxuries of an Indian life after captivity, that they might be well fatted. Upon the gala day they were brought forth one by one, taken to the summit of the temple and laid upon an altar before their slayer. A keen knife was drawn over the chest, the heart torn from its enclosure and hastily conveyed below to be hung before the god for whom sacrifice was made. Bodies were then sliced, cooked and the feast spread. During the year preceding the Spanish entrance, their records show that 20,000 had met their fate in this way.

Aztecs were a social, kindhearted people when on friendly terms and always respected a superior in intellect, from whom they were eager to obtain knowledge.

DISCOVERY PERIOD.

EARLY EXPLORERS.

FRENCH MISSIONARIES in the seventeenth century were resolute workers and came to America to seek and to save souls among the Indians. The headquarters for their missions were at Montreal where a cathedral was built and a school established. Thither others of France flocked, some devoting their attention to teaching, some to trading, while others consecrated their exclusive time to the welfare of the Red Man.

Catholic priests, called Jesuit Missionaries, early penetrated westward as far as safety would permit, at the same time allow a speedy return at almost any moment. They traversed the regions of the Great Lakes and established missions in various localities. All these did much good and gained popularity with traders who soon followed. Lovable natures, tender words and honest intentions can soften even the heart of a savage and the good these devoted men did can never be questioned.

Discovery.—Among the missionaries who journeyed hundreds of miles beyond the most distant points reached by Englishmen was Father Allouez. Impatient and anxious to learn more of the condition of the inhabitants, he had traversed much of the lake region and made inquiry about the tribes beyond. In 1667 he learned of the Illinois Indians whom he greatly desired to visit, and it is said that he penetrated southward through Wisconsin, reaching the north-west boundary of the present State in search of the " Mesasippi " (Great River).

On returning he conceived the propriety of holding a great peace conference on Green Bay for the purpose of uniting the tribes of the West and getting a permit to visit them. For' this purpose he sent Nicholas Perrot to the site of the present city of Chicago to invite a tribe in that region to the meeting. Perrot arrived at this now busy spot in the fall of 1670 and was proba-bly the first white man to set his foot upon Illinois soil. As no written description was given nor maps drawn, and as the dis-coverer did not penetrate into the State, but little importance is attached to the event.   .

MARQUETTE AND JOLIET.

The First Explorers of Illinois were Marquette and Joliet; the former a Jesuit priest, the latter a French trader. They were desirous of visiting the Indians along the Mississippi and the river bearing the same name as the tribe. Accordingly these two gentlemen joined company, procured men and, May 13, 1673, left Mackinaw for the mouth of Fox River, which they ascended as far as possible, when they shouldered their ca-noes and scanty supplies and carried them to the Wisconsin, but four miles distant. In talking over the long journey before them the guides lost courage and, believing the stories they had heard of the huge monsters inhabiting the banks of the stream farther south and of the dangerous whirlpools, they refused to accompany the expedition any farther, trembling at the idea of any mortal undertaking such a hazardous trip. After bidding the Indians a friendly farewell and thanking them for their kind warnings and information, Marquette and his party glided slow-ly down the untried stream.

The spectacle before them was indeed a beautiful one. The broad stream was almost without a ripple, while the soft breeze kissed their faces and occasionally stroked their hair; on either bank were the vine clad hills and nature's forests alive with sing-

ing birds whose notes broke the monotonous stillness of the valley; upon the prairies beyond the graceful deer were feeding,
now and anon raising their heads as if their confidence in perfect peace were weak even in their beautiful pastures where all
nature seemed to unite for the promotion of their welfare. Such
scenes led them to think of the beauties they were yet to behold;
of the great river they hoped to explore.

THE MISSISSIPPI.—June 17, 1673, their curiosity was dispelled,
for before them lay the long-talked-of stream. The color of
the water betokened far off regions different from any they had
yet seen and they determined that this land, too, should be united to New France and belong to the crown of the mother country forever. The indications were that it had once been a larger stream than as they beheld it. The channel wound through
a valley, probably two miles wide, bounded by bluffs that had
the appearance of having formerly been its banks. "Where
does this river originate and into what does it flow?" was eagerly asked. "We will find out," said Marquette, "but we must
not forget our mission, the souls of the Red men of the forest."
Their bark moved out upon the stream. On every turn in its
course the men gazed forward as far as their eyes could reach,
but only to rest them upon bluffs. They watched the banks for
human beings with whom they desired to mingle, purchase supplies and gain a full description of the country through which
they were passing, in order to complete a map of the newly discovered territory. The presence of savages to the early settler
was a horror but to the explorer it was regarded as a benefit.

THE ILLINOIS.—Their careful search was rewarded, when a
hundred miles below the present northern boundary of the State,
by the sight of footprints which told them they were near inhabitants. Carefully securing their canoes by fastening them
to trees, they ascended the bank and followed a path through
the forest. They soon discovered a village of happy Indians
whom they approached with open hands and friendly hearts.
Four elder Indians advanced to meet them. We would do great
injustice to the men of the forest if we were to accuse them of
acting in the least selfish toward their white visitors. The
men were conducted to the town where they enjoyed the fullest

confidence of their hosts. They were presented to the chief
with all the dignity of an introduction to a higher officer in a
civilized nation. He questioned them regarding their countrymen of the East and assured them of an everlasting friendship.
He presented the peace pipe and thereupon, that bright June
morn, Frenchmen smoked with the Illinois Indians whom
early traders and missionaries had longed to visit. It was
urged upon them to visit another village where the Great
Chief of the Illinois resided, and as they journeyed thither, many
followed, gazing upon the priestly costumes and watching their
graceful movements as compared to their own rude manners.
Their visit was announced to the "Great Chief" who sat in his
large tent surrounded by dignitaries of the tribe. The French
told him of their journey westward to visit the tribes along the
Great River, talked about the power of their ruler in Canada
and of his subduing Iroquois and other Eastern tribes. Western
nations were glad to hear of the conquest of this nation, whom
they feared because of power and skill in warfare, as taught them
by Englishmen. This increased the warmth of the reception. He
said that their presence added flavor to his tobacco, made rivers
calmer, the sky more serene and the earth itself more beautiful;
besides gave encouragement for a happy and peaceful future.

A FEAST.—The chief ordered a feast to be spread before the
strangers and as the party had journeyed for many days in a
wilderness on scanty food, the well-prepared repast of hominy,
fish, deer, buffalo and dog's meat was indulged in with relish.

Upon benches arranged in a semi-circle the guests were seated
and conversed freely with the hospitable hosts. Servants busied
themselves bringing the smoking morsel and, after cooling by
blowing their breaths upon it, sometimes tasting to make sure
of not burning, placed the food into the hungry mouths.

OTHER DISCOVERIES.—Endeavors were made to persuade
the French of dangers in continuing farther down the river,
fearing they would form treaties with other tribes along the
route, thus depriving them of a full advantage in trading;
also give to others a protection proffered them. Finding persuasion impossible they gathered about the French to the number of 700 or 750, in military array, and formed a complimentary

escort to the river. After a kind farewell they watched the boats until they vanished from view down the stream.

Illinois River did not then receive their attention but upon reaching the Missouri they were puzzled. Here poured forth another large stream of muddy water in a strong current, bearing trees and other rubbish. Its source must be in an unknown land. Soon after passing the Ohio they saw another tribe upon the banks, beckoning for them to land. Again they were treated kindly, but made to believe it would only require ten days to reach the mouth of the river.

HOSTILE INDIANS—Some days after, on nearing Arkansas River, their attention was again called to the bank by a party of Indians in a hostile attitude and who put out in boats as if to capture them. At once the French realized their danger and were on the verge of destruction when chiefs appeared, directed them to land and commanded the braves to be patient. The chiefs conducted the party to camp and listened to their story attentively. They kept them over night, giving them their best bunks. In the morning they were allowed to depart and amid friendly demonstrations, besides messengers had been sent ten miles below to apprise the Guachoya tribe, in whose territory DeSoto died 130 years before, of the arrival of Frenchmen. Here, the following day, July 2, they were again highly reverenced, though in the midst of a most barbarous tribe. Men wore no clothing and women only girded themselves with animal skins. Food was of the coarsest quality and such as only a brute or savage would enjoy feasting upon. These dishes arrived before the visitors in almost countless numbers, and not to have partaken of them would have been an insult to their hosts. Notwithstanding the unpleasant surroundings, upon finding an Indian that could speak the Illinois tongue, Marquette proclaimed to them his doctrine of the Christian faith and told them of the God above, who witnesses all that is said and done. This they received in astonishment which, together with the information about Canada, led them to consider the French a great people and to wonder at their knowledge.

At this juncture the party questioned the propriety of continuing farther south. They feared Spaniards, whom they learned

were somewhere near, even more than Indians and, July 17,
departed for the Illinois, having been on the river nearly five
weeks. When nearing Illinois Marquette became ill and lingered some days before being able to resume his journey homeward. They learned that by going up Illinois River they could
reach Lake Michigan by a shorter and easier route. In so doing
they were able to add to the map more interior and give a better
description of the finest prairie country of the globe. Several
tribes were visited as they passed through the State, among them
the friendly Kaskaskias who proffered the service of guides to
the lake.

Marquette remained at the mission on Green Bay and Joliet
hastened to Canada with the maps and papers describing the
expedition. Misfortunes increase as we near the end. When
at the rapids above Montreal, and within a few miles of its destination, the boat capsized. All documents together with two
men found a watery grave, and Joliet barely escaped being
also drowned. He, however, told his story which caused all
Canada to rejoice, and the news, in glowing colors, conveyed to
France. Marquette returned to Illinois to establish a mission at
Kaskaskia, departing from Mackinaw with two companions,
October 25, 1674. He sailed down Lake Michigan to Chicago
River, upon the banks of which he took hemorrhage and died
before reaching the missions again. Joliet never returned.

LA SALLE, TONTI AND HENNEPIN.

New France.—In their early discoveries and settlements
Frenchmen had confined themselves to more northern regions
and especially along St. Lawrence River. All territory in America belonging by right of discovery, had been christened New
France and began enlarging to unlimited boundary. Of this
Couracelles was Governor until 1672, when Frontenac, a bold
General, succeeded him. Governor Frontenac was a kind-hearted,
liberal man. He desired to improve and increase the French
domain and welcomed to his audience persons with plans for
pushing farther westward.

La Salle, a young man not yet thirty years old, had gained
the favor of Governor Frontenac by his good demeanor and

prudent plans for western colonization. The Iroquois Indians of New York were at war with the western tribes and as the former were trading with the English, La Salle argued that the latter should be secured as allies of the French. He became enthusiastic upon the subject and in 1673 erected a fort at the head of Lake Ontario near the source of St. Lawrence River and named it Frontenac in honor of his friend, the Governor. At that time French settlers were forbidden the erection of like defences but the plans of La Salle were in accordance with the better judgment of leading officials; thus nothing was done in opposition and the fort was allowed to stand. He visited France the following year (1674) to secure aid from the king in establishing missions and trading posts throughout the country beyond the Great Lakes, but his projects were defeated by persons secretly plotting against him. For several years he was a disappointed man.

Preparations for the West.—In 1678 La Salle again visited France with new plans, new arguments and a better knowledge of the broad field stretching westward, which he laid before the king. His ideas were approved and he was given a company of thirty men, among whom were skilled tradesmen and hardy laborers; a good store of tools for the building of vessels and forts; and supplies in the shape of blankets, provisions, and trinkets with which to trade with the Indians. By a liberal expenditure of his own money, together with this outfit, he was well equipped for the enterprise. Upon St. Lawrence River he erected a vessel to carry supplies and trade between Fort Frontenac and Niagara Falls. The boat was of 10-ton burden, contained a deck and departed on its first trip Nov. 17, 1678. At Niagara the erection of a fort was begun, but owing to hostilities of Seneca Indians of that lacality, incited by personal enemies, only a store house for shelter was completed. Another vessel was ordered built to sail from Niagara Falls to the western extremity of the lakes. About the time all material was in readiness La Salle was called to Montreal where he was detained by conspirators trying to destroy his reputation and credit by circulating false stories.

He had brought with him on his return from France an Ital-

ian, Henri Tonti, who had lost a hand in the Sicilian wars, but
a noble and trustworthy young man. He was of great value in
this undertaking because of his firm, reliable disposition and was
well qualified to carry out the plans of his senior in office. To
him was entrusted the building of the vessel above Niagara Falls
and which was afterward known as the Griffin. Material for
this boat was carried a distance of twelve miles, up rocky
heights, to a point above the cataract, where it was deposited
and work commenced. Before it was completed a band of Senecas set it on fire but it was only partially consumed before the
flames were extinguished. All damages were repaired and a
few days after the return of La Salle it was finished, presenting
a beautiful appearance. It was mounted with five cannons
pointed through port holes. Upon the prow was the carving of
an animal partially resembling an eagle and partially resembling
a lion. This peculiar looking figure amazed the Senecas who
regarded it with awe.

The First Vessel upon the Great Lakes beyond
Niagara was the Griffin, launched August 7, 1679, in the presence of almost the entire tribe of Senecas. Cannons were fired
as she spread her sails to the breeze and she smoothly glided
westward toward the Land of the Illinois. Her sails shone at a
great distance and as she sped across Lake Erie savages stood
upon the shores, gazing in wonder at the strange spectacle.
Her course was directed to the Jesuit settlement on the Strait of
Mackinaw. Here the crew landed and returned thanks for
their safe deliverance, for they had encountered severe storms,
especially upon Lake Huron.

Difficulties.—Arrests.—Before the expedition started, fifteen men had been ordered to Lake Michigan with merchandise to trade with the Indians, directed to take all furs received
to the Illinois tribes where they were to remain until the commander could arrive with his men upon the boat. Instead of
carrying out these plans some of the party sold their furs and
joined other traders. Information of this perfidy was gained
by La Salle when he arrived at Mackinaw. He at once proceeded to arrest the offenders, four of whom he captured without much difficulty and two others were taken by Tonti at the

Straits of St. Mary. This was a bold move as the traders at Mackinaw mission were jealous of him, fearing he would take from them honors that they themselves wished to enjoy. The Indians were also incited against him, yet his daring, forward manner prevented any from laying hands on him or carrying out plans for assassination.

Immediately after Tonti's return the party with "boat fort," as the Indians termed the Griffin, sailed into Lake Michigan. They visited a small island in Green Bay where they met a few more of the fifteen traders that had been sent West before them. These had been faithful to their commander, having collected large stores of furs and deposited them in a safe place until the proprietor's arrival. It afforded a happy moment for a dark hour. Much money had been expended and no income derived to satisfy creditors who already began to complain. To make amends and insure future loans the Griffin was laden with a cargo sufficient to make La Salle a rich man. It was in the middle of September and the danger of sailing a vessel, especially a frail one, was great, yet nothing could change the orders. Parting salutes were fired from the vessel as she bade adieu to the West.

DANGERS UPON LAKE MICHIGAN.—La Salle and his men departed for the mouth of St. Joseph River, Michigan, where Tonti and men had promised to arrive, coming overland. They were now in small boats upon turbulent Lake Michigan threatened with destruction. Often the little barks were on the point of sinking, but, through desperate exertions of the men, water would be bailed out before exposed to another dip. Gales blew on several occasions for two days before abating, rendering it impossible for them to eat their saturated food, or land amid bounding breakers for fresh supplies.

TROUBLE WITH INDIANS.—At one landing indications of aborigines were visible though none put in an appearance until one of the number shot a bear. The report was heard by a band of hunters who followed the men to camp. They waited until nightfall, then crept to the beach where the valuables had been stored, and carried off several articles. However, a dusky form was seen sneaking near and an alarm given. When it became evident that they had been discovered they made apologies, saying they were only trying to discover if the party were friends or foes, and desired to smoke the calumet of peace. It was not until they had departed that the theft was discovered; then, taking a few men, La Salle started in pursuit. Two warriors were captured but one was released to carry a message to his chief, stating that the stolen goods should at once be returned or the captive would be put to death. As part of the articles had been lost on the way it was impossible to return all, so the chief determined to re-capture the prisoner. La Salle drew up his little band upon an eminence where no rock nor tree afforded shelter for the savages and awaited the attack. It was evident to the Indians that they could not reach their adversaries with arrows without exposing themselves to the deadly fire of the rifles. Father Hennepin was then sent to them, clothed in his priestly gown, when they proposed to return what goods they could and pay for the others. Thus the affair terminated satisfactorily.

SCARCITY OF FOOD.—On landing at St. Joseph River the hearts of the little company failed them. They wanted to push forward to the Illinois tribes to procure corn for the approaching winter, that locality having lately been visited by famine; but La Salle could not agree to this, for he had sent Tonti another route and he, with his men, had not yet arrived. In order, largely, to keep his men in good spirits he apprised them of the importance of a fort at the point where the Griffin was to return, now St. Joseph, and set them to work in its construction, contrary to their wishes. However it served as a barrier to despondency, though the delay caused great suffering for want of food and proper shelter at that season.

On the expiration of twenty days a portion of Tonti's men arrived without food nor merchandise, but sore and tired. By December 3, 1679, all had arrived. Without completing the fort, named Miami in honor of Indians near by, this small band of French explorers and traders, numbering in all thirty-three persons, set out for the great hunting grounds of the Illinois although winter had already stripped the forests of green foliage and begun forming ice upon rivers.

LA SALLE LOST.—The route taken was up St. Joseph

River to the site of South Bend, Indiana, thence by land to the headwaters of Kankakee River. With the company was a Mohegan hunter, for a guide, who also helped to supply them with meat. As he was out hunting, La Salle undertook to find the path leading from one river to the other without awaiting his return. He started boldly into the forest but, becoming bewildered, lost the directions and could not find his way back. Encountering a swamp, he endeavored to make its circuit and reach camp, but evening came on, thus frustrating his design. By firing his gun he aroused an Indian who had built a fire and had cuddled down beside it. He called in several dialects, but the poor fellow was evidently frightened and fled. On coming up to the spot a nice bed of grass dexterously arranged and yet warm lay before him. He took full possession and was soon wrapped in deep slumbers. In the morning he resumed his journey and reached camp in safety, carrying two opossums which he had killed with a club. During his absence Tonti and his men had engaged in a diligent search for him and it was with much joy that they welcomed his arrival.

Land of the Illinois.—The journey was resumed the day following La Salle's return and, Dec. 12, 1679, they first beheld the present State of Illinois, their course being along Kankakee and Illinois rivers. During this interval of twenty-one days, their encouragements alternated with discouragements. When the Mohegan hunter returned he was not laden with game; on the contrary had been wholly unsuccessful. They had been out of meat for some time and the men were growing weak and faint. Their spirits were only kept up by the grandeur of the country spread before them. Here a cliff studded with rocks and shrubbery, sometimes rising to a considerable height; there a level prairie stretching away toward the horizon, upon which could be seen, in the distance, animals for the chase—large buffalo, tender deer and savage bear, any of which they would have devoured with a keen relish; while on every hand lay unmistakable signs of a country rich in facilities if the proper means were employed to improve upon these gifts of nature. La Salle, too, had a monopoly on buffalo skins, as none but he could ship them. At times they could see, as far as the eye could reach, camp fires burning brightly and forms about them cooking and devouring what they themselves so much desired, fresh meat with a flavor they knew would even satisfy the appetite of King Louis. At one time they found a huge buffalo bull mired in snow and mud, struggling to escape. He was killed and with the united force of twelve men and the use of pulleys was extricated from his prison. The flesh was sliced and served them for food several days.

Father Hennepin Hears Mass.—Out in the wilderness, hundreds of miles from civilized people, they did not forget their Maker, but on January 1, 1680, landed and heard mass. Though the day was as cold as Illinois winters usually get, they bowed reverently to their God and with thankful hearts arose, wishing each other a happy new year. Father Hennepin, a Jesuit priest and then typical of Father Marquette, conducted services and after mass gave a lengthy talk, especially impressing upon them the importance of keeping together, dwelling upon the bravery required to endure the hardships of wilds by which they were completely surrounded. He spoke of honors to be conferred upon them upon their return to France; but overlooked the thought of reverence to be paid them by future generations, and how much their kind acts would be treasured as historical gems.

Welcome.—The first sign of inhabitants of the country was a deserted village near the present town of Rock Port, La Salle County, where they arrived December 26, 1679. Here a principal city of the Illinois stood as a summer residence but its inhabitants had evidently migrated to a different locality. Corn was found secreted in a cave. To this they helped themselves, taking in all fifty bushels, in hope of finding the owners and amply rewarding them.

January 3, 1680, they reached the expansion of Illinois River, now known as Peoria Lake, and shortly afterward beheld smoke rising from the forests below, knowing themselves to be in presence of human beings. An Indian village was pitched just south of the lake and was surrounded by snow-covered hills. At this little village, immediately where Peoria now stands, La Salle landed. By his tact and straightforward manner, he secured kind treatment after allaying the fright of the inhabitants at the strange, warlike appearance of his band. After presenting the calumet of peace the men were taken within tents and were even caressed, while a rich feast was being prepared. When the meal was ready, servants fed the party from their hands, placing within the mouths bit after bit. Others took off their shoes, washed their feet and annointed the soles with bear's oil. As may be imagined this warm reception was heartily appreciated by the French. La Salle immediately entered into negotiations to establish a trading post at this point and erect a fort. This privilege was at first denied him, but upon telling them he would pass on down the river and trade with Osage Indians, as he had offered to do with them, the requests were granted from the fact that they were jealous of that tribe; also they believed the French might prove a benefit to their future prosperity in buying furs and assisting them to prevent an Iroquois invasion.

Rebellion.—Up to this time, although La Salle's task had been wearisome and his journey beset by dangers, he had generally been prosperous: he had pushed forward into a wilderness 1,500 miles beyond any settlements; he had examined the country, erected forts and gained the friendship of many savage tribes. Now fortune seemed to frown upon all his undertakings: his men were almost exhausted and appeared utterly disgusted with the expedition; they doubted that any good would result from this, to them, aimless wandering in the wilderness, cut off from all friends, surrounded by savages and exposed to hunger and cold. Finally this dissatisfaction grew to open murmurs against their leader whom they condemned as a foolish adventurer.

La Salle perceived that discontent had sprung up which might result in mischief if not at once quelled, that a storm was impending and must be calmed. He went into their midst and assuring them of his good intentions and the certainty of ultimate success; he pointed them to the prospect of glory and of wealth; he reminded them of the success of Spaniards in Mexico and Peru, but they were not to be appeased. A doubt was expressed that they would ever receive any reward for such protracted slavery, misery and indigence other than hardships, starvation and an unknown grave; they asked what could be expected as the result of a ramble, almost to the confines of the earth, but to be obliged to return poorer and more miserable than ever; they said the only means of avoiding the impending calamity was to return while they had sufficient strength for the journey. They proposed to abandon La Salle to his laborious and useless discoveries, as they termed them, but feared that he, by his intelligence and influence, would find means of apprehending and punishing them as deserters; besides it was impossible to proceed without provisions or resources of any kind. It was then suggested to cut up the tree by the roots—to end their misery by the death of its author. They finally determined to incite the Indians against him, hoping to reap the advantage to be derived from his murder without actually appearing to have participated in the crime.

The intriguers approached the Indians with false stories; telling them that La Salle had entered into negotiations with the Iroquois, their greatest enemies, who would descend upon them in mighty hosts. This story was generally believed. La Salle, discovering that something was wrong among his hosts by their expressions and lack of trust, inquired into and learned the cause of the fresh trouble. He assured them of the impossibility of his being in league with a tribe at so great a distance. His manner quieted them and their suspicions were lulled for the time.

This peace was of short duration. An emissary had been secretly sent from a neighboring tribe, the Mascoutins, to the Illinois to stir them up against La Salle and his party. By great art he almost convinced them that this man was in alliance with the Iroquois, and well nigh succeeded in his efforts to induce them to destroy the whole band, his story tallying with the one previously circulated by the disaffected among their own company. The suspicions which La Salle, by his candor and address, had allayed were revived and the chiefs spent the night in deliberation. In the morning all the delusory hopes he had entertained, on the apparent return of confidence, were dispelled. He perceived the cold reserve of the chiefs, the ill-concealed distrust and indignation of all, but his endeavors to discover the immediate cause of the change were unsuccessful and he began to think of the propriety of intrenching his party in a fortification.

Alarmed and surprised, unable to remain in suspense, he boldly advanced into the midst of the Indians, gathered here and there in groups, and, speaking their language sufficiently well to be understood, he demanded the cause of the coolness and distrust visible upon their brows. He said, " Last evening we parted in peace and friendship; today I find you armed and some of you ready to fall upon me. I stand here in your midst, unarmed and alone, a willing sacrifice to your vengeance if I can be convicted of any designs against you."

Moved by his open and undaunted demeanor, the Indians pointed to the deputy of the Mascoutins who, they said, had been sent to apprise them of schemes and connections with their enemies. Rushing fearlessly toward him, La Salle demanded his evidence or reason for this alleged plot. The Mascoutin coldly replied, that in circumstances where the safety of a nation was concerned full evidence was not always required to convict suspicious characters; that the slightest circumstances often justified precautions, and that he considered it his duty to remove all possibility of harm from his friends.

La Salle finally gave sufficient assurance of his honest intentions, lack of hostile designs against them and the utter impossibility of any connection with the Iroquois. A good understanding with this tribe was at length restored and his own men became so far reconciled that they agreed to remain at the fort on duty. Notwithstanding, they were still inclined to defeat the object of further expeditions, at one time venturing so far as to attempt the destruction of leaders by putting poison in the food.

Fort Crevecœur (Broken Hearted).—Seeing all other plans fail to induce La Salle and his followers to abandon an expedition down the Illinois River, thence exploring the Mississippi from its source to its mouth, as previously planned, the chiefs invented fabulous stories of the great river. They described dangerous whirlpools, huge serpents and fierce animals of monstrous size that infested its waters and its banks. To these stories La Salle gave no credit, but his men, generally, believed them and gave vent to fear of journeying into a region so inhabited. Several had already deserted and as fear was entertained of others leaving, also being wearied by difficulties, La

Salle abandoned his expedition for some time and determined
upon the erection of a fort at the foot of the lake. The position was a favorable one being in the center of a thickly populated locality where there were seventeen flourishing Indian
villages. The work did not progress very rapidly but was completed in February, 1680, to which date Peoria may properly
date her history and Illinois her first fort. The site was about
two hundred yards from the lake between two ravines, and the
structure was formed by throwing up dirt to a considerable
height, then surrounding it by palisades at least twenty-five feet
high. La Salle at this juncture was despondent and named it
Crevecœur, a French word meaning broken hearted. He had
received no word from the Griffin on which he expected material for another boat to sail upon Illinois and Mississippi rivers;
his men were rebellious; his fortune gone. Thus ended his
first expedition.

Separation.—La Salle firmly believed that he was on the
right course to discover a short route to India and that the Mississippi emptied its waters into the South Sea (Pacific Ocean).
If true, he reasoned, they could transport pelts to that country
and obtain articles of value for trading with the savages. These
bright prospects were sufficient to strengthen him. He desired
to visit Fort Frontenac to learn of the fate of the Griffin, and if
lost to replace it by another. He also concluded to send a party
with Father Hennepin up the Mississippi; but the Indians were
still hostile to further western explorations. He saw the propriety of leaving his men in perfect contentment and of having
friendly relations restored between them and the Red Men. In
this he was greatly puzzled until an incident occurred that enabled him to become master of the situation. While out hunting, one cold, dismal day, they chanced to fall in with a young
Indian returning from a war journey. The poor fellow being
faint and weary, the party took him to camp and gave him re-
freshments. They questioned him regarding the West, the rivers, the forests and the hunting grounds. As he had heard
nothing of the plans of the chiefs who told the fabulous stories,
he revealed all that he knew of the country. Presents were
given him in return for a pledge of secrecy concerning the in-

terview and allowed to return. When he had departed, La Salle, with six men, set out for the Indian camp to proclaim to the chiefs his knowledge of the West and of the "Great River." They were feasting upon bear's meat at the time, but without ceremony he boldly confronted them and told the news he had received from the Master of Life, besides accusing them of falsehood—charging them with what he himself was guilty of on this inteview. The chiefs were astounded at his knowledge and confessed their guilt. By way of apology they said they wanted the French to remain with them and did not wish them to mingle with other tribes. This was a happy circumstance. Setting his men to building another vessel and sending Father Hennepin with a few of the bravest on an expedition up Mississippi River, he arranged to return East. Two days after Hennepin's departure, La Salle, with the Mohegan hunter and four men departed March 2, 1680, up the stream for Lake Michigan. Spring had not yet opened out the rivers nor melted the snow from off the land, yet they pushed forward. While ascending the river he fell in company with several Indians, one of whom was the leading chief of the Illinois tribes. With him he made peace on easy terms by telling the good-natured old fellow that he was on his way East to procure arms to defend them against Iroquois, a then dreaded foe. This chief agreed to send food to the men in the fort and to see that they were well cared for. La Salle had carefully examined a high rocky eminence, known afterward as Starved Rock, and directed Tonti, who had been left in charge of erecting a new boat, to fortify it if possible.

The First Chapel was built of logs at Fort Crevecœur immediately after La Salle's departure for the East and by his instructions. Father Gabriel Ribourdi and Father Membre were left with Tonti to instruct the savages and convert them to their faith. The reverend gentlemen worked diligently, but upon learning more of savage life saw more of depraved humanity than they had ever anticipated, became disheartened and discouraged, but their good influence was unbounded.

Bad News.—After the middle of March, La Salle and party arrived at the present site of Joliet, where they left the stream and traversed by land to Lake Michigan, following the course of the Chicago River for some distance and to its mouth where busy Chicago now stands. They then journeyed around the shores of the lake to St. Joseph River, reaching it on the 24th. Let no one pronounce himself victor until the conflict is ended. The fort was reached but only reached to learn that nothing had been heard of the Griffin. What could be the trouble? True, he knew not whom to call friend in this wilderness, where homesickness and savagery only seemed to exist. Here he met men he had sent to ascertain the fate of his missing vessel. He directed these men to report to Tonti while he with his party journeyed across the present State of Michigan to Lake Erie where they launched a canoe and in all haste sped to Niagara only to learn more sad news. A cargo of merchandise belonging to him, valued at $400, had been lost by the sinking of a vessel in the Gulf of St. Lawrence.

We find everywhere a class of persons sanguine in hope, bold in speculation, always pressing forward; besides, they are quick to discern the imperfections that exist, while disposed to think lightly of the risks and inconveniences which attend advancement. This was the disposition of La Salle, Columbus and John Smith. Each had difficulties to surmount—they were followed and surrounded by bands of men that clung with fondness to what was ancient, even though they were in a new land. They feared the western wilds, though convinced by overpowering argument that the sooner they established trading posts therein the better for the mother country and for themselves, but consented to no advance only with misgivings and forbodings. La Salle learned at Frontenac that his creditors had seized upon his goods and that he was almost penniless in a new land strange to him and his countrymen. He pushed on to Montreal where, by his indefatigable efforts, with a will equal to almost any emergency, a supply of goods and fresh men were procured at the expense of friends and the Government. In haste he returned to Frontenac, but there met messengers with intelligence of fresh trouble in Illinois and other Western points.

War in Illinois.—TONTI WITH THE INDIANS.—Scarcely had La Salle passed out of sight and Tonti had taken command of the remaining men than the heartless wretches rebelled against their commander. They destroyed the boat in progress, burned the fort, seized all valuables and left Tonti with seven followers in the wilderness and at the mercy of treacherous Indians. Two of the men were sent, post-haste, to inform La Salle of what had taken place. The remaining articles were gathered together and taken to an Indian camp for safe-keeping while the men were to employ themselves in hunting and exploring until the return of their master.

ATTACK BY THE IROQUOIS.—The Iroquois Indians of New York had learned from the settlers in the Colonies and from British traders, with whom they were on friendly terms, much of the arts of war. Being powerful and selling a portion of their lands in New York and Pennsylvania, they began pushing westward for more territory. Already they had conquered the Eries and destroyed the Hurons, while the Miamis had been persuaded to join them in an attack upon the Illinois tribes; thus a force was organized that could completely annihilate them. The attack was to be a surprise but a friendly Indian, who had been visiting in Illinois, met the army, his countrymen, on their western march. He hastened back and apprised them of their danger. The tribes flew to arms. Women began gathering together the camp material for safe-keeping while men applied the war paint and joined in the dance to encourage the timid who were fearful of the coming contest.

TONTI WOUNDED.—The lives of Tonti and his men were now in peril. La Salle being in the East, rumor soon spread that he was with the Iroquois, guiding them to the West—in fact the messenger declared he saw him leading the hosts, mistaking the chief who was partially clothed in European costume. Thus they believed Tonti and his band were acting as spies to inform the enemy of their position and true condition. Tonti could not speak their language fluently, furthermore they would not listen to his pleadings but looked upon him with a suspicious eye. As the alarm was given only one day before the Iroquois arrived preparations for battle were made hastily. In the evening a company of warriors gathered about Tonti and his comrades demanding their lives. This was pressing them hard. Nothing could appease their wrath but a faithful promise to enter

into the fight with them, and this only secured a postponement
of their probable fate until after the battle. The return of
scouts at all hours of the night kept the camp in utter confusion.
In the morning intelligence was received of the near approach
of the foe and the warriors sallied forth, September 11, 1680.

As the enemy far outnumbered the Illinois, Tonti took it upon himself to attempt a negotiation of peace and advanced with
a belt of wampum. The enemy, supposing that he was an Indian, endeavored to kill him. He received a number of severe
wounds, one, a stab near the heart that gave him great pain.
When their mistake was discovered he was taken to the rear
and attended by the Indian doctors who carefully dressed his
wounds and gave him medicine. He told the chiefs that the
Illinois were under the protection of the French; that there
were 1,200 warriors, beside sixty French ready to assist when
called upon. This story frightened the Iroquois and they sent
Tonti to make peace. Taking advantage of this turn of affairs
the Illinois retired across the river. The Iroquois, however, remained in the neighborhood, encircling the Illinois camp on various pretenses as occasion presented.

It became evident that the only safety was in flight and the
sooner the better. Accordingly, when the Iroquois were at sufficient distance, the village was fired and its fugitives escaped
down the river, leaving the enemy in undisputed possession of
the field. When its truth was revealed to the Iroquois as to the
number of their adversaries, they fell upon Tonti demanding an
explanation of the matter. This was difficult, but by various
artifices he succeeded in satisfying them for the time: however,
the following day he and his party were ordered to leave the
territory.

MASSACRE.—The Illinois divided into many small bands and
departed from their country, save a party of Tamaroas, who believed that the Iroquois's plan was only to occupy these rich
hunting grounds and that no harm would befall them: hence
remained at the mouth of Illinois River. A band of 700 warriors
fell upon them. Men fled leaving helpless women and children
in the hands of their blood-thirsty assailants, who tortured them
at the burning stake, with scalping-knives and tomahawks, and in

all ways that savage cruelty could devise.

THE FRENCH ESCAPE.—As nothing more could be done to avert the savage warfare, the little French band started up the river, but the boats were leaky and they landed for repairs. During this delay they witnessed the most savage brutality that man could imagine. No wonder their blood curdled at the thought of their situation. The grave yard was visited by the Iroquois and hundreds of bodies exhumed to destroy the future state of the dead. Their hatred was so intense that, at times, they ate the putrefied flesh. While awaiting repairs the French party was reduced to four by the murder of a friar, Father Gabriel Ribourde, who was out viewing the beauties of the country and praying earnestly to his Maker, when he was scalped by a band of Kickapoos in search of Iroquois scalps. The old man was never again seen but the fact was afterward learned when his scalp was exhibited in the Indian camp.

Tonti and his men pushed on up the river without making any more discoveries of note, their object being to reach the Pottawatomies, a friendly tribe in the vicinity of Green Bay, Wisconsin. Their march was perilous and impeded by sickness. Tonti himself was attaked with a fever and was unable to make further progress for some weeks. December was fast approaching before they reached Green Bay. Here they were hospitably entertained. The chief frequently asserted that there were but three great generals—himself, Tonti and La Salle.

La Salle Returns West with twenty-three French and thirty-one Indians, departing from Frontenac, August 10, 1680, and was accompanied by La Forest. They traversed by way of the lakes, to the mouth of St. Joseph River; sailed up that stream to the site of South Bend, Indiana; crossed over to the Kankakee and thence to Illinois River. Our prairies were clothed in their green garb while all was joy and mirth. At times they encountered vast herds of buffalo, and laid up a quantity of meat for future use, which, with other supplies, they fancied would please the lonely Tonti and his companions. On approaching the site of the village where they had left the Illinois Indians in all their glory, they were surprised and disappointed. Nothing was left to tell the story, save the exhumed bodies which the buzzard by day and the wolf by night were greedily devouring. Standing upon poles driven into the ground were human skulls, and where tents had once stood the ground was covered with ashes—no crops to grace the fields, no storehouse of supplies. This told the story in part. What had become of their friends? Had the whole Indian tribe, so lately inhabiting these lands, become extinct?

Three of their number hid among rocks for a few days while La Salle and the four remaining men, who had not been left at trading posts along the way, rowed on down the stream to ascertain the fate of those in whom they were much interested. Before reaching the river's mouth they passed the scene of the previously described carnage. Half charred bodies of women and children were yet standing by stakes but it was evident that the men had fled almost instantly, as no dead bodies were found to tell the tale of their bravery in defending the helpless. Here no trace of Tonti and his men could be discovered. Being near the Mississippi they pushed on and for the first time La Salle beheld that mighty stream. The men were eager to explore it but their leader thought too much of his brave General to give up his search and would not yield to their requests. Returning by rowing night and day they soon reached settlements, the Illinois having returned in their absence. A few men were left to rebuild Fort Crevecœur, while La Salle and the remainder continued their journey up the stream. They left marks along the way to indicate to their friends the path they had taken, but none had been left to tell them of the whereabouts of their missing companions.

Return to Fort Miami.—On the afternoon of January 6, 1681, a small hut was discovered by the party in search of Tonti, on Kankakee River, a short distance above its juncture with the Des Plaines. This led them to believe that something could be learned at Fort Miami at the mouth of Joseph River. Thither they hastened journeying through snow that drenched them to their armpits, all in anxiety to get the expected news; but on their arrival they were disappointed, for no tidings had been received.

Plans for Confederation.—While at Fort Miami La

Salle met fugitives from King Philip's war of the East, who desired to join him and his Indian allies. As trouble began brooding between the French and English in matters of trading, and as Iroquois were hostile to the Illinois, it occurred to La Salle that it would be a good plan to form a confederation of these fugitives, the Miamis and Illinois. To strengthen this confederation he thought it best to unite the different nations within one region. Of a better location than the land of the Illinois he did not know and whether or not these tribes would consent to a union he had not learned. He remained in Michigan but a few days and returned to Illinois. Traveling was yet difficult although the spring sun would effect an occasional thaw. On reaching the Kankakee the leader and two of his men became snow-blind and could not proceed further until sight was recovered. During this delay a band of Foxes, hunting in their neighborhood, told of Frenchmen that put La Salle on track of both Tonti and Hennepin. On arriving among the Illinois he laid his plans before them. The tribes were in sore need of allies and were so rejoiced at his project that they prepared a grand feast and supplied him with provision. The only difficulty now lay in effecting an alliance with the Miamis.

La Salle resolved to again visit Miami towns while La Forest went to Mackinaw. On approaching the principal village he encountered Iroquois whom he bitterly rebuked for their actions in Illinois. They were ashamed of their conduct and slunk away during the night to avoid meeting him again, while Miamis were astounded at the power of his will. This was a favorable circumstance and the next day he completed an alliance amid shouting and great rejoicing. He then set out for Canada where he arranged plans accordingly and returned by water in canoes. It was on a still November day when he approached Fort Miami, which he discerned at some distance, as the autumn leaves had fallen. Columns of smoke arising from the forest told of a recruited colony awaiting his return. When he landed he was received with shouts of exultation, being hailed as chief. Selecting a few of his braves he proceeded to the mouth of Illinois River, traveling most of the distance by means of sledges, where he arrived February 6, 1682.

Father Hennepin's Expedition up the Mississippi River was a success as to its designs. Though Marquette had paddled in a canoe along a portion of this stream, he had left much yet to be examined before a complete map of the great river of New France could be drawn. The party descended the Illinois River in perfect security and were ascending the Mississippi, near the Wisconsin, when a band of Sioux Indians surprised them and took them prisoners, April 11, 1680, conducting the explorers over the route they wished to journey, but as prisoners. Though in the hands and at the mercy of a brutal enemy the men were delighted with nature's gifts about them. Here they were in the midst of a mighty stream, flowing in a wide channel between rocky heights studded with shrubbery and mounted occasionally by fertile soil. The ascent of these cliffs would often reveal rich prairies upon whose broad expanse large herds of buffalo were feeding. These scenes they witnessed for hundreds of miles.

They named the falls of the Mississippi, now almost in the heart of Minneapolis, St. Anthony. Upon this famous spot, now occupied by the largest flouring-mills of the world and where the stream is girded by bridges, the party lingered for some days. While detained with the Siouxs, Hennepin occupied his time in studying their language and teaching them his few simple medical remedies. Early in 1681 he and his two companions were permitted to return to their countrymen, traveling by way of the Mississippi, Wisconsin and Fox rivers to Green Bay thence to Quebec where Hennepin embarked for France.

The Lower Mississippi was the next object of La Salle's attention. He awaited about two weeks at its confluence with the Illinois for the spring freshets to subside, then departed for the South. The main object of this expedition being to discover the mouth, they landed but few times either to examine the country or learn of its natives. They, however, visited the Natches Indians and were apprised of customs similar to those of the Aztecs of Mexico. Proceeding on down the river, examining only a few of the larger tributaries, he reached the Gulf, April 6, 1682, and completed his explorations upon the " Father of Waters " from St. Anthony Falls to the Gulf of Mexico.

Though Spain had taken possession 143 years previous and claimed the region by right of De Soto's discovery, La Salle returned to a suitable spot, landed and took possession in the name of France uttering the following harangue:

"In the name of the most high, mighty, invisible and victorious Prince Louis the Great, by the grace of God, King of France and Navarre, fourteenth of that name, I, this 9th day of April, 1682, in virtue of the commission of his Majesty, which I hold in my hand, and which may be seen by all whom it may concern, have taken, and now do take, in the name of his Majesty and of his successors to the crown, possession of this country of Louisiana, the seas, harbors, ports, bays, adjacent straits, and all the nations, peoples, provinces, cities, towns, villages, mines, minerals, fisheries, streams and rivers, comprised in the limits of the said Louisiana."

The name was given to this vast country by La Salle in honor of Louis XIV, king of France. When the ceremony had ceased a volley of musketry rent the air while every voice joined in shouts of joy, and the little party prepared to return to Illinois.

At different times in the ascent their progress was impeded by hostile Indians, who had heard of the Whites taking possession of lands in the East and were fearful lest they, too, should be molested and despoiled of their hunting-grounds. La Salle fell sick on the way and remained for some time at a small fort he had built in the descent of the river. The news was sent to Membre who departed for France to proclaim the result of this expedition. La Salle felt that his presence was almost indispensable in New France as his men could not be depended upon and the Iroquois were yet hostile.

Conspirators began doing effective work as the influence of La Salle spread throughout the West. He had gathered over 20,000 Indians around his banners, among whom missionaries were laboring faithfully while peace and harmony reigned supreme. The English traders did not approve of French missions and posts in these regions for they had heard Illinois favorably mentioned. La Salle and Governor Frontenac had enemies both in France and New France that were more reluctant than wise. During the progress of the Lower Mississippi expedition

Frontenac was removed from office (1682) and superseded by De La Barre, an enemy to La Salle and all that was progressive. He began from the first of his administration to oppose the former plans and withholding aid in a time of necessity. La Salle was poorly equipped and now an expedition was being planned by the Iroquois against his allies. Not only did La Barre withhold ammunition, arms and other supplies but kept messengers sent him, as prisoners. After La Salle returned from the South he ordered Fort St. Louis built upon the height afteward known as Starved Rock, which became the headquarters for his confederation. This rock is situated eight miles below Ottawa, on Illinois River. Further improvement was deemed unnecessary until word could be received from the Governor. The following was taken from La Salle's last letter to him:

"The Iroquois are again invading the country. Last year the Miamis were so alarmed by them that they abandoned their towns and fled, but on my return they came back, and have been induced to settle with the Illinois at Fort St. Louis. The Iroquois have lately murdered some families of their nation and they are all in terror again. I am afraid they will take flight and so prevent the Missouris and neighboring tribes from coming to settle at [Fort] St. Louis, as they are about to do. Some of the Hurons and French tell the Miamis that I am keeping them here for the Iroquois to destroy. I pray that you will let me hear from you, that I may give these people some assurances of protection before they are destroyed in my sight. Do not suffer my men who have come down to the settlements to be longer prevented from returning. * * * * But Monsieur it is in vain that we risk our lives here, and that I exhaust means in order to fulfill the intentions of his Majesty, if all my measures are crossed in the settlements below, and if those who go down to bring munitions, without which we cannot defend ourselves, are detained, under pretext trumped up for the occasion. If I am prevented from bringing up men and supplies, as I am allowed to do by the permit of Count Frontenac, then my patent from the king is useless. * * * I have only twenty men, with scarcely 100 pounds of powder, and I cannot long hold the country without more."

This letter, as others, was never answered. La Barre was jealous and wrote to the King, stating that La Salle had never made the discoveries he reported and was lavishly spending fortunes on useless forts and expeditions.

La Salle Recalled.—The letters containing falsities, written by La Barre, of this great and magnanimous man caused his ruin. The king ordered him to return to France in early spring (1683). When the news reached Fort Frontenac all his goods were seized and an officer sent post-haste to take command of Fort St. Louis, of which Tonti had charge. The officer chanced to be a kind-hearted man and, contrary to orders from La Barre, allowed him and his men to remain at the fort, with certain liberal privileges in hunting and exploring expeditions. La Salle immediately embarked for France to answer charges against him.

La Salle's Last Voyage and Death.—On his arrival in France he was received with warmer favor than he had anticipated and was given an audience by the King. He succeeded in convincing the ruler that he had received false reports of him; also, that his plans were unquestionable. He was again commissioned to return to the New World.

In August, 1684, he set sail with 280 colonists to found a settlement at the mouth of Mississippi River. On the way he and his Captain disagreed as to the course they should take, though it was afterward found that La Salle had been right; but contrary to his directions they were carried about 800 miles too far west. As their discussions grew to anger, each wanting his way, and the Captain being an enemy to him from the first, the party was landed out in the wilds of Texas with scant ammunition and provision. As the Indians were hostile it was thought best to erect a fort. Reconnoitering parties sallied forth in every direction to ascertain their location, but without avail. The men grew disobedient, causing dissensions. Bitter feelings became so intense that secret plots were laid against their commander. Finally one of the leaders of a hunting expedition was killed and the body hidden. La Salle, attracted by buzzards flying about, was making his way to the spot when attacked and slain, January, 1687. Thus perished a man who had pushed his discoveries to such an extent that his efforts were only surpassed by those of Columbus.

Tonti learned from people in the East of La Salle's arrival in the South and, upon hearing no news of him, sent a body of men southward. Though inquiries were made far and wide no intelligence was received of the new-comers. However, a few men were stationed at the mouth of Arkansas River to learn, if possible, of their whereabouts.

The assassins made their way to Fort St. Louis and informed Tonti that he was in Texas, well and hearty. They presented a forged order for a large amount of fur which they took with them, sold for money and clothing, and departed for France. They were finally imprisoned but regarding their execution our histories are silent.

The spots visited by La Salle and his comrades, which were sacred to him are sacred to the people to-day. Little did he dream of the future city at the foot of Lake Peoria; at the mouth of Chicago River; at a short distance below the mouth of the Missouri; at the Falls of St. Anthony and a few miles below, and upon the spot where he took possession of the vast Territory of Louisiana. Illinois not only owes a namesake but a monument to the enterprising La Salle.

STORIES.

Indian Torture.—At the same time that La Salle discovered the Niagara Falls, with McGalinee and men, he went southward into what is now New York State and visited the Seneca Indians. They were treated as friends and given comfortable apartments in one of the larger tents.

On the evening of their arrival a party of warriors returned from the valley of the Scioto River where they had captured a young man of the Shawnee tribe. He was treated kindly but kept as a captive and confined in a tent adjoining that occupied by the French party.

Shortly afterward three women entered, began heaping evil epithets upon him and threatening him with death. This conduct was alternated with bitter weeping. On inquiry concerning the difficulty, the French learned that the older squaw was the mother of a young man who had been killed, and that according to custom the captive had been given her by the captors to place in the stead of her son, upon whom she was allowed to have revenge; if she chose to have him tortured her request would be granted. She had decided upon the latter, selecting the following morning for the execution.

This savage custom was too brutal for kind-hearted Frenchmen and they set about to dissuade the Indians from their intentions, but all in vain; they offered to purchase the man and use him for a guide but he could not be bought; they said it had always been a custom of their fathers and this they dared not abandon.

Early the next morning two Indians came hurriedly into the Frenchmen's tent as messengers stating that the ceremony would soon begin. They again endeavored to save the Shawnee from a horrible death pronounced upon him, a death he fully realized as he, too, had probably often participated in like amusements. Upon sight of the French the poor fellow begged piteously for them to save him. Once more a sum was offered for his release but the offers seemed to enrage the cannibals and the torture began.

He was tied to a tree and a fire kindled near by, in which lay an iron rod heated red hot. When all preparations were complete one of the largest and most solemn dignitaries of his tribe advanced with the red-hot iron and first touched it to the captive's foot, then slowly moved it up his leg, burning an unsightly track in the ascent. The screams of the sufferer seemed to arouse the bystanders who rent the air with shouts and danced for joy. The iron was thus drawn over all parts of his body, though care appears to have been taken not to touch any vital part that the torture might last the longer. This continued for six hours and as the last vestige of life was ebbing away the victim was struck with a rock and his savage torturers fell upon him, cutting off different members—one the head, another a limb, others pieces of flesh until the body was completely annihilated. These bits were cooked and eaten as the most delicious food, some of which they offered their visitors saying that human flesh was the best meat in the world.

When evening came the entire tribe turned out with clubs, beating tents and yelling vociferously to drive away the dead man's spirit. La Salle and party becoming alarmed at these demon-strations, also noticing some signs of ill-will among their hosts, became fearful of next falling victims to savage customs and accordingly took their departure the following morning.

The Illinois Give to Marquette and Joliet a Formal Reception.—"A trail," uttered by one awoke the quiet occupants of small birch-bark canoes as they glided slowly down with the strong Mississippi current. Just what they hoped to find! Boats were paddled to shore and the party landed to examine it. Surely there must be a powerful tribe near by, they said, and a visit was planned; the men being left in charge of the boats while Marquette and Joliet undertook the dangerous journey. A trail was followed for six miles where they beheld by the side of a beautiful meadow a group of wig-wams with all the surroundings of an Indian village. Beyond this village, in the distance, they beheld another but more thickly populated.

After bowing reverently and commending themselves in prayer to their God, they suddenly emerged from their hiding place in open view to the Indians, shouting loud and long. This threw the nearer village into a commotion and after a brief conference, during which time the missionaries were in anxious suspense, four aged men advanced toward them. No one uttered a word as they approached but each held a large peace-pipe which he kept swinging as a token of friendly intentions. When these men came near enough the following dialogue was begun by Mar-quette, dressed in a long black gown as when performing priestly ceremonies:

"To what nation do you belong?"

"We are Illinois and have brought you our pipes to smoke. We also invite you to our village where all await you and we can all enjoy the day together."

The six then proceeded together to the village. Here were two Frenchmen 600 miles from Whites that could render them assistance if necessary; unarmed and helpless in the midst of savages never before visited by Europeans. But these tribes had heard of the "Black Gowns," as Indians usually called the priests, and from the first believed Marquette to be one. They looked to him as a teacher who would instruct them as they had done others at the missions and posts farther east. These villages were on the west bank of the Mississippi, near its junction with the Des Moines. They learned from their escorts that the nearer town was called **Pe-ow-a-sea** and the other Moing-we-na.

As was a custom among Indians of these regions, to show that no weapons had been secreted about the person, one stood in the door of a larger tent, where the leading chief dwelt, entirely naked. He was pointing to the sun and said:

" How beautiful the sun shines, O Frenchmen, when you come to visit us! All our people welcome you, and you shall enter our homes in peace." The men were then presented to the chief to whom they addressed their mission and who responded: " I thank thee, Blackgown, and thee also," pointing to Joliet, " for coming to visit us. Never has the earth been so beautiful and never has the sun shone so brightly upon us as to-day. Never has our river been so calm and free from rocks. Your canoes have swept them away. Never has our tobacco had so fine a flavor, nor our corn so promising as we see it to-day, now that you are with us. Here is my son," giving to the Frenchmen a little boy whom they had captured from another tribe and one the chief had adopted. " I give him to you that you may know our hearts. I implore you to take pity upon me and all my followers. You know the Great Spirit who has made us all. Ask him to give life and come and dwell among us that we may know him." At the time he presented the little boy he also presented a peace-pipe and said: " This is the sacred calumet. Wherever you bear it, it signifies peace. All our tribes will respect it and it will protect you from harm."

They then visited the other village where they met with a similar reception and the great feast was spread. That night they slept secure in the wigwams of the Illinois.

Adopted by Indians.—At two o'clock, April 11, 1680, when rowing up the Mississippi near the mouth of the Wisconsin, the exploring party, consisting of Father Hennepin, Michael Ako and Anthony Auguelle, espied thirty large bark canoes filled with savages, evidently on a warring expedition, near them rounding a bend in the river. It was too late to escape. As soon as the warriors discovered them they raised a tremendous shout and pushed forward with great speed.

Father Hennepin stood erect in his boat and waved the calumet of peace, but was not heeded. They surrounded the helpless band, seized the peace-pipe and drew the boat ashore amid deafening yells. Contrary to most other tribes, these Indians refused to treat with the Frenchmen and the anxiety became great. The two leading chiefs conferred together, while younger warriors demanded their lives. Thus they parleyed until Hennepin seized an axe and advanced into their midst, presenting it to the chiefs and indicating by signs that they might kill him if they wished. This act caused a feeling of admiration in the savage breast.

The band proved to be of the Sioux tribe from the Upper Mississippi. When thirty miles south of the falls (Minneapolis) a decision was made. The men were to be adopted by chiefs who had lost children and their goods were divided. This journey proved long and tedious, the destination being 150 miles above the falls. When near this point the men were separated, chiefs with whom they were to live residing at different villages. Father Hennepin's new father was met by five of his wives in canoes when about three miles from home. Hennepin was presented as a son and the children were told to call him brother.

Father Hennepin was so exhausted that he could not rise from the ground without assistance. The chief ordered that he should be taken through a peculiar course of medical treatment. He was carried into a hut similar to "dug-outs" of western prairies, the top and sides being covered with skins. By use of hot stones its temperature had been raised to almost oven heat. Four medical attendants surrounded him, spatting and rubbing his flesh until a perspiration flowed in great drops, at the same time yelling vehemently to drive out the evil spirits. This was kept up, at intervals, for two weeks when he had regained his former strength although living in a large one-roomed wigwam filled with the wives and children of the chief.

During this captivity these self-installed parents feared their children would escape and guarded them very closely. Hennepin more than the others amused his chief by various artifices, and when visited by his friends he always brought forward his newly adopted son to show what he could do. Father Hennepin had paper and ink with him and whenever he heard a new word wrote it down and in conversation referred to his paper. This was mysterious to the simple-minded savages who thought the Great Spirit told him the meaning of their words.

BIOGRAPHICAL.

Jacques Marquette was a man of rare accomplishments, good in purpose, strong in character and full-hearted in all he undertook. Deaf to the din of theological controversy, hid from assemblies of prejudiced pretended Christian workers, we have a few faithful ones who seek, in remote quarters, a retirement to labor, not for honor or riches but for elevating the human race.

Jacques Marquette was born in France in 1637, of wealthy parents. He was given a careful training and developed an interest in books. At the age of seventeen he resolved to abandon the world of riches and rank to enter the ministry in the Catholic faith, and at the age of nineteen began teaching, following the profession twelve years, when elected to the priesthood. He came to America in 1666 and began his labors almost immediately after his arrival, September 20. His first efforts were among the Hurons and Ottawas, then among tribes upon the western border of New France. His exertions were appreciated and in 1671 he built a chapel on Mackinaw Strait. The next year he wrote to friends at Montreal of his success and said " Ready to seek new nations toward the South Sea [Pacific Ocean] who are still unknown to us, and to teach them of our great God." The Indians to whom he referred were those of Illinois who, he had learned, inhabited the Mississippi regions. He desired to be the first Frenchman to behold this mighty stream, and longed to be the first missionary among the barbarous tribes inhabiting its banks. It was not difficult for him to get permission to take this trip, for Allouez and others had long been advocating the idea of pushing farther westward.

During his stay in America he labored faithfully in his one grand purpose—to convert the savages. Not a single account has ever been written of his once wavering in his work.

His first trip to Illinois served him only as an introduction.
When about to begin his work and while on the second expedition, sailing down Lake Michigan, the exposure to storms and
damp autumnal winds were more than his frail constitution could
bear and he was taken with violent hemorrhage soon after entering Chicago River. A hut was built and the little band prepared for winter, and a long winter it was to them. " With the
return of spring his disease relented, when he descended the
Illinois River to the Indian village below Ottawa, where he
gathered the people in a grand council, and preached to them
concerning Heaven and hell, and the virgin, whose protection
he specially invoked. A few days after Easter he returned to
Lake Michigan, when he embarked for Mackinaw, passing
around the head of the lake beneath the great sand-dunes which
line the shore, and thence along the eastern margin to where a
small stream discharges itself into the great reservoir south of
the promontory, known as the ' Sleeping Bear.' Marquette had
for some time lain prostrate in the bottom of the canoe. The
warm breath of spring revived him not, and the expanding buds
of the forest did not arrest his dimmed gaze. Here he requested
them to land. Tenderly they bore him to the shore, and built
for his shelter a bark hut. He was aware that his hour had
come. Calmly he gave directions as to the mode of his burial,
craved the forgiveness of his companions if in aught he had
offended them, administered to them the sacrament, and thanked
God that he was permitted to die in the wilderness."

Marquette died May 18, 1876, but his name was cherished by
the Indians, who knew him best, many years afterward. If a
storm overtook them while out upon the water, they would call
upon the name of Marquette. Legends had it that the winds
would immediately quell. He was, indeed, a good man.

Rene Robert Cavelier de La Salle was one of the
greatest, if not the greatest, explorers of the American continent. It is a pleasure and a benefit to study the lives of men of
push; men that hold up a single mark and strive over all that is
difficult to win; men convinced of the value of an object and are
willing to lay down their lives for its success; men that desire to

see the world moving and their nation growing in honor, strength, riches and morality; yea, men that make our nations what they are.

Our subject was born in Rouen, Normandy, France, November, 22, 1843, and was reared almost in the shadow of the great Catholic cathedral of that ancient capital. Studious and quiet in his youth, he naturally loved books which were his constant companion at the age of seven and until he grew to manhood. During his boyhood he manifested a strong will of purpose and his friends looked to the time when he would become one of the foremost in Christianizing the world. He was given a thorough training for the Jesuit priesthood that had for its motto " Ad majoram Dei gloriam." After finishing his education he went to Canada to engage in missionary labors but spent more time in studying the dialects of the Indians, learning their customs and effecting bargains with them, than looking after their souls' welfare. He soon became master of seven of these dialects, and gained the friendship of several tribes.

The young lord was given territory where La Chine now stands, near the rapids of St. Lawrence River, upon which he built a fort, established a trading post and prepared to found a settlement. He soon relinquished the settlement plan because of a love of further adventure yet slumbering in his bosom. He had entertained a band of Senecas at his fort during the winter of 1668-9, from whom he had derived much information of the " far West " and of its grandeur. Especially did they talk about Ohio which took its rise in their territory and flowed westward a distance of nine months' travel by canoe.

Accordingly, on July 6, 1669, with fourteen men, he set out for the purpose of exploring the Ohio River. They ascended the St. Lawrence to Lake Ontario, along its shores to the Niagara where they beheld the mighty cataract, to the Seneca town (See story), thence to the Ohio which they followed till in the locality of Louisville, there learning that the Ohio emptied into a great river that flowed on and on until it was lost in the far South. This news offered an opportunity for more discoveries and greater fame to the mind of La Salle, but it was not thus received by his men who mutinied and deserted him in a body.

Thus left in the wilds without friends or food, subsisting upon roots, twigs and the hospitality of Red Men, this young man of culture and fortune made his toilsome journey through the wilderness to the eastern settlements. He lingered with tribe after tribe, learning their language and customs; of the extent of territory and its richness, until he had gained a fair idea of the interior of this vast region and of its prospects in colonization, becoming better posted upon such topics than any other man among his contemporaries, though he was then but twenty-seven years old and had spent but four of them in America.

The remainder of his life has been briefly scanned in the preceding pages of this work, but too much for his favor can not be added. He was a bold man. Like Columbus he was studious and thoughtful in youth, in manhood earnest, patient and determined, resolutely overcoming every obstacle in the way to success; yea, nature endowed him with more: in address he was pleasing, in appearance noble, in discernment keen and accurate. The Cabots took the shortest route and easiest assignment, La Salle the more difficult and hazardous, with no guides but treacherous Indians and no followers but rebellious ones. Ponce de Leon sought to retrieve his lost fame, increase his wealth and immortalize his youth; La Salle forsook kindred, fortune, ease and supine pleasure for hardships, ignominy and premature old age in his zeal to elevate the condition of the Western wilds and give to his native country a new world. De Soto sought wealth, La Salle sought peoples whom he strove to harmonize; the one was feared by savages the other regarded with reverential love. Thus we may compare the life and character of this man with others of his day and find in him a noble character without an evil intention; striving for his aim in life, a martyr to thieves and sluggards by whom he was assassinated in January, 1687.

Louis Hennepin was born in Belgium in 1640. He preached for some time in Holland and came to America with La Salle. He was first stationed at the Indian mission of Ft. Frontenac, then joined La Salle's expedition to Illinois. Upon his release by the Sioux Indians he went to Quebec, thence to France. Here he published accounts of his travels which grew to be popular. Though ordered to America by church authorities he refused and fled into Holland. He then went to England where he was taken up by King William who cajoled and flattered him until he prevailed upon him to write another account of his discoveries in the New World. In this work many previous statements were modified and Hennepin was given the honor of first descending the Mississippi to its mouth. King William wished to present some specious reason for his claim to the territory of Louisiana and merely used Hennepin as a tool. In early life Father Hennepin was a good man but trying captivity had seemingly disheartened him and he became a traitor to all but personal interests.

Louis Joliet was born in Quebec, Canada, in 1645 and was of French parentage. He early displayed literary talent and was educated in a Jesuit college for the priesthood but abandoned his studies and began life as a trader. When but twenty years old he received a commission from Governor Frontenac to explore the Mississippi River and set out for the western missions where he joined Father Marquette. He had been a trader for several years and was versed in the Indian languages. La Salle greatly desired the appointment but for certain reasons was defeated. Having procured a permit for making discoveries he was given the credit and to him, only, was granted the Anticosti Islands for services. He never returned West but devoted his attention to trading on his domain. He died in 1700 with the title of Seigniory of Joliette which title was transferred to his family.

SETTLEMENT PERIOD.

EARLY HISTORY.

NATURAL ADVANTAGES.— Word spread to the remotest parts of civilization regarding the grand discoveries made by La Salle and Marquette in beautiful regions of the "far West." People were eager to learn more about the prairie country; not that they believed it adapted to the raising of grain, cattle and other domestic animals, but they loved the prospect of making their homes in a land of plenty where they could communicate with civilized nations by navigable rivers; gather together abundant supplies of furs without much labor and transport them to the mother country with but little expense. In Illinois they believed were the richest mines of the world, which idea was not abandoned for many years. In fact the Government reserved certain sections in the sale of public lands believing them to be richly provided with silver. Every advantage or indication of advantage offered settlers in this portion of the New World was examined closely.

Broad nature pointed the early explorers and settlers to a vast territory lying farther westward. The similarity of the Lower Mississippi and the Missouri River, both in waters and channel indicated this; while the Upper Mississippi was decidedly different. This led the

French to believe that the **Missouri** was the head waters of the Great River while the Upper Mississippi was a separate stream. Had the idea been so prevalent among the French as with the Spaniards, the former would not have been satisfied to settle in Illinois but would have ascended the Missouri in search of the gold mines of the Northwest, as described by the Aztecs to Cortez: they believed themselves to be in possession of those regions.

The trade carried on from the fruits of the hunt was quite extensive. Many animals found in Illinois were treasured as of great value and it became a fashion with European people to prefer furs made of pelts brought from America. Whole cargoes were shipped directly to Paris and sold at high prices. The animals most common in Illinois were the prairie wolf, deer, squirrel and rabbit; the grey wolf, brown bear, fox, raccoon, opossum, gopher, muskrat, otter and beaver were also quite common, while the black wolf, panther and wildcat were occasionally killed. A few wild horses also roamed the prairies but were seldom seen; though at times, the early settlers captured a number and broke them to service. These sold from $15 to $25 each.

The First Settlement was that of Kaskaskia, near the mouth of the river that bears the same name and but a few miles from the Mississippi. The first permanent fort was that of St. Louis, on the Illinois River near Ottawa, where a mission was established, but the Whites dwelt in tents or within the fort as if intending to remain only temporarily.

When La Salle floated down the Mississippi he found a tribe dwelling upon the banks, who were not in the least hostile. On accompanying them to their village he was surprised at the beautiful locality and complimented the inhabitants upon their fine town, beautiful surroundings and pleasant location. He at once resolved to bring hither persons from Canada to locate and trade with these friendly people. This was done in 1682. Records confirm this. In the cathedral of Kaskaskia there is a book that contains a record of baptisms performed when the place was only a mission. The first baptismal record reads about as follows: " In the year 1695, March 10, I, James Gravier, of the Society of Jesus, baptised Peter Ako, newly born of P. Michael Ako. Godfather was D. de Hautchey, Godmother was Mary

Arami, Mary Jane was grandmother of the child."

Michael Ako was with Hennepin in his expedition to the Upper Mississippi and as there is no account of his returning with him to France, he no doubt came with La Salle to this place where afterward the priests located; the first of whom was the above named gentleman, succeeded by Julian Bindeau, June 13, 1697, he in turn ruling until 1699, when Gabriel Marest took charge.

Jesuit Life, in the wilderness, was similar to Indian life, and they ruled themselves for several years. A mission was also established at Cahokia and called St. Sulpice, where mills were built for grinding corn and sawing boards. Here a mansion was erected in the center of a large farm. Like some Norman castle, encircled by the humble homes of the peasantry, this dwelling stood surrounded by the wigwams of the Indians. The fields were worked in common.

These people were happy; no taxes to pay, no bonds to be lifted, no mortgages coming due and no politics to discuss. They raised all they ate and made most of what they wore, paying the priest for his masses and the fiddler for his tunes. These compensations were small and the people were always lighthearted and free. Bancroft says, " The gentle virtues and fervid eloquence of Mermet made him the soul of the mission of Kaskaskia. At early dawn his pupils came to church, dressed neatly and modestly, each in a deer-skin or robe sewn together from several skins. After receiving lessons they chanted canticles; mass was then said in presence of all the Christians, the French and the converts—the women on one side and the men on the other. From prayers and instructions the missionaries proceeded to visit the sick and administer medicine, and their skill as physicians did more than all the rest to win confidence. In the afternoon the catechism was taught in the presence of the young and the old, where everyone without distinction of rank or age, answered the questions of the missionary. At evening all would assemble at the chapel for instruction, for prayer and to chant the hymns of the church. On Sundays and on festivals, even after vespers, a homily was pronounced; at the close of day parties would meet in houses to recite the chaplets in alternate choirs, and sing psalms till late at night."

A Mission Established at Peoria.—In 1711 Father Marest still preached to the people of Cahokia, and by strenuous efforts converted many Indians. On one occasion there chanced to be present a chief residing near Lake Peoria, who was converted to the faith and insisted upon the good priest paying his tribe a visit. After thinking the matter over, Father Marest was unable to abandon the idea and in the cold of spring set out for the village, 150 miles distant, to establish a new mission. In speaking of this trip he says: "I departed, having nothing about me but my crucifix and breviary, being accompanied by only two savages who might abandon me from levity, or might fly through fear of enemies. The terror of these vast uninhabitable regions, in which for twelve days not a single soul was seen, almost took away my courage. This was a journey wherein there was no village, no bridge, no ferry-boat, no house, no beaten path; and over boundless prairies, intersected by rivers and rivulets, through forests and thickets filled with briers and thorns, through marshes, in which we sometimes plunged to the girdle. At night repose was sought on leaves, exposed to the winds and rains, happy if by the side of some rivulet whose waters might quench our thirst. Meals were prepared from such game as might be killed on the way, or by roasting ears of corn."

He preached to these tribes with good result. Soon others followed and, in 1712, a trading post was founded. In 1732 the work at this point had so increased that a chapel was built but was burned by the Cherokees four years afterward.

New Orleans the Capital.—The same year (1711) that Father Marest established his mission with the Peorias, the capital of Illinois was changed from Montreal to New Orleans as this locality was to be included in Louisiana. The outlet for commerce from Illinois was through the Mississippi. Thus the French resolved to settle the valley, and fortify themselves against the English of the East. To accomplish this a commerce was to be established first.

At the head of these plans the king placed Sieur Anthony Crozat, a man of great wealth and ability, also an officer of the royal household. The King was favorable to the enterprise and said, " From the information we have received concerning the situation and disposition of Louisiana, we are of opinion that there may be established therein a considerable commerce, of great advantage to France. We can thus obtain from the colonists the commodities which hitherto we have brought from other countries, and give in exchange for them the manufactured and other products in our kingdom. We have resolved, therefore, to grant the commerce of Louisiana to the Sieur Anthony Crozat, our Counselor and Secretary of the household and revenue, to whom we entrust the execution of this project. We permit him to search, open and dig all mines, veins, minerals, precious stones and pearls throughout the whole extent of territory, and to transport the proceeds thereof into any port in France, during fifteen years. And we grant, in perpetuity to him, his heirs and all claiming under him, all the profits, except one-fifth of the gold and silver which he or they shall cause to be exported to France. We also will that the said Crozat, and those claiming under him, shall forfeit the monopolies herein granted should they fail to prosecute them for a period of three years, and that in such case they shall be fully restored to our dominion."

Crozat, however, did not find in his grant the country he supposed. The mines which he particularly relied upon proved a failure. Though many expeditions were sent out in search of these, they returned almost empty handed and with unfavorable reports. This darkened his sole ambition. Fur trade was monopolized by the English of the East, who had so won the Indians by liberal trading that, had it not been for the priests, Crozat and his grasping companions would have had no commerce at all. As it was he had spent 450,000 livres and had realized but 300,000. His men began deserting him for he could not pay them promptly. He petitioned to the King to allow him to retire from the position though his fifteen years had not expired. To this King Louis agreed and in 1717 placed the control immediately under the crown.

The White population of Illinois now numbered about 200. Several were engaged in agriculture but the people, generally,

lived as the Indians, save a few scattering traders and workers
of the northern mines in the present Jo Daviess County.

"South Sea Bubble."—In 1715 Louis XIV, King of
France, who had reigned seventy-two years, died. The Government was transferred to his son, Louis XV; but the father
had left a debt of 3,000,000,000 livres. He had been lavish with
his money and by extravagant living had incurred this enormous
liability which the new Government decreased at first 1,000,000,-
000 livres by contracting the currency. France was at the height
of her ambition for speculation. People had become entangled
in heavy debts and were unable to pay them. The colonies of
the Mississippi Valley became a theme of conversation, for the
people believed that vast fortunes lay slumbering in the New
World, notwithstanding the failures in trying to find them.

In 1716 John Law, a Scotch gambler, arrived in France
with a new scheme. He had studied the financial condition
of Europe over which he wandered in his degraded profession. His knowledge of finance added to the inspiration of
the ideal wealth of the New World aided him in perfecting his
plan. By permission he established a bank based on the indebtedness of the country, with a fair promise of success. The
Regency of the young King gave him encouragement and in
1718 the Government made his institution a royal bank. To
this was united a company that had exclusive control of the
commerce of the Missisippi River. Rumors were circulated of
the discovery of gold and silver in the new regions, when the
shares of the company sold for double and treble their par value.
The commerce of the Indies and of Senegal in Africa were
united to that of America. France was to be rich in a day and
John Law was controlling general of all this success. Bills were
issued to the amount of eighty times the worth of all the coin in
the kingdom and the whole system rested upon credit. People
from all parts of the globe flocked to France and lavishly specu-
lated in the shares. Buildings were enlarged and hotels built to
accommodate the mighty throng; England took up the project
and desks were placed upon the streets of London where were
sold large tracts of the country; vessels bound for America were
laden with emigrants and large cargoes; settlements grew rapidly

and the Valley of the Mississippi was under headway to soon become thickly settled. But the aspect changed.

" South Sea Bubble " was a phrase that caused many hearts to ache. At the first demand for specie the whole system fell. Persons that believed themselves rich became beggars in a day. Whole fortunes were lost. Lords, ladies, bishops, priests and all classes had been lured into the project. Law, who had been regarded a saint, was now stoned by the people and was compelled to take refuge with the King. So popular had he become at one time and so desirous were the people to see him that various artifices were practiced. According to orders a coachman drove over a curbstone near Law's residence and upset the carriage. The mistress pretended to faint and was carried into his house. When she had finished her pretended swoon she arose and purchased stock of him.

The Multiplied Settlements was the only good that resulted from the above speculations. Those in the North were located principally between the Kaskaskia and Illinois Rivers. By 1730, 5,000 Whites and 2,000 Negro slaves were in Illinois. In 1721 the Jesuits built a college at Kaskaskia and established a monastery at the same place. These brought over monks and nuns who aided in establishing a permanent home in the West.

Arranged Massacre.—In 1726 M. Pierrier was given the Governorship of Illinois and a large portion of the Valley. His rule was looked upon with jealousy by the Indians who were sometimes punished for trivial faults, while their country was being rapidly filled with settlements. A secret plan was put on foot to bring about a general massacre of all Whites in the Valley. The plot was well arranged. The new of the moon was the signal for preparation and each tribe was given a number of sticks to indicate days thereafter—when a day expired a stick was drawn. Unfortunately for themselves the Natchez received a smaller bunch than the others. Hence an attack was begun by them and not carried out along the whole line, Illinois remaining quiet. For this warfare the Natchez were severely punished. Women and children were unmolested but the men were mostly captured and sold as slaves. Thus the tribe perished.

Progressive Illinois.—In 1732 the charter was surrendered and King Louis issued a proclamation stating that Louisiana was free to all his subjects and thereafter operations would be conducted by the Royal Governor under the control of the Crown. The mining fever gradually subsided and agriculture was noticed more than formerly, Illinois becoming the most popular section of the entire tract. Settlers began working for themselves instead of, as had been the custom, a company of wild speculators. Villages grew to be towns and tents were replaced by houses. M. Pierrier remained Governor-General over the country but appointed councilmen under him to see to different sections. The Illinois settlements were under D'Artaquette, a noble Frenchman of high rank. He succeeded in establishing peace and harmony throughout his command. But the Indians of the South under other leaders began withholding their trade from the French, giving it to the English. On the other hand those of Illinois were faithful to their friends, remembering the kindly lessons taught by Jesuits.

War with the Chickasaws.—First Battle.—The Chickasaws of Kentucky and Tennessee had not forgotten their hatred for the French and implored the Illinois tribes to join them in making a complete sweep of all the White settlers. With these appeals the sturdy sons of Illinois not only refused to comply but secretly sent word to the French of the interview. A council was held between the commanders of Ft. Chartres (military headquarters for Illinois) and New Orleans. Arrangements were made for Bienville, who had taken the Governor-Generalship of Louisiana in 1736, to assemble the forces of the South and, with his few Indian friends, proceed northward by way of the Tombigbee River, thence by land, joining D'Artaquette, who was to collect the settlers of this State with all the Indian allies possible. Bienville was successful in his march northward, having collected a larger army than was anticipated. On his arrival at the head of the river he added to it a company of Choctaws to whom he offered a liberal reward for scalps. These were very impatient for an advance, not being satisfied to await the arrival of forces from the North. Skirmishing began almost immediately, making it impossible to refrain longer from attacking their fort. The signal for this was given May 16, 1737. The fort proved to be a skillfully arranged barrier, having been under the supervision of the English in its erection, and too much of a defense for the Governor-General and his allies. The object, they said, in beginning the attack early was to surprise the enemy; but every Chickasaw was at his post and well prepared. Again they made a desperate assault and again they were repulsed. Finally, with thirty-two killed and sixty-six wounded, the southern forces retired from the field retreating rapidly homeward. Bienville was sorely mortified and believed the Chickasaws able to withstand twice the forces he would be able to raise. He disbanded his army, threw his cannon into the river and returned to New Orleans a defeated man.

The Illinois troops under D'Artaquette had already made their attack and had been repulsed. The Indians were so impatient to rush upon their foe that the commander could not persuade them to await the arrival of the army from the South. They would push on closer and closer until a skirmish ensued and then the Indian blood began to boil. Fearless at the onset, they fought with true courage and would have gained the victory had it not been for the loss of their unfortunate commander who was wounded in the first of the attack. This confused his Indian allies who fled without a halt until out of danger.

GOVERNOR D'ARTAQUETTE AND DE VINCENNES BURNED AT THE STAKE.—D'Artaquette was sore from his wounds and could not retreat. With him the noble DeVincennes and others who remained with their wounded commander rather than flee for their lives quietly submitted, when captured. The captives were treated with courtesy at first, the captors hoping to get a ransom for their deliverance in good condition. When they learned, however, that the enemy had returned home and being encouraged by their successes in vanquishing the southern forces their savage barbarity assumed sway and they resolved upon an old-time jollification. D'Artaquette and his comrades were tied to stakes and slow fires kindled about them. The heat scorched their bodies; the flesh became crisped, then disappeared from the lower limbs, and slowly death ascended. Prayer was the only relief for these poor unfortunates, miles from any source of help.

In this manner two of the noblest men, with their comrades, perished while their tormentors danced about and spit upon them.

SECOND BATTLE.—A knowledge of the barbarous treatment of the northern leaders reached Governor Bienville at New Orleans through colonists of the East. He was mortified and resolved upon revenge. Sending his plans to France, he obtained permission to fit out another expedition against the Chickasaws. Though he was not a little chagrined at his former misfortune, his last expedition was almost as barren as the first one had been.

In 1740 the army departed. The strength from Illinois numbered 200 French and 300 Indians, commanded by La Buissoniere. The forces from the South were 1,000 French and 200 Indians. A fort was built near St. Francis River for storage and to serve as a place of refuge. Here fever set in and the army was not fit for duty. On the approach of winter the disease abated but the supplies were exhausted and the troops were threatened with famine. When spring came the sun, instead of smiling upon a powerful force, shed its kindly rays upon a handful of fugitives with small pretensions to an army. M. Celeron, of the Illinois country, however, believed in his own ability and with a few soldiers sallied forth to meet the foe. The Chickasaws, mistaking this for a strong force of the enemy, sued for peace. A long conference was held in which the French followed up the advantage gained by the mistake. The Chickasaws thereupon agreed to trade with them and never again patronize the English. If called upon they declared they would send troops to aid in the protection of the French in time of war. Besides this they were to be on friendly terms with the Indians that had been aiding the settlers of the Valley. Thus ended the Chickasaw war.

Review.—There is no government so dear to an American as one made and conducted by the people. These privileges were almost entirely allowed the early French residents of Illinois. Happy they were if ever people were happy; careful in duty and always ready to perform any religious requirement put upon them. They had congregated in settlements where they worked in common, their sole aim being a healthy subsistence with comfortable surroundings. Homes were usually built in fertile regions where good land was plenty and fresh water convenient; besides, the timber lands were hunted where fuel was handy and building material abundant. Houses were usually made of logs; if otherwise, of stone. In many instances a number of families resided under the same roof, frequently eating from the same table; also, a large field was kept for agricultural purposes near every settlement. This field was divided into sections and apportioned according to the energy and strength of the persons who labored. Beyond this field were the pastures for their flocks. Yearly, 600 barrels of flour were exported to New Orleans. Besides this the colonists shipped from the country quantities of corn; hams of hogs, deer, bear and buffalo; pickled pork and beef; wax, cotton, leather, tallow, tobacco, skins, furs, venison and numerous other articles. Quantities of lead were also obtained from the mines of the present Jo Daviess County.

By 1730, 150 families had collected together in five settlements, the most important of which were Kaskaskia, on the Kaskaskia River six miles above the mouth, first settled in 1682; Cahokia, situated at the mouth of Cahokia Creek and five miles below the site of St. Louis, settled in 1686; Fort Chartres, twelve miles above Kaskaskia, the fort having been built in 1718; and within four miles of the fort, St. Philip colony was situated.

"FRENCH AND INDIAN WAR."

The term "French and Indian War" was given to this seven years' struggle by English historians because the French and a portion of the Indians united to prevent them from extending their claim beyond the Alleghanies. It might more properly be called the French and English Boundary War.

French and English Jealousies sprung up between the two nationalities in America from two causes: First, England and France had been at war for several years and the bitter feelings toward each other had been carried to the New

World. Second, a boundary line had never been agreed upon.
The English were rapidly pushing westward and occupying the
lands, while traders penetrated hundreds of miles beyond their
frontier. These occasionally came in contact with the French
who claimed all territory west of the Alleghanies and east of
the Rockies, lying between the North Ocean and Gulf of Mexico. When the French positively refused these traders the use
of their lands a feeling of vengeance flew through every English nerve and trouble became apparent.

In order to gain a better plea for their pretended claim upon
the same territory, the English assembled the Iroquois Indians
of New York, at that time yet powerful, and purchased from
them all western lands to which the Iroquois had no right. This
purchase was made in 1744. Had it not been for the French
power in Canada, the English would have taken possession un-
ceremoniously, but they well knew they would have an army
of not only French but Indians to contend with were they to
make such an attempt.

The French Take Action.—The inhabitants of the Mississippi Valley, especially those of the present State of Illinois,
were looked upon by their kinsmen in Canada as possessing the
most fruitful regions in the New World. As exports were
gradually growing in value, they felt it their duty to maintain
them and protect their colonies. Then, too, it was upon the
lands traversed by Marquette and La Salle, who had prepared
maps of the country, taught the natives Christianity, traded with
them, built forts and established commerce before any Englishman knew of the country; or, had he known, it is doubtful that
he would have dared to put a foot upon the soil.

In 1749 the authorities of Canada cast plates of lead upon
which was engraved their claim. These plates were laid by
mounds, at the mouths of rivers and various other points in the
disputed territory. However, this move had no tendency to
check the English. The same year they erected a trading post
upon Miami River, in the Ohio Company's territory of which
Lawrence, Augustus and George Washington, together with
five wealthy English gentlemen, were the proprietors. They
began collecting stores, ammunition and artillery as rapidly as

possible. They went so far as to seize two English traders and later captured a post. When the English learned of this they called the Iroquois in council, reminded them of the land purchased in the West, of the former treaties they had made, and informed them that the French had encroached upon the privileges granted by them. They also tried to show that it was the Iroquois's duty to assist in righting the wrong the French were now perpetrating. They soon learned, however, that a Frenchman was held in higher esteem, even by an Iroquois, than an Englishman. After various means of persuasion and several arts of strategy had been played, a chief replied to Easton, spokesman for the English, by saying, "The Indians on the Ohio left you because of your own fault. When we heard the French were coming we asked you for help and arms, but we received neither. The French came; they treated us kindly, and gained our affections. The Governor of Virginia settled on our lands for his own benefit, and when we wanted help he forsook us."

The kindness with which the French had treated the Indians bound them closely, and hand in hand they vowed to bar out their Eastern intruders. Thus the "Land of the Illinois" and neighboring localities not only brought about strife in America but the quarrel was taken up in Europe.

Jumonville Killed.—In 1754 Washington with 200 men encountered Jumonville among the rocks near Fort Du-Quesne, now Pittsburg, Pennsylvania, and an engagement followed in which the latter was killed and his forces routed. For this Washington has long been criticised by the French, even charged with being an assassin. Jumonville had been sent, they claimed, with a written statement of rights and grievances, and was on his way to the English headquarters when the skirmish took place. If this were true Washington was ignorant of the fact. The echo of the first musket shot of the engagement, said to have been fired by Washington himself, encircled the globe. It began the long war that drove France out of America and made a warlike people of the colonists of the East. When the news reached the Old World it threw England and France into a state of excitement, especially the latter. The people of Illinois were likewise enraged. At no time since they came to America had they displayed so much determination to settle a question with the musket and connon.

Capture of Fort Necessity.—Fort Chartres, Illinois, was the French headquarters for all military equipments of the West, Macarty being in command. M. de Villiers, a subordinate officer at this place, was a half brother of Jumonville, recently killed. Collecting an army of French and Indians, he proceeded down the Mississippi to the Ohio, thence up that stream to Fort Du Quesne where he took command shortly afterward. Washington was advancing upon this post but on learning of the superior forces he would have to encounter, retreated, pursued by De Villiers to Fort Necessity where he fortified himself. His army was insufficient, however, to withstand an attack and he was allowed to retire honorably, leaving behind his artillery and prisoners taken at the time of Jumonville's defeat. This was an event that called forth general rejoicing in Illinois.

Defeat.—The turn of affairs was a signal for action on the part of the British ministry who decided to send aid to the colonies. General Braddock was given the chief command and arrived in America in 1755. He led an attack on Fort Du Quesne, Washington being in command of the American troops. The French and Indians lay concealed in a ravine ten miles from the fort. The English were again routed and the French remained in possession of the fort until in 1758 when it was burned and abandoned, but was immediately rebuilt by English.

The French were unsuccessful at other points also. The year of Braddock's defeat (1755) all settlers had been driven from their homes in Acadia; parent separated from child, husband from wife, and scattered in various parts of the wilds. By 1760 all other posts had surrendered and the settlements were in the hands of the English, though a treaty was not perfected until three years later.

Pontiac's War.—DETROIT.—Pontiac, who ruled with a commanding hand over many tribes, planned a general massacre of the English. If an attack upon the frontier fortresses were a success, then they could fall upon the unprotected inhabitants, and drive the English from the land forever. He sent word for a general assault upon all the forts from the east to the west, from the north to the south; he to strike the first blow. He told his people that the King of France had been sleeping, but now had awakened to a sense of his duty and was sending a large number of men in war canoes down the St. Lawrence to assist his children in the forests. The English afterward accused the French of Illinois of encouraging this idea. All the tribes agreed to assist him in the desperate plot, the equal of which had never been undertaken. Thousands of helpless people were to be slain; scalps hanging about were to be the only remnants left of the English then in America. The fruits of the assault, he said, would be far superior to those of Braddock's defeat. Dancing and joy prevailed. He had so inspired his savage warriors that they were ready to follow wherever he might lead. He spoke of the kindness of Frenchmen and the cruel disposition of Englishmen; he dwelt upon the prospect of getting back their lands that were now occupied by cruel strangers: and how pleasant it would be to have the old hunting days return, with the French who had taught them so much and had given them the beautiful ornaments they wore; he spoke of the certainty of their power being restored by the great French king who would protect them from all dangers, and added, " Now I go to Detroit to learn of the situation at the fort."

The plan was to massacre the garrison. It would have been a triumph on the part of the savages had not the desperate plot been revealed by an Indian girl (See story) who deserves more praise for the lives she saved than the famous Pocahontas in protecting a man she admired. The attack was then turned to a siege lasting forty days, when the Indians abandoned the hope of taking this point.

IN OTHER LOCALITIES the Indians had been more successful. At Fort Miami, on the head waters of the Maumee, an Indian girl told the commander that a woman was dying just outside. A Miami town being near, he was lured thither and seized. The savages at once entered the fort and completed the destruction of its garrison with the scalping knife.

At Mackinaw a band of Indians engaged in playing ball and

were watched by the entertained soldiers. After the game had been in progress for awhile one side seemingly drove the other to the fort. Finally the ball was thrown over the stockade. A goodly number scaled the works to get it, but no sooner were they within than they began to slaughter the inmates. The commander, Major Henry, was writing at his desk when he heard the shrieks of the dying men. Hastening to the woods he made his escape but was closely pursued.

Not only were these depredations carried on at the forts but the English people were attacked in their homes, and hundreds were killed. Women were compelled to stand and see the brains of their children beaten out while awaiting their turn. Throughout Pennsylvania rapine and carnage abounded on every hand. A large Indian force entered the State and spread terror wherever it went. People took refuge in the larger towns which were fortified. The colonists were wholly unable to put down the war for the time being, as the organization was too complete —Illinois, the refuge for homeless French and many Indians, could not easily be reached and the English Regulars had returned home; besides it would have been murderous to kill off the tribes.

Illinois Disturbance.—British Getting Possession. —When the English came to take possession of the forts they found the Indians yet hostile. The French had always treated the Indians with the greatest of respect. They visited each other and were generous in all their dealings, though it was sometimes difficult for Frenchmen, somewhat refined, to endure the uncouth, filthy disposition of savages. To these rude ways the English would not submit and contemptuously hurled bitter reproaches upon them for their ill-bred manners. The impatience on their part and endurance on the part of Frenchmen made the Indians lasting friends to the latter and bitter enemies to the former.

The Illinois forts had been left under French commanders as it was not regarded safe for the English to take charge immediately after the close of the late war. Thither came large numbers of Indians complaining of their mistreatment and threatening vengeance upon their late rulers. In 1763 a treaty had been signed at Paris by which France gave up all her possesssions in

America, east of the Mississippi, reserving only two small islands off the coast of Newfoundland for fishing purposes. At the same time Spain ceded Florida to Great Britain, leaving her in undisputed possession of this vast territory, so far as the relations of civilized nations were concerned. The only perplexing question now before her was how to pacify the Indians and gain possession of the forts in Illinois.

The same year the treaty was signed Major Loftus, with a force of 400 men, undertook the arduous task. He sailed to New Orleans, where he embarked in small boats, with the dignity of a Sir Walter Raleigh, to take command of Fort Chartres. He did not reach Illinois. When a short distance on his way the warriors of Pontiac congregated upon the shores and fired into his fleet, killing several soldiers at the outset. As the river was out of its banks Loftus saw no means of dispelling his foe and immediately steered homeward, indignant because of defeat. He sought to blame the French who were ignorant of his approach. Thus ended the first attempt to take command of the Illinois forts.

PONTIAC'S SPEECH.—In 1764 Pontiac again tried to arouse the Illinois Indians to action. He also visited the French at Fort Chartres, and to the commanding officer made a speech. He said: " Fathers, we have long desired to see you and enjoy the pleasure of taking you by the hand. While we refresh ourselves with the soothing incense of the friendly calumet, we will recall the battles fought by our warriors against the enemy which still seeks our overthrow. But while we speak of their valor and victories, let us not forget our fallen heroes, and with renewed resolves and more constant endeavors strive to avenge their death by the downfall of our enemies. Father, I love the French, and have led hither my braves to maintain your authority and vindicate the insulted honor of France. But you must no longer remain inactive and suffer your red brothers to contend alone against the foe, who seek our common destruction. We demand of you arms and warriors to assist us, and when the English dogs are driven into the sea, we will again in peace and happiness enjoy with you these fruitful forests and prairies, the noble heritage presented by the Great Spirit to our ancestors."

GENERAL GAGE was appointed to succeed General Amherst as commander of all the English provincial forces. He, too, saw the difficulty of reconciling the Indians to English rule, especially while the forts in Illinois remained in possession of the French. He therefore planned to send a force westward, not by the way of New Orleans, but down the Ohio. In order to prepare the natives for their coming, he sent, in February, 1765, two men, who were as equal to the emergency as any, to frighten them and get them to receive the troops with courtesy. The result was decidedly opposite that expected. The men were not given an audience and were obliged to flee for their lives in disguise, being aided by the French who barely saved them from destruction. The army never took the westward march.

The English then began studying methods used by the French in gaining Indian friendship. They had heard of the moral lessons taught them, but were averse to allowing the clergy the honor of quelling this people. They decided to do as the French occasionally did—distribute presents among them, but to excel all former generosities they loaded a cargo of costly, beautiful articles, such as had never arrived in Illinois. The goods were slowly towed up the river, manned by Frenchmen who were to tell the savages about English wealth and of a large stock of such articles in store for them. Word of the approaching boat reached Pontiac first. The chieftain gained all possible information and when it landed, the Indians, not backward in the least, jumped aboard, took possession of the cargo, whipped the Frenchmen and distributed the articles themselves.

PONTIAC'S WAR ENDED.—The late disturbances were somewhat agitated by a few French traders who forged letters from the King telling of preparations to aid his red children of the forest. They manufactured stories of English mistreatment and kept the savages instilled with ideas not conducive to peaceful relations. These things were kept from the higher authorities who knew nothing of the doings of traders.

General Amherst wrote M. de Villiers to make known to the Indians the change of government and to attend to it at once. In a letter to Pontiac, Villiers said: " You can not expect further assistance from the French; they and the English are now at peace and regard each other as brothers. The Indians should abandon hostilities which are leading to no good results." This Pontiac took as an insult on the part of the French.

Pontiac Assassinated.—This daring leader met his death at the hands of an assassin, in 1769. While at St. Louis he learned that a feast was in progress at Cahokia, given to the Indians and settlers by the British. He resolved to attend and at once set out. He found the red men nearly all drunk, and was soon intoxicated himself. An English trader, seeing an opportunity to get Pontiac out of the way, employed an Indian to kill him, promising a reward of a barrel of whiskey for his services. His offer was accepted and a tomahawk was buried in the brain of the great warrior, who had spread terror through the land for many years, who was revengeful when enraged and who exerted an influence over the tribes that were ready to be foes of the English on every pretext.

Thus perished a great chief. One who, it might be said, was semi-civilized; one with a broad heart and tender disposition unless inflamed with revenge; one who was conversant on higher topics and sought the society of leading men of the nation. He first favored the French when but a boy and in his last speech he was frank to say, "I love the French."

British Governors.—Although New France and that portion of Louisiana lying east of the Mississippi were taken by force of arms in 1760 and ceded to Great Britain in 1763, literal possession of Illinois was not secured until 1765 when Captain Sterling arrived at **Fort Chartres.** Previous to his arrival M. Ste. Ange de Belle Rive departed for St. Louis followed by many af his countrymen.

Captain Sterling died soon after assuming control and Major Frazier took his place but did not rule to suit the Government. Soon after Colonel Reed took charge but ruled with a tyrannical hand and made himself odious to the people. Colonel Wilkins was then placed in command but the settlers had learned to complain and were not yet suited. The displeasure reached its climax when he announced that the judicial department should be in the hands of the people in the execution of civil laws. Seven Judges were appointed from among the citizens to hold their court monthly, the first session opening December 6, 1768. This the people could not understand—a court to be made up from the people, who knew but little about law, was to them the height of folly. Every verdict was questioned and no other court existed to which the dissatisfied could appeal for a more learned decision. The former court was re-established in 1774.

Another authority Wilkins took upon himself was the distribution of lands. Notwithstanding orders had been given by the Government not to sell any territory beyond the head waters of the rivers flowing into the Atlantic Ocean, he began almost immediately to apportion the land of the Illinois to the English. He believed that the laws of England were just in depriving an alien of the right to own property: hence he divided the possessions vacated by French, but hesitatingly allowed those who so desired to remain upon the farms they had occupied for half a century, though they would swear allegiance to Great Britain. That portion of the country not to be sold was to be reserved for the Indians, but Wilkins called together a council of chiefs at Kaskaskia, in 1773, also a posse of traders, and of them obtained two large tracts, about one-eighth of the present State. For this purchase he agreed to give 250 blankets, 260 stroudes, 350 shirts, 150 pairs of half-thick stockings, 150 breechcloths, 500 pounds of gunpowder, 4,000 pounds of lead, 144 knives, 30 pounds of vermilion, 2,000 gunflints, 200 pounds of brass kettles, 200 pounds of tobacco, 30 gilt looking-glasses, 144 fire steels, 168 garterings, 144 gun worms, 288 awls, 10,000 pounds of flour, 500 bushels of corn, 12 horses, 12 cattle, 20 bushels of salt, 20 guns and 5 shillings in cash. The deed for this land was recorded at Kaskaskia, September 3.

Government Removed.—Fort Chartres was destroyed by the freshet in 1772, in which one side was torn away. The stream had been gradually washing toward the fort for many years because of a sand bar that formed near the mouth of the Kaskaskia, which bar has since become an island. The English garrison abandoned the building entirely, taking up their abode at Fort Gage on the opposite side of the river, which they occupied the remainder of their stay. The Governor moved his office into Kaskaskia.

The old fort gradually crumbled away, the inhabitants making use of the timber. On this spot many nights were spent in peace; many were spent in sorrow. Thousands of miles from their kindred and mother country, that little band could but grow lonesome when thoughts of them would arise. Surrounded by savages, yet it was home; it was a dear home for it was a place of freedom and refuge. Upon this historic spot trees are now growing that are at least thirty inches in diameter, while no vestige of the defense remains to be preserved as a memento.

The Condition of Illinois under British rule was far from being improved. No attention was directed to her save to keep the Indians quiet. Wilkins's Government did not last long. The French left the country one by one and Indians by degrees discontinued their frequent visits until the once busy towns appeared deserted save the presence of an English garrison that finally dwindled away entirely. Before the Government had been changed one year the entire population numbered but 3,000 souls, the original number at Kaskaskia.

IMPROVEMENTS.—The first water-mill was built at Kaskaskia by Mons. Paget who was killed by Indians in 1764, one year after its completion. The wealthiest man in these settlements was Mr. Beauveair, an English arrival, who owned a large plantation and kept eighty slaves to work upon it. His annual shipment of flour is said to have been 86,000 pounds. Some Frenchmen had held one of 200 acres on which were many cattle and a brewery. This was sold to Englishmen in 1765, when it was improved and enlarged. But the most marked event under the rule of British Governors was the establishment of a store at Cahokia by Charles Gratoit, in 1774. This was the first place for trade in merchandise opened west of the Alleghanies, but was the forerunner of others. The proprietor, a young man, afterward married a daughter of Pierre Chateau, the founder of St. Louis, to which place he then removed.

REVOLUTIONARY WAR.

A Struggle for independence from Great Britain had arisen through a desire of the colonists of the East to bring about favorable action upon a set of grievances they had drafted to the King. The ensuing warfare so encouraged the colonists that the Continental Congress drafted a Declaration of Independence at Philadelphia, July 4, 1776. This document set forth a plan for a new Government " for the people and by the people," and for the success of this they vowed to give up their lives if need be. The victories alternated between them and the King's forces until 1777 when Burgoyne was captured. This was a master stroke for the loyalists and led to an alliance with France a few months afterward.

Situation in Illinois.—During the first two years of the Revolution our quiet little settlements remained at peace; but as it progressed British agitators worked among the inhabitants—English, French and Indians, creating a hatred for the colonists and injuring their cause. They said these people were desperate characters, the most inhuman wretches that ever existed. They narrated, falsely, instances in which women and children were brutally treated without the slightest degree of mercy. They said that the Virginians would enter houses and, without a word, scalp the inmates; that the long knives of these blood-thirsty people penetrated every heart within their reach, and that the western inhabitants should be on the lookout for them. Men unaccustomed to military affairs were drilled continually to be prepared to meet the " Long Knives," as they were taught to call the Virginians, and Indian warriors were kept near by. The priests taught their flocks to be patient and endure the worst without a groan if such must come.

Clarke Commissioned by Patrick Henry.—George Rogers Clarke, who afterward became famous as an opposer of Benedict Arnold, had spent much of his time of late years among the western tribes and knew of their feelings toward the British. He conceived a plan of attack along a line of forts of the West, and believed they could be easily won to the American cause, thus preventing trouble from that quarter, for the source of Indian barbarity appeared to be Detroit, Kaskaskia and Vincennes where the British supplied them with arms. He was a native of Virginia, and thither he hastened in December, 1777, to impart his plans to Patrick Henry, then Governor. All was going on well. He learned of the surrender of Burgoyne and at once caught the inspiration of the colonists—"give me liberty or give me death." Filled with patriotic zeal he laid his plans before the Governor. Patrick Henry saw in Clarke a man whom he could trust in performing the duties of so important an undertaking, and seating himself soon after the interview, penned the following commission:

"You are to proceed with all convenient speed to raise seven companies of soldiers, to consist of fifty men each, officered in the usual manner, and armed most properly for the enterprise; and with this force attack the British force at Kaskaskia. It is conjectured that there are many pieces of cannon and military stores to a considerable amount at that place, the taking and preservation of which would be a valuable acquisition to the State. * * * It is earnestly desired that you show humanity to such British subjects and other persons as fall into your hands. If the White inhabitants of that post and neighborhood will give undoubted evidence of their attachment to the State, for it is certain they live within its limits, by taking the test prescribed by law, and by every other way and means in their power, let them be treated as fellow-citizens, and their person and property be duly respected. Assistance and protection against all enemies, whatever, shall be afforded them, and the commonwealth of Virginia is pledged to accomplish it. But if these people will not accede to the reasonable demands, they must feel the consequences of war, under that direction of humanity that has hitherto distinguished Americans, and which it is expected you will ever consider as the rule of your conduct, and from which you are in no instance to depart. The corps you are to command are to receive the pay and allowance of militia. The inhabitants of this post will be informed by you that in case they accede to the offers of becoming citizens of this commonwealth, a proper garrison will be maintained among them, and every attention bestowed to render their commerce beneficial; the fairest prospects being open to the dominions of France and Spain. * * * * Wishing you success, I am your humble servant. P. HENRY.

The March Westward was begun by Colonel Clarke

on February 4, 1778, almost immediately after receiving his commission. He proceeded to Pittsburg where he was re-enforced and received supplies, but a scanty amount of each—of the former, that they might be reserved for assistance in the East; of the latter, that the troops might not be overburdened with baggage. He received re-enforcements also from Kentucky, but then he had only one-half the men required by his commission. Disappointment beset his way. When opposite the site of Louisville, at Corn Island which he fortified, he told his men the object of the expedition and the ends to be accomplished. This proved too much for a large number who had enlisted from Kentucky, and in spite of all precaution he had taken to prevent desertion several made their escape. Loyal men were sent after the deserters with instructions to compel them to return or shoot them. The recesses and thickets formed excellent hiding-places for the runaways and but few were captured. At another time a Kentucky company received orders to return because of threatened peril in the State. This left Clarke with but 152 men, yet every one was reliable.

They had already dropped down the Ohio from Corn Island when a total eclipse of the sun occurred, June 24, 1778. About this time a messenger from Virginia overtook the little army tand told them of the unbounded joy that was diffusing itself throughout the American army and the homes of patriots. France had acknowledged America's independence and troops were on their way to assist in the struggle. This acknowledgment was made February 6, but the news did not reach the West until the latter part of June, a period of 140 days, a marked contrast to electric speed.

Near the mouth of the Tennessee, Clarke halted. By chance, and a fortunate one it was, he met hunters who had been in the vicinity of Kaskaskia but a short time previous. From one, John Duff, whose services Clarke procured as a guide, he learned the state of things in the Illinois settlements: That a militia had been drilled and that spies had been stationed along the Mississippi to give the alarm should the enemy approach; also, that the fort commanding the town was kept in order as a place of retreat, but had no regular garrison. He listened with pain

to the vile stories circulated in those wilds where strangers seldom visited. Now he was to overcome such an organized resistance within their own country and surrounded by works with
which they were perfectly familiar. It was evident to him that
the advance should be made secretly and the attack a surprise,
or his little band would be overwhelmed and cut to pieces by
superior numbers. The distance by land through the wilderness was nearly 130 miles but that was not sufficient to dishearten
a man with the energy of Colonel Clarke. Slowly and cau-
tiously he led his men through the pathless forests, choosing
an unfrequented route that they might not be discovered. Once
they believed their guide to be a traitor and were on the verge
of putting him in irons when the poor fellow proved his inno-
cence. Finally they reached the outskirts of the settlement of
Kaskaskia where they made a halt until night should drop her
sable curtain upon the earth.

Attack upon Kaskaskia.—When the inhabitants closed
their eyes on the evening of July 3, 1778, little did they suspect
the proximity of their dreaded foe silently awaiting a favorable
opportunity to descend upon them. Fearless, they retired to
their couches without taking any precaution against an attack.
The Indians were their friends and had agreed to assist if their
services were required.

Clarke and a company of men were to secure the fort while
two divisions were to rush upon the citizens. In the dead of
night the troops quietly stole upon the town. No sentinels were
on duty to give the alarm and their approach was not suspected
until a signal was given to tell the others that the fortress had
been taken. The soldiers then rushed into the streets with hideous cries. No imagination can picture the feelings of those poor
French when they were awakened by the yells of the troops
and the dismayed cry of their neighbors,—" Les long couteaux!
Les long couteaux!" (the Long Knives).

Should these terror-stricken creatures escape, Clarke feared
that they would spread the alarm throughout the country and
bring down upon him a large force of French and Indians.
They were therefore driven back into their homes and compelled to remain. It was five days before Clarke could allay

the fears of these superstitious people. He then said to the priests: "My countrymen disdain to make war upon helpless innocents. It was to protect our own wives and children that we penetrated the wilderness and subjugated this stronghold of British and Indians, who have practiced barbarism, and not our object to plunder your homes. We do not war against Frenchmen. The King of France, your former ruler, is the ally of the colonies; his fleet and arms are fighting our battles, and the war must shortly terminate. Embrace whichever side you deem best, and enjoy your own religion, for American law respects the believers of every creed and protects them in their rights. And now to convince you of my sincerity, go and inform the inhabitants that they can dismiss their fears concerning their property and families; that they can conduct themselves as usual and that their friends who are in confinement shall immediately be released."

The few that had been taken prisoners were now released and the old cathedral bell rang joyfully. Shouts for Independence resounded from all parts of the town, while the priests hastened to Colonel Clark to apologize for their misconception of the Americans.

Other Posts were also visited and taken without the shedding of blood. Even the vilest opposers of the American cause became its supporters. Clarke was highly esteemed and the name of Governor Henry was pronounced for the first time in Illinois. It may properly be said that Patrick Henry was a Governor of infant Illinois, for she passed under the control of Virginia, July 4, 1778, two years after the signing of the Declaration of Independence.

Having learned that the army was to proceed to Cahokia, influential citizens offered their services to conduct the expedition thither. Together the escorts and soldiers marched upon the settlement, not under cover of darkness but by daylight (July 10). Here, too, was a cry of "The Long Knives," but upon seeing the French from Kaskaskia the commotion was checked and soon the people were shouting for "Liberty and Freedom."

Fort Vincennes was as easily taken. M. Gibault, a priest at Kaskaskia, also officiated at Vincennes. From him he learned that Governor Abbot had gone to Detroit on business, that a military expedition against the place was unnecessary, and that the inhabitants were mostly under his supervision. He pledged himself to bring them over to the American cause if permitted to do so. The offer was accepted and through his agency the inhabitants threw off their allegiance to Great Britain, compelling the garrison to surrender the fort and abandon the place.

For these services the Legislature of Virginia voted Colonel Clarke complimentary resolutions, the following November, and authorized him to hold the territory as a vassal of Virginia.

Peoria.—Three soldiers were sent to Peoria Lake to apprise the settlers of the change in Government. The first residence, they learned, was built in what is now Peoria by Robert Maillet, in 1761. This was followed by several others and the town was called La Ville de Maillet, in honor of the founder. Two block-houses were erected. These were used but a short time, there being no immediate danger, as the neighboring tribes were on friendly terms with them. The visitors described the town as composed of narrow streets and log houses, stretching along the lake for a considerable distance. They told of a vineyard and winepress in good order, the latter having a cellar beneath in which to store wine to give it age. A church, beautiful in comparison with the average places of worship, stood at the entrance of the town. A large wooden cross was set upon the roof, while over the door were gilt letters in French. A windmill had been erected for grinding grain and there were several buildings stored with goods for barter. The Peoria customs were similar to those of Kaskaskia though none could speak the English language, the inhabitants being French, Indians and half-breeds.

Vincennes Taken and Re-taken.—When the news of Clarke's invasion reached Hamilton, the British Governor at Detroit, he hastily collected a force of British, French Canadians and Indians, numbering in all about 480 men, and set out in the fall of 1778 to re-capture Vincennes. The garrison now consisted of one private and one officer. However, the brave commander, Captain Helm, determined against allowing the Indian allies full sway in their barbarity, stood in the gateway beside a

loaded cannon and, as Hamilton advanced to within hailing distance, ordered him to halt. The British, not knowing the
strength of the garrison, paused while Hamilton demanded his
surrender. Helm replied that he must first know the terms.
Thereupon he promised the honors of war and a capitulation
was agreed upon, when Captain Helm and one private marched
out, December 14, 1778, and the British again unfurled their
flag over the defences.

Clark fully realized the danger of allowing this post to remain in the hands of the enemy, knowing their attention would
next be directed to Kaskaskia and Cahokia, and that, as soon
as the spring floods would sufficiently subside to allow an easy
expedition. Accordingly, February 7, 1779, he commenced the
march thither with 175 men, Captain Rogers having been sent
with forty-two men and two four-pounders in a boat to a point
below the mouth of White River upon the Wabash. His orders
were to allow no one to pass in either direction.

Clarke and his men endured many hardships on this trip.
Swamps were numerous and filled with water; rivers and creeks
were overflowing the land and running in strong currents, while
the party were poorly equipped and the march had to be performed without delay. They arrived at the mouth of the Little
Wabash on the 13th only to find the country submerged in a
continuous sheet of water from two to four feet deep through
which they waded for a distance of fifteen miles. To keep the
men in good spirits and nerved for their difficult journey Colonel
Clarke devised and encouraged many little pleasantries. A lively
Irish drummer boy, who was versed in the songs of his country,
chanced to be in the command. He was the right fellow in the
right place. While the others were wading water to their armpits, he was perched upon the shoulders of the tallest man, playing
his drum and singing comic songs. On the evening of the 18th
they arrived at the mouth of the Embarras River and, having
no means of crossing, were detained two days. Fortune again
smiled upon them. On the 20th a party of Indians chanced to
be passing in a boat which was borrowed to transport the men
to the other side. Here they were within sound of the morning
and evening gun at the fort. They learned that the people were

wholly unaware of their approach. Now came the last full day's march, it being the most hazardous of all. Clarke says, " I unfortunately spoke in a serious manner to one of the officers; the whole were alarmed without knowing what I said. I viewed their confusion a minute, then said to those near to do as I did. I immediately put some water into my hand, poured powder on it, blackened my face, gave the war whoop and marched into the water. The party immediately followed, one after another, without uttering a word of complaint. I ordered those near me to sing a favorite song, which soon passed through the line and all went cheerfully." During the night they rested on dry land but in the morning another and the last deep sheet of water lay before them. This they were to cross to meet death, captivity or victory, they knew not which. Clarke says, " We had observed several men out on horseback shooting ducks and sent out active young Frenchmen to decoy and take one of them prisoner, in such a manner as not to alarm the others. Being successful, in addition to the information which had been obtained from those taken on the river, the captive reported that the British had that evening completed the wall of the fort, and that there were a good many Indians in town. Our situation was truly critical. No possibility of retreat in case of defeat, and in full view of the town, which, at this time, had 600 men in it— troops, inhabitants and Indians. * * * * I determined to commence operations immediately, and wrote the following placard to the people of the town. 'To the inhabitants of Vincennes: Gentlemen, being now within two miles of your town with my army, determined to take your fort this night, and not being willing to surprise you, I take this opportunity to request such of you as are true citizens, and willing to enjoy the liberty which I bring you, to remain still in your houses, and those, if any there be, who are friends of the King, let them instantly repair to the fort and join the hair-buyer General, and fight like men. And if any of the latter do not go to the fort, and shall be discovered afterward, they may depend upon severe punishment. On the contrary, those who are true friends to liberty, may depend upon being well treated, and I once more request them to keep out of the streets, for every one

I find in arms on my arrival shall be treated as an enemy.'"

This letter filled the enemy with dismay and made the capture less difficult, though not without an engagement in which the British could not bring their guns to bear directly upon their foe because of their elevated position, thus overshooting. Whenever a port-hole opened, aim was brought upon it by half a score of rifles. This disheartened the garrison and secured a speedy capitulation, on Washington's birthday, February 22, 1779. This ended the Revolutionary War in the West.

Illinois County.—COUNTY FRAMED.—In October, 1778, the General Assembly of Virginia erected the conquered country, embracing all the territory northwest of Ohio River, into the County of Illinois. This is said to have been the largest county in the world. It included what is now Ohio, Indiana, Illinois, Michigan and Wisconsin, an area of 250,000 square miles. The following is the substance of a few ordinances for the government of this county passed in the session of 1783:

That the French and Canadian inhabitants, and other settlers of the Kaskaskias, St Vincents, and the neigboring villages, who have professed themselves citizens of Virginia, shall have their possessions and titles confirmed to them, and be protected in the enjoyment of their rights and liberties. That a quantity, not exceeding 150,000 acres of land, promised by this State, shall be granted to the then Colonel, now General George Rogers Clarke, and the officers and soldiers of his regiment, who marched with him when the posts of Kaskaskia and St. Vincents were reduced, and to the officers and soldiers that have since been incorporated into the said regiment, to be laid off in one tract, the length of which is not to exceed double the breadth, in such place on the northwest side of the Ohio as a majority of the officers shall choose, and to be afterward divided among the said officers and soldiers in proportion according to the law of Virginia.

GOVERNOR-GENERALS.—Colonel John Todd of Kentucky was appointed by Patrick Henry, Governor-General over this territory and was implored to deal mildly with the Indians and make friends with them; to settle all questions of boundary, if possible, in their favor; to allow the Catholics and other creeds, if such there were, full benefit of their religious rights; in other words, make the land a home of peace and liberty, returning, as nearly as possible, to the former mode of living.

In June, 1779, Colonel Todd arrived at Kaskaskia which he made the capital of the whole county. He ruled with a mild hand and was a favorite among the people, frequently going East to learn of the best forms of government under the circumstances. In his consultations he gained the best advice as he sought the most enlightened men upon self-government. He had command of the troops of Kentucky, which position he had not resigned on receiving his appointment in Illinois. In 1782 he fought a desperate battle at Blue Licks in that State where he was killed.

Timothy de Montbrun, a Frenchman, was appointed Todd's successor. Little in known of this ruler as the settlements were comparatively forgotten and even the important events were allowed to sink into oblivion until 1787, when the jurisdiction of Illinois passed under the government of the Northwest Territory. General Clarke remained military commander until 1783. No attempt had been made by the British to continue the contest after the surrender of Cornwallis at Yorktown and a final peace was this year established by which the colonies were acknowledged independent and there was no further need of an army in the West.

New Settlements were added to the county. In 1781 an expedition started from Maryland for Western lands, intending to erect homes in the wilderness. James Moore, Shadrach Bond, Robert Kidd, Larken Rutherford and James Garretson, afterward all prominent men, were among the number. After crossing the Alleghanies they took canoes and floated down the Ohio to the Mississippi which they ascended to what is now Monroe County, about half way between Kaskaskia and St. Louis. The three former settled in the " Great American Bottom," but the two latter chose a more frequented spot—Bellefontaine.

In early days certain places were chosen by those journeying from one settlement to another as suitable for camping and recruiting. Here also engagements were filled for trade or consultation and public gatherings were held. Bellefontaine, so named because of a crystal fountain bubbling up cool and sparkling by the roadside between Cahokia and Kaskaskia, was not of the least favored of these points. Near by was a beautiful grove in which James Garretson and Larken Rutherford erected their humble dwellings; but pleasanter, more inviting homes it would be difficult to find.

STORIES.

Pontiac's Plan.—A greater leader than Pontiac, chief of the Ottawas, probably never lived in the United States. But he was treacherous—could not be depended upon by persons he regarded as enemies. He had formed a strong attachment for the French and when the English came to take possession of the western forts, after the Boundary War, he stood a barrier in their way. At the time of the Indian outbreak in 1760, this chief was commander of the warriors about Detroit where Major Rogers was ordered to take command. He says, " As I approached Detroit at the head of a military force I was met by an embassy from one who came to let me know that Pontiac was at a small distance, coming peacefully; and that he desired me to halt until he could see me with his own eyes. His embassador had also orders to inform me ' that he was Pontiac the king and lord of the country I was in.' When we afterward met he demanded my business in his country, and how I dared to enter it without his leave. I informed him that it was not with any design against the Indians that I came, but to remove the French out of the country who had prevented the friendly intercourse between the English and the Indians. He thereupon told me that he stood in my path and gave me a string of wampum as much as to say, ' you need not march further without my leave.' At the second meeting we smoked the calumet together and he assured me that he had made peace with me and my detachment, and that I might pass through his country unmolested and relieve the French garrisons."

Soon after Major Gladwin took command at Detroit, Pontiac and forty warriors presented themselves at the fort and offered to entertain the garrison with a dance. Having been admitted, the dance began while a few skulked about, peeping into every nook to ascertain the condition of the surroudings, the commander and his troops not suspecting the fiendish designs of the jolly crowd. The plan was to again visit the fort with concealed weapons and then, at a given signal, they were to kill the officers while many other warriors would scale the ramparts from without.

When Pontiac returned to camp he told his men all about the fort and the manner of the attack. While in their midst he began the war-dance and was soon joined by the entire assembly. This was the signal to prepare. Savages would congregate in bodies and enumerate the scalps they would bring to the village, while the women and children listened attentively to their boasting remarks. But among them was a faithless girl who shuddered at their designs. She had occasionally visited the fort and on the day previous to the intended attack told the commander of the plot.

That evening the still air bore distant sounds of war-whoops and dancing to the inmates of the fort. The girl's story was confirmed. Next morning as the mists cleared away, Pontiac and his men departed upon their mission of destruction. Sixty advanced to the fort and applied for admittance. Beneath their long cloaks were secreted weapons intended for use when once within the walls. The gates were opened and the array of large dignified warriors filed in. They were greatly surprised on entering to find lines of armed men on all sides ready for action. All the soldiers were in full uniform and traders had assembled to assist if needed. The fierce looks cast about by the chiefs further verified the story of the beautiful Indian girl, though an attack was not feared. Not so easily changed in his intentions was Pontiac. Several times he was in the act of giving the signal, previously agreed upon, but each time changed his mind and finally gave orders to pass out. The Indians hiding about the fort were surprised at receiving no order to advance and when the chiefs returned without the spoils of a massacre their thirst for blood could not be restrained.

Two days later the place was again surrounded by Pontiac and his allies, when a siege was begun. Burning missiles were hurled into it from all sides which set fire to the buildings threatening destruction. The garrison dug wells to get sufficient water to quench the flames. They finally succeeded in clearing away the trees and rocks, behind which the Indians secreted themselves, thus putting an end to the destruction. This siege was continued forty days. For the sustenance of the warriors Pontiac gave the inhabitants of the locality a form of note on birch bark which were afterward all paid.

An Indian Legend is generally far from being reliable but in relation to the destruction of the Illinois tribes, much of the following is true. The correct account of the death of Pontiac has been given in a previous topic. The legend is as follows:

After the close of the war, at Detroit, Pontiac and his tribe had located upon territory belonging to the Illinois on Kankakee River. After remaining for some time as if intending to make it their permanent abode, they were ordered off by the owners of the land. Not complying, the Illinois threatened war against them. On one occasion a party of hunters (Ottawas) were attacked by them. After this a council was called at which Kineboo, the Illinois chief, became enraged at the remarks of Pontiac and stabbed him. This nerved not only the Ottawas but the Chippewas, Shawnees, Kickapoos and Miamis, who joined in an attack upon the Illinois proper.

All their villages were destroyed except La Vantum, the principal town, which was well fortified and was the abode of the chief and his bravest men. This being left, the Illinois had about abandoned the fear of further trouble, when, in the midst of a marriage feast, their foes appeared with the skull and crossbones of Pontiac upon a pole, emblemating a vow to share the fate of their leader or have revenge.

The Illinois fought bravely and repulsed them time and again though they were outnumbered three to one. Night came on; the warriors concluded they could not stand another battle with

an adversary that fought so well and were still receiving re-
enforcements. Accordingly they retreated to the opposite side
of the river and fortified themselves upon a rocky height, which
unfortunate move christened it "Starved Rock," once the location of La Salle's Fort St. Louis and where he received word
of his downfall.

Here they were attacked but in their commanding position
could repulse the allied tribes who were then satisfied to turn the
attack into a siege. Provisions then grew short and this once
energetic tribe was reduced to starvation rather than brutally die
at the hands of their unmerciful enemies. Gradually death relieved them until the dreaded tomahawk put on the finishing
stroke. Thus, in 1769, the nation was annihilated and its members strewed over the fields where they had once been so prosperous and happy.

TERRITORIAL PERIOD.

NORTHWEST TERRITORY.

EPARATED.—The tract of country known as the County of Illinois was separated from Virginia and ceded by her to the United States in 1784; Thomas Jefferson, Thomas Lee, James Monroe and Samuel Hardy being the delegates to Congress to enact the cession. Virginia was re-imbursed for the sum she had expended in establishing the new Government and in its maintenance. The territory lay west of the Alleghanies and north of the Ohio River. Great were the expectations of the people as to the future prospects of this vast and beautiful region.

Laws.—Following is a brief summary of the principal ordinances passed July 13, 1787, for the government of the newly organized tract under the name of the Northwest Territory. They were not enforced until 1790, when Governor St. Clair arrived:

I. The territory might be divided at some future time into two divisions.

II. Congress should appoint a Governor whose office would continue three years unless that body chose to revoke the appointment. Congress should also appoint a Secretary and Judges, the former under the same conditions as the Governor, the latter during good behavior.

III.   The Governor was made Commander-in-chief of the
army.

IV.   When the census of the territory would reach 5,000
inhabitants, Representatives should be chosen, one for every 500
free male citizens over twenty-one years of age.

V.   Representatives were to serve two years.   In case of
death the Governor should call an election in that district to fill
the vacancy.

VI.   There should be formed in the territory not less than
three nor more than five States, and the boundaries stand as follows: The western State should be bounded by the Mississippi,
the Ohio and the Wabash rivers, a direct line drawn from the
Wabash and Post Vincents, due north to the territorial line between the United States and Canada, and by the said territorial
line to the Lake of the Woods and Mississippi River. The middle
State should be bounded by the said direct line, the Wabash from
Post Vincents to the Ohio, by the Ohio by a direct line drawn due
north from the mouth of the Great Miami to the said territorial
line.   The eastern State should be bounded by the last mentioned
line, the Ohio, Pennsylvania and the said territorial line.   It was
further declared that the boundaries of these three States should
be subject so far to be altered, that, if Congress should thereafter find it expedient it should have authority to form one or
two States in that part of said territory which lies north of an
east and west line drawn through the southernly bend or extreme
of Lake Michigan. And whenever any of the said States should
have 60,000 free inhabitants therein, such State should be admitted, through its delegates, into the Congress of the United
States, on an equal footing with the original States in all respects
whatever; and should be at liberty to form a permanent constitution and State Government.

VII.   Slavery was in a manner prohibited.   Slaves brought
into the State were compelled to sign an agreement to work for
their masters a certain number of years; if they did not sign this
the master had sixty days in which to sell them.   Those under
age were to work for their masters thirty-two years and then
become free.

First Territorial Government.—Governor St.

CLAIR.—The Governorship was given to Arthur St. Clair, on October 5, 1787. On July 9 this venerable gentleman, who had been an esteemed officer of the Revolutionary War, arrived at Marietta, in the State of Ohio, where he began his administration, thus changing the capital of Illinois to a point outside the present State, where it remained until the territory was divided. St. Clair's administration was a success. In the following summer, after taking command, the Governor and his three Judges met at the capital and framed a code of laws, by which to act in their dealings with citizens at variance and for the enforcement of peace and morality.

PUNISHMENT.—The only punishment by death was for murder, treason and arson. Pillories were not sparingly used in those days, neither was the whip—most frequently for larceny, burglary, perjury and robbery. Drunkenness was subject to a fine, and if not paid, the offender was placed in the stocks for a specified time according to the misdemeanor. For a great offense by a person not able to pay the fine, the sheriff had the power to sell the person to an idividual who would treat him as a slave, often requiring his services for a period of seven years.

PRESIDENT WASHINGTON'S REQUEST.—Up to 1788 little had been done for the welfare of the settlers of Illinois, yet the people of that locality were not entirely idle. This year the Governor was authorized to direct his attention to the settlement of Vincennes and especially those along the Mississippi River. He gave the French deeds for the lands they occupied, provided they would swear allegiance to the United States. Of this Washington was not wholly ignorant, for he referred to the matter on several occasions; once, especially, when he wrote, in 1789, "You will proceed, as soon as you can with safety, to execute the orders of the late Congress respecting the inhabitants of Post Vincennes, at the Kaskaskia and other villages along the Mississippi."

This called forth immediate action on the part of Governor St. Clair who, in February, 1790, departed upon his mission, accompanied by Secretary Sargeant. He made many acquaintances from whom he learned much about the most valuable and unknown territory over which he had control. Upon his arrival

in Illinois he found the country greatly reduced from the condition
in which he had expected to find it.   Many people of enterprise
had died and others had moved away; disputes had arisen as to
the limits of claims and there was no authority by which to de-
cide the matter.   In consequence the people had no ambition to
go on in the arduous task of building up the country and yet
maintain a subsistence.   The bison by this time had all been
frightened from east of the Mississippi; Indians were not so flush
with game as in the days of La Salle; trade with them had diminished and a few tribes were hostile to the settlers, especially
so to the colonists who had lately arrived from the East.

The Survey Question.—The present plan for the survey of the Northwest, instituted by Thomas Jefferson, had been
authorized by Congress.   P. Gibault, the priest who did so much
for Colonel Clarke on his mission of bringing over the western
posts to the cause of Independence, was yet living and, on Governor St. Clair's visit, presented to him in a friendly manner the
following with eighty-eight signatures:

" The memorial humbly showeth, that by an act of Congress
of June 20, 1788, it was declared that the lands heretofore possessed by the said inhabitants, should be surveyed at their expense; and that this clause appears to them neither necessary nor
adapted to the quiet minds of the people.   It does not appear
necessary, because from the establishment of the colony to this
day, they have enjoyed their property and possessions without
disputes or lawsuits on the subject of their limits; that the sur-
veys of them were made at the time the concessions were obtained from the ancient kings, lords and commandants; and that
each of them knew what belonged to him without attempting
an encroachment on his neighbor, or fearing that his neighbor
might encroach upon him.   It does not appear adapted to pacify
them; because, instead of assuring to them the peaceable possession of their ancient inheritances, as they have enjoyed it till
now, that clause obliges them to bear expenses which, in their
present situation, they are absolutely incapable of paying, and
for the failure of which they must be deprived of their lands.

" Your Excellency is an eye-witness of the poverty to which
the inhabitants are reduced, and of the total want of provisions

to subsist on. Not knowing where to find a morsel of bread to nourish their families, by what means can they support the expenses of a survey which has not been sought for on their parts, and for which, it is conceived by them, there is no necessity? Loaded with misery and groaning under the weight of misfortunes, accumulated since the Virginia troops entered the country, the unhappy inhabitants throw themselves under the protection of Your Excellency and take the liberty to solicit you to lay their deplorable situation before Congress; and as it may be interesting for the United States to know exactly the extent and limits of their possessions, in order to ascertain the lands which are yet at the disposal of Congress, it appears to them, in their humble opinion, that the expenses of the survey ought more properly to be borne by them for whom it is useful, than by them who do not feel the necessity of it. Besides, this is no object for the United States; but it is great, too great, for a few unhappy beings who, Your Excellency sees yourself, are scarcely able to support their pitiful existence."

Orders were issued for a general survey but this did not remove the obstacle in the way of development of the French colonies and they gradually dwindled away, having learned to live in an Indian fashion. But few descedants of the first settlers of Illinois are anywhere to be found.

FRONTIER WARS.—1783-1794.

Cause.—Though a treaty had been agreed upon, in 1783, that restored peace between England and the colonies, by which the latter also gained their independence, yet the British agents were not idle in arousing the Indians against the settlers of the Northwest—the Mississippi River formed the western boundary of the United States, and Great Britain entertained the fond hope of finally making the Ohio the northern. Her subjects continued to trade with the Indians of this region, whom they found jealous of the settlers and in a rebellious spirit. They not only encouraged warfare, but advocated the scalping knife upon all White settlers found west of the Alleghanies and north of the Ohio. Their efforts were not barren of results. A confederation of all the tribes was formed and a thoroughly organized campaign arranged, but the attacks naturally fell upon the present States of Ohio and Indiana.

The Kickapoo Wars began in 1785 and continued two years. Their old chief Pecon thought he could subdue the settlers of the West and began hostilities. To his surprise he found some good fighters ready for him. The Indians sallied forth in bands of from ten to fifty, stealing upon the Whites unawares.

In 1786 they made prisoners of two children of William Garretson, whom they took to Salem Fork on the Sangamon. Here the children were found, but their captors would only consent to release them upon the payment of a liberal ransom. The same year they attacked the settlement at Bellefontaine, Monroe County, killed five of the number and took several prisoners.

To prevent these depredations the people formed a society known as Rangers. Whenever the Indians made an attack the members of the organization were notified by messengers, and soon a body of armed men would be in hot pursuit. The Rangers, together with the block-houses, proved of great benefit in vanquishing these foes.

Illinois Warfare.—Through the untiring efforts of Governor St. Clair a treaty was formed with several tribes, but they were broken by dissensions. Daily the war cloud grew thicker and darker. Finally the savage thirst for blood, plunder and revenge burst forth with all its fury. Father would be killed in the field, mother and children at their homes. The innocent and helpless were scalped that the marauder might take his wigwam trophies to prove his worth as a destroyer of lives. Frequently individuals were taken prisoners and, at times, treated with courtesy.

In a contest at Bellefontaine, in the early spring of 1788, between a band of Kickapoos and four settlers, John Villis was killed and William Biggs taken prisoner. The latter was treated kindly and even offered the daughter of a chief in marriage. He was afterward liberated through the influence of French traders and allowed to return to his home. Mr. Biggs became a noted citizen, occupying a seat in the Territorial Legislature and afterward chosen Judge of the County Court. Three boys were attacked near a block-house. Two escaped, but one was struck with a tomahawk and scalped. He was not fatally injured, however, and finally recovered.

In 1790 James Smith, a Baptist minister, was attacked by a band of Kickapoos who took him prisoner while engaged in prayer for a poor woman and child whom he saw them killing. They had intended to destroy him also, but seeing his attitude of prayer and hearing him sing, they thought he was in intercourse with the Great Spirit and the scalping knife was for once spared. He was laden with plunder and compelled to march by their side until he sunk beneath the hot sun and heavy burden. Again they consulted, uncertain what to do with him, when he laid bare his bosom and told them to kill him if they wished, at the same time pointing toward Heaven. This move of fearless submission touched their savage hearts; he was unloaded, thereafter treated with the greatest respect, and ransomed by the settlers of New Design. The same year a party of the Osage tribe attacked a settlement and led off many horses. In an attempt to recapture the property one of the party was killed.

In 1791 John Dempsey was fired upon, but escaped injury and gave the alarm. A company collected and started in pursuit under the leadership of Captain Hall. A fight ensued in the proverbial Indian fashion, both parties taking to the trees. The red skins were driven from the neighborhood with the loss of five while the settlers escaped even a scratch.

Another band of Kickapoos entered the American Bottom (Mississippi bottom opposite St. Louis) and stole nine horses. This was in the vicinity of Captain William Whitesides, who gave chase. An engagement followed in which several Indians were killed. So vigorous was the onset, that the terrified savages, believing themselves surrounded by an overwhelming army at once surrendered the stolen property and sent an aged chief to negotiate for peace. When this brave leader learned of the insignificant number of the adversary he called to his comrades to renew the contest, but they were already beyond reach of his voice, fearing that the wrath of the Whites could not be appeased. The chief was then disarmed and told to flee for his life. This locality was not again disturbed. In 1795, however, Captain Whitesides led an expedition against a band of warriors,

encamped on the bluffs near Belleville.   In the engagement the
Captain was shot in the side, he thought fatally.   As he fell he
exhorted one of his sons near by to fight bravely and not allow
an Indian to touch him.   Another son was shot through the arm
and disabled.   He crept to his father whom, he expected, would
soon expire.   In examining the wound he traced the course of
the bullet around the ribs to a spot near the spine where he found
it lodged.   Taking out an old pen-knife he cut the lead out and,
holding it up, exclaimed, "Father, you are not dead yet."   The
old veteran sprung to his feet and said, " Come along boys, I can
still fight them."

In the same year (1795) the family of Mr. MacMahan was
attacked when his wife and four children were killed before his
face and their bodies laid in a row on the floor.   Making
prisoners of Mr. MacMahan and a grown daughter, they
departed for their towns.   On the second night of their encampment MacMahan, finding the Indians asleep, put on a pair of
their moccasins and made his escape.   He arrived at the settlements just as the neighbors were burying his family.   They had
enclosed the bodies in rude coffins and were engaged in putting
the sod on their graves as he came in sight.   He looked on the
newly-formed hillocks, and raising his eyes to Heaven in pious
resignation said, "They were lovely and pleasant in their lives,
and in death they are not divided."   His remaining daughter
was afterward ransomed by the charitable contributions of the
settlers.

Indiana Warfare.—GENERAL HARMER'S EXPEDITION.
—As the confederation of tribes was some time in forming, so
it took a long while to break up the war without bringing large
armies into the West and completely annihilating the Indians.
Records show that over 1,500 Whites were murdered or carried
into captivity between 1783 and 1790 in the Northwest Territory
alone.   British traders yet kept up a continual agitation of war
among the savages, assuring them that their king would unite
with the Indians and assist them to drive out the intruders.
These busy bodies even held forts which they claimed to be places
of refuge for themselves and the settlers, but, when war broke
out, they closed doors on the helpless people and revealed all their

knowledge to the Indians. This was clearly shown in an expedition against the towns on the headwaters of the Wabash and upon the Maumee, led by General Harmer, in the autumn of 1790. The General unsuspiciously sent word to the British at Detroit, that the expedition was exclusively against the Indians. The fact was revealed to the savages who deserted their towns, only leaving what they could not take with them.

BATTLE OF THE WABASH—Other expeditions were sent out but few, however, were successful. The most disastrous was that led by the Governor himself. He had become old and infirm and at the time of this battle was so afflicted with the gout that he could neither ride nor walk, but was carried at the head of his men on a litter, from which he issued orders.

When twenty-nine miles from Fort Jefferson and while passing through a deep ravine, the channel of a tributary of the Wabash, November 4, 1791, he was suddenly attacked by a large force of Indians in ambush, commanded by Little Turtle. They were well managed. . Hardly had the engagement commenced until they were pouring a deadly fire upon the Whites, an army of backwoodsmen, who became panic stricken and took to flight. Of the 1,400 engaged, 900 were slain and left strewed upon the ground to be devoured by the scavengers of the air and forest.

EFFECT.—This victory was an encouragement to the foe and long did they dance that evening about their spoils—plunder, scalps and the dying. General Wayne afterward camped upon the spot where this carnage took place and, though a period of three years had elapsed, over 600 skulls were in view and it was necessary to scrape the bones away to prepare a place for campfires. A peace commission asked to negotiate with the Indians after this but in council at the Maumee Rapids in which sixteen tribes were represented, the following was the reply:

"Brothers: We shall be persuaded that you mean to do us justice, if you agree that the Ohio shall remain the boundary line between us.   *   *   *   Money to us is of no value; and to most of us unknown; and, as no consideration whatever can induce us to sell the lands on which we get sustenance for our women and children, we hope we may be allowed to point out a mode by which your settlers may be easily removed and peace thereby obtained.

"Brothers: We know that these settlers are poor, or they never would have ventured to live in a country which has been in continual trouble ever since they crossed the Ohio. Divide, therefore, this large sum of money which you have offered to us among these people. Give to each, also, a proportion of what you say you would give to us, annually, over and above this very large sum of money; and as we are persuaded, they would most readily accept of it in lieu of the land you sold them. If you add, also, the great sums you must expend in raising and paying armies, with a view to force us to yield you our country, you will certainly have more than sufficient for the purpose of repaying these settlers for all their labor and their improvements.   *   *   *   We want peace. Restore to us our country and we shall be enemies no longer."

This speech was dictated by British traders who hoped to secure the land for themselves. The object was not to take the land from Indians but to keep the British from the territory, who deserved punishment for their wholesale crime. The Americans desired to enforce a treaty similar to that with the Illinois and Wabash tribes. This gave the Indians control of the land save what had been previously purchased and no other would be taken without the payment of a sum agreed upon.

BATTLE OF THE MAUMEE.—After the defeat of Governor St. Clair, General Anthony B. Wayne, who won the appellation of "Mad Anthony" by his daring bravery, was placed in command. Little Turtle declared that he was a leader who never slept and advised peace; but the Indians rejected his counsel, and a desperate battle was fought on the Maumee, August 20, 1794. The savages were completely routed and pursued for fifty miles, Wayne laying waste their towns and villages for some distance.

PEACE.—A treaty was then made by which the Indians gave up all of Ohio and a portion of Indiana. In the same fall Mr. Jay effected a treaty with Great Britain by which the traders were withdrawn; thus the British were no more among the red men arousing them against the settlers. General Wayne told the warriors before leaving them, that, if they violated the treaty even after he was dead, he would arise and fight them. These parting words also had their effect and the peace was lasting.

Noble Women.—The settlements had been greatly aided in overcoming their difficulties by a number of noble women who were always anxious to preserve peace if possible. Among these during the late Indian wars was Mrs. LeCompt. Her first husband was St. Ange; second, LeCompt; and last, Thomas Brady. She was generally known, however, as Mrs. LeCompt. She possessed the wonderful power, so lacking among the early settlers, of inducing the Indians to listen to her and acquiesce in her provisions for peace. Often when an enraged band appeared before the village in which she resided, when the settlers were all in arms, the women and children weeping lest they should all be scalped, this woman would hasten out unarmed, unprotected and meet the foe. Soon she would return with a number, sometimes twenty of the chiefs, and a peace contract would be signed. She never failed to bring about a reconciliation. She also possessed many friends among the Indians who would lay down their lives rather than see Mrs. LeCompt suffer the slightest torture. These friends frequently informed her of intended attacks; and thus the people would be on their guard. Her sole ambition was the welfare of her people and an affectionate friendship with the Indians. Only one true to such a cause, would venture out in the dead of night to meet a band of blood-thirsty hounds ready to lick the blood of their foes.

New Settlements were made in Illinois during the time that it was a part of the Northwest Territory, notwithstanding the horrors of Indian warfare. In 1790 Joseph Motte, a Frenchman, established a ferry across the Wabash at Vincennes. Though there was much difficulty in defending himself against the Indians, he was successful and gained the patronage of an extensive travel in a few years. This caused settlers to venture to the Illinois side of the river.

The same year (1790) Jean Baptiste, a slave residing with his master near Lexington, Kentucky, made good his escape; and taking with him his master's gun, fled to the Indians in Illinois.

As he had once been a captive and lived among them a few years, he had learned their manners, customs and language. In an Indian village on the Des Plaines he was united with a squaw in marriage, at which place he remained until 1796, when he departed with his family for the mouth of Chicago River where he made his home. Thus the first white settler of the metropolis of the West was a negro with his red and black family. At this point Baptiste traded with the Indians for several years.

James Piggott of Connecticut arrived in Monroe County in 1783 and built a fort, afterward known as Fort Piggott. In 1790 forty-three families had congregated at this place, which proved a safe refuge for them, and the settlement continued to prosper for many years. In 1795 the same man established a ferry at St. Louis, which became the main point of communication between the Spanish settlements on the west side of the river and the English and French on the east. From this date the present Monroe County was a favorite locality for settlement.

Cahokia was, from 1780 to 1800, the leading Indian headquarters for all western tribes. Julian Dubuque lived here for several years but in 1788 purchased a tract of land near the city that bears his name. Other traders made Cahokia their rendezvous and the town often had many strangers within its limits.

A New County.—The settlements of Illinois had been converted into one county, known as St. Clair. The census of 1790 showed a white population of 1,200 and the people were distributed over a large sweep of territory. In 1795 a divison was made, the line extending eastward about midway between Kaskaskia and St. Louis. All the territory lying north of this line was styled St. Clair County and all south, Randolph County.

INDIANA TERRITORY.

Formation.—The census of 1790 showed a population of 1,200 Whites in Illinois and in the whole territory it amounted to 12,000. The White population in Ohio alone numbered over 5,000 at the close of 1796. This entitled the people to a first class territorial government. In 1798 Governor St. Clair issued an order for an election of Representatives. The large tract of land included in the Northwest Territory was divided May 7, 1800. All that portion lying east of the line drawn from the mouth of the Kentucky River through Fort Recovery to the British possessions, west of Pennsylvania and north of the Ohio, was included in Ohio Territory, and the remainder known as Indiana Territory.

July 4, of the same year, the law passed into effect and the capital was located at Vincennes. William Henry Harrison, afterward President of the United States and long known as " Tippecanoe Harrison," was chosen Governor; John Gibson, Secretary; and William Clark, John Griffin and Henry Vanderburg, Judges. These were able men, under whose administration the country made rapid progress. Governor Harrison did not arrive until the following January and the office was filled by Mr. Gibson, the Secretary. Upon his arrival he set about organizing and arranging a code of laws. He called together the Judges, and the law making body continued in session two weeks.

Increased Domain.—Up to 1800 all the territory west of the Mississippi was owned by Spain, of which there were over a million square miles. It was known as Louisiana Territory and was ceded back to France, the original claimant. In 1803 the United States purchased this large tract of Napoleon who was, at the time, in need of money to carry on the war in Europe which he had set about to conquer. The amount paid was $15,000,000.

In 1804 all the possessions of the United States west of the Mississippi were included in Indiana Territory. This union lasted only one year, when Louisiana was detached and formed into a separate territory. The purchase of this domain was a signal for much rejoicing throughout the West, for the Mississippi became entirely under the control of the States. For a few years after Indiana Territory had been established a series of treaties, including a large land-purchase, were made with the Indians.

Fort Dearborn Erected.—The colonization of the northern part of the State remained dormant for many years while the southern portions were being rapidly settled. Though a few persons had established their homes at the mouth of Chicago River with Baptiste, yet they were traders and thought of no other resource by which they might gain a livelihood than trading with the Indians. In 1804 the Government began erecting a fort at this point known as Fort Dearborn, named in honor of Harry Dearborn, Secretary of War, under whose orders it was probably built.

Territorial Election.—Two classes of territorial government were in vogue at this time. Under the second class the Governor, selected by Congress, had exclusive control as a law executor; the first class gave a privilege to the people to choose Representatives to work, as law makers, in harmony with the appointed Governor. There appeared to be an opposition to the first class government and to bring out the wishes of the people, when the census had attained a sufficient number, the Governor called an election, which was held on September 11, 1804, and gave a majority of 138 votes in favor of the first.

Territorial Legislature.—A Territorial Assembly was called at Vincennes, January 30, 1805. The choice for Representatives of Illinois were, Shadrach Bond and William Biggs of St. Clair, and George Fisher of Randolph. The new Legislature convened July 29, 1805. Governor Harrison read his annual message advocating changes. In this message he spoke against selling liquor to the Indians. He said: "You have seen our towns crowded with drunken savages; our streets flowing with blood; their arms and clothing bartered for the liquor that destroys them; and their miserable women and children enduring all the extremities of cold and hunger. Whole villages have been swept away. A miserable remnant is all that remains to mark the situation of many warlike tribes." Mr. Harrison was true to his conviction, having previously sold a distillery at reduced figures because he saw the misery it was creating.

Everything passed off smoothly under the new form of government until the taxes were to be collected. This was a novel arrangement to many, especially to the French who held a meeting at Vincennes and agreed to support no one who advocated the first class territorial government. Little attention was paid to this and soon the "Ship of State" was again smoothly sailing with a good breeze. About this time a book of laws was published for Indiana Territory and generally distributed.

Separationists and Anti-Separationists.—In 1805 Michigan (then included the present State of Wisconsin and a portion of Minnesota) was separated from Indiana Territory, and in a short time thereafter the question came up whether or not it would be expedient to form a separate division of Illinois. Two parties sprung up known as the Separationists and Anti-Separationists, the former being the stronger in Illinois and the latter in Indiana though both parties had strong foot-holds in each of the localities.

The doctrine preached by the Anti-Separationists was that the expense in running the Government would be greater if divided; that the territories would work in unison if they remained as one, and a stronger resistance could be maintained if the defense of life were required; besides, those living about Vincennes knew the capital would be removed from that locality if a division were effected, because of its situation at the side of the territory. The Separationists claimed that the country was being rapidly settled and that the sooner each Territory could be arranged as it would be admitted into the Union the earlier it would become a State; that the settlements were too remote from each other to make laws that would suit both localities; that the long journeys through the wilderness was dangerous; that, should an out break occur, the Government could immediately act for the safety of the people. During the discussion of these questions other points would be bought up, the argument wax warmer; then would follow taunts, threats, blows; and not unfrequently these debates ended in bloodshed and assassination. So marked were the party lines that persons of one persuasion of mind would only associate with those entertaining similar views. In fact, the people became very much like modern politicians.

Election.—In order to strengthen the Separation party, an Indiana Representative who was also Speaker of the Legislature, Jesse B. Thomas, was chosen delegate to Congress. He greatly desired to go to Congress but, in order to be elected, had agreed to represent the sentiments of the Separationists,

although a majority of his supporters resided in Illinois. The new settlements increased more rapidly in Indiana than in Illinois from the fact that the timber was better and the distance not so far from the more thickly settled States. Thus the new member's task in Congress was comparatively easy and he succeeded in forcing upon the assembly the fact that, as the population had increased to such an extent in Indiana it would be advisable to divide the territory. Accordingly February 3, 1809, Illinois became a separate division and was known as Illinois Territory, bounded by the Mississippi on the west, and on the east by the Wabash to Vincennes, thence north to a line drawn west from the south bend of Lake Michigan. This was the year the "Army President," James Madison, took his seat and about the time the merciless savages again began their depredations upon the frontier.

ILLINOIS TERRITORY.

Rulers.—The Governor chosen for the new Territory was Ninian Edwards; Judges, Jesse B. Thomas (moved to the State soon after his appointment), Alexander Stuart and William Spriggs. Nathaniel Pope, a relative of Mr. Edwards, was appointed Secretary.

Governor Edwards managed the affairs of State in a satisfactory manner. Though the people were far from being reconciled to the separation, he went to work upon his own responsibility, manifesting no desire whatever to favor either party. On clearly taking in the situation he applied himself with the zeal of a President of the United States. His efforts told. The law-making power was called together at Kaskaskia June 16, 1809. The first task was a re-organization of the militia for the impending crisis of defense.

Tecumseh War.—British were again busying themselves among various tribes, to induce them to again take up arms against the settlers, then numbering about 11,500 in Illinois Territory. As in former wars the brunt fell upon territory east and northeast of us, but the people were without an army and thus subject to small bands of skulking Indians who fell upon those residing remote from thickly settled communities, block-houses or forts.

CONFERENCE WITH TECUMSEH.—The first manifestation of an outbreak was led by Tecumseh, chief of the Shawnees. He prepared to form an alliance of all tribes against the Whites and offered to lead the Indian legions. Several tribes agreed to follow at his bidding. Governor Harrison of Indiana Territory called a conference at Vincennes, August 12, 1810. Tecumseh, accompanied by warriors, appeared. The discussion became heated to the extreme. Tecumseh maintained that the Whites had no right to make treaties with the several tribes but that all Indian nations owned the land in common. Therefore, when lands were purchased, the transfer would be valid when agreed to by the entire race. In Mr. Harrison's response he alluded to a grievance, Tecumseh had narrated, in a bantering manner which thoroughly aroused the chief who sprung to his feet and threatened to prostrate the speaker. Upon this the warriors all arose, with tomahawks in hand, ready to pounce upon the Whites who were entirely defenseless. An awful silence ensued until the Governor broke it by continuing his remarks in a fearless tone. Tecumseh and his followers retired soon after, but still indignant. Not only did they threaten to break the treaty but declared their intentions for revenge.

THE POTTAWATOMIES, about this time, penetrated into the new country of Missouri where the young warriors not only stole horses and other valuables but fell upon inhabitants and committed several murders. For these depredations the Governor of that territory requested a permit from Governor Edwards to secure the guilty parties if possible. For the mission Captain Levering was selected. On his visit to the chief he found him rather indifferent regarding the matter, but Levering was not the man to succumb to obstacles without a bold effort on his part to overcome them. Finally he effected a partial compromise in which several horses that had been stolen were delivered and a promise made to send others to Captain Heald of Fort Dearborn.

BATTLE OF TIPPECANOE.—Tecumseh departed for the South in July, 1811, where he sought to persuade the Creeks,

Choctaws and Chickasaws to second his plans. Governor Harrison of Indiana regarded this the time to strike a blow to establish peace. Accordingly he set out for Prophet's town (Tippecanoe) where he arrived November 6. The Indians were under command of the One-Eyed Prophet who sent out deputies to meet Harrison, thus averting immediate action, but it was only to strengthen his own army and be better prepared to take his enemy at a disadvantage. The deputies prevailed upon the troops to encamp upon high ground, but the Whites had a leader too shrewd to be caught in such a trap. The Indians acted suspiciously and a strong guard was kept at the outposts to maintain a careful watch during the night while the entire army, 700 strong, was ready for battle.

Their plans were not for naught but might have been better. They were aroused by the Indian war whoop while it was yet dark. The foe came into camp upon them with all the fury common to a savage onslaught when confident of success. After a fierce struggle the assailants were driven from the camp but not until many had been killed on both sides. In this battle Joe Daviess fell victim to the tomahawk.

Earthquake.—In 1811 an earthquake, frightfully felt in Illinois, concentrated its force at New Madrid on the Mississippi below the mouth of the Ohio. The phenomenon occasioned great fear among the settlers. The ground opened in several places emitting sulphurous gases, and then closed again with a loud sound. Mud was thrown into the air and in places the ground sunk several feet.

Election.—February 15, 1812, Governor Edwards issued an order for an election, allowing the people a privilege of deciding whether they would adopt the first class territorial government or not, i. e. choose a form of Legislature to work in harmony with the Governor chosen by Congress. The polls were open for three days, allowing all a favorable opportunity to cast their ballots, and the election resulted in favor of the affirmative by a large majority. In the following September the Governor and Judges added three new counties which then divided the Territory into five—Randolph, St. Clair, Madison, Gallatin and Johnson.

October 8, 9 and 10 an election was held and the following officers chosen: Delegate to Congress, Shadrach Bond; Legislative Council, Pierre Menard of Randolph, William Biggs of St. Clair, Samuel Judy of Madison, Thomas Furguson of Johnson and Benjamin Talbot of Gallatin; Representatives, George Fisher of Randolph, Joshua Oglesby and Jacob Short of St. Clair, William Jones of Madison, Philip Trammel and Alexander Wilson of Gallatin and John Grammar of Johnson.

First State House.—The elected members convened December 25, 1812, in the new capitol at Kaskaskia. The building was made of limestone and resembled an old-fashioned church of a rural, rocky district, contrasting only in the fact that it had an upper story. It is needless to search for contrasts between that quiet little body to the stormy Legislature of tricky lawyers and politicians of to-day, or the little limestone State house and the capitol building of the present, constructed of hewn stone and almost every kind of granite in the world, one of the handsomest in the world. Suffice it to say, however, it was in the most thickly settled community of the West while the present one would have been in a wilderness seventy-five miles from any settlement.

Roads and Defenses.—The roads through the country consisted of mere trails or paths, the most frequented leading to Kaskaskia. The Kaskaskia & Detroit trail led from the former place diagonally through the State passing out at Danville. The Kaskaskia & Vincennes trail became noted after 1779 when Colonel Clarke marched through that region. Lake Peoria trail extended from that vicinity through Terra Haute. The most prominent Indian trail was from Fort St. Louis, near the present city of Ottawa, to the Indian village visited by Marquette when he passed down the Mississippi. In 1800 and for several years after, a trail that led from Lusk's Ferry on Ohio River to Kaskaskia was much used. When the country became more thickly settled several of these trails were converted into mail-routes, along which settlers would first pitch their cabins.

The only inhabited districts that enjoyed any degree of safety from the Indians were in the neighborhoods of Kaskaskia, Cahokia and Vincennes, because of the many settlers in unison and the number of block-houses in which the inhabitants could take refuge should a band of the enemy appear. Several families had settled in the Saline regions of Vermillion County, near Danville, but were scarcely known to the savages, and were engaged in the manufacture of salt. Those at Chicago, outside of Fort Dearborn garrison, were half-breeds and lived with the Indians. In Jo Daviess County were a few miners who usually abandoned their homes, in case of danger, and took refuge with the settlers down the river. Thus the most defenseless settlers were in the interior of the State, especially in the vicinity of Lake Peoria. Not only were they in danger of savage barbarity but many of the French, who were unfriendly to the new form of Government because of taxes to be paid, were yet living at Peoria and might co-operate with the Indians.

A Conference.—Governor Edwards still entertained a hope of allaying the war by treaty. In March, 1812, he called together a council of Indian chiefs at Cahokia which convened April 16. The following were present and were addressed by the Governor in person: Gomo, Pepper, White Hair, Little Sauk, Creat Speaker, Yellow Son, Snake, Maukia, Ieman, Bull, Neckkeenesskeeskeckee, Ignance, Pottawatomie Prophet, Pamousa, Iskkeebee, Manwess, Toad, Pipe Bird, Cut Branch, The South Wind, Black Bird, Little Deer, Blue Eyes, Sun Fish, Blind of An Eye, Otter, Makkak, Yellow Lips, Dog Bird, Black Seed, Mittitasse, Desskagon, Malshwashewii and White Dog. They listened attentively to all that was said and selected Gomo to reply to the speech, which he did on the following day in an eloquent and friendly manner. To make his speech more forcible he exhibited several half-clad, miserable-looking squaws, brought along for the occasion, to show how poor they were and their great need of help. They were only practicing deceit, having no intentions of peace whatever.

INDIAN WARS OF 1812.

The second war with Great Britain began in earnest in 1812. The large armies did not reach Illinois but the people were at the mercy of a more barbarous foe, spurred on and equipped by British who made a desperate effort to secure a complete confederation of the tribes.

Alarm in Illinois.—Settlers who had gone into the wilderness a few miles from block-houses, realized an insecurity, and most of them abandoned their homes for the thickly settled communities. Several took their wives and children to block-houses but remained themselves upon their claims; others accompanied their families and occasionally visited their deserted homes. During the absence of a husband and father the remaining members of his family would be chilled at the approach of every messenger, lest he came with the intelligence that their dear one had fallen victim to the tomahawk.

Fort Dearborn Massacre.—The only settlement of the northeast at this time was at Fort Dearborn (Chicago, then in Michigan Territory). At this place the Indians, half-breeds and garrison were on friendly terms though the former had been solicited to take up arms against the latter. There were friendly chiefs in this locality who kept the garrison and the three or four families, who were generally in the fort, informed of all that was taking place. The command was under Captain Nathaniel Heald, recently from Kentucky. He came to Chicago, with his wife shortly after their marriage, each riding a beautiful bay pony.

The summer of 1812 found Captain Heald in command of but seventy-five men, one-half of whom were wholly unfit for duty because of sickness. At this critical moment orders came from General Hull to evacuate the fort and retire to Fort Wayne on the Maumee. The Captain being an obedient officer, wished to comply with the request and accordingly set about arranging for the departure.

The Indians having been steadfast in their friendship, Heald still looked upon them as allies and hoped to deal with them as man should deal with his fellow man, at the same time forgetting the British influence in inciting them against the Whites, as at Mackinaw and elsewhere. Had he been left free to follow the dictates of his own judgment, all would probably have been right, but his plans were questoned from first to last. The subordinate officers opposed an evacuation because, they said, they could never escape; besides, the buildings would be reduced to utter waste. However, Heald remained steadfast and considered

it best to disguise no movement from the Indians whom he regarded his friends.   Accordingly a conference was called and
the entire plan revealed.   All the ammunition, extra arms, liquor,
etc., were to be left for the red men to divide among themselves
and they in turn to furnish a safe escort to Fort Wayne.   The
officers again remonstrated and persuaded Mr. Heald that such
proceedings would insure their utter annihilation.   To furnish
the Indians liquor to craze their brains and then provide them
with ammunition, would be putting weapons into their hands by
which to slay the donors.   Secretly the treaty was broken by
the Whites who took the liquor kegs to the river, broke in the
heads and emptied the contents; the ammunition was thrown into
a well, while the arms were broken and then pitched in after it.
This transaction was found out by the Indians who regarded it
a failure on the part of the Whites to keep their word and at the
same time deprive them of the promised liquor.

On the morning of the 15th of August, 1812, with drums beating and colors flying, the garrison moved out in battle array for
the distant fort on the Maumee.   They were headed by Captain
Wells who had with him an escort of friendly Indians from Fort
Wayne.   Following these and at the head of the garrison, Captain and Mrs. Heald rode upon their fine palfreys.   Immediately
behind the troops were the wagons in which the women and
children were transported, also the sick of which there were
many.   Last of all marched a band of 500 Indians who claimed
to be escorts for a short distance, but who proved to be a band of
scalpers ready to join another band secreted ahead on the lake
road supposed to be the one the Whites would take.

The first indication of trouble was at least two miles form the
fort, when the Indians began forming in front.   Captain Wells
detected their movement and immediately rode back and informed Mr. Heald of their fiendish designs.   The wagons were
hastily arranged that they might protect the sick and helpless as
well as serve for breastworks.   Behind these the handful of soldiers gathered to defend themselves the best they could.

During the fight Captain and Mrs. Heald were separated.
Soon after Mr. Wells rode up to her with the blood streaming
down his face.   He said he feared he had been mortally wounded

and requested her to tell his wife that he had fought bravely. At that moment his horse was shot and the lifeless animal fell upon him in such a manner that he could not, in his exhausted condition, extricate himself. In this position he killed another Indian, making eight in all, when he was overpowered and scalped. His heart was cut out, sliced and devoured by the savages while yet warm. Mrs. Heald was a witness to this sickening transaction.

All were massacred but twenty-seven who laid down their arms and consigned themselves to their fate—prisoners of war in the hands of savages. Had it not been that among these were chiefs, friendly to the Whites, all would have perished, either at the hand of the scalpers or burned at the stake. Mr. Heald was captured by one party and his wife by another. But they were both purchased from the captors and delivered to an Indian trader who secured a Frenchman to row them to Mackinaw as prisoners of war where they were delivered to the British. The commander at this post chanced to be a Mason as was Heald, thus they were uncommonly well cared for. They only remained here for a short time when ransomed and allowed to return home. Other captives were liberated, several not until the following spring, however, but the wounded were tortured.

When the news went abroad that the fort was to be abandoned, warriors assembled from all directions and for miles distant. A band of these from the regions of the Wabash did not arrive for several days after the bloody work.

Thus ended one of most inhuman massacres, on a spot where thousands now hurry to and fro daily, ever recorded in history. The only land-mark to point out the site of this tragedy is a large cottonwood tree standing on 18th Street, between Prairie Avenue and the lake.

Peoria Campaign.—FIRST EXPEDITION.—In October, 1812, Governor Edwards sent an expedition to Lake Peoria. The entire State militia numbered but 350 able-bodied men and with the troops from Vincennes only 400 could be spared. They were composed mostly of young men who had entered the ranks with a view to having a good time, considering the trip a novelty; and, had it not been for the fear in which Governor Edwards was held by the Indians, the undertaking would have been marked by more thrilling warfare, but as it was, the foe fled at sight of the armed troops, leaving nothing for them to do but to plunder and burn the stores and wigwams.

The most notable occurrence was the encounter with the French. When Governor Edwards discovered that there was nothing left for him to do, he sent word to Captain Craig, in command of the supply boat, to make preparations for a return. When a short distance below Peoria the boat was fired in the night by Indians who could be traced to the village, and evidence tended to prove that the French had harbored the incendiaries. Craig burned the town, took about seventy-five of the residents on board and landed them near Alton where he left them without food. These reached St. Louis a few days thereafter in a half-starved condition. Shortly after the French returned to Peoria and rebuilt the town.

A SECOND EXPEDITION to Lake Peoria was planned in the summer of 1813. The troops, while in Indian localities, were in constant alarm; at the slightest indication of danger they would become fear-stricken and shoot at random, on one occasion killing a comrade—though there was not a foe within eighty miles, —and leaving their tents and stores behind. The army numbered about 900, a large per cent of whom were from west of the river where depredations had been committed by the same tribes that were giving our settlers trouble. Though no decided engagement took place the Indians harbored about Lake Peoria were driven from the settlements. Fort Clark was built at this point and the country traversed by Rangers until the savages were overawed and for a short period the people enjoyed quiet.

Last of the War.—In 1814 the troubles in the West became more desperate than formerly, from the fact that Perry's victory on Lake Erie and the successes of General Harrison had driven the Indians westward. About this time the savages entered the homes and scalped men, women and children. But gradually they were overpowered and the warfare subsided. October 18, 1814, the troops were all disbanded.

The People of 1814, when the war closed, turned their attention to improving their farms and homes, and promoting the general interests of the country.' New settlements were formed and many immigrants arrived from the East. From this forward Illinois society assumed a new phase as there was a marked change in the manners and customs, imitating those of eastern colonies.

The church was undergoing a change likewise. The Catholic organization remained about as formerly. A few families arrived from Canada and several from the East, but the early French settlers, their number having dwindled to about one-fifth of the population, were the main supporters of this church. Protestants began to flourish under the supervision of the old-fashioned ministers who delivered their illiterate, lengthy sermons in a " sing-song tone." Great excitement prevailed at these meetings, often held in the forests otherwise in dwellings or humble churches. The good influences of these sincere people will go with us through generations. Even the eloquence of the early orators may be heard at times to-day while the economic living of the people, to be honest and upright, are worthy examples that should be impressed upon the minds of the present and coming generations.

Marriage engagements were somewhat binding upon the male that he might not flirt with his lady friends, and he was compelled to fill out the following form three months prior to the " wedding-day:"

" Know all men by these presents that I,................... ...., am held and firmly bound unto ...., Clerk of .... County and Territory of Illinois, in the just and full sum of five hundred dollars, by which payment well and truly to be made, I bind myself, my heirs, and assigns for and in the whole, sealed with my seal, and dated this .... day of .... 1814.

" The condition of the obligation is such, that whereas the above bond .... has this day made application for license to join together in bonds of matrimony with .... Now if the said .... does well and truly marries the said .... without any fraud, partiality or illegality attending the said marriage, then this obligation to be void, otherwise to be and remain in full force and virtue in law.

Bondsmen $\left\{\begin{array}{l}\dotfill \\ \dotfill\end{array}\right.$

Criminal laws were revised in 1812, remaining to that time the same as were used in Indiana Territory. In 1815 a thorough revision was made and they were rudely printed in book form by Matthew Duncan.

A Territorial Bank was established at Shawneetown in 1816. Its capital was not to exceed $300,000 and the Territory was authorized to subscribe one-third of the stock. The institution enlivened business and remained the only bank in the Territory for several years.

The First Newspaper published in the State was the " Herald " at Kaskaskia, established in 1814; it was a three-column folio, but in 1816 was enlarged to a four-column. In 1817 it was purchased by Cook & Blockwell, in whose hands it remained until moved (1820) to Vandalia. No other paper was published until 1818, when an Anti-Slavery organ sprung up at Shawneetown, known as the " Emigrant." In 1819 a third paper, and also of Anti-Slavery persuasion, was printed at Edwardsville, known as the " Spectator."

Territory to a State.—From the great Northwest Territory two States had been admitted—Ohio in 1802 and Indiana in 1816, while Illinois was following close after them in population. The people of the latter were becoming energetic and grew anxious to make their Territory a State, and when a State, of the foremost in the Union. For such an outcome the Territory bade fair. Lead mines appeared numerous and inexhaustible; coal had been discovered as early as 1721; along the streams timber grew in abundance, while in certain localities were forests of considerable size. The greatest drawback in the minds of the early settlers were the vast swampy prairies, the breeders of ague. In early days when travelers returned from visits to Illinois they told of the landscape over which wild animals roamed in large herds; of frolicking brooklets and navigable rivers, of the rich mines and prospects for coal—but they took no fancy to the prairies covered with grass and dotted with marshes. To-day, when the traveler returns from his trip through the State, he tells of the beautiful farms fenced in as it were with green arbors, interspersed here and there with groves of shade and orchard, if here in the month of June he fails not to describe the fields of golden grain alternating with the waving rows of crisp thrifty corn. He tells of large cities that have sprung up as if by magic—cities that defy the world for business and enterprise, while their stately mansions stand in magnificent splendor forming long avenues; of the manufactures, a yet growing industry; of traffic and travel carried with lightning speed from town to town, city to city, and through the State from State to State on tracks more numerous, according to size, than in any other in the Union.

But such was not the condition of affairs in 1818. The population had not yet reached the required number, 60,000, to be admitted as a State, there being but 38,000. Most all the present counties of the South and Southwest had inhabitants within their borders. In the East but few had yet taken up their abodes, most of the inhabitants of this locality preferring to remain east of the Wabash where they could demand immediate protection of the Government. The colony in the neighborhood of Danville was composed of but two or three families; Chicago had not yet taken its boom though a few houses had been erected; scattered along the Mississippi as far as Alton were settlements, thence a wilderness to Jo Daviess County which was not then within the present boundaries; on the Illinois was Peoria, with her few inhabitants; also other villages farther north on Rock and Kankakee rivers. Three or four families had pushed out into the central portion, settling the Counties of Sangamon and Macon, while in other districts hunters had wandered, built their cabins and remained alone in the forest, only seeking a subsistence; not even desirous of claiming the land upon which they were living.

The ruling power was held in the Southern half and other settlements were seldom consulted upon political topics. Further than this but little interest was manifested in other settlements; the people had retired to these secluded spots more to be let alone than to take pride in advancing the new country in just laws, moral customs and progressive industries. In fact, many were wedded to Indians and hoped rather to dwell in the wilds as mediators between the two races—Caucasian and American. Consequently we must credit the Southern portion with the rapid development of the Territory, and to them is due the honor of putting the State machinery in good working order.

During the year 1817 a petition was circulated by the citizens soliciting Congress to admit Illinois into the Union as a State with privileges equal to those of other States. This document was received by the people with due regard, bearing as it did their sentiments and designed to bring about their wishes. Nathaniel Pope was yet the delegate to Congress, and when he departed by river and stage, in the fall, he bore with him many injunctions from the people in regard to the matter. In the following January he received the precious document, but could not get a hearing in Congress until in April.

Northern Boundary Changed.—It was first necessary to secure an enlargement of the State. By the ordinance of 1787 the Northwest Territory was to be divided into three divisions (See previous page), or Congress might have the power to form one or two States north of a line drawn east and west by the south bend of Lake Michigan, and might change the boundary as it would see proper. To adopt the former boundary would deprive her of the extreme northern mines and the port at Chicago, the head of a canal to the Mississippi already talked about. Illinois was situated in the Center of the United States. She had access to the navigation of the Ohio, Wabash, Mississippi and Illinois rivers. Judge Pope easily persuaded those honest old fathers in Congress, faithfully laboring for the good of the country and not for "machine politicians," that to deprive her of the harbors of Lake Michigan would be to rob her of the advantages awarded by nature itself, leaving her without the facilities of becoming a foremost State, for railrods were then unknown. Accordingly the boundray was fixed at 42 degrees 30 minutes.

First Constitutional Assembly.—As authorized by Congress, in an act becoming a law April 18, 1818, the people chose Delegates who assembled at Kaskaskia in July, 1818, and prepared a Constitution which was completed and signed August 26. Jesse B. Thomas, former Delegate to Congress, was chosen President and William C. Greenup, Secretary of the convention. The following are the Delegates who represented the counties then organized:

St. Clair—Jesse B. Thomas, John Messenger, James Lemon.

Randolph—George Fisher, Elias K. Kane.

Madison—Benj. Stephenson, Jos. Borough, Abraham Prickett.

Gallatin—Michael Jones, Leonard White, A. F. Hubbard.

Johnson—Hezekiah West, William McFartridge.

Edwards—Seth Gard, Levi Compton.

White—Willis Hargrave, William McHenry.

Monroe—Oldwell Carns, Enoch Moore.

Pope—Samuel O'Melveny, Hamlet Furguson.

Jackson—Conard Will, James Hall, Jr.

Crawford—Joseph Kitchell, Edward N. Cullom.

Bond—Thomas Kilpatrick, Samual G. Morse.

Union—William Echols, John Whitaker.

Washington—Andrew Bankson.

Franklin—Isham Harrison, Thomas Roberts.

The principal worker in this assembly was Elias K. Kane who afterward became United States Senator. Mr. Kane was brilliant and far-sighted in reasoning. He early began the study of law and had become distinguished in his profession. He was one of the first opposers of imprisonment for debt and Illinois was the first State to abolish the practice.

State School Fund.—Judge Pope was an able lawyer and to him is due the honor of inducing Congress to provide a State fund for the promotion of education. Though he had lived in the Territory only since 1815 and had been a Delegate to Congress two years since that time, he was well posted upon the necessities of the people he represented. As he suggested another amendment was put upon the laws. Formerly a certain per cent of the fund from the sale of land was taken to improve the roads, but this was lavishly wasted in throwing logs into the mud and in building grades not sufficiently drained to keep them from becoming water-soaked. By the amendment the people were to make their own roads and the five per cent was to be appropriated to schools; one-sixth of which was to be used exclusively for a college.

The Election took place on the third Thursday, Friday and Saturday of September, 1818. There being no party contest all hearts turned to Shadrach Bond of St. Clair for Governor and Pierre Menard of Randolph for Lieutenant-Governor.

STORIES.

Mrs. Gilham's Captivity.—On a fair June morning, 1790, while the noble James Gilham was laboring in his fields with his elder son Isaac, on his little farm in Kentucky, a party of Kickapoo Indians, from this State, slunk around the house where Mrs. Gilham was busy about her household affairs and the children were engaged in play. They watched a fair opportunity and captured the mother with her three children, the elder being twelve and the younger but four years old.

When the savages entered the house Mrs. Gilham was so frightened that she fainted away and could but remember the words of her son, "Mother, we are all prisoners." They took what provisions they could find and all the clothing possible for them to carry, emptying even the feathers from the feather bed.

The Kickapoo town, for which they set out, was situated near the center of the present State of Illinois and in a locality far from any White inhabitant. In their journey thither they avoided all settlements lest they should be discovered and pursued. This rendered all hope of escape impossible and the captives heroically submitted to their sad fate. The children's feet began getting sore and were badly bruised from the rapid journey through the pathless wilderness. To ease the pain of the little ones, the mother tore pieces from her dress and bound around their feet as best she could. The Indians had with them a small quantity of jerked venison which they were kind enough to give to the children when the other provisions were exhausted, whilst they and Mrs. Gilham partook of no food for several days; when one of the party was sent out to get meat, but only returned with one gaunt raccoon. Mrs. Gilham, who had become alarmed lest the children when on the verge of starvation should all be killed, afterward said, " The sight of that poor raccoon did me more good than stores of wealth."

The animal was dressed by singeing the hair from the body and emptying the contents of the entrails. It was then chopped to pieces and, with head, bones, skin and intestines, boiled in a kettle and made into a kind of soup. The savages and their captives sat around the kettle and devoured the contents, helping themselves with spoons made of bones and forks, of wood; thus obtaining relief from immediate starvation.

The Ohio was approached with caution as the Whites frequently passed up and down this stream. Through the day they camped in a thick wood near the present site of Hawksville, Kentucky, where they made a raft of logs, lashing them together with red elm bark. At night they crossed the stream undiscovered. After they had gone a few miles beyond the river they relaxed in speed and soon satisfied their appetites. Keeping to the east and north of the settlement of Vincennes, they crossed the Wabash near the present site of Terre Haute and marched through the present counties of Clark, Coles and Macon, finally reaching the town on Salt Creek, about twenty miles northeast of Springfield.

The field in which Mr. Gilham was at work being some distance from the house, he did not discover the misfortune that had befallen his wife and little ones until he returned at dinner time. Then the Indians had placed many miles between him and them, having hastened away with all possible speed. On his approach he was startled at the appearance of his lonely home. No smoke was curling up from the chimney to remind him of the savory meal in preparation; no happy children running to welcome him home; no wife awaiting him upon the threshold: instead, all was silent and hushed. He entered the house, where were many indications of the scene enacted early in the morning. Here empty boxes, there the contents that had not been worth taking strewed upon the floor; and over all, the indications of a hurried departure. At once divining the situation he gave the alarm and soon willing neighbors had joined with him in the search. The trail to the edge of the timber could easily be detected but soon this disappeared and they were compelled to give up the pursuit. In the morning that husband and father was a peaceful farmer striving to lay up stores for the future; in the afternoon, a bereaved man hunting for his loved ones.

He sold his possessions in Kentucky, then visited the settlements of Vincennes and Kaskaskia with· the hope of securing the aid of the French traders, who had a fair knowledge of all tribes then in the Northwest. War continued between the Whites and Indians rendering his efforts hopeless. Five years passed and yet no tidings came, but he did not fail to converse with every trader he saw and his labors were not without result. He finally learned from one of these that his wife and children were with the Kickapoos. With two Frenchmen for interpreters and guides, he visited the Indian town on Salt Creek and there found his family alive and well. Clemons, the younger son, could not speak a word of English and it was with difficulty, after living five years among the red men that he could be persuaded to leave them for a new home.

In his visit to Illinois Mr. Gilham had become so favorably impressed with the country, that in 1797, two years after the recovery of his family, he became a resident of the Territory and spent the remainder of his days in Madison County, followed by other noted persons of his State. In 1815 Mrs. Gilham's name was brought before Congress and she was given a quarter section of land for the suffering she had endured while in the wilderness.

Lively and Huggins.—When the Indians became hostile, during the War of 1812, two settlers, Messrs. Lively and Huggins, were living in the wilderness twenty-five miles from any settlement. Huggins desired to move to a fort at Hill's Station, in Randolph County, but Lively fearlessly objected, asserting that there was no danger. Finally Huggins departed for the settlements leaving Lively and his family in the wilderness without any means of defense.

Mrs. Lively suffered untold miseries from imaginary scenes of Indian warfare, but she could not persuade her husband to depart. His stock were kept in an enclosure for safety from the savages and wild beasts. Disturbances at night were frequently noticed, which were regarded as an indication of trouble and added misery to the frightened family, consisting of parents, two sons and two daughters; also a hired hand was with them. On several occasions, when the stock were uneasy and the dogs barking viciously, Lively seized his rifle and proceeded from the house to ascertain the trouble, but he always told his family that it was wild animals that caused the disturbances. This did not satisfy her and she finally persuaded him to move. They were to take their departure in the night and on the evening set all things were being made ready. Mr. Lively directed his son and hired hand to get up the horses from the pasture, while his wife and daughters busied themselves in milking the cows and about the extra labor in making ready to depart. They were truly light-hearted; in another day, if all went well, they would be in a place of safety.

When the boys departed for the pasture Mr. Lively was seated on a stump, rifle in hand, guarding the premises. They had not proceeded far, however, until the report of a rifle caught their ears. Hastening back toward the house, they soon ascertained the trouble. The view that met their eyes haunted them for many years. A large band of hideous, demon-like savages had surrounded the house, dancing, yelling and brandishing the tomahawk. They had begun their dastardly work and soon father, mother, daughters and younger son were slain. Thus perished one of the first families that settled in Washington County. The remaining son and hired hand reached the settlements in safety and spread the alarm. Rangers took the trail, overtook the party, killed several and recaptured some of their plunder.

Gomo's Speech.—The following is the speech delivered by Gomo in response to Governor Edwards, at Cahokia in March, 1812:

" You see the color of our skin. The Great Spirit, when he made and disposed of man, placed·the Red-skins in this land, and those that wore hats on the other side of the big waters. When the Great Spirit placed us on this ground, we knew nothing but what was furnished to us by nature. We made use of our stone axes, stone knives and earthen vessels, and clothed ourselves from the skins of the beasts. Yet we were contented! When the French first made large canoes they crossed the wide waters to this country, and on first seeing the red people, they

were rejoiced. They told us that we must consider ourselves
as the children of the French, and that they would be our fathers; the country was a good one, and they would change goods
for skins.

"Formerly we all lived in one large village, there was only
one chief, and all things went on well; but since our intercourse
with the Whites, there are almost as many chiefs as we have
young men.

"At the time of the taking of Canada, when the British and
the French were fighting for the same country, the Indians were
solicited to take part in that war—since which time there have
been among us a number of foolish young men. The Whites
ought to have staid on the other side of the waters and not
troubled us on this side. If we are fools, the Whites are the
cause of it. From the commencement of their wars they used
many persuasions with the Indians; they made them presents
of merchandise in order to get them to join and assist in their
battles—since which time there have always been fools among
us, and the Whites are blamed for it.

"The British asked the Indians to assist them in their wars
with the Americans, telling them that if we allowed the Americans to remain upon our lands they would in time take the whole
country, and we would then have no place to go to. Some of
the Indians did join the British, but all did not; some of this
nation in particular did not join them. The British persisted in
urging upon us that if we did not assist them in driving the
Americans from our lands our wives and children would be miserable for the remainder of our days. In the course of that war
the American General [Clarke] came to Kaskaskia, and sent
for the chiefs on this river to meet him there. We attended,
and he desired us to remain still and quiet in our villages, saying
that the Americans were able of themselves to fight the British.
You Americans generally speak sensibly and plainly. At the
treaty of Greenville, General Wayne spoke to us in the same
sensible and clear manner. I have listened with attention to you
both. At the treaty of Greenville General Wayne told us that
the tomahawk must be buried, and even thrown into the great
lake; and should any white man murder an Indian, he should be

delivered up to the Indians; and we on our part, should deliver up the red men, who murder a white person, to the Americans.

"A Pottawatomie Indian, by the name of Turkey Foot, killed an American, for which he was demanded of us; and although he was a great worrior, we killed him ourselves in satisfaction for his murders. Some of the Kickapoos killed an American. They were demanded, were given up, and were tied up with ropes around their necks for the murders. This is not what the chief, who made the demand, promised, as they were put to death in another manner. Our custom is to tie up a dog that way when we make a sacrifice. Now listen to me well in what I have to say to you.

"Some time ago one of our young men was drunk at St. Louis and was killed by an American. At another time some person stole a horse near Cahokia. The citizens of the village followed the trail, met an innocent Kickapoo on his way to Kaskaskia and killed him. Last fall, on the other side, and not far from Fort Wayne, a Wyandot Indian set fire to the prairie; a settler came out and asked him how he started the fire. The Indian answered that he was out hunting. The settler struck the Indian and continued to beat him until they were parted, when another settler shot the Indian. This summer a Chippewa Indian at Detroit was looking at a gun, when it went off accidentally and killed an American. The Chippewa was demanded, delivered up and executed. Is this the way General Wayne exhibited his charity to the Red-skins? Whenever an instance of this kind happens, it is usual for Red-skins to regard it as an accident. You Americans think that all the mischiefs that are committed are known to the chiefs, and immediately call on them for the surrender of the offenders. We know nothing of them; our business is to hunt in order to feed our women and children. It is generally supposed that we Red-skins are always in the wrong. If we kill a hog we are called fools or bad men; the same, or worse, is said of us if we kill a horned animal; yet you do not take into consideration that, while the Whites are hunting along our river, killing our deer and bears, we do not speak ill of them. * * * * *

The desires of the chiefs and warriors are to plant corn and pursue the deer. Do you think it possible for us to deliver the murderers here to-day? Think you, my friends, what would be the consequence of a war between the Americans and Indians. In times passed when some of us were engaged in it many women were left in a distressing condition. Should war now take place, the distress would be, in comparison, much more general. This is all I have to say on the part of myself and warriors of my village. I thank you for the patient attention to my words."

BIOGRAPHICAL.

William Henry Harrison, Governor of Indiana Territory, was the son of Benjamin Harrison, a noted man in Revolutionary times. In speaking of the father we are carried back to old Virginia, the "Mother of Presidents," his associates being the Washingtons, the Randolphs, the Lees, the Masons, the Henrys, the Jeffersons, the Madisons, the Monroes and their great compatriots. In the council of these men, sacred to American history, he often mingled and himself serving three terms as Governor of that State and earlier as a member of the Continental Congress.

The beautiful banks of the Potomac and James are well known and upon the latter William H. was born February 9, 1773, being the third son of the family. He was given the opportunity for a good education and made the best use of it until eighteen years of age when his father died. After this period he became unsettled but his early training was lasting. Near his home the mortified Cornwallis handed his sword to Washington when our subject was but eight years old; when the convention met to frame the Constitution he was fourteen; when Washington was inaugurated President he was sixteen.

He early resolved upon the study of medicine and began a course at Philadelphia. Shortly after this he joined an expedition westward to fight the Indians and was put in command of a pack-horse train bound for Fort Hamilton, near Cincinnati. The trip being a hazardous one and coming with a commission from President Washington, his boy-like appearance attracted unusual attention among the officers, and especially from Governor St. Clair. He was shortly after advanced to a Lieutenancy and fought his first battle with General Wayne on the Maumee. For bravery and good judgment he was promoted to a Captaincy. In 1798 he resigned his position in the army and accepted the appointment of Secretary of the Northwest Territory, in which position he remained until in 1800 when the Territory was divided into Ohio and Indiana territories, he being appointed Governor of the latter.

As Governor he saw this vast domain rapidly increase in inhabitants. His principal work while in this capacity was dealing with the Indians, negotiating in all, thirteen treaties, some were broken and some kept, but in which 60,000,000 acres of land were involved. It was during this official capacity that he won the appellation of " Tippecanoe Harrison " by gaining a decisive victory in the bloody battle at Tippecanoe, Indiana.

After this battle he figured prominently in United States service. He was made commander of the army of the West in the War of 1812, and together with Commodore Perry broke its back-bone, completing this work in a decisive victory over Proctor and Tecumseh in the Valley of the Thames, Canada, where the latter was killed and his followers hopelessly disheartened. He was first elected to Congress in 1816, from this forward figuring prominently in politics and in 1840 was nominated by the Whigs for the Presidency. March 4, 1841, he was inaugurated, serving but one month in this high office when he died, April 4.

Ninian Edwards, to whom the Governorship of Illinois Territory was entrusted, afterward United States Senator and also State Governor, was born in Montgomery County, Maryland, in March, 1775, where he lived until he grew to manhood. His parents took pleasure in giving him a thorough education, and procured the services of a private instuctor. When young Edwards grew older he fell into bad company and was on the road to ruin, having plenty of money at hand and mild parents who only hoped for a change in the morals of their son, anticipating a time when the young man would have " sown his wild oats," though that time does not arrive until the vigor of active life is sometimes past.   Not so with young Edwards.

In 1798 he was licensed to practice law.   When he had been in this profession but a few months he saw, as many do, a necessity for a better education, but he did not wait for a better opportunity; he went to work in earnest.   His labors told and he became widely known throughout the states of Kentucky and Tennessee as an able lawyer.   His society and council were early sought by politicians, though he was not a lover of their profession.   For a time he carried on a frindly correspondence with Henry Clay who aided him to secure his appointment in Illinois.

In 1802 he returned to Maryland on a visit to his parents and friends, when he married Miss Elvira Lone, a noble and highly esteemed young lady of the neighborhood, who proved to him a worthy helpmate.

When he was but thirty-two he had filled the positions of Representative to the Kentucky Legislature, Presiding Judge of the General Court, Circuit Judge, Fourth Judge of the Court of Appeals and Chief Justice of the Supreme Court of Kentucky; the latter he was filling when appointed to Illinois.

He was tall and of a commanding appearance, conveying an impression of power; his writings were pleasing and in address he was fluent.   In after life he became sober and earnest, and Illinois owes much of early distinction to the efforts of Ninian Edwards.   He died July 20, 1833.   (For his career in State service and efforts of his son, Ninian W., who resides in Springfield, see State Period.)

CHICAGO IN 1833

STATE PERIOD.

CONSTITUTION.

MODIFIED laws for a temporary purpose are not lasting. The first written Constitution presented to and read before the Convention required the Governor and Lieutenant-Governor to have been citizens of the United States thirty years before eligible for the office and were the only State officers to be elected by the people. The other four officers—Secretary of State, Treasurer, Auditor and Attorney-General—were to be appointed by the former and confirmed by the State Senate.

As the people, generally, desired Pierre Menard to be Lieutenant-Governor, the Delegates took the liberty to shape a provision accordingly. Colonel Menard was a Frenchman and had taken out his naturalization papers but a year previous. It was therefore agreed that a two-years' resident of the State was eligible to the office.

Great power was vested in the Governor as to appointments. In order to weaken his power in this direction it was agreed that the General Assembly could make certain appointments if it chose. This was done in order to get Elijah C.

Berry for Auditor of Public Accounts, as it was generally supposed that Shadrach Bond would be the next Governor and that
he would not appoint Mr. Berry to the named office.   The above
provisions were the weakest points of the Constitution.   They
were weak from the fact that there was no stability in the controlling ordinances.   When the Governor and General Assembly were on good terms the former could make the appointments,
otherwise the latter would attend to this business.

   The salaries for Governor and Judges of the Supreme Court
were $1,000 each; Secretary of State, $600.   Slave laws were
about the same as under territorial government save that children
born of slave parents should be free when of age.

----◆•●•◆----

BOND'S ADMINISTRATION.—1818–1822.

Governor,	-	-	Shadrach Bond.
Lieutenant-Governor,	-	-	Pierre Menard.
Secretary of State,	-	-	Elias K. Kane.
Auditor,	-	-	Elijah C. Berry.
Treasurer, { 1818–20,	-	-	John Thomas.
{ 1820–22,	-	-	R. K. McLaughlin.
Attorney-General, { 1818–20,	-	Daniel P. Cook.
{ 1820–22,	-	William Mears.
Speaker of { 1st House, -	-	John Messenger.
{ 2d " , -	-	John McLean.
United States Senators, { E. L.,	-	Ninian Edwards.
{ T. L.,	-	Jesse B. Thomas.

1 Representative in Congress; Population in 1820, 55,211.

   The First General Assembly convened at Kaskaskia, October
3, 1818, one day before Governor Bond assumed the duties of
his office, and remained in session until October 13, when it took
a recess until it should be empowered by Congress with all the
rights of a State Legislature.   No business was transacted save
the choosing of the above State officers and electing two United
States Senators.   Matters of interest were discussed and plans
mapped out for the organization of the new State.   The Assembly consisted of fourteen Senators, representing the fourteen

counties, and twenty-nine Representatives.

Illinois having been declared by Congress a State of the Union, December 3, 1818, the Legislature again convened January 4, 1819. Governor Bond's message was brief and contained but few points for action other than putting the machinery of the State Government in working order.

Internal Improvement was regarded as the first and most important step to be taken. The canal from Chicago to the Mississippi was warmly advocated and a lack of immediate cash only prevented its being pushed through with all possible speed. Where a town had not yet been started and the Legislature believed there should be one, laws were enacted accordingly. The following is the ordinance, passed January 9, 1818, for the building of Cairo:

" AND, WHEREAS, the said proprietors represent that there is, in their opinion, no position in the whole of the extent of the Western States better calculated, as respects commercial advantages and local supply, for a great and important city, than that afforded by the junction of the Ohio and Mississippi rivers. *

*   *   *   *   And, whereas, the above named persons are desirous of erecting such city, under the sanction and patronage of the Legislature of this State, and also of providing for the security and prosperity of the same, and to that end propose to appropriate the one-third of all the moneys arising from the sale of and disposition of the lots into which the same may be surveyed, as a fund for the construction and preservation of such dykes, levees and other embankments as may be necessary to render the same perfectly secure; and, also, if such fund shall be deemed sufficient thereto, for the erection of public edifices and such other improvements in the said city as may be, from time to time, considered expedient and practicable; and to appropriate the other two-thirds part of the said purchase moneys to the operation of banking."

Finances, Habits and Customs.—Early in the administration a crisis in financial affairs was impending that pointed to an embarrassment of the young State. But few persons foresaw it. The ignorance of a true conditon of the State, on the part of the people in general, was due to their secluded, economic mode of living, their principal occupation being agriculture.

It was difficult to dispose of the surplus products because of tedious ways of transportation. Commerce was carried on principally by way of the Mississippi and the ascent was slow and laborious. Occasionally goods were brought over the mountains in lumber wagons drawn by four, six or eight horses, thence floated down the Ohio to the Mississippi, up which they were towed.

The settler purchased but few articles, consequently any business beyond his farm received but little attention, in speculation he seldom indulged. His wife and daughters spun and wove his winter clothing from the wool produced by his sheep; summer clothing and also dry goods were made from flax or hemp. Tan yards were scattered throughout the State where hides and pelts were made into leather which the shoemaker manufactured into boots or shoes for a few bushels of corn or wheat. In building his house he piled up logs—hewn if time permitted and tools were accessible; if not, they were left as they were cut in the forests—between which mortar and sticks were placed until the crevices were all or partially filled; doors were swung by leather hinges and fastened with wooden latches. Tools were loaned and borrowed, persons often awaiting for weeks to secure the use of those engaged ahead. With these and by the assistance of a neighboring blacksmith, they made their own plows, harrows and wagons; besides, their bedsteads, chairs, tables, cupboards and candlesticks were all of home manufacture. Lands cost them $2 per acre provided they bought from the Government, one-fourth of which was cashed. On purchasing from speculators they paid more but cashed a smaller per cent.

Payment for many of these purchases were beginning to come due (1819) and there was an increasing demand for money. Immigration had been encouraged until persons were enticed into the State, without money nor resources from which to obtain any. These, too, were equipped with a farming outfit and provided with homes, accomplished by an exchange of labor.

To meet the increasing demand for cash, a State bank was formed in 1821, without money and issued bank notes of one, two, three, five, ten and twenty dollars. Heavy loans were made and the State either took personal or mortgaged security. Legislators firmly believed that they had contrived a means by which they would get the State out of her difficulty, while neighboring States were being swamped in bold speculations and would all break. Ford gives the following anecdote of Lieutenant-Governor Menard, when the latter put the vote to the Senate for resolutions to Congress to get that body to honor the bank money in reception for the purchase of land: "Gentlemen of de Senate, it is moved and seconded dat de notes of dis bank be made land-office money. All in favor of dat motion say aye; all against it, say no. It is decided in de affirmative. And now, gentlemen, I bet you one hundred dollars he never be made land office money." The Speaker of the House also believed this a useless move and resigned to make a speech against the bill. Of course their bank currency was not made landoffice money and the wild legislating was keenly felt in the following administration.

Capital Changed.—Prospects were discouraging for Kaskaskia ever to become a large city because of its unfavorable surroundings, and as the location was distant from the center of the State, it was deemed prudent by the Legislature of 1819 to remove the capital to a more suitable locality. A committee was chosen to select such a spot. These men discovered, in a vast wilderness, what seemed to them a fine site for a flourishing town, and because of the classical significance of an Indian word "vandal" they named the "future city" Vandalia. Here the Second General Assembly convened December 4, 1820.

Kaskaskia suffered in the extreme from a loss of the law-making body. Her population at that time numbered 7,000; to-day there are but 300 souls in that once thriving town of the wilderness. The change has been more particularly from a freak of nature. Land in that locality is mellow and because of frequent inundations from the rivers the Kaskaskia has formed a new channel, leaving the "Ancient City of Illinois" upon an island, the banks of which are gradually wearing away. Thus the town that has furnished so much historical romance to the people of the West will shortly be no more.

Slavery in Illinois.—In 1819, when the State government was forming, a new a code of slave laws was instituted in order to prevent rebellion. These with a few slight modifications took the name of Black Laws. It was enacted that no negro or mulatto should reside in the State until he had procured a certificate of freedom, and given bond, with security, for good behavior, and not to become a county charge. No person was to hire or harbor a negro or mulatto who had not complied with the law under the penalty of $500 fine. All such free negroes were to cause their families to be registered. Every negro or mulatto not having a certificate of freedom, was to be deemed a runaway slave; was liable to be taken up by any inhabitant; committed by a Justice of the Peace; imprisoned by the Sheriff; advertised; sold for one year; and, if not claimed within that time, was to be considered free, unless the master should afterward reclaim him. Any person bringing a negro into the State to set him free, was liable to a fine of $200. Riots, routs, unlawful assemblies and seditious speeches of slaves, were to be punished with stripes, not exceeding thirty-nine, at the discretion of any Justice of the Peace; also, slaves were to be punished with thirty-five lashes for being found ten miles from home without a pass from their master; also, it was made lawful for the owner of any dwelling or plantation to give, or order to be given, to any slave or servant coming upon his plantation, ten lashes upon his bare back; and persons who should permit slaves and servants to assemble for dancing or reveling, by night or day, were to be fined twenty dollars. It was made the duty of all Sheriffs, Coroners, Judges and Justices, on view of such an assemblage, to commit the slaves to jail, and to order each of them whipped, not exceeding thirty-nine stripes on the bare back, to be inflicted the next day, unless the same should be Sunday and then on the next day after. In all cases where free persons were punishable by fine under the criminal laws of the State, servants were to be punished by whipping, at the rate of twenty lashes for every $8 fine. No person was to buy of, sell to, or trade with a servant, without the consent of his master; and for so doing was to forfeit four times the value of the article bought, sold or traded.

The propriety of keeping slaves had been discussed since early in United States history, but in 1820 the question was urged with more or less bitter feeling. The neighboring State, Missouri, was applying for admittance and, as the people therein were about equally divided on the slavery issue, the question was brought up in Congress whether it should be admitted as a free or a slave State. Henry Clay then brought forth a compromise bill by which it was admitted in 1821 as a slave State but the practice was to be prohibited in all other territory lying west of the Mississippi River and north of 36 degrees 30 minutes. Illinois took up the question, for slavery was not prohibited and the State was Pro-Slavery on a test election. The census of 1810 showed but 158 slaves in the entire Territory; of 1820, 917; but in 1830 the number had diminished to 748, while in 1850 there were none.

Counties Admitted.—The settlements increased rapidly. People flocked from all parts of the globe and the newer portions were being rapidly filled. The Legislature of 1821 added seven new counties to the nineteen already formed—Fayette, Montgomery, Sangamon, Green, Pike, Lawrence and Hamilton.

Election—Four candidates were placed in the field, of which two were of slavery persuasion and two anti-slavery. Of the latter were Edward Coles, Land-Office Registrar of Edwardsville, and General James B. Moore, of the State militia; of the former, Joseph Phillips, Chief Justice of the Supreme Court and Thomas C. Brown, Associate Justice of the Supreme Court. The election was held in August, 1822, and resulted in favor of Mr. Coles by fifty majority. Five candidates were in the field for Lieutenat-Governor, A. F. being elected.

BIOGRAPHICAL.

Shadrach Bond, first Governor of Illinois, was born in Frederick County, Maryland, in 1773. His father was a planter and engaged quite extensively in that branch of occupation, devoting more attention to his farm than to the education of his children. There were but few places where the youth might be instructed in the days of young Bond, and he received but a meagre idea of the world, studying only the common branches the few days he attended school. He, however, became a close observer and in time his knowledge was only surpassed by his intelligent reasoning and careful decisions. His complexion was dark but his eyes hazel. Always jovial and apparently in good humor, he never failed to please his companions, becoming a favorite, especially with the ladies.

On his arrival in Illinois he engaged in farming, but was soon called to fill positions of trust, his first calling being to serve as a Delegate to the Indiana Territorial Convention. In 1812 he was a Delegate to Congress and, in company with his wife, made the trip to Washington on horseback. In 1814 he was receiver of public money; after his Gubernatorial position, land-office registrar at Kaskaskia, near which place he lived. Here his career was ended April 12, 1832, and here his remains were interred. These, together with those of his wife, were removed by the State to Chester and a beautiful monument was erected to their memory.

COLES'S ADMINISTRATION.—1822–1826.

Governor,	- - -	Edward Coles.
Lieutenant-Governor,	- -	- Adolphus S. Hubbard.
Secretary of State,	- - -	(3 changes)
Auditor,	- - -	Elijah C. Berry.
Treasurer, { 1822–23,	- -	R. K. McLaughlin.
{ 1823–27,	- -	Abner Field.
Attorney-General,	- - -	James Turley.
Speaker of { 3d House, -	- -	Wm. L. Alexander.
{ 4th " , -	- -	Thomas Mather.
United States Senators, { E.L., { 1818–25,		Ninian Edwards.
{ 1825–31,		Elias K. Kane.
{ T.L., 1823–29,		Jesse B. Thomas.

1 Representative in Congress; Population in 1825, 72,817.

The Third General Assembly convened December 2, 1822, and continued in session until February 11, 1823. The State was in a political blaze when the new administration took the reins of Government.

Slavery Agitation.—In his inaugural address Governor Coles advocated the emancipation of slaves held by the French. This aroused the party that believed it had the power to carry out measures at its own hand. The question that had been agitating the minds of the settlers seemed ready to come to a focus. Both parties had established newspapers in the principal towns, and had for their correspondents the dignitaries of the State.

The Legislature was about equally divided on the question, and the elections had been close. It was thus in Pike County, a large territory lying between the Illinois and Mississippi rivers and extending north to the boundary. Nicholas Hanson and John Shaw each claimed the seat in the General Assembly, the former representing Anti-Slavery and the latter Pro-Slavery.

The time of Jesse B. Thomas as United States Senator having nearly expired, the people desired his re-election. It was learned that Hanson, in spite of his Anti-Slavery views, would vote for him while Shaw would not because of personal animosities. In order, therefore, to re-elect Thomas, Hanson was allowed to take his seat in the Legislature; but immediately after the election for Senator he was compelled to give place to his opponent, having been a member for a period of only two months—the party now wishing to change the Constitution, a Pro-Slavery man would best answer their purpose. The motto, " Convention or death " became common.

Everything was now to be carried by storm. In the evening after this transaction a company of ratifiers entered the streets of the capital. The procession was headed by Judge Phillips, Judge Reynolds, Lieutenant-Governor Kinney and members of the Legislature. The party, in every respect, resembled a party of modern ratifiers. Tin horns were blown, drums beaten, guns fired, while those with good lungs exercised them in deafening shouts.

The Pro-Slavery members lacked one vote for the necessary two-thirds majority to change the Constitution and the matter was laid before the people to vote upon at the coming election. Excitement ran high. Both parties immediately set to work for a thorough organization. On election day there was a general turn-out. Voters were brought to the polls on stretchers when too ill to be otherwise conveyed; the lame were not absent, neither the blind nor the deaf; boys suddenly became of age, though father maintained them several years thereafter and postponed giving them the promised cow, horse or land, when of age.

The election returns showed 11,772 votes polled, of which 4,950 were for and 6,822 against a Constitutional Convention. This was the last effort to make Illinois a slave State.

Finance.—As previously stated the State organized a bank in 1821. Almost any one could borrow money and in a short time $300,000 had been lent. Soon the notes began to fall below par; the first fall was 25 cents, thence down the scale until the value was but 30 cents on $1. In consequence of this fall, although the Government declared a debtor not obliged to pay a debt for a space of three years were he refused the acceptance of bank notes, money from other States naturally took its place and there was more Ohio and Kentucky currency in circulation than our own. The crisis from this visionary statesmanship was reached in 1824, in which year alone the State lost $100,000.

School and Road Laws were enacted by the Fourth General Assembly (1824) that were somewhat similar to those of to-day. These laws were not favorably received. Objections were especially raised by those who had been compelled to labor five days upon the highways but under the new law pay a few cents per capita. They also complained of the school tax, probably because their children were being educated free of charge. Such rebellious clamors were raised against the system that the next Legislature repealed the law.

The Illinois & Michigan Canal was incorporated by an act of the Legislature in the spring of 1825. Its capital stock was to be $1,000,000 with an understanding that it was to be completed in ten years; the corporation to receive the benefit of tolls and donated public lands for fifty years, when both were to be transferred to the State and six per cent interest paid for the use of the money.

Daniel P. Cook, in honor of whom Cook County is named and the only Representative from the State then in Congress, defeated the measure for the time. He said that the rich harvest which it was destined to yield, should go into the treasury

of the State; that in less than thirty years it would relieve the
people of taxes, and leave a surplus to be applied to other works
of public utility. Through his efforts 224,320 acres of land were
granted to Illinois by Congress, in 1827, in alternate sections along
the proposed canal route.

Governor Coles Arrested.—Party spirit was again
aroused, in 1825, when it was learned that Governor Coles had
wilfully violated the laws and Constitution of Illinois. Anyone
bringing slaves into the State and freeing them was to give bond
of $200 each as a guarantee for their good behavior. The Gov-
ernor brought with him ten negroes whom he freed, paying no
attention to the laws. His county brought suit of $2,000 against
him and got judgment for the amount, but the Legislature inter-
fered by changing the limitation of the statutes. The Judge
could not accept the change and the matter was taken to a
higher court where, through strategy, the decision was reversed.

Lafayette's Visit.—In 1825 the State was honored by a
visit from General Lafayette, General Washington's friend and he
who fought hand in hand with the patriots in their struggle for
Independence, although he was a resident of France. He had
grown old in years but he was carried back to his younger days
on meeting a few of the veterans he had once known. He was
given a reception at Kaskaskia and at Shawneetown, being the
guest of the Governor. At the latter place his path was car-
peted from the landing to Rawling's mansion and flowers were
showered upon him by little girls arranged along the way. This
house yet stands.

Election.—The Presidential vote of 1824, in Illinois, stood
as follows: Whigs, John Quincy Adams, 1,541, and Henry
Clay, 1,046; Democrats, Andrew Jackson, 1,273, and John C.
Calhoun but a very small vote. Mr. Crawford, announced him-
self as a fifth candidate subject to no convention nomination.
Being a personal friend of Governor Coles, he received 218 votes.

In the campaign of 1825 there were three Gubernatorial candidates in the field—Ninian Edwards, Thomas Sloe and Adol-
phus F. Hubbard. The candidates for Lieutenant-Governor
were ministers of the gospel—William Kinney, a resident of the
State from 1797 and a member of the Baptist church; Samuel

H. Thompson, a Methodist. Edwards of Madison, and Kinney of St. Clair were elected.

BIOGRAPHICAL.

Edward Coles, second Governor of Illinois, was a man of polished ideas and a refined gentleman but subject to whims peculiar to himself. He was born in Albemarle County, Virginia, December 15, 1786. He received a thorough common school education and afterward attended William and Mary College from which he graduated. In early life he became an associate of Patrick Henry, Thomas Jefferson and James Monroe. He was also private secretary of President Madison for several years. In 1847 he visited Russia on a mission for the President. His taking up his residence in Illinois was merely accidental. It was anticipated that the candidates for President in the coming election would be John C. Calhoun and Secretary of Treasury Crawford. The Senators from Illinois were divided—Edwards supporting the former and Thomas the latter—and to overbalance the influence of Edwards, Mr. Coles was sent to the State, getting the appointment of land-office registrar at Edwardsville through the influence of Mr. Crawford.

Governor Coles was an uncompromising opposer of slavery. Having been a planter in Virginia, when he moved to Illinois he emancipated his slaves, giving to each a piece of land they might call their own. He became enthused upon the question and during his Gubernatorial career directed most of his efforts in this direction. He figured but little in politics after retiring from this office. In 1833 he moved to Philadelphia where he died July 7, 1868.

EDWARDS'S ADMINISTRATION.—1826–1830.

Governor, - - - -		Ninian Edwards·
Lieutenant-Governor, - - -		William Kinney.
Secretary of State, { 1826–28, -	-	George Farquer.
{ 1828–39, -	-	Alexander P. Field.

Auditor,	·	·	·	·	Elijah C. Berry.
Treasurer, { 1823–27,	·	·	·		Abner Field.
{ 1827–31,	·	·	·		James Hall.
Attorney-General,	·	·	·		George Farquer.
Speaker of { 5th House,	·	·	·		John McLean.
{ 6th "	·	·	·		"

	E. L.,	1825–31,	Elias K. Kane.
United States Senators, { T. L.,	{ 1823–29,	Jesse B. Thomas.
	{ 1829–30,	John McLean.

1 Representative in Congress; Population in 1825, 72,817.

The Fifth General Assembly convened December 4, 1826, and continued in session until the following February 9.

Governor Edwards took charge of the State Government at a disadvantage, yet he did justice to the people holding the reputation he had already gained and at the same time conducting his own administration. In his campaign speeches he denounced public men who labored for self gain by robbing the people of their dues. For this he endured the enmity of politicians and many employes of the civil service. Standing alone he publicly exposed the duplicity and carelessness of the cashier, T. W. Smith, of the Edwardsville branch of the State bank. He told of the great burden that was oppressing them because of a reckless banking system and advocated a change. This was striking at the very base of political favoritism which was too much for the guilty who heaped maledictions upon him from every quarter, referring to the time in particular when he had publicly accused Mr. Crawford, Secretary of the United States Treasury, of the embezzlement of Treasury funds for campaign purposes—but in this he was backed by the President himself and other men of prominence.

In his inaugural speech he suggested an immediate examination of the Edwardsville branch of the Illinois bank, enumerating reckless loans, also loans to officers that had never been entered upon the books. The Legislature chose an investigating committee, made up of Mr. Edward's enemies, who reported the bank in good condition.

The Circuit Judges were regarded by him as of no consequence under the circumstances, and he advocated the holding of court by the Supreme Judges twice a year with an increase

of salary, dispensing with Circuit Judges entirely. This proposition met with favor, from the fact that many of the defeated candidates for the office were in the Legislature, and they
greatly desired to see their opponents ousted. (See Territorial
Period for a sketch of the early life of Ninian Edwards.)

Winnebago War.—ORIGIN.—In the summer of 1827
two keel boats, sent with supplies to Fort Snelling, stopped at a
large camp of Winnebagoes a short distance above Prairie du
Chine. Getting the warriors drunk the boatmen enticed squaws
on board and set sail, but on their return they were attacked by
the outraged Indians. The contest was warm, several Whites
and many Winnebagoes being killed.

EXPEDITION.—A few days after this Lewis Cass, by previous
agreement, was to meet this and other tribes to negotiate a treaty
with them, but not an Indian appeared. Realizing that something was wrong he repaired to Prairie du Chine where he
found the Whites had taken shelter within the barracks and
learned that the Winnebagoes, Sacs and Siouxs had begun scalping the helpless and innocent. He then proceeded down the
river and warned the settlers of their danger. For the safety of
the Galena settlements General Tom M. Neale, of Sangamon
County, was sent against the Indians. Red Bird, a Sioux chief,
surrendered. He and other chiefs were taken to Prairie du
Chine and lodged in jail. Several were acquitted and several
hung while Red Bird pined away and died from humiliation
and close confinement.

Public Land Scheme.—In the session of 1827 the question of reducing the price on public lands came up and it was
thought best to petition Congress to make the price easier. The
Governor suggested a surrender of the lands in Illinois to the
State where he claimed they properly belonged and not to the
United States. His proposition was at first thought unreasonable.
In his message to the Sixth General Assembly he brought up
the matter again with a considerable degree of eloquence. The
politicians believed this a good opportunity to gain notoriety; the
resolution passed and a petition, that received general approval,
was dispatched to Washington. The result was only as was
formerly anticipated—the United States disposed of the lands.

Origin of "Sucker."—The Illinoisans ran up the Mississippi River in steamboats in the spring, worked the lead mines during warm weather, and then down the river again to their homes in the fall, thus establishing a similitude between their migratory habits and those of the fishy tribe called suckers. For this they were called "Suckers," especially by the Missourians. Analogies always rebound. So the Illinoisans by way of retaliation, called the Missourians "Pukes." It had been observed that the lower lead mines in Missouri had sent up to the Galena mines whole loads of uncouth ruffians, from which it was inferred that Missouri had taken a puke and had vomited to the upper lead mines all her worst population. By these names, "Suckers" and "Pukes," the Illinoisans and Missourians are likely to be called forever.

Election.—The Legislature of 1829 changed the mode of voting, which had been most of the time by ballot, to "viva voce" to prevent fraudulent voting by impositions upon the illiterate.

No party lines were drawn in the political contest at the close of Edward's administration; the only decision to be made was in the choice between the men, who were both Democrats, as were most of the people of the State. They were William Kinney, the Lieutenant-Governor, and John Reynolds, an ex-Associate Justice of the Supreme Court; candidates for Lieutenant-Governor were Rigdon B. Slocumb and Zadok Casey, the latter an intelligent man and a fluent speaker, but was possessed of a limited education. Reynolds and Casey were elected.

————:o:————

REYNOLDS'S ADMINISTRATION.—1830–1834.

Governor,	-	- -	- John Reynolds.
Lieutenant-Governor,	{ 1830–32,	-	Zadok Casey.
	{ 1832–34,	-	W. L. D. Ewing.
Secretary of State,	-	- -	Alexander P. Field.
Auditor, -	-	- -	James B. T. Stapp.
Treasurer,	{ 1827–31,	- -	James Hall.
	{ 1831–36,	- -	John Dement.

Attorney-General,   -   -   -   George Farquer.

Speaker of { 7th House, -   -   -   W. L. D. Ewing.
          { 8th   "   , -   .   -   Alex. M. Jenkins.

United States Senators, { E. L., 1831–35, -   Elias K. Kane.
                        { T. L., 1830–35, -   John M. Robinson.

1 Representative in Congress; Population in 1830, 157,447.

The Seventh General Assembly convened December 6, 1830, and continued in session until the following February 16.

Reynolds vs. Legislature.—As the Senate was made up principally of Jackson men, Reynolds being opposed to Jackson, a disagreement manifested itself when the latter began making appointments. Henry Eddy, Sidney Breese, Alfred Cowler and Thomas Ford were all Prosecuting-Attorneys and had served the people satisfactorily, yet the Senate removed all but the latter. The Governor re-appointed and still the Senate was not satisfied. Finally when the Legislature adjourned the former appointments were again made by the Governor.

A Timid Legislature.—This Assembly might well be called the fearless-timid Legislature—fearless upon the enactment of certain laws but timid when rebuked by the stay-at-home politicians. They passed a bill for the establishment of a penitentiary, doing away with the pillory and the whip, but it was by a request of the people. The notorious State bank was yet in existence, but in no better condition than it had been one year after its establishment; besides, the notes were coming due and no former Legislature had acted upon the matter. Something must now be done or the State would sink into bankruptcy. Accordingly the State borrowed $100,000 at 6 per cent, which was known as the "Wiggins Loan." This turn produced confidence. Although it was the best move they could have made, the members slunk home as if they had committed a sad blunder.

THE DAWN OF A NEW ERA.—Population had increased to 157,447 but civil authority had changed but little. The people remained under a form of Government only for sake of fashion, not realizing the importance of proper legislation as to the moral welfare of the citizens or the advancement of the State in industry and enterprise. If a plan were introduced it was looked upon as mere child's play and the whole scheme would fall to pieces. The same drawback was common in those days that exists and flourishes to-day in certain localities; the people had lived neighborly for years, determined in their minds upon the styles of the institutions they desired, but they were to be just what George Washington, Thomas Jefferson or John Adams approved. Continual war was waged between the non-progressive and the spirited elements; frequent quarrels would be aroused and would often end in fights. Men learned to disagree both politically and religiously.

Ministers of the gospel would often be disputed. They were not required to be learned gentlemen but men that could take a text, begin in a low, humiliated tone verging upon a singsong—then decidedly singsong, increasing in volume—, swinging the arms and body until a perspiration began to flow, when they would " haul their coats " and, in shirt-sleeves, finish a long and difficult harangue. The loudest sermons were pronounced the best and if a minister could display a more or less degree of sadness and shed a few tears he was pronounced sincere and his sermon a convincing one. The people regularly attended church and would talk over the sermons for days after hearing them. As the denominations were new in popular patronage, each member thought his creed was the right one, thus bitter church disputes arose.

In 1820 the first educated ministers arrived but they were long looked upon with a jealous eye by the older people and especially by uneducated ministers who claimed that these brothers were "selling the gospel." But as they were a sort of missionary from the Eastern States and were paid principally by people of that locality, a place was given them, generally in villages and towns while the old-fashioned clergy were retained in the country circuits.

Justice, in point of law, was dished out equally peculiar. There were two or three lawyers who had given careful study to this profession though the bulk were men, picked up, who had natural faculties to become LL. D's., but had never been placed in positions to master their subjects, nor learn little arts of trickery. The usual places for holding court were in log houses and in close rooms similar in size to those where our Justices of the Peace transact business to-day, because of which the people were usually obliged to stand. If it were a summer day when an important case was to be tried the people would congregate in squads outside until the clerk would appear with the usual information, " Come in, boys, Old ———— is going to hold court;" on hearing this there would be a rush for the best positions, to find a seat if possible or a place to lean against. Judges were sedate and dignified, exceedingly careful that they did not offend any one lest they should grow unpopular. They would seldom allow cases to be tried before them that required their decision, always demanding a jury on which they gravely placed all responsibility, frequently refusing to instruct this body as the law required them to do.

A man had been tried for murder before a prominent Judge, and after the jury rendered a verdict of " guilty of murder," the Judge thus addressed the young man: " Mr. Green, the jury in their verdict say you are guilty of murder, and the law says you are to be hung. Now I want you and all your friends down on Indian Creek, to know that it is not I who condemns you, but it is the jury and the law. Mr. Green the law allows you time for preparation, and so the court wants to know what time you would like to be hung." He was compelled to set the time, however, for the prisoner answered, " May it please the court, I am ready at any time; those who kill the body have no power to kill the soul, my preparation is made, and I am ready to suffer at any time the court appoints." After twisting about, the Judge stammered out, " Mr. Green, you must know that it is a very serious matter to be hung, it can't happen to a man more than once in his life, and you had better take all the time you can get. The court will give you until this day four weeks. Mr. Clerk, look at the almanac and see whether this day four weeks comes on Sunday." Upon the clerk's ascertaining that " this day four weeks" came on Thursday the Judge proceeded, " Mr. Green, the court gives you until this day four weeks, at which time you are to be hung."

Prior to the year 1830 the people dressed in costumes similar to those worn by the earlier settlers, giving little or no thought to art, science or refinement—in fact those out of the regular custom of the country were pronounced foppish or flippant if they went to one extreme, vulgar, if to the other. About this time the trade of Illinois with other States brought merchants from the East into the larger towns; merchants went to New York or Philadelphia almost every year for goods; commerce was established upon the rivers by means of steamboats, carrying people to and from the older States in much less time than formerly. These associations brought about a marked change, but the older people of the State looked upon it as being a ruination to the country and especially to the young who paid " too much attention to neatness and dress."

The bowie-knife was gradually omitted from the belt, people became more ambitious and industrious, inventions were studied, railroads were talked about and the progressive looked forward to a further development of the State.

BLACK HAWK WAR.

Scarcely had the Legislature adjourned until hostilities with the Indians broke out and a war began that terminated only when the lives of many innocent settlers and vengeful savages had been sacrificed. This was the noted Black Hawk war.

Cause.—A large tract of land had been purchased from the Sacs and Foxes, by the Government in a conference at St. Louis, in 1804, Governor Harrison conducting the treaty in person. This treaty was confirmed by Black Hawk (Mucata Muhicatah) and Keokuk in a conference, in 1815, with Governor Edwards; but on the demand, in 1830, for the tribe to remain west of the Mississippi and cease insults, Black Hawk denied the validity of the treaty and manifested a rebellious spirit. He declared that the chiefs were made drunk and signed a paper when too stupid to know the importance of the document. Keokuk declared the treaty just, remaining at home with the tribe that was under his influence, while Black Hawk, impatient for revenge upon the settlers with whom he would never trade in time of war, and 300 warriors crossed the river and took up their residence in an old Indian town on the river bank that had once accommodated from 6,000 to 7,000 of this tribe.

Hostilities Opened almost immediately after the Indians

crossed the river, when warring parties sallied forth to commit depredations upon the Whites. The settlers laid in a complaint to the Governor who at once set about to right the matter. The people had been undisturbed in their peaceful habitations for nearly twenty years. The counties in the South and Southwest had become thickly inhabited, but in the remainder of the State the settlements were few and far apart.

General Gaines's Treaty.—General Gaines was sent, in June, 1831, to Rock Island where he learned that war could not be averted and immediately requested Governor Reynolds to send 700 volunteers. The number being raised, Joseph Duncan of the State militia, afterwards Governor, was placed in command. They proceeded to the mouth of Rock River where they met General Gaines in a steamboat but by some misunderstanding or bad management, the Indians escaped at a point now known as Rockport. As General Gaines threatened to continue the war even across the river Black Hawk and his frightened chiefs sued for peace and the expedition returned with but the satisfaction of having burned a deserted town.

Battle of Old Man's Creek.—The treaty was observed, on the part of the Indians, but a few months when those desiring warfare re-crossed the river and visited the Pottawatomies and Winnebagoes, a part of whom they easily persuaded to join them. It took only a few days for the settlers to arm themselves, and soon 1,800 men were in pursuit. They marched to Ogee's Ferry, established for the crossing of emigrants on their way to and from the Galena mines and where a post office was in charge of John Dixon, the veteran mail carrier between Ft. Clark (Peoria) and the mines. Here, now known as Dixon, a halt was made to secure provisions and to learn, if possible, the position of their enemy. General Samuel Whitesides was put in command of the entire army, it having been recruited and numbering 2,000 strong.

A company of frontier men from the counties of McLean, Tazewell and Fulton, who were eager for a fight, offered their services, 275 in number, to find the Indians. After a few days' search they succeeded in capturing three of the foe, but lost ten or twelve men of their own number. They came back to camp at

Dixon in post-haste, one or two dropping in at a time, Major Stillman, the commander, having lost all control of his men.

Army Disbanded.—The army was without food, save a few cattle they had received from John Dixon, and grew almost mutinous in their anxiety to be discharged, having left home and business without preparations; yet they marched against the enemies' camp, from which Stillman's men beat a rapid retreat, but not an Indian was to be found. The forces returned to Ogee's Ferry (Dixon) and were discharged by the Governor, their time of three months' enlistment having expired. A few companies remained to guard the country until fresh volunteers could arrive.

Indian Creek Massacre.—On the 21st of May, 1832, shortly after the troops had been disbanded and before another army had been raised, a party of Indians fell upon the settlement on Indian Creek, a tributary to the Fox River, and massacred fifteen persons—men, women and children, in three familes of Davis, Hall and Pettygrew; also taking two girls, Sylvia and Rachel Hall, prisoners, whom they conveyed into Wisconsin where they were afterward ransomed by the payment of $1,000. The account of this horrible butchery was given by the Indians themselves. They told the story of the deed with much interest, laughing at the shrieks and groans of their victims as the spears and tomahawks were thrust into the vital parts of the bodies. They told of the amusement they had had in mutilating the dead and leaving them in grotesque positions. The remains of this brutal carnage were carefully gathered together by General Whitesides and buried in one common grave.

Battle of Burr Oak Grove.—While the new army was being raised Indian depredations continued throughout the State. June 15 the forces assembled at Beardstown and Hennepin, intending to scour the country. General Whitesides, having been relieved of his command, enlisted as a private. The work was continued for a short time in bands of skirmishers.

An attack was made on Captain Snyder's forces while encamped at Burr Oak Grove, June 17, by a party of seventy Indians. As a portion of the troops had just returned from pursuing a small band of the enemy, the camp was surprised and began beating a hasty retreat when Captain Snyder called upon General Whitesides, then a private, to assist him in rallying his men. The General raised his gun and threatened to shoot the first man that ran. His words turned the tide of battle and in a short time he proved his skill as a marksman by shooting the leader, when the Indians retreated with a slight loss on either side.

Battle of Apple River Fort.—An attack was made on Apple River Fort at the present town of Elizabeth, near Galena, when the latter was a village of but 400 inhabitants. This fort was only a place of refuge for the tweny-five settlers of that immediate locality. When Black Hawk and his allies arrived the people fled to the fort and all worked diligently. Women molded bullets and the men fought vigorously for fifteen hours, when the siege was raised. A short time afterward forces arrived from Galena, that had been notified by a man secretly dispatched for that purpose, and pursued the Indians for a considerable distance but without result.

To Arms!—Three men were killed in a lead mine near Fort Hamilton by a party of eleven savages. General Dodge of Wisconsin started in hot pursuit, overtook them and killed the entire party who sung the death song while they fought desperately.

Captain Stephenson of the same locality pursued a party of Indians with less success. The latter took refuge in a thicket and repulsed the Whites who were mortified at their defeat and made a second desperate assault, but with the loss of five men, were compelled to abandon the attempt to drive them from their thick covert.

Such atrocities were constantly being committed all over the country that the settlers saw an immediate necessity to rally and put a stop to such continual and petty warfare.

Major Demont's Engagement.—Major Demont, in command of a battalion of scouts, was sent in advance of the main army. On the 25th of June he learned that a force of 500 warriors, under command of Black Hawk, was near at hand. The troops were filled with excitement believing an engagement with the entire Indian force was at hand. Demont accordingly pushed forward to entice them into battle though General Atkinson was with the main command at Dixon.

He had proceeded but a short distance when a few of the enemy's scouts were discovered, and some of his men, eager for a fight, started in pursuit contrary to orders. In his endeavors to recall these soldiers, he, with but twenty men, ventured a mile away from the main army. Here he was attacked by 300 warriors lying in ambush. Slowly retreating and by sending orders to his men, he collected his forces near a group of log buildings which they entered, and being thus fortified were able to repulse the assailants after an hour's siege.

Suffering of the Army.—SEARCHING FOR A FOE.— When the news of the attack on Major Demont reached General Atkinson at Dixon, men under Alexander were dispatched to the vicinity of Galena to prevent the Indians from escaping across the river while he advanced toward a region known as the Four Lakes. Reconnoitering parties were sent out to scour the country but each returned empty handed and without any information regarding the enemy. A band of Pottawatomies now joined the Whites and about the same time Major Dodge arrived with a company from Wisconsin. The army wandered about for eight weeks without finding a foe or trophies of warfare. They endured fatigue and hardships. Often the food became scarce and before fresh supplies could arrive the troops would be almost famished.

THE TREMBLING LANDS were now entered. These are immense flats of turf, extending for miles in every direction, from six inches to a foot in thickness, resting upon water and beds of quicksand. A horseman or even a single soldier passing over produces a quivering motion. Horses would sometimes, on the thinner portions, force a foot through and fall to the shoulder: yet so great is the tenacity of the upper surface that in no instance was there any trouble in getting them out. In some places the weight of the earth forces a stream of water upwards, which carrying with it and depositing large quantities of sand, forms a mound. The mound, increasing in weight as it enlarges, increases the pressure on the water below, presenting the novel sight of a fountain in the prairie pouring its clear stream down the side of a small mound, then to be absorbed by the sand and returned to the waters beneath. While in this locality comfortable encampment and rapid march were impracticable.

Campaign for 1832.—No United States troops having yet arrived, the army was composed principally of Illinois men; a few troops, however, from Wisconsin and Missouri aided. It was divided into three detachments: General Posey to go to Fort Hamilton; Colonel Ewing, to Dixon; Henry, Alexander and Dodge, to Fort Winnebago, situated at the point of greatest proximity between the two rivers—Fox and Wisconsin; while General Atkinson was to have command of the entire force and was to first build a fort at Lake Kush-Konong.

Alexander's division became mutinous, would not march as directed and was sent back to remain with General Atkinson; Dodge complained that his horses were tired out from a recent march and it would be difficult to proceed; Henry's men likewise protested when they saw so many odds against them and all the officers of Colonel Fry's regiment signed a protest which they presented to General Henry who acted upon the matter by putting the dissatisfied officers under arrest to be sent to General Atkinson. This was too much for the commanders who pleaded earnestly to remain, swearing allegiance to their leader in all he chose to undertake, and with tears in their eyes implored him to take no further action in the matter. Fresh horses arrived for General Dodge, and confidence being restored, the little army took up its march July 14. General Henry was first in command; White Pawnee, a Winnebago chief, and Poquette, a half-breed, acted as guides.

Treacherous Indian Guides.—White Pawnee and Poquette were false to the Whites and led them astray in several instances, which was, however, detected by a lucky occurrence. It seems that they reported the enemy up the river about twelve miles from the fort and that two men, with Little Thunder as guide, were sent south to inform General Atkinson of the fact; but when a few miles on their journey the messengers discovered a trail over which Black Hawk had passed a short time before. Their threats alarmed Little Thunder, who fled back and informed White Pawnee and Poquette of the discovery. They all attempted to escape but their designs were discovered by an officer who immediately reported to General Henry. Fearing trouble, should the affair be known to the soldiers, they were reprimanded and threatened privately. This led to a truthful revelation of the whole matter, and the exact position of Black Hawk and his forces.

A Stampede took place among the army horses, July 12. A fright was caused by an unknown means and every animal tore loose, bounding over the prairie at full speed. In this over a hundred horses were lost, either by death or inability of the owners to find them.

Black Hawk's Retreat.—The chase now began. All set out in good spirits; those deprived of horses were at times relieved by those who were in possession of them. Few were encumbered with baggage, unnecessary articles having been cast aside. When the troops got sight of the plain trail they were eager for the chase. Every article found along the way that had been abandoned by the retreating enemy, forced a smile from one to the other; it was an evidence that revenge, so sweet, was soon to be tasted, and there was a prospect for the speedy termination of the war. Their joy was clouded by suffering on many occasions. The second night they were exposed to a severe thunder-storm, when the torrents of rain poured upon them in fearful flood; fires could not be built, clothing could not be dried nor food cooked. It was a repetition of the hardships of war endured by every soldier. The next was more favorable. Rain had ceased, food had been prepared, and they enjoyed a refreshing sleep beneath the broad dome of Heaven with only an ethereal covering between. When morning dawned the troops were again in the distinct path of their retreating foe. A repeated command was, "Close up ranks," "Close up ranks," when the men on foot were even in a run to keep up with horsemen. The advance guard was seldom very far ahead of the main portion of the army. Limbs grew tired but hearts lightened as an occasional sick Indian was overtaken, having been left behind to await his fate at the hands of an enemy he had once defied. Then cooking vessels were found along the trail, an occasional blanket and various other articles that had a tendency to hinder a rapid retreat.

Finally the advance of our army came in sight of the rear of the savages, then all disappeared and nothing was left but a trail to indicate the course they had taken. It became evident that a general battle was not far distant, though Black Hawk endeavored by every means in his power to reach Wisconsin River. Skirmishing parties were repeatedly left behind to annoy the pursuers and thus hinder their rapid advance. They reached the broken country, but the savages were unable to effect a crossing under such pressing circumstances.

Battle of the Wisconsin.—The Indians secreted themselves along a deep ravine and when the Whites came up poured a rapid fire into their ranks. At this juncture Major W. L. D. Ewing, commander of the advance battalion, and Major Dodge, in charge of Wisconsin troops, halted awaiting the arrival of General Henry who soon came up with the bulk of the army and formed them into line of battle. A charge was ordered along the whole line. This was promptly obeyed, sending Black Hawk and his forces to the long grass in the bottom, where they made another resistance, but as night came on the fighting was discontinued. In the morning the troops were again in arms and ready for the conflict but the savages had retreated across the river and were out of immediate reach.

Sixty-eight Indians were left dead on the battle-field, while many were afterward found who had died from their wounds in the course of their march. General Henry, knowing from experience in previous engagements that the savages had been instructed to aim high, ordered all the cavalry and officers to dismount and leave their horses in the rear. Thus the Indians in obeying orders had overshot their mark, having killed but one man and wounded eight.

The success of this engagement was not made public by General Henry but by Major Dodge and his friend, Doctor Phillio, editor of the "Galenian;" consequently the Wisconsin gentleman, afterward Governor, took upon himself the honors that should have been loyally given another. The correction was first made public by Governor Ford in a lecture of February 17, 1843, which was then generally published by the press.

A Race for the Mississippi.—On the day following

the battle of the Wisconsin, as soon as new guides could be procured, General Henry and his command retired to the Blue
Mounds, where they received provisions and were joined by the
remainder of the army under General Atkinson. After a few
days spent in recruiting, the entire army started in pursuit of the
Indians.

At this time an indignity was put upon the most efficient officer and his brave men. General Henry had done all in this
expedition that had yet been done to capture the barbarous enemy, but his entire command was placed in the rear during the
march and ordered to take charge of the baggage now being
drawn with difficulty over the hilly country. They keenly felt
the insult but were too gentlemanly to retaliate, knowing that
just dues would finally rest where they belonged. But the opportunity again presented itself in which the young General
clearly demonstrated his superiority as a commander over any
yet in the field.

Four days pursuit led the army to the bluffs of the Mississippi,
the enemy not yet having effected a crossing. On the 29th of
July they made the attempt but were frustrated in their designs
by the timely arrival of the steamer Warrior, which opened such
a deadly fire upon them that several were killed and the remainder frightened.

Battle of Bad Axe.—Here Black Hawk by skillful ma-

neuvering led General Atkinson into a trap. In order to keep
the Whites back and allow his braves time to cross, this great
chief, with twenty picked warriors, hid in the woods and when
the forces came up began an attack. Atkinson formed his men
into line and made a charge, the Indians retreating toward the
river but three miles above a point where the others were
crossing.

When General Henry, with his baggage train, arrived at the
spot where the engagement had begun, he discovered that Atkinson had been out-generaled. By consent of the principal
officers he left his baggage and horses, and pursued the trail
which soon led them to the river where about 150 warriors were
crossing. On these they charged to prevent them from escaping

any farther than to an island in the river. Atkinson, hearing the firing in the distance, perceived what mistake had been made and, to prevent Henry from reaping an entire victory, came hastily upon the field—leaving his twenty Indians—and made a charge on the few helpless fellows that had reached the island.

Scott's Army.—General Scott was sent West with United States troops but being prevented by Asiatic cholera, which swept off a large number of his army, did not arrive until a treaty had been made. Four steamers—Henry Clay, Superior, Sheldon Thompson and William Penn—were chartered for the passage of the troops. So desperately did the cholera rage that two were abandoned before they reached their destined point on Lake Michigan—Chicago.

The army, after landing, passed through Gilbert's Grove and Elgin; thence to Beloit, Wisconsin, where the army went into camp and several more soldiers died. At this place news reached them that the war had ended. They then started on their homeward march, going by way of Rockford, and down Rock River to Fort Armstrong, thence by steamer to their homes. It might be here mentioned that many of the soldiers were so delighted with the country through which they passed, that but a few years elapsed before they returned with their families and friends to make their homes in Illinois.

Peace.—The Battle of Bad Axe virtually ended the war, Black Hawk being captured a few days thereafter and taken into custody. The soldiers returned to their homes and settled down to domestic affairs.

The Eighth General Assembly convened December 3, 1832, and adjourned the following March 3. This session proved an interesting one, the project of building railroads being warmly discussed. The building of the Illinois Central road from Peru to Cairo was introduced by Speaker Alexander Jenkins, and a survey across the State through Springfield, now the Wabash, was proposed by George Farquer.

Election.—In August, 1834, four candidates were in the field for Governor and four for Lieutenant-Governor; the parties were Whig and Democrat. Joseph Duncan of Morgan County, an Anti-Jackson man but generally supposed to be a warm friend to him (he was then in the United States Senate and the people could not exactly determine his political belief), was chosen Governor and Alexander M. Jenkins, Lieutenant-Governor.

BIOGRAPHICAL.

John Reynolds, the fourth Governor of Illinois, was a native of Pennsylvania, born in 1788, of Irish parentage, and moved to Illinois in 1800, subsequently residing in Tennessee in which State he was educated, returning for that purpose after his parents had taken up their residence in this State. Though he received a classical education his nature failed to grasp it in that light. He was addicted to profanity and thoroughly detested those who chose to select their language. However, this brusqueness was ameliorated in a great measure by a kind disposition. He was a staunch Democrat and a warm admirer of Buchanan, though he preferred Lincoln to Douglas. He was a member of the Charleston convention and was greatly respected because of his age. His days were ended at Belleville in 1865.

General Henry, the hero of the Black Hawk War, was an earnest, sober-minded man of ability and worth. He was of a sensitive nature, never retaliating but making the most of a civil attack. In disposition, he was distant—even his more intimate friends knew little of his early life. Two years after the close of the Black Hawk War he went to New Orleans for health, having symptoms of consumption. At this place he lingered for many months, being unknown to his attendant who not once dreamed of being in the presence of a hero whose record helped make another a Governor. He had never married and died March 4, 1843, and not until then was his whereabouts known. Papers were found on his person that revealed the mystery and stranger.

Black Hawk was born in a large Indian village on the Rock River near its mouth, in 1768, and was of Sac parentage. He attained the high position of chief by his daring bravery and vigorous manhood. He despised the colonists and helped to secure many scalps during the War of 1812 as well as in the

Black Hawk War. He raised a family of children to whom he was always kind as he was also to his wife. He dearly loved his tribe and reverenced his ancestors, to whom he would often refer. He was captured in 1832, soon after the Battle of Bad Axe, by a company of Winnebagoes who delivered him to the Whites. He was taken to Washington before President Jackson whom he addressed as follows: "I am a man and you are another. We did not expect to conquer the white people. I took up the hatchet to revenge injuries which could no longer be borne. Had I borne them longer, my people would have said, 'Black Hawk is a squaw. He is too old to be a chief. He is no Sac.' All is known to you. Keokuk once was here; you sent him back to his nation. Black Hawk expects that, like Keokuk, he will be permitted to return too." The President assured him that when there was no more danger of another outbreak he might return but for the present it was best for him to remain in bondage. He was taken to Fortress Monroe where he remained until June, 1833, when he was given his liberty.

He was an object of interest to the people who made much ado over him during his imprisonment. He became attached to the commander, General Eustis, and upon leaving presented him with a bunch of white eagle feathers and a hunting-dress, asking him to keep them in remembrance of Black Hawk. This noted warrior died October 3, 1838.

DUNCAN'S ADMINISTRATION.—1834-1838.

Governor,	-	-	-	Joseph Duncan.
Lieutenant-Governor,	{ 1834-36,	-	Alex. M. Jenkins.
	1836-38,	-	W. H. Davidson.
Secretary of State,	-	-	-	Alexander P. Field.
Auditor, {	to 1835,	-	-	James P. B. Stapp.
	1835-41,	-	-	Levi Davis.
Treasurer, {	1831-36,	-		John Dement.
	1836-41,	-	-	Charles Gregory.
Attorney-General,	-	-	(four changes)
Speaker of {	9th House,	-	-	James Sample.
	10th "	-	-	"

United States Senators, $\begin{cases} \text{E.L.,} \begin{cases} 1835-37, & \text{W. L. D. Ewing.} \\ 1837-41, & \text{Richard M. Young.} \end{cases} \\ \text{T.L., } 1835-41, \cdot & \text{John M. Robinson.} \end{cases}$

3 Representative in Congress; Population in 1830, 157,447.

The Ninth General Assembly convened December 1, 1834, and continued in session until the following February 13. An extra session convened December 7, 1835, adjourned the following January 18. This term might properly be called the "administration of internal improvement." Two days after the Legislature convened, Joseph Duncan took the oath of office.

New State Bank.—The State was now in a prosperous condition. People were flocking to Illinois by hundreds; peace had been made with the Indians and the State could cash her indebtedness. Peace and prosperity reigned. The Legislature grew wild over the outcome. The Governor wanted a State bank; the members of the Legislature began thinking they did too, and before the honorable body adjourned (1836) another bank had been established without submitting the question to the people for discussion. This State bank was to be chartered with a capital of $1,500,000 and shares sold principally to residents of the State. The privilege of increasing the capital $1,000,000, if deemed necessary, was also granted. Six branches were instituted and the old bank at Shawneetown again opened.

Principal stock holders were, Godfrey, Gilman & Co. of Alton, the intended rival city of St. Louis; Thomas Mather, of Kaskaskia; John Tillson, of Hillsboro, and Samuel Wiggins of Cincinnati. T. W. Smith also held shares and endeavored to capture the presidency of the institution but was defeated in his aspirations by the Alton firm, the partners having their shares sufficiently divided to hold the balance of power among the different factions of stockholders, and Thomas Mather was chosen.

Internal Improvements.—ALTON, had early aspired to becoming the capital, but Sangamon County being represented, in particular, by the famous "Long Nine," (Abraham Lincoln, Ninian W. Edwards, etc.) and Springfield being a candidate, she was willing to give up the project in order to become the metropolis of the State. Great excitement prevailed and a special session of the Legislature was called. Heavy loans were made to Alton and in 1837 the city tried herself. She bought all the lead mines that the article might be shipped from her warehouses. The price of lead nearly doubled at first but it soon ran down and new lead was preferred to that stored in damp cellars, which finally sold at a discount. By Alton's wild speculation the State lost about $1,000,000.

THE ILLINOIS & MICHIGAN CANAL question was once more sprung upon the people and after several attempts, a loan of $500,000, with the State for security, was arranged; in 1836 work was begun. Estimates were called for as to actual cost of the structure, which was placed at $4,043,336.50, while it was calculated that a railroad over the same line would cost but $1,-052,488.19. The channel was to be made forty feet wide at the bottom, and to hold sufficient water for the largest vessels to pass through; thus making the structure of National importance as well as of State. This would naturally bring an extensive travel and thoroughly animate cities along the way, especially Chicago.

Tenth General Assembly.—Arrangements had been made for a multitude of people at the capital and little Vandalia was indeed crowded. This Assembly, like the preceding, held two sessions: First from December 5, 1836, to the following March 6; second, from July 10 to July 22. It was made up of such members as Abraham Lincoln, Stephen A. Douglas, James Shields, Augustus C. French, John Hardin, Ninian W. Edwards, W. L. D. Ewing, John Dement, John Dougherty, John Whitesides, O. H. Browning and Cyrus Edwards. The Legislature grew wild on the question of internal improvement, as did the Internal Improvement Convention, and passed many resolutions they would not have thought of doing under more quiet circumstances.

Internal Improvement Excitement.—Provisions were made for railroads to be built from Galena to the mouth of the Ohio; from Alton to Shawneetown; from Alton to the east boundary of the State; from Quincy through Springfield to Wabash River; from Peoria to Warsaw. The rivers Kaskaskia, Little Wabash, Illinois and Rock were to be thoroughly dredged and perfectly fitted up for navigation.

People began thinking they had committed a great error in not undertaking the matter before, and were impatient to see a general means of transportation in operation. Accordingly the work was at once begun, regardless of cost or without looking at the dark side of the undertaking. Boards of Commission were appointed and $12,000,000 appropriated by loan, which was but one-twentieth of the amount required for the improvements as then planned. The road built from Illinois River to Springfield alone cost $1,000,000, and when finished was not worth to the people one-hundredth part of its cost. But few roads ever were completed. Work was ordered and begun at both ends, and at points where the lines crossed rivers, upon which material could be transported; but only embankments remain to tell of the wild schemes of the people when Illinois began to assume its present standing in the civilized world.

The State bank capital was now increased to $3,100,000 by making the State a stockholder, which was to have a larger portion of the stock, but the people to remain the majority of the stockholders. In the spring the United States suspended specie payment and the State did likewise. To protect the internal improvement system, a special session was called as above stated; but under the circumstances the system would not be protected, and the Legislature assisted to tear down plans already on foot.

Magic Cities.—CHICAGO.—The history of this great city properly begins with the construction of the canal. After Fort Dearborn massacre (1812) the place was deserted save by two Indian traders and several half-breeds. In this condition the settlement remained until in 1816, when the fort was rebuilt; but the few people who were then added to the little colony did nothing toward laying the foundation of a future city, and in 1823 the United States troops abandoned Fort Dearborn, and the Government factory was sold and converted into a fur depot. Chicago was again of no importance.

In 1825 new houses were built and the number increased to fourteen; taxes paid amounted to $79.72; in 1830 the election returns of Chicago precinct of Peoria County showed but thirty-two votes polled, including territory within a twenty-mile radius, Chicago population numbered ninety-eight. Cook County was organized in March, 1831, with Chicago the county seat, but even then it was far from being a town of any note. As General Scott's vessels landed at its port in 1832, the town became somewhat known abroad and the following year Congress appropriated $25,000 to dredge the river and remove a sandbar from the mouth, that large ships might enter the harbor. By aid of a freshet in 1834 the work was completed.

The year 1835 is said to have been one of the most remarkable in its growth, when the population sprung up, as if by magic, from a few hundred to 3,265. At this time a number of towns were surveyed and incorporated. Speculation began on sale of lots. From June to December, 370,043 acres of land were sold in the northeast part ot the State, and mostly in the vicinity of Chicago. To accommodate the traveling public, old hotels were enlarged and new ones built and by 1837 the resident population had so increased that she was ranked with the cities.

OTHER CITIES were fast following in the wake of Chicago and the work already begun made people frantic throughout the entire State. Meetings were held in every county and resolutions passed upon the subject; an Improvement Convention was arranged to convene at the same time the Legislature assembled. Most counties responded to the call.

Indians all Removed.—The Pottawatomies were the last to be removed from Illinois. They annually assembled at Chicago to receive their annuity of $30,000 in goods for lands previously sold. Frequent propositions were made by the Government for a purchase of their remaining lands in the State, but the nation dearly loved their old hunting grounds and earnestly protested. In one conference Meta, their chief, said:

"My father, you know that we first came to this country a long time ago, and when we sat ourselves down upon it, we met hardships and difficulties. Our country was then very large but now it has dwindled to a small spot, and you wish to purchase that. This has caused us much reflection, and we bring all our chiefs and warriors, and families, to hear you. [Numbering in all 3,000 persons.]

*   *   Our old people have all sunk into their graves; they had sense. We are all young and foolish and would not do anything they could not approve, if living. We are fearful to offend their spirits if we sell their lands, we are fearful to offend you if we do not. We do not know how we can part with the land.

" Our country was given to us by the Great Spirit, to hunt upon, to make corn-fields, live on, and, when life is over, to spread down our beds upon, and lie down. That spirit would never forgive us if we sold it. When you first spoke to us at St. Marys we said we had a little land and sold you a piece. But we told you we could spare no more; now, you ask us again. You are never satisfied. * * Take notice it is a small piece of land where we now live. It has been wasting away ever since the White people became our neighbors. We have now hardly enough to cover the bones of our tribe."

After a conference of two weeks, in 1836, they sold all their lands east of the Mississippi and were removed west of that stream soon after. In this transaction 5,600,000 acres were purchased and the last of the first known inhabitants of Illinois removed from within her borders.

Election.—In the fall election of 1838, a Legislature advocating internal improvement was chosen. The Democrats and Whigs each had a strong ticket in the field, the former headed by Thomas Carlin for Governor and S. H. Anderson, Lieutenant-Governor; the latter, by Cyrus Edwards for Governor and W. H. Davidson, Lieutenant-Governor. The question of internal improvement was favored by the Whigs but the Democratic candidates failed to define their exact position and were elected by a large majority.

BIOGRAPHICAL.

Joseph Duncan, fifth Governor of Illinois, was born at Paris, Kentucky, February 23, 1794. He early displayed a military talent and took an active part in the War of 1812, in the Black Hawk War and in several other Indian difficulties. His education was meager but his natural abilities were great. He was a good General and his services in this position were invaluable; as a statesman, he was brilliant; as a Governor, firm. He died at Jacksonville, Florida, January 15, 1844.

CARLIN'S ADMINISTRATION.—1838–1842.

Governor,	· · · ·	Thomas Carlin.
Lieutenant-Governor,	· ·	· Stinson H. Anderson.
Secretary of State, { 1838–40,	·	· Alexander P. Field.
{ 1840–42,	·	· Stephen A. Douglas.
Auditor, { 1835–41,	· ·	· Levi Davis.
{ 1841–43,	·	· James Shields.
Treasurer, { 1836–41,	· ·	· John D. Whitesides.
{ 1841——,	·	· Milton Carpenter.
Attorney-General, { to 1840,	· ·	Geo. W. Olney.
{ from "	·	Josiah Lamborn.
Speaker of { 11th House,	· ·	W. L. D. Ewing.
{ 12th "	· ·	"
United States Senators, { E.L., 1837–43,	·	Richard M. Young.
{ T.L., { 1835–41,		John M. Robinson.
{ 1841–43,		Samuel McRoberts.

3 Representatives in Congress; Population in 1840, 404,000.

The Eleventh General Assembly convened December 3, 1838, and continued in session until the following March 4. An extra session was called which met in the new capitol, December 8, 1839, and adjourned the following February 3.

River Improvement.—The retiring Governor advocated the relinquishing of the improvement system but Governor Carlin spoke only against its too extensive application, saying, " Under the present mode of proceedings, however, nearly $2,000,-000 have [already] been expended and whatever diversity of opinion may now exist as to the expediency of the system as originally projected, all must admit that the character and credit of the State forbid its abandonment." But the Legislature made other appropriations. Illinois River was to be improved to Ottawa; $20,000 were appropriated for the Embarras River, and the same amount for the Big Muddy; besides, others more insignificant received their share of attention.

Railroads.—EARLY HISTORY.—The first reference made in our records to the construction of a railroad in Illinois was that of January 27, 1831, when the Legislature passed an act to construct a railroad or canal from the Mississippi bluffs across the

American Bottom to the present East St. Louis. In December, 1832, the Legislature incorporated the Springfield & Alton Turnpike Road Company "to transport, take and carry property and persons upon the same [road] by the power and force of steam, of animals, or of any mechanical or other power, or of any combination of them which the said company may choose to employ." At the same session the Rushville & Beardstown Turnpike Road Company was also incorporated and in the fall of 1834 the Chicago & Vincennes Railroad Company.

In his address to this Legislature Governor Duncan said, " Of the different plans proposed experience has shown [that] canals to be much more useful and generally cheaper of construction than railroads; they require less expensive repairs and are continually improving, and will last forever, while railroads are kept in repair at a very heavy expense, and will last but about fifteen years." The first road was built over the American Bottom and the cars were drawn by animals. The rails were made of sawed scantling upon which straps of iron were nailed.

THE FIRST ENGINE used in the State for drawing cars was run eight miles east from Meredosia toward Springfield, November 8, 1838, and was celebrated as a novel event.

Springfield the Capital.—A bill for removing the capital came before the Legislature in 1838; but, this assembly being composed of policy members, to bring about certain improvements, it became a difficult question, calling out many and long debates in favor of different localities.

The first ballot stood as follows: Springfield 35, Vandalia 16, Alton 15, Jacksonville 15, Illiopolis 6, Decatur 4, Carrollton 3, Bloomington 2, Mt. Carmel 2, Paris, Palestine, Grafton, Shawneetown, Pittsfield, Kaskaskia, Shelbyville, Hillsboro and Caledonia, each 1.

The fourth and last ballot was, Springfield 63, Vandalia 16, Jacksonville 11, Peoria 8, Alton 6, Illiopolis 3, Hillsboro, Caledonia, Grafton, Essex, Bloomington and Shawneetown, each 1.

In 1839 a new State house was completed and all records were removed to Springfield where the Legislature first convened December 9, 1839. This building stands in the center of the city and is now used as the Sangamon County court house.

Governor-Senate Contest.—A bitter party contest arose, in this administration, regarding the appointment of a Secretary of State. Alexander P. Field had been filling this position since his appointment by Governor Edwards; as he was not deemed the best man for the office, also being a Whig, Governor Carlin desired his removal and claimed his power to appoint a new Secretary. In this he made a number of attempts but the Senate rejected all and he was doomed to disappointment. When the Legislature adjourned he again appointed Mr. McClernand, who demanded the office but was refused. He brought the matter into court where it was decided against him, as the Supreme Court was made up of Wilson and Lockwood, Whigs, and Smith and Brown, Democrats—the latter, being a relative to McClernand, declined to vote. The Democrats now set about to change matters, by which, in the next election, they secured a majority of their party for the Legislature and thus placed in office a man of their choice, Stephen A. Douglas.

In 1835 Circuit Courts were re-established and were presided over by five Judges. These courts were entirely abolished, during this administration and the Judges added to the Supreme Bench, giving Democrats a majority.

Arranged Duels.— HARDIN-DODGE.— Partisan feeling was so intense at this time that many bitter quarrels arose that threatened to end in duels. The most prominent of these were disputes over the additional Judges and between parties holding opposite views on the slavery question. Hon. J. J. Hardin and Hon. A. R. Dodge, of Peoria, thought they could not get along together without resorting to a duel, but the matter was happily arrested by friends.

SMITH–MCCLERNAND.—The same year (1840) in making a speech against the Supreme Judges, John A. McClernand, who yet resides in Sangamon County, referred to the alien decision, on the part of Whig Judges, in such a manner as to excite a reprimand from Theopholus W. Smith, then one of the Judges. The matter was thoroughly investigated when it was found that McClernand was getting too close upon facts and the difficulty merged into a personal quarrel. A letter was sent which McClernand received as a challenge, and accepted it as such, naming

Missouri as the place of combat, the weapons to be rifles and the parties to stand at a distance of forty paces. The civil authorities getting hold of the matter, a warrant was issued for the arrest of Smith which ended the quarrel.

LINCOLN–SHIELDS.—Another quarrel took place in 1842 which figured more prominently than either of the other two. Times grew very dull and people could scarcely pay their debts; the only money in circulation was so depreciated in value that it took two dollars to amount to the value of one in specie, while the law of 1837 permitted the authorities to collect taxes in specie or its equivalent. Accordingly Governor Carlin, Auditor Shields and Treasurer Carpenter ordered collectors to collect as above privileged. A clamor of dissatisfaction was raised and the collection of taxes was ordered postponed until the next Legislature convened.

September 2, an article was written to the " Sangamo Journal " by Abraham Lincoln, entitled " The Lost Township, August 27 " and signed " Rebecca "—an article containing language that Mr. Lincoln would not have thought of using in later years—in which the State authorities were sneeringly attacked and their actions denounced as absurd, even going so far as to dub one a conceited dunce, who was caricatured in such a manner that all believed the reference was to James Shields, and which that gentleman took upon himself. Mr. Shields demanded the name of the author of the article, and upon receiving the desired information, in company with General Whitesides, he departed for Tremont, Tazewell County, where Mr. Lincoln was attending court.

Short notes were sent between them which resulted in the choosing of seconds. Mr. Lincoln, however instructed his friend, Dr. Merriman, whom he had named as his second, that in case it were possible to adjust the affair amicably he would offer the following for publication:

" I did write the ' Lost Township ' letter which appeared in the ' Journal ' of the 2d inst., but had no participation, in any form, in any other article alluding to you. I wrote that whole for political effect. I had no intention of injuring your personal or private character or standing as a man or gentleman; and I did not then think, that that article could produce or has produced that effect against you; and had I anticipated such an effect would have forborne to write it. And I will add that your conduct towards me, so far as I know had always been gentlemanly; and that I had no personal pique against you, and no cause for any."

His instructions to Dr. Merriman were that if a compromise should be effected he would leave it with his judgment as to how much of the above should be published, otherwise the preliminaries of the fight should be:

1. Weapons—Cavalry broad swords of the largest size, precisely equal in all respects and as are now used by the cavalry company at Jacksonville.

2. Position—A plank ten feet long, and from nine to twelve inches broad, to be firmly fixed on edge, on the ground, as the line between us which neither is to pass his foot over on forfeit of his life. Next a line drawn on the ground on either side of said plank, and parallel with it, each at the distance of the whole length of the sword and three feet additional from the plank; and the passing of his own such line by either party during the fight, shall be deemed a surrender of the contest.

3. Time—On Thursday evening at five o'clock, if you can get it so; but in no case to be at a greater distance than Friday evening at five o'clock.

4. Place—Within three miles of Alton, on the opposite side of the river, the particular spot to be agreed on by you.

Any preliminary details coming within the above rules, you are at liberty to make at your discretion, but you are in no case to swerve from these rules or pass beyond their limits."

The parties had all crossed the river and weapons were at hand when General Hardin and Dr. English succeeded in compromising the affair.

BUTLER–SHIELDS.—William Butler, a friend of Mr. Lincoln, then took up the quarrel and continued to annoy Mr. Shields, when he, too, received a challenge to fight with rifles, at sunrise, one mile north of the State house. As the answer did not come until late at night, the matter was dropped.

WHITESIDES AND MERRIMAN now quarreled about the affair

and challenges were interchanged. However **this** was terminated by the parties not agreeing upon a location; one desired
St. Louis and the other Louisiana, Missouri.

Arrival of Mormons.—A religious sect known as Mormons, sometimes called Latter Day Saints, arrived on the east
bank of Mississippi River in the present Hancock County, in
1839-40, and erected a town which they named Nauvoo. Because of depredations and selfishness for their own people, and
because of the practice of polygamy they had been driven from
Missouri where they settled at an earlier day (See Smith's biography, Ford's administration). A special charter was granted
by the Legislature in 1840, giving them special privileges in
government.

While in Missouri they voted with the Democratic party,
though afterward persecuted by them—opposed by a Democratic Governor and denied protection by a Democratic President of the United States. On coming to Illinois, they allied
themselves with the Whigs, then striving for power and whose
growing strength and proffered sympathy had induced them to
recross the river rather than go farther west.

The city was organized in 1841 with Prophet Joseph Smith
as Mayor. They were allowed a militia to act independent of
the State militia, and in short they were treated as a persecuted
people who deserved sympathy. The same year the Governor of
Missouri demanded the arrest of Smith, but he was shielded in
various ways and not delivered to that State. Afterward a
Nauvoo ordinance was passed that protected its citizens from arrest and which the State was bound to respect. Before the close
of this administration, however, they allied themselves again
with the Democrats, the party most likely to win, and from
whom they craved protection. In consequence attention was
directed to their customs by the Whigs and from this forward
their stay in Illinois was far from peaceful.

A Crash.—The visionary enterprise of internal improvement, voted for by brilliant men, kept the State in constant
excitement for four years, when it fell with a crash, causing
financial depression and leaving the State in debt about $15,000,-
000, with but a meagre recompense. In February, 1842, the

State bank went down and others soon followed. Statesmen knew a crisis was coming yet they were devoting more attention to National politics than State interests; and from the election of 1840 to the present, National politics have drawn the party lines.

Through this unwise and imprudent statesmanship the State became financially embarrassed; hard times set in; people could not pay their debts, nor could they buy, as the long and expensive transportation to an ordinary market required almost the value of their produce.

Colleges, by the close of this administration, were in active operation in different localities. A Presbyterian college was established at Jacksonville; Shurtleff, at Alton by Baptists; McKendree, at Lebanon by Methodists; a nunnery, at Kaskaskia by Catholics; a seminary, at Mount Morris by Methodists; also Knox College, at Galesburg, and one at Macomb were doing telling work.

The Election, in 1842, for State officers was close and party lines for the second time in the history of the State were closely drawn. The Democrats nominated for Governor, Thomas Ford; Lieutenant-Governor, John Moore. The Whig candidate for Governor was ex-Governor Joseph Duncan; for Lieutenant-Governor, W. H. Henderson. The former candidates were successful.

STORY.

Murder of Lovejoy.—For many years the slavery question was more or less agitated in Illinois. Rev. Elijah P. Lovejoy started a religious paper in St. Louis in the interest of the Presbyterian church; but in it he strongly denounced slavery and, as it was feared that the press would be destroyed, it was removed to Alton in 1836, and the name changed to Alton "Observer." Here he became a firm Abolitionist and because of his uncompromising sentiments which he expressed in the strongest possible language he became a victim of mob violence and at four different times his press was entirely destroyed. Parties threatened to tar and feather him, but he fearlessly continued his publications.

The Alton authorities ordered him to discontinue his paper

that peace might be restored, as his sympathizers were fewer than his enemies and even the pulpit began denoucing him for his war-like spirit, but he faltered not in a work he believed himself called upon to perform. Meetings were called in which his presence was requested and where the situation was discussed with much bitterness. In a volume compiled by Rev. Edward Beecher, brother of the Brooklyn divine, is found a lengthy discussion between the State Attorney-General and Mr. Lovejoy.

A fourth press was ordered and arrived by boat, November 7, 1837. The following is given by Mr. Tanner, a friend to Mr. Lovejoy and an eye-witness of the evening riot of this day:

" The fourth press had been shipped to Alton from Cincinnati, and had been received in the dead of the night, in presence of the Mayor, and taken to its final destination. We were fully prepared to receive and defend it, having, in the building, about sixty men, well armed and drilled, stationed on different floors in squads or companies of sufficient strength to do full execution if the mob should attempt to take the press when landed.

" All was quiet in the city and we considered the press free from harm, as it lay on storage with the most responsible and most respected firms in the city. As night approached we gathered in the building to talk over the situation, and congratulated each other on peace. About nine o'clock the company of men began to disperse to their homes, when Mr. Gillman asked if some few of the number would not volunteer to remain through the night with him, for he intended staying, as a precaution in case the warehouse was attacked. Nineteen men answered the call, and the devoted little band prepared themselves for whatever might occur. An hour elapsed before any signs of disturbance were noticed, but then it was evident that a mob was gathering. Messrs. Keating & West asked permission to enter the building to confer with Mr. Gillman, and being admitted, informed us that unless the press was given up the building would be burned over our heads. We had, early in the evening, selected for our Captain, Enoch Long, who had seen some service, thinking that occasion might require concerted action on our part. His method of defense was much milder than some of us advocated, for we considered it best to fire on the mob and make short work of it; but he commanded that no one should shoot without his order, an order which, from mistaken motives of mercy, he hesitated to give until it was too late to intimidate the besiegers.

" The crowd gathered and attempted to force an entrance, but were temporarily checked in consequence of the order of our Captain to one of his men to fire upon them in return for their shot, which had entered the building. Our shot proved fatal, killing one of the mob, whose name was Bishop. The lull was short; the mob returned, re-enforced by ruffians who had been drinking, and with savage yells they shouted that they would ' fire the building and shoot every d—d Abolitionist as he tried to escape!' No orders were given for concentrated fire at any time; it was all hap-hazard, and every man did as he thought best. At this juncture the Mayor appeared, and we asked him to lead us out to face the mob, and, if they would not disperse upon his command, that he should order us to fire upon them. His answer was, that he had too much regard for our lives to do that, but at the same time he most distinctly justified us in our defense. He attempted, afterward, to disperse them himself, but his power was gone—they merely laughed at his authority, as his weak and nervous treatment of them on former occasions had destroyed all his influence as a magistrate.

" Attempts were now made to fire the building, and against one side, in which there were no openings, a ladder was placed to reach the roof, on which a man ascended with a burning torch. Captain Long called for volunteers to make a sortie, in order to prevent the accomplishment of their purpose, and Amos B. Roff, Royal Weller and Elijah P. Lovejoy promptly stepped forth to execute his order. As they emerged from the building shots were fired from behind a shelter, and five balls were lodged in the body of Mr. Lovejoy, others wounding Mr. Roff and Mr. Weller. Mr. Lovejoy had strength enough to run back and up the stairs, crying out as he went, 'I am shot! I am shot! I am dead!' When he reached the counting-room, he fell back into the arms of a bystander, and was laid upon the floor where he instantly passed away without a struggle and without speaking a word."

The press was then destroyed and thrown into the river while its defenders were allowed to retire unmolested. The building had been set on fire but the flames were extinguished without much damage. A beautiful monument now marks the resting place of Mr. Lovejoy.

BIOGRAPHICAL.

Thomas Carlin, the sixth Governor of Illinois, was born, as most of his predecessors in office, in Kentucky, July 18, 1789. His parents were Irish and his early education was neglected; but in after years he read much and became well versed in political affairs. He was a brave officer in the Black Hawk war, commanding a spy brigade. In 1834 he was appointed to receive public money at Quincy. After serving his term as Governor he removed to his old home at Carrollton, where he died February 14, 1852, having moved to that place in 1825 from the bank of the Mississippi opposite the mouth of the Missouri.

FORD'S ADMINISTRATION.—1842-1846.

Governor, - - - -	Thomas Ford.
Lieutenant-Governor, - - -	- John Moore.
Secretary of State, { 1842-43, - -	Lyman Trumbull.
{ 1843-46, - -	Thomas Campbell.
Auditor, { 1841-43, - - -	James Shields.
{ 1843-46, - -	W. L. D. Ewing.
Treasurer, - - - -	Milton Carpenter.
Attorney-General, { to 1843, - -	Josiah Lamborn.
{ from " -	- James A. McDougall.
Speaker of { 13th House, - -	Samuel Hackelton.
{ 14th " -	- Wm. A. Richardson.
United States Senators, { E.L., 1843-49, -	Sidney Breese.
{ T.L., { 1841-43,	Samuel McRoberts.
{ { 1843-47,	James Semple.

7 Representatives in Congress; Population in 1845, 528,000.

The Thirteenth General Assembly convened December 5, 1842, and adjourned March 6, 1843. But few important questions were acted upon save peaceful measures in the promotion of the welfare of the people. As the greater portion of the inhabitants were from the older States, Eastern customs began to predominate. The State was deeply in debt and on the verge of Mormon trouble when the new Governor came into office and to this he devoted most of his attention.

MORMON WAR.

First Arrest of Smith.—Early in 1843 a Missouri Constable appeared before Governor Ford with an indictment against Joseph Smith, the Mormon leader and a pretended prophet, for a conspiracy to murder Governor Boggs of that State. A permit for his arrest being granted by our Governor, a Constable of Hancock County in company with the Missouri officer proceeded to Nauvoo to take in custody the "Prophet," but on learning that he was on a visit near Rock River, proceeded thither and served their papers.

Before they succeeded in getting him out of the State, they were overtaken by a party of Mormons who overpowered them and rescued him. This transaction aroused the State authorities who issued a new writ for his arrest, but when the case was brought before Judge Pope, a Whig, he was released presumably on party principles. This release led the Mormons to believe they were to be favored thereafter and as their membership in Illinois alone now numbered 16,000, they became offensive to their neighbors.

Smith a Presidential Candidate.—As the State had permitted Nauvoo to act independent of the regular Government and no apparent authority manifest, the Nauvoo bigots were still more inflated with confidence. In 1844 Joseph Smith announced himself a candidate for the Presidency of the United States, subject to the vote of the people. His followers believed that he would meet with success and preached their faith in various parts of the country.

Nauvoo Riot.—As Smith became more tyrannical in his precepts and revelations, dissensions arose in their own ranks. He claimed a doctrine had been revealed to him on one occasion, which held that a woman could not get to Heaven unless she were a wife or a concubine of an elder of her choice. An attempt was then made by him to take the wife of William Law, one of the leading Mormons, who bitterly fought the practice. Law not only censured Smith but procured a printing press and issued a paper among the brethren denouncing the matter. Only one issue was circulated, however, before the press and office were completely demolished. From this time it was dangerous for William Law, his brother and one or two others to remain in Nauvoo and they fled to the neighboring town of Carthage, where a writ was issued for the arrest of the destroyers of the office under the charge of riot. This exposure of Nauvoo life followed by mob violence helped to arouse a feeling of indignation among the people. Living in a country that boasted of its liberty they claimed a free press to be one of the constituents of a good government.

When the news reached Nauvoo that complaint had been made against the elders, a committee was dispatched to Carthage to explain the matter and make right the wrong if possible. On close questioning it was ascertained that the reports circulated throughout the country in many cases were true and that the "Latter Day Saints" were caring more for present pleasures than future salvation. It was also learned that kidnapers had been sent into Missouri to capture persons who would be likely to prove strong witnesses against Smith and a few of his elders, should they ever be brought to justice.

The Governor's Investigation.—The Governor made Carthage a visit to ascertain the truth concerning the difficulties and learn what he could of the condition of affairs. He found the citizens in arms throughout the adjoining counties, ready to expel this independent sect if necessary; meetings were being held, where stringent resolutions were passed. In one at Warsaw the citizens resolved to exterminate or otherwise rid the State of the entire Mormon population. But all did not join in this rigid movement; a few believed in peace and hoped to establish it even with these people. This third element was called "Jack Mormons," an appellation received by them with indignation. The Governor tells the following:

"On the morning before my arrival at Carthage, I was awakened at an early hour by the frightful report, which was asserted with confidence and apparent consternation, that the Mormons had already commenced the work of burning, destruction and murder; and that every man capable of bearing arms was instantly wanted at Carthage for the protection of the country. We lost no time in starting, but when we arrived at Carthage we could hear no more concerning the story. Again, during the few days that militia were encamped at Carthage, frequent applications were made to me to send a force here and a force there, and a force all about the country, to prevent murders, robberies and larcenies, which, it was said, were threatened by Mormons. No such forces were sent; nor were any such offenses committed at that time, except the stealing of some provisions, and there was never the least proof that this was done by a Mormon. Again, on my late visit to Hancock county I was informed by some of their violent enemies, that the larcenies of the Mormons had become unusually numerous and insufferable. They indeed admitted that but little had been done in this way in their immediate vicinity. But they insisted that sixteen horses had been stolen by Mormons in one night, near Lima, in the county of Adams. At the close of the expedition, I called at this same town of Lima, and upon inquiry was told that no horses had been stolen in that neighborhood, but that sixteen horses had been stolen in one night in Hancock County. This last informant being told of the Hancock story, again changed the venue to another distant settlement in the northern edge of Adams."

Second Arrest of Smith.—Shortly after the Governor's visit martial law was inaugurated at Nauvoo, under the direction of the leader, Joseph Smith. All members of the sect assembled under arms, and no one was allowed to pass in or out of the town without a permit. The Governor now issued an order that if Nauvoo would surrender she should be protected, but if not the whole force of the State should be called out against her if necessary. The Constable, with ten men, was sent to conduct those charged with riot to Carthage. Upon his arrival at Nauvoo, he found the parties professedly willing to go with him, but they requested that they might be allowed to await the next day, stating that at eight o'clock they would be before the Carthage Justice.

The morning dawned, but no one came; eight o'clock arrived, and yet no Mormons responded to the summons, when it was given up that they had promised, to get rid of the officers. Another summons was sent them and with it an order to surrender the State arms which had been entrusted to them, but of which they had proved themselves unworthy. In obedience, Joe Smith, his brother Hiram, and members of the Nauvoo Council appeared at Carthage and were tried for riot. They were bound over to Court by a Justice and discharged to appear at Circuit Court.

Lodged in Jail.—Before the Smiths could leave Carthage a second writ was issued for their arrest and they were thrown into jail. This building was constructed of thick stone walls, and was divided into three departments: one with small cells well barred and secured; another with commodious rooms and better furnished; while the third was occupied by the jailer and his family.

The Governor in Nauvoo.—When the Smiths were thrown into prison the cry of the people was for an examination of Nauvoo in search of apparatus with which counterfeit money could be manufactured, as it was believed that a large portion then in circulation came from that place. An expedition publicly known was not deemed expedient, but the Governor decided to visit the place under a different pretext; namely, to talk to the inhabitants. Accompanied by an escort of dragoons, he made his visit, addressed the people, and called for a vote from those assembled as to whether they would support the laws of the State or their leader if the matter came to a test. It was carried unanimously in favor of the laws. It not being deemed best to make any further examination, the party departed for Carthage.

Joe Smith Assassinated.—Trouble was imminent in the vicinity of Carthage. Before leaving for Nauvoo Mr. Ford placed a strong guard over the Mormon prisoners under the command of General Demming, instructing him and his men to defend the prisoners even at the peril of their own lives.

The troops lately discharged were from the vicinity of the

difficulties and, instead of returning to their homes as directed, arranged for mob violence. Eight guards were left at the jail while General Demming and his men encamped upon the public square. The troops deserted him almost in a body, and the General was soon helpless in the midst of a furious mob of enraged people; besides, most of the troops remaining with him and all the guard had joined the conspirators.

On the afternoon of the 27th of June, 1845, a black spot was placed upon Carthage history that never can be erased. Here a group of men engaged in deep and mysterious conversation; there an individual hurrying from place to place as if on important business, while on close scrutiny others could be seen creeping along under cover of fences, hedges or bushes, and culminating near the jail. At about five o'clock the fence around the building was scaled by 150 masked men who were fired upon by the guard with muskets loaded with blank cartridges—a part of the pre-arranged plot. They at once proceeded to break open the door but found it securely held by parties within. Retreating a few paces they took deliberate aim and, at a given signal, the door was completely riddled with bullets. A thud and moan were heard from within. Hiram Smith and Messrs. Taylor and Richards, two friends on a visit, were killed. The door then being easily forced open, the way remained clear to seize the "Prophet," who had secreted himself under the bed. He had been provided with a six-barreled revolver and at once opened fire upon his assailants, wounding three of them. Having discharged the contents of his weapon, he tried to escape by jumping from the window; but was discovered by his watchful foe and, with his body pierced by many balls, expired before the cloud of smoke had lifted. Thus perished the founder of the Mormon church which is yet giving the people of the United States so much concern.

Effect.—About dusk when the Governor, with his escort, had proceeded a distance of two miles on his return from Nauvoo, he was met by two messengers who told him of what had befallen the "Prophet." Hastening to Carthage he found the story too true. The people were preparing to leave the town, fearing an attack from Nauvoo, and the Governor departed for

Quincy to hold himself in readiness to raise an army if necessary and at the same time be out of immediate danger to himself.

But all were surprised at the result, for the entire Mormon population went into a season of mourning and did not offer to avenge the deed. Instead of the cause of Mormonism being weakened by the death of the " Prophet " the membership was greatly increased. His injunctions pronounced before his departure from Nauvoo and his dying words, "O Lord, my God," remained with his people and they pronounced him a martyr equal in humility to Christ. The story spread that he had died without a moan and without resistance; that he had arisen from the dead; that he had been seen to ride across the heavens on a great white horse while the brightest of flames of fire descended and rested upon his head, at sight of which his murderers were dumfounded and could not move. Elders were sent all over the United States and to Europe to preach the cause of the dead "saint," and the population was claimed to have reached 200,000; yet not one-tenth of that number were ever in Nauvoo at any one time.

Mormons Driven from Illinois.—After the death of Joseph Smith the two parties remained comparatively quiet until in 1845, when the bitter rivalry was kindled afresh, causing the Mormons to seriously ponder over the propriety of journeying farther westward where they could worship unmolested, and their religion would be allowed to thrive. In the fall of 1845, as they were on the verge of departing, conventions were held in the adjoining counties by the anti-Mormons and measures were adopted by which the "saints" were to depart for the West in the spring. Most of their possessions were purchased. For transportation 14,000 wagons, mostly from the timber of which the temple and other structures had been built, were manufactured. During the winter indictments against many of the " apostles," were instituted, principally for handling counterfeit money. In consequence of which and fearing an immediate arrest, the more fearful crossed the Mississippi while it was yet frozen over, and in early spring a long train was started on its westward journey. About 1,000 could not find purchasers for their property, and thus remained for the time being.

Many persons from other States had purchased the property of those already gone and, not knowing the condition of affairs in the neighborhood, settled in the midst of this strange people surrounded by hostile parties.

In September, 1846, a writ was issued for the arrest of several Mormons, unprovoked perhaps, and put into the hands of John Carlin to execute; but the pusillanimous officer called together a posse of men and attempted the matter in a cowardly manner. An engagement took place in which several parties were killed on both sides.

It was finally decided that these people should leave Nauvoo immediately, and then the unmerciful Brockman was not satisfied, but with 800 men and fully as many spectators entered the city, forcing even the helpless to leave on a few hours notice. This was in a sickly season and scores perished before they had journeyed fifty miles from their once comfortable abode. Besides this several new-comers had been driven from their homes and were not permitted to return until a force of State militia appeared upon the scene. A company of 350 of these troops were kept in the neighborhood until the following December. (For early history of Mormons see biography of Joseph Smith).

Election.—Six candidates for Governor were placed before the Democratic convention that met at Springfield in February, 1846: Lyman Trumbull, John Calhoun, Augustus French, A. W. Cavarly, Richard M. Young and Walter B. Scates. The contest lay between the two former who, being nearly a tie, were both withdrawn and the majority of ballots were then cast for Augustus C. French. The contest for Lieutenant-Governor was likewise warm and terminated in the nomination of J. B. Wells.

The Whigs, being in a minority, at first declined holding a convention, but it was regarded as a complete failure not to bring out candidates, while the national party greatly desired that they should hold a convention and place men in the field. This was done on the 8th of June at Peoria, the choice falling upon Thomas M. Kilpatrick of Scott County and Nathaniel G. Wilcox of Schuyler.

In the campaign the Whigs did all in their power to injure French by bringing up his record during the Internal Improvement war, but the election in August stood 58,700 to 36,775 in his favor.

BIOGRAPHICAL.

Thomas Ford, seventh Governor of Illinois, was born in Pennsylvania in 1800. He was a half brother to George Farquer, whose father died in 1791. After his death the mother married Robert Ford, a man of considerable importance, who was killed in the mountains by robbers. In 1803 Mrs. Ford, with her children, departed for St. Louis to enter land in the Spanish domain; but on finding the price higher than she anticipated, settled in Illinois.

Thomas was brilliant when but a boy. He gained distinction as a lawyer and finally became Judge of the Supreme Court. After serving his term as Governor, he moved to Peoria where he wrote a history of Illinois from 1818 to 1847, but did not live to see it published; this was attended to by his friend, James Shields. He died November 2, 1850.

Joseph Smith, the founder of the Mormon religion, was born in Sharon, Vermont, on the 23d of December, 1805, of humble parentage. Smith claimed, that when he was but fourteen years old he began to reflect upon the importance of a preparation for the future state. He went from one denomination to another, but in none could he find a religion that satisfied him; yet all claimed to be on the right track. He then withdrew to secret places and engaged earnestly in prayer. On one occasion near Palmyra, New York, a bright light from above approached him. He, as other prophets, at first became frightened, but soon ascertained that no harm was intended him and listened attentively to a voice which told him that his sins were forgiven and his prayers heard; that the covenant which God had made with ancient Israel was about to be fulfilled; that the time was at hand for the gospel to be preached in its power and fullness to all nations, and that he was chosen to be an instrument in the

hands of God to assist in bringing about the divine purpose in
this glorious dispensation; that the American Indians were a
remnant of the tribe of Israel and had given up their religion
many years previous; that the records that had been kept by man
were all destroyed, but that God had preserved a complete history, engraved by his faithful follower, Mormon, upon plates of
gold; that these were buried in the ground along the highway
between Manchester and Palmyra, about three miles from the
former. He proceeded to secure these accounts and found them
enclosed in a case of stone. These gold plates were thin, fastened together with rings and resembled a book. While here an
angel appeared to him and directed his sight, when he beheld
the devil with a large army of demons.

   The news of his claims to discovery got abroad and, in order
to escape the mobs, he was compelled to move to Pennsylvania,
where by divine inspiration he translated the characters, resembling Egyptian hieroglyphics, and published what has ever
since been known as the Book of Mormon. It was not difficult
to find followers and soon a number began preaching the gospel,
claiming to have seen the plates. Governor Ford in his history
says: " The story is remarkably well gotten up, and may yet
unhappily make the foundation of a religion which may roll
back upon the world the barbarism of eighteen centuries passed
away. Whilst there are fools and knaves, there is no telling
what may be accomplished by such a religion."

   The first church was founded at Manchester, April 6, 1830,
by Smith and his followers. In 1833, with many new additions,
the sect moved to Jackson County, Missouri, where they became
very impudent, claiming the State was theirs and for that matter
the world, they being saints. They laid the foundation of Independence, a few miles east of Kansas City, and another band
established themselves at Kirtland near Cleveland, Ohio, where
Smith made his home and where he established a bank which
broke in a few years, leaving the people who had deposited
with him in destitute circumstances. They then decided to
leave Ohio and assembled in Missouri where they built the city
of " Far West." Here they began plundering the neighborhood
and taking their spoils to a place which they called " the Lord's

Treasury." The County Clerk was a Mormon, so it was finally arranged that he should favor his people, who agreed not to abide by the laws of Missouri, denouncing them as unjust. The citizens and Mormons came together in a pitched battle in which several were killed. This aroused the indignation of the State and its Governor sent an armed force against them, which, though in arms, drove them to their main town, "Far West," where the leaders were captured, among whom was Smith himself. They were promised their freedom, provided they would leave the State, except the principal leaders who were condemned and sentenced to be shot, but this was afterward rescinded. (For later history see Mormon War.)

FRENCH'S ADMINISTRATION.—1846–1853.

Governor,	-	Augustus C. French.
Lieutenant-Governor { 1846–49,	-	Joseph B. Wells.
{ 1849–53,	-	William McMurtry.
Secretary of State,	-	Horace S. Cooper.
Auditor,	-	Thomas Campbell.
Treasurer, { 1841–49,	-	Milton Carpenter.
{ 1849–53,	-	John Moore.
Attorney-General, 1846–49,	-	David B. Campbell.
Speaker of { 15th House,	-	Newton Cloud.
{ 16th "	-	Zadok Casey.
{ 17th "	-	Sidney Breese.
United States Senators, { E.L., { 1843–49,		Sidney Breese.
{ 1849–55,		James Shields.
{ T.L., 1847–53,		Stephen A. Douglas.

7 Representatives in Congress; Population in 1855, 1,050,000.

The Fifteenth General Assembly convened December 7, 1846, and adjourned March 1, 1847. The Sixteenth held two sessions; January 1, 1849, and October 22 they were convened. The State Constitution having been changed that the election for Governor and the other higher State officers, save Treasurer and Superintendent of Public Instruction, might be elected at the time of Presidential election, Governor French was re-chosen to fill out the short term of three years; thus the Seventeeth

General Assembly also came under his administration, convening
January 6, 1851, in the week required by the new Constitution.
As the Convention failed to make any provision for Attorney-
General the office became extinct when Mr. Campbell's time
expired; but was again instituted in 1865, when R. Ingersoll
was appointed. This might properly be called the "First War
Administration."

WAR WITH MEXICO.

Cause.—At the time Governor French entered upon the
duties of his office the United States was engaged in war with
Mexico. Texas having rebelled, in 1837, from Mexico, the
country to which she originally belonged, secured her independence and shortly afterward applied for admission to the United
States; but the people of the latter were divided on the question,
and it was made an issue in the election of 1844, when a plank
was inserted in the Democratic platform to that effect. James
K. Polk, the candidate of that party, being elected decided the
wishes of the majority.

A bitter dispute then existed between the two countries regarding the boundary, Texas claiming the Rio Grande for the
line while Mexico asserted that it was the Nueces River, confining it to a much smaller strip than had rebelled. On the annex-
ation of Texas the Mexican minister departed from Washington
and threatened war, while the United States endeavored to settle
the matter by compromise; but the former would not listen to
any negotiations for peace. Accordingly General Taylor with
United States troops was sent to the disputed territory, in 1845,
where hostilities had begun.

Preparing for War.—The call for troops was divided
principally among the Western and Southern States, the demand
from Illinois being for three regiments. The response was
liberal and four were ready for action almost immediately. The
troops assembled at Alton where they were inspected by General James Shields. Choice for Colonel of the First Illinois
fell upon General John J. Hardin; Second, William H. Bissell;
Third, Captain Forman, of Fayette; Fourth, Hon. E. D. Baker.

United States forces were divided into three divisions, known as General Taylor's Army, General Scott's Army and General Kearney's Army. The 1st and 2d Illinois left Alton July 17, 18 and 19, on the steamers, Convoy, Missouri and Hannibal. Abandoning these at a convenient point on the lower Mississippi, they marched overland to San Antonio, where they went into camp for a few days. The 3d and 4th departed July 22 and 23, the former on the Glencoe and John Aull, the latter on the Sultana and Eclipse, reaching Comargo, their destination, the latter part of September.

Long March of the 1st and 2d Illinois.—As these troops were called to the "Sunny South" when the great luminary shed its light in vertical rays upon them, the marches were destructive to life and health; more troops died from exposure to the scorching heat and from change of food than at the hands of the enemy. The 1st and 2d regiments were called upon to endure the greater suffering because of their long journeys on foot. They were to join General Taylor's Army, but before being permitted to remain with him were sent with a detachment, numbering in all 3,000 men, under General Wool, to pass through several northern states of Mexico, where the inhabitants were on the verge of rebelling as Texas had done. They took up the march September 26, 1846, and crossed the Rio Grande at San Juan, or the ancient Jesuit town, Presidio, distant 182 miles from San Antonio, and reached the city of Santa Rosa October 24. This place is situated at the base of Sierra Gorda mountains which they were unable to cross with their cannon, provisions and other accoutrements. This ended the enterprise having accomplished nothing. In many towns the people were willing to feed the troops but none gave indications of deserting their country.

1st and 2d Illinois at Buena Vista.—The 1st and 2d Illinois joined General Taylor's division in time to take an active part in the battle of Buena Vista. General Bissell with the 2d regiment, was brought into the heat of the engagement—in short, the battle would have terminated differently had it not been for the coolness of this commander and his troops. The conflict began on the morning of the 23d of February, 1847, and all that long day the heaviest charge was directed against that portion of the army in which the Illinois troops were stationed. They and a portion of the Texans faced this galling fire as they took deliberate aim, and by the aid of the batteries, strewed the ground on which the enemy stood with the dead and dying; yet the Mexicans did not waver but pushed forward to rout this destructive division. At one time the troops were nearly surrounded, but when Colonel Bissell saw the danger of being captured he gave command to cease firing. Orders were next given to wheel about; then the decisive "Forward march," which was obeyed and the troops retreated to a new position, where the command was given to halt: every man stood at his post, the contest was renewed and finally the enemy forced to retreat. When evening came General Taylor's forces occupied about the same position they did at the beginning of the engagement, and in the night Santa Anna stole away, leaving the field in undisputed possession of the United States. The loss of the 1st Illinois regiment was 29 killed, 16 wounded; 2d Illinois, 62 killed, 69 wounded. Of the entire Union force but 264 were killed—almost two-fifths from Illinois. The loss of the Mexicans aggregated at least 2,500.

3d and 4th Illinois at Vera Cruz.—General Scott conducted the attack on Vera Cruz, in which the 3d and 4th Illinois took an active part, though not one of their number was lost in the engagement. March 9, 1847, the troops were landed, and they considered it fun to drive the Mexicans from hill to hill in their irresistible advance upon the city. Various means were tried to induce the enemy to surrender, but for some time without success. After waiting two weeks a destructive bombardment was opened upon their stronghold, in which 2,500 tons of ammunition were thrown into the city, discharging its mission with terrible precision, when it surrendered.

3d and 4th Illinois at Cerro Gordo.—The march was now taken up for Cerro Gordo where Santa Anna had collected 15,000 troops after his defeat at Buena Vista, having marched thither with all possible speed. There was but one road by which the Union army could gain the interior. This was upon what is known as the national road, leading through a deep gorge, the passage of a river through the mountains, 2,000 feet below the heights encompassing it, upon which the Mexicans were perched ready to pour shot and shell down upon their foe. By keeping the enemy's attention on pretended attempts to pass this road a new one was nearly completed before the design was discovered. In the night the 3d and 4th Illinois regiments succeeded in getting a 24-pound battery to these heights and in the morning the engagement began along the whole line. The enemy's left was given to the Illinois troops to capture. They discharged their work nobly and reached the Jalapa road, thus preventing a retreat in that direction. In the storming of a battery General Shields was shot through the lungs. Though his obituary was published in many papers he survived the injury.

This was the last engagement in which the Illinois troops fought during the Mexican war. As the time for which they had enlisted had about expired and as they all desired to return, their services being no longer necessary, they were soon discharged and arrived at home by the first of June. However, the war did not close until a few months afterward, when the city of Mexico surrendered.

The Illinois Troops in this war gained distinction worthy of note: they had engaged in the severest battles, had furnished more men than any other State save Texas, and were the heaviest losers; beside, they stood the brunt of the assaults and defied the most destructive charges. The 5th and 6th regiments were also organized and departed for the scene of conflict, but owing to the early capture of Mexico their services were not needed to guard the country for the bringing of supplies, as was originally intended.

The Second Constitutional Convention was called and convened June 7, 1847, with Zadok Casey President pro tempore. Newton Cloud was elected President and Henry W. Moore, Secretary.

MEMBERSHIP CONTEST.—A bitter contest was sprung in the Legislature upon the question regarding membership of this Convention; the slavery controversy being the principal point

at stake, politicians naturally divided.   The majority of the earliest settlers came from slave States, taking up their abode in the
southern portion, while the northern part was settled principally
from anti-slave States.   These immigrants arriving later, as a
natural consequence made their homes in the newer portion—
the north.   Owing to this a party line was drawn across the
State regarding apportionment.   The North wanted the census
of 1845, which showed a population of 662,125, while the South
desired that of 1840, the population then numbering 476,183.
The point was carried in favor of the former, 162 delegates
being chosen.   The principal Democrats were, Thomas Campbell, Willis Allen, Anthony Thornton, Walter B. Scates,
John Dement, John M. Palmer and Zadok Casey; Whigs,
Stephen T. Logan, David Davis, Jesse O. Norton, Henry O.
Dummer, Archibald Williams and Cyrus Edwards.

SALARY RESOLUTION.—The following were the principal
resolutions adopted in convention which were submitted to the
people for approval and carried in a contest that called out a full
vote: That the salary of the Governor should be $1,500: Secre-
tary of State, $800; Auditor, $800; Treasurer, $800; Judge of
Supreme Court, $1,200; Judges of Circuit Court, $1,000; that
no one should be subject to a draft but free, able-bodied citizens
between the ages of eighteen and forty-five; that members of
the Legislature were to receive two dollars per day when not
in session over forty-two days; days of session after that, one
dollar; also an allowance of ten cents mileage each way. Result of the vote, 49,066 for and 15,859 against.

SLAVERY RESOLUTION.—The convention likewise submitted
the vote as to whether free negroes should be admitted into Illinois or not, or whether they should be brought into the State at
all and freed by their masters.   The vote stood 20,884 for and
49,066 against their admission, becoming known as the foundation of the " Black Laws."

DEBT RESOLUTION.—A tax of two mills upon taxable property, over and above other taxes, for cancelling the State debt,
was also submitted and the returns stood 41,017 for and 30,586
against.   It was a wise measure and became the means of early
liquidating the indebtedness that had for several years been a

burden. It also showed the position of the people as to honesty and integrity. On the first Monday in March, 1848, the vote was taken and went into effect the following month.

STATE ELECTIONS.—The new Constitution required State elections to be held on the day and year of Presidential election.

Illinois and Michigan Canal.—During this administration the Illinois and Michigan canal was completed and navigation commenced in 1848. Since 1825 it had been the pet scheme of our ancestors for enriching the State, but when finished upon the narrow plan did not prove the benefit to the country that had been anticipated. In consequence of the drainage of ponds and the opening of channels, by settlers throughout the country, the water of the rivers flowed off more rapidly; thus it followed that the Illinois River was not navigable for the entire season and the through trade naturally sought some other channel. Hence the tolls of the canal reached but $173,327; otherwise they would have doubled that amount.

The Bloody Island Dike question was brought up in 1849 for settlement. A sand bar that had collected in the Mississippi river opposite the landings of St. Louis was proving a detriment to the interests of that city and would in all probability eventually obstruct the landing of boats. The city built a dike from the above island to the Illinois shore, and while the operation was in progress an injunction was laid upon it by the State of Illinois; but the matter was compromised after armed men had appeared upon the scene and the work continued.

Gold Fever.—In 1850 gold was discovered in California and soon a great emigration poured over and from the State, seeking the fields of fortune in the far west. The plains were thronged with vehicles—principally covered wagons—making their way westward. Illinois lost a large per cent of her population through the excitement and many farms that were being put under cultivation were abandoned; but most of the pilgrims to the strange land had returned before the next census was taken; many no richer, a few with gold.

State Policy War.—CAUSE.—Illinois was jealous of Missouri because the then great commercial center of the West, St. Louis, was located in that State. In 1849 this gave rise to

the " State Policy " which lived and flourished for several years
and was not wiped out of existence until 1854. It not only
assisted to divide the State into North and South but greatly
impeded the prosperity of certain sections of the country and
is felt in the extreme southern portion of Illinois to this day.
A company had under construction a railroad between Terre
Haute, Indiana, and Jacksonville, the only one allowed the South
across the State. Repeated afforts had been made to secure
roads to St. Louis, which point received much of the Southern
Illinois trade, but all without avail.

THE FIRST GRIEVANCE CONVENTION was accordingly
called in June, 1849, to bring out the sentiments of the people
residing in the south third of the State. Over 1,000 delegates
assembled, and at least 3,500 spectators to witness the transactions
of this great meeting having for its object a point of interest in
their common welfare and fortune. Zadok Casey presided.
Earnest speeches were made and a writ of grievances submitted,
which emphatically depicted the wrong perpetrated upon the
southern counties by those of the north for the sole purpose of
aiding certain cities, while, by so doing, they were neglecting
the commercial interests and ruining the early settled portion of
their State.

STATE POLICY CONVENTION.—Illinois papers, also those of
other States, took up the cause and commented upon it; the people generally believed that the State would call an extra session
of the Legislature, and it was deemed advisable to hold a convention in opposition to the one previously held. Accordingly
July 20, 1849, delegates assembled at Hillsboro, Montgomery
County, at which time an immense barbecue was prepared and
13,000 people were in attendance. Among these were Joseph
Gillespie, Cyrus Edwards, General Thornton and W. D. Lat-
shaw. At this meeting the negative side was produced: St.
Louis was a rival city, and for the State to build railroads that
would aid in furthering her advantages would be folly; Illinois,
it was claimed, was already paying annually $15,000 to her fund
for a license to sell produce within her corporation.

LEGISLATIVE ACTION.—The Policy Convention had its
effect upon the Legislature that convened in October, 1849.

Not only did this assembly reject the claims of the people of the southern counties, but passed strong resolutions upon the question of "State Policy." This act called out severe criticisms upon the Legislature by newspapers of the United States. Following is the strongest explanation:

"RESOLVED, I. That the geographical position of the State of Illinois, considered in connection with the construction of railroads within her limits, is one of the greatest natural advantages which she possesses, and which under a judicious system of Legislative policy must be very instrumental in promoting her general welfare as a State.

II. That the prosperity of a State or nation consists, not only in the virtue and intelligence of a brave and energetic people; in the richness of her soil and mineral resources, but also in the extent of her flourishing towns, cities and villages.

III. That any internal improvement, whether constructed under a general or special law, tending in its operation to impede the growth and prospects of cities, towns and villages within our own borders, ought not to be encouraged.

IV. That the construction which should be given to the sixth section of the tenth article of the Constitution is, that the General Assembly shall encourage improvements that are of an internal character and advantage, and not such as are mainly intended to promote external interests.

V. That a railroad commencing at our eastern boundary, running across the State and terminating at a point on the Mississippi opposite St. Louis, and also uniting with continuous lines of railroads extending eastwardly through our sister States, either to Cincinnati or the Atlantic cities, would be immensely advantageous to St. Louis, at the same time that it would impede the growth and prosperity of the cities, towns and other localities on the Illinois side of the Mississippi River.

VI. That the connection of the Mississippi River by continuous lines of railroads with the Atlantic seaboard is of vital importance to the whole Union, and we willingly invite the construction of railroads passing through other States, to our eastern boundary, promising to grant to them the right of way, and reserving to ourselves only the privilege of fixing the termini; a

privilege we constitutionally claim, and which we are entitled
to exercise by reason of our geographical position.

VII. That the construction of the great Central Railroad is
a subject of vast importance to Illinois, and all laws, having for
their object the completion of the same on proper principles,
ought to be encouraged; providing such laws do not infringe too
much upon our natural advantages growing out of the geographical position of the State.—[Laws of special session, 1849.

Our statesmen were willing and even anxious for railroads to
be constructed from the Atlantic coast westward but they reserved the right to name their termini when passing to or through
the State.   In 1850 a new Legislature was elected, which
body, in its session of 1851, granted a charter to the Ohio &
Mississippi company.   Senator Douglas took up the question
also by writing letters home referring the people to the fact that
they should be more liberal in their views; that in the northeast
part of the State was a city (Chicago) that was growing from
the resources of the great Northwest which was becoming rapidly settled; that the people should not give preference to the
towns but to the agricultural interests upon which the towns
depended.

SECOND GRIEVANCE CONVENTION.—As the Salem Convention of 1849 had been successful in securing the Ohio &
Mississippi railroad another convention was called, setting forth
further grievances, especially a necessity for other roads.   Honorable Zadok Casey was again President, and Sidney Breese
was appointed Chairman of a committee to draft an address to
the Governor, setting forth the propriety of calling a special
session.   The Governor complying, the special session convened
in February, 1854, which was more liberal than the former and
the "State Policy" died its death.

Illinois Central Railroad.—To this administration
belongs the construction of a railroad that has brought into the
State more revenue than any other industry—the Illinois Central. It had been proposed to build a road from the terminus of the
Illinois and Michigan Canal to the junction of the Ohio and
Mississippi Rivers, but the matter remained a question in the
minds of the people until in 1850, when Congress granted to

Illinois 3,000,000 acres of land through the State along the contemplated line, to aid in building it. All this grant lay in alternate sections, and the United States immediately raised the price of her remaining alternate sections from $1.25 per acre, the then market price, to $2.50 per acre and disposed of it earlier than she would otherwise have done had the grant not been made.

Work was almost immediately begun upon both ends of the main line, which was to be built first. The work being in fair progress a question arose among the people along the route as to the proper place for the Chicago branch to connect with the main line. After the cities had parleyed over the matter and various offers made it was decided to build the branch from a point where the least amount of land had yet been sold. Accordingly Centralia was selected. The Government also made a similar grant to other new States south, and thus a line of railroad, reaching from the Great Lakes to the Gulf, would soon be in full operation. Work was hurried forward and by 1856 the road was completed from Dunleith (East Dubuque) to Cairo; also the branch line connecting the latter city with Chicago. Seven per cent of the gross earnings have been pouring into the State Treasury ever since and if the Legislature steers clear of bribery, the institution will ever continue to be of vast importance to the financial interests of Illinois.

State Bank.—The first act of the Legislature of 1851 was to work upon a bill to re-establish the State bank. Notwithstanding the Government was in the hands of the Democratic party, which had repeatedly inserted in its platform the belief that all former financial crashes had their origin in the reckless banking system, yet the bill for re-establishing this pretended enemy, passed by a goodly majority. The reason for this move, as offered by those in favor of the bank was, that the State had been flooded with money from other States, some of which was greatly depreciated, and it had become a source of annoyance to the people to be able to tell the worthless from the genuine; beside it was not an indication of stability for other States to furnish the circulating medium. When submitted to the vote of the people, the question carried by a large majority.

Election.—In the election which took place at the close of

French's administration three tickets were placed before the people from which to choose. The Democrats nominated Joel A. Matteson for Governor, Gustavus Kœrner, Lieutenant-Governor; Whigs, E. B. Webb, Governor, J. L. D. Morrison, Lieutenant-Governor; Abolitionists, Dexter A. Knowlton, Governor, and Philo Carpenter of Cook, Lieutenant-Governor. The Democratic ticket was successful.

BIOGRAPHICAL.

Augustus C. French, eighth Governor of Illinois, was born at Hill, New Hampshire, August 2, 1808. His parents were in moderate circumstances, but both died when he was only nineteen years old, leaving four younger children for him to maintain. He discharged his mission in a noble manner; at the same time found spare moments for his own mental improvement and even attended college a few terms. He studied law and in 1831 was admitted to the bar. He early became a warm friend of Stephen A. Douglas, was also an elector for President Polk. After his gubernatorial career he became professor in McKendree College at Lebanon, where he died, September 4, 1864.

MATTESON'S ADMINISTRATION.—1853-1857.

Governor,	Joel A. Matteson.
Lieutenant-Governor,	Gustavus Kœrner.
Secretary of State,	David L. Gregg.
Auditor,	Thomas Campbell.
Treasurer,	John Moore.
Speaker of { 18th House,	John Reynolds.
19th "	Thomas Turner.

United States Senators, { R. L., { 1849-55, James Shields. 1855-61, Lyman Trumbull. T. L., 1853-59, Stephen A. Douglas.

9 Representatives in Congress; Population in 1855, 1,050,000.

This might well be called the "Administration of Immigration." The rapid sale of land and the many laborers employed in working on the Central railroad were the means of bringing many new settlers; the population increased from 851,470, as given in the census of 1850, to 1,711,955, as shown by the census of 1860, while Chicago in 1855 numbered 80,000.

Free School System.—The most important act of the Eighteenth General Assembly was the establishing of the free school system as it exists to-day. Various laws had been enacted and repealed until the State authorities themselves hardly knew the test result of all their legislating upon this branch. Free schools had been prevented from flourishing by the sale of school lands in 1828, but what was realized by these sales had accumulated to a round little sum, of which the township fund, in 1855, amounted to $1,441,477 and yielded an interest of $111,191 annually.

Two large conventions were held in 1853, one at Jerseyville and one at Bloomington, as it was contemplated that a special session of the Legislature would be called. Home school system and those in use abroad were discussed, the results compared, until it was not difficult to distinguish the different workings of school laws then in vogue. This convention had its desired effect and the Legislature took a wise step in this direction. This important branch of State government had been in the Secretary of State's hands, and having other matters on his mind of a more political nature, our free school system had been grossly neglected. Accordingly the office of Superintendent of Public Instruction was created; salary, $1,500 a year. The Governor appointed Ninian W. Edwards, son of Governor Ninian Edwards, to make an investigation of the schools of the State, report their condition and suggest, if possible, a future course. When his report was made a bill was prepared and passed the Legislature by almost a unanimous vote, February 15, 1855.

Temperance.—"Maine Liquor Laws" passed the Joint Assembly in 1855, for a submission of the question to a vote of the people. These laws prohibited the sale or manufacture of intoxicating liquors. The passage of the bill was brought about by various circumstances: In 1853 a law took effect that prohibited an individual from drinking liquor in the same building where it had been sold or given to him; also, a dealer was not allowed to sell or give away liquor in quantities of less than a quart. These restrictions met with bitter opposition and they were repealed by the next Legislature. The temperance people, full of enthusiasm, held conventions at the Capital, though refused the use of the State house, and resolutions were framed by them similar to the "Maine Law." By the next General Assembly a new Legislature had been elected and the temperance people were favored by the passage of the bill.

LIQUOR RIOTS.—As this bill forbade all licensing of saloons and as saloon men of Chicago were then paying $300 yearly, they claimed that from the passage of the bill they would be exempt from taxation until after the election, and accordingly refused to pay their fines. They were arrested but a number of friends quickly organized themselves into a mob while the trials were in progress, which was not quelled until several had been killed and the militia called out. On the following day the city was put under martial law. When the vote on the question was submitted to the people the liquor element had gained such a hold on them, especially in Chicago, that the bill was lost.

A National Question.—A new party was now fast gaining popularity, based principally upon the slavery question, and partially made up from those dissatisfied with the old party that had been holding the reins of Government almost since its foundation was laid. The discussion of various questions that brought forth this party would necessitate a National discussion rather than of State, but that young readers may better understand the divided opinions of the people, we refer them to the introduction of slavery in 1619; to the "Missouri Compromise" of 1820 and to the repeal of the same law in 1854; to the "Fugitive Slave Act" of 1850; and to the "Kansas Struggle" of 1854. The party opposed to slavery had existed for many years before any token of organization was given. All bitter disputes had been virtually settled by the Missouri Compromise, as it allowed Territories permitting slavery to be admitted into the United States lying south of a line drawn westward from the southern boundary of Missouri, while this right was prohibited north of that line, Missouri excepted. When Texas was to be admitted in 1845 a dispute arose as to whether it should be free or slave though it lay south of the named line—the anti-Slavery party

claiming it was not a part of the United States when the compromise was made. The admission of Texas was the means of
organizing a party spirit which had not yet died away when
Kansas desired admission, but the people of that Territory were
divided in their wishes and apparently averse to settling the
matter peaceably. Senator Douglas of Illinois, in his endeavor
to quiet the new disturbance, only kindled it afresh by advocating "squatter sovereignty." He introduced a bill to that effect
which became a law in May, 1854, and virtually repealed the
Missouri Compromise by giving a Territory the right to choose
whether it would become a free or slave State. This aroused
the indignation of the anti-Slavery party, especially in Illinois.

Douglas Denied Free Speech.—On the return of
Senator Stephen A. Douglas from Congress, the city of Chicago
was in a ferment of excitement, one faction upholding him in
his work and the other threatening his life. His opponents had
learned to fear him because of his power and eloquence. He
had reversed public sentiment on several occasions almost by a
single speech, and now the Democratic party wished to have
him explain the Kansas-Nebraska bill, which he had introduced
and which was intended to gain favor with the people. When
he attempted his address in Chicago, free speech was denied him.
He had been warned not to appear in public, as announced for a
certain evening in August (1854), but he paid no attention to
either threats or warnings.

He took his place in front of North Market Hall as announced, and where at least 10,000 people had assembled. He
began by alluding to the threats and comments upon the occasion, but when he merged into the political situation there was an
annoyance of hissing which culminated in yells. He folded his
arms and stood staunch and firm until the tumult had subsided,
when he launched forth again, but his voice was once more
drowned. Thus for four hours he stood before a mob and was
at last compelled to abandon his undertaking, notwithstanding
a desperate attempt on the part of his friends to restore order.

Senatorial Contest.—In the Senatorial contest of 1856
the canvass waxed warm. On first ballot James Shields received
41 votes; Abraham Lincoln, 45; scattering, 13. These men

had been bitter antagonists even before their threatened duel in 1842. On the fifth ballot Shields received 42; Lincoln, 34; scattering 23. On the seventh Shields's name was withdrawn and Joel A. Matteson received 46; Lincoln, 27; scattering, 25. On the tenth (Mr. Lincoln's name having been withdrawn on the ninth) Trumbull received 51; Matteson, 47; scattering, 1. Trumbull, of anti-Slavery persuasion, was thus chosen.

Political Parties.—First Republican Convention. —The first meeting of the new party in Illinois was held in Jacksonville in 1853 by but seven members. However, the present name was not agreed upon until in 1854 at a meeting in Bloomington, when the appellation, " Republican," was adopted on motion by John Lynch. From this time forward the party grew rapidly, with the following papers of the State its staunch advocates by 1856: The Jacksonville Journal by Paul Selby (now editor of State Journal, Springfield); Quincy Whig, V. Y. Ralston; Chicago Tribune, C. H. Ray; Rock Island Advertiser, O. P. Whorton; Peoria Republican, T. J. Prickett; Staats Zeitung, George Schneider, Chicago; Princeton Post, Charles Foxon; Lacon Gazette, A. N. Ford; Dixon Telegraph, B. F. Shaw; Decatur Chronicle, W. J. Usrey. The editors of these papers met in Decatur in February and arranged for a convention, which was held in Bloomington in May, where John Wentworth, John M. Palmer, Richard Yates, Lyman Trumbull and O. H. Browning figured as prominent personages. W. H. Herndon, Springfield, and R. J. Oglesby, Decatur, were also present. The State ticket stood as follows: Governor, W. H. Bissell; Lieutenant-Governor, Francis Hoffman; Secretary of State, O. M. Hatch; Auditor, Jesse K. Dubois; Treasurer, James Miller; Superintendent of Public Instruction, W. H. Powell.

Democratic Convention.—The Democrats felt that a contest was at hand and early rallied to meet the onset. Almost a year before the election a convention was held and the following State ticket nominated: Governor, W. A. Richardson; Lieutenant-Governor, Colonel R. J. Hamilton; Secretary of State, W. H. Snyder; Treasurer, John Moore; Auditor, Samuel K. Casey; Superintendent of Public Instruction, J. H. St. Matthew.

ELECTION.—The entire Republican ticket was successful by 4,729 votes on the head of the ticket.

BIOGRAPHICAL.

Joel A. Matteson, ninth Governor of Illinois, was born in Jefferson County, New York, August 8, 1808, being the only child of a farmer in ordinary circumstances. Young Matteson early became an adventurer. First going to Canada, he remained there a few years, when he returned home and entered an academy. After finishing his course in this school, he departed for the purpose of visiting several cities, returning by way of St. Louis, through Illinois and back to his home, paying his expenses by honest labor. After returning to his native land he married, sold his farm which he had partially improved, it having been given him by his father, and moved to the country of his choice —Illinois. In a locality where there were but two neighbors within a radius of ten miles, he selected his homestead. On this he erected a house, leaving his wife and child twelve miles distant while doing so, and sleeping at night under a pole shed. Upon awaking one morning he found a huge rattlesnake occupying a part of his bed. Without help, it was with much caution that he succeeded in deserting his visitor without being bitten. After improving his farm he became a heavy speculator. When first elected to the Legislature, in 1842, he was proprietor of large woolen mills at Joliet.

Mr. Matteson was not an orator, but he was a good Governor though he was afterward charged with being a defaulter; yet the State never lost a cent through the charged fraud. Governor Matteson died at Chicago in January, 1873, a disheartened and poor man though once wealthy.

BISSELL'S ADMINISTRATION.—1857–1861.

Governor,	{ to 1860,	·	·	W. H. Bissell.
	{ from " ,	·	·	John Wood.
Lieutenant-Governor,	-	·	·	John Wood.
Secretary of State,	·	·	·	O. H. Hatch.

Auditor,   •   •   •   Jesse K. Dubois.
Treasurer,   •   •   -   William Butler.
Supt. of Public Instruction, { to 1859, William H. Powell.
                             { from " , Newton Bateman.
Speaker of { 20th House,   -   .   John Reynolds.
           { 21st   "   .   -   Thomas Turner.
                           { E.L., 1855–61,   Lyman Trumbull.
United States Senators, {   { 1853–59, Stephen A. Douglas.
                       { T.L., { 1859–61,   "
9 Representatives in Congress; Population in 1860, 1,711,955.

Governor Bissell took the oath of office in the Governor's mansion, being unable to proceed to the capitol because of nervous prostration. The members of the Legislature proceeded thither for opening ceremonies, escorted by a company of soldiers. The Governor was not able to deliver his message and gave the manuscript to a member who read it to the Joint Assembly upon convening in the hall of Representatives.

A Stormy Legislature.—The Twentieth General Assembly was a stormy one. In the Senate the Democrats had one majority; the House stood 38 Democrats, 31 Republicans and 6 Americans (Know-Nothings), who usually voted with the Republicans. But few questions for the welfare of the State were discussed, most of the time being spent in political bluster —the discussion of each other and the character of the party— and for the melee the members appeared primed. On the organization of the House the first matinee occurred.

Peoria District Contest.—In the Peoria district C. M. Eastman had received the majority of votes but several ballots had the initials of his name wrong. By throwing these out the Democrats could seat their man, Mr. Shellebarger, which was accordingly done. This gave them the number as stated above; otherwise the Republicans would have had a majority. Both sides fully realized the importance of securing the speaker. Mr. Bridges, a Republican and former clerk, was present and made an attempt to call the House to order, but the Democrats were ready for the battle and John Dougherty was nominated speaker pro tempore; the nomination was put to vote, declared carried, and both gentlemen made a desperate effort to secure the attention of the members. A motion was put and declared carried for the Sergeant-at-arms to eject Bridges, which he did amid a tumultuous uproar. The Democrats were then in charge and seated their member, retaining the control until organized.

ATTACK ON THE GOVERNOR.—After the reading of the Governor's message, a motion was made to order 20,000 copies of it printed, when the tumult was again begun by John A. Logan, then Democratic member, who amended the motion by substituting 10,000 copies, following with a two days' speech in which he severely rebuked the Governor, and the party for supporting him in his alleged violation of the Constitution by taking the steps he did in the Bissell-Davis affair. [See biographical sketch of Governor Bessell] The amendment carried. The Governor of the people's choice was bitterly assailed throughout his administration, as he should have been were the charges preferred against him true. The following is an extract from General Logan's speech:

"I am lost in amazement —standing before the people with falsehood upon his lips, and averring his own guilt of a reckless disregard of all that can inspire confidence in man; * * * I warn young men and old against the example set. I pray God that we may never again witness such an occasion. Virtue and truth bereft of all their charms, while the hideous and hateful gods of vice hold dominion over the people."

Lincoln and Douglas Senatorial Contest.—IN-

TELLECTUAL AND POLITICAL IMPORTANCE.—No student can afford to grow into maturity without a careful study of these two men. His labor will not be thrown away. Gaining, as they did, a world-wide reputation in the times when our nation was tottering, their works live to tell of the spirit each threw into his undertaking, stimulated by vigor and determination to win; supported by natural ability and tact. The arguments, comparisons and applications in their speeches were sound; their retorts quick and cutting. The times called for action and they were prompt to obey; each, grappling his fire brand, held it aloft beyond any mortal achievement, and the kindled flames were for the time bedimmed by the glaring eloquence of adversaries never before or since surpassed or equaled in a political canvass.

CHALLENGE.—Another United States Senatorial term was

drawing to a close, which was being filled by Hon. Stephen A. Douglas who had held the position eleven years and was aspiring to a re-election. Abraham Lincoln also desired the appointment. July 24, 1858, the latter sent the former a challenge to address the same audiences in a joint discussion over the State. As Mr. Douglas had already arranged with the Democratic Central Committee to stump the State, he replied that until he could consult that committee, being anxious to accept the challenge, he could give no definite answer. It was finally arranged and seven discussions were held: Ottawa, August 21, 1858; Freeport, August 27; Jonesboro, September 15; Charleston, September 18; Galesburg, October 7; Quincy, October 13 and Alton October 15.

When the contest ended the men were enemies. Douglas was the successful candidate for the Senate, but Lincoln's name and sentiments had become known to the people of the United States and he was selected by Republicans to be their candidate in the Presidential election of 1860, when he was successful. Douglas was also a candidate but there being two Democrats in the field, Northern and Southern, he made no effort to meet with success.

Election of 1858.—The tickets in the election of 1858 were headed by Treasurer and Superintendent of Public Instruction. Parties for this year stood as follows: Buchanan Democrats, favoring the introduction of slavery into Kansas; Democrats, favoring Douglas in his introduction of slavery where a majority of the people desired it; Republicans, favoring the abolition of slavery though not then asserting it. To give an idea of the political standing of the times we give the result of the election.

TREASURER.		SUPT. PUBLIC INSTRUCTION.	
James Miller, r	125,430	Newton Bateman, r	124,556
William F. Fondey, d	121,609	Augustus C. French, d	122,413
John Dougherty, b d	5,071	John Reynolds, b d	5,173

Republican Congressmen were elected in the First, Second, Third and Fourth districts; Democratic, in the Fifth, Sixth, Seventh, Eighth and Ninth.

An Apportionment Bill was brought before the Legislature in 1859 which caused another terrible scene in the House. Lincoln and Douglas had so awakened the people of the State by their stirring eloquence, that when the bill came up not the least point was left undisputed; the Democrats were losing ground and the Republicans were anxious to gain all they could. As matters stood on the introduction of the bill the popular vote was on the side of the Republicans but according to the arrangement of districts the Democrats were likely to get a majority in the Legislature. This bill provided for the opportionment in such a manner that Republicans were not allowed as many Representatives in the Legislature as they thought they were entitled to have, claiming that the south portion of the State had more per capita than the north; thus confining them to thirty-three Representatives while the Democrats would be given forty-one. By every means possible the bill was retarded and kept back; when it finally passed, the Lieutenant-Governor was careful to be away and did not sign it for several days; then when received by the Governor he retained the document a week before putting his veto upon it. When the Governor's private secretary began reading the veto in the House a regular stampede ensued. In vain the Speaker attempted to restore order, asserting that there was not a quorum present and requesting the removal of the secretary. The clerk would not receive the document which was tossed about and almost destroyed before it was rescued. Business was brought to a dead lock and many bills were never brought before the Assembly.

Canal Script Fraud.—In 1859 the Canal Script Fraud, claimed to have been perpetrated by ex-Governor Matteson, came to light. On investigation it was found that that gentleman, who had conducted the affairs of State through with glory and pomp, was a defaulter to large amounts by taking old bank script from a sealed box and re-issuing it. When charged with the crime, Governor Matteson turned all his property over to the State without a word of defense, save the assertion that he had been imposed upon, and thus died, fourteen years later, a poor man; yet when he took his seat at the Capital he was well-to-do.

Death of the Governor.—March 18, 1860, Governor Bissell died and Lieutenant-Governor Wood became his successor for a term of ten months. He had been in poor health during the entire term of office and upon being attacked by politicians, probably unjustly, his condition did not improve. His funeral was attended by a large crowd from all parts of the State. This is the first and only Governor who passed away while in office.

Election.—STATE.—The Republican State Convention met at Decatur, May 9, 1860, and nominated the following ticket: Governor, Richard Yates; Lieutenant-Governor, Francis A. Huffman; Secretary of State, O. M. Hatch; Auditor, Jesse K. Dubois; Treasurer, William Butler; Superintendent of Public Instruction, Newton Bateman. The Democrats met at Springfield, June 13, and selected the following ticket: Governor, J. C. Allen; Lieutenant-Governor, L. W. Ross; Secretary of State, G. H. Campbell; Auditor, Bernard Arntzen; Treasurer, Hugh Maher; Superintendent of Public Instruction, Dr. E. R. Roe. They approved of the nomination of Stephen A. Douglas for President. The Breckinridge Democrats also put in nomination a State ticket. The result of the election was in favor of the Republicans, the gubernatorial vote resulting as follows: Richard Yates, R., 172,196; James C. Allen, D., 159,153; T. M. Hope, B. D., 2,049; scattering, 2,905.

NATIONAL.—Abraham Lincoln and Stephen A. Douglas each received a nomination for the Presidency, as previously stated, while Breckinridge was supported by the Buchanan Democrats (the South). The canvass was warm and stubborn. In Illinois Lincoln received 171,126; Douglas, 158,254; Breckinridge, 2,293 and Bell, 4,819 votes.

BIOGRAPHICAL.

William H. Bissell, tenth Governor of Illinois, was born near Painted Post, New York, April 25, 1811. His parents were quiet, industrious people, desiring only a neat, comfortable home and caring little for worldly pleasures or luxuries as they traversed the path of virtue and honesty, in which they carefully trained their children to follow. William being of an energetic disposition, acquired an ordinary literary education in an academy, after which he studied medicine and began the practice of his profession in Monroe County, Illinois. On visiting a court room he became infatuated with the excitement which generally arises at trials, became a frequent visitor at the various courts and held several conversations with leading lawyers upon the subject now taking possession of his hitherto unsatisfied mind. In 1830 he began the study of this profession and was admitted to the bar in 1841, serving a term as Democratic member in the Legislature the following year. About this time his wife died, leaving to him the care of two daughters. He was subsequently married to the daughter of Elias K. Kane who survived him but a few days. Governor Bissell will ever be remembered as a good lawyer, a charming speaker and an excellent Colonel, having been the hero of Buena Vista in 1847, at the head of the Second Illinois. While in Congress, in which he served two terms, a bitter dispute arose between him and Jefferson Davis: the latter gentleman endeavored to reap laurels for valor in the Mexican War, that were not due him, especially in the battle of Buena Vista. The replies of Bissell which were cutting and powerful gave him a national reputation. The contention increased in warmth until Davis challenged him to a duel which he is said to have quietly accepted, though the matter is not understood as the following oath was required of him by the State unless previously changed:

"I do solemnly swear that I have not fought a duel, nor sent or accepted a challenge to fight a duel, the probable issue of which might have been the death of either party, nor been a second to either party, nor in any manner aided or assisted in such duel, nor been knowingly the bearer of such challenge or acceptance, since the adoption of the Constitution; and that I will not be so engaged or concerned, directly or indirectly, in or about such duel during my continuance in office: so help me God."

When elected Governor he was a Democrat but of anti-Nebraska persuasion. Soon after assuming the reins of Government he was stricken with nervous prostration and died before his term of office expired, March 16, 1860. He was a devoted believer in the Catholic faith to the last, and the funeral services were accordingly in charge of the denomination of his choice.

Abraham Lincoln was a descendant of an English family that migrated to Massachusetts in 1638, whose posterity lived first in Pennsylvania, then in Virginia and afterward moved to Kentucky. The following is an autobiography written for J. W. Fell of Bloomington:

"I was born February 12, 1809, in Hardin County, Kentucky. My parents were both born in Virginia of undistinguished families—second families, perhaps I should say. My mother, who died in my tenth year, was of a family of the name of Hanks, some of whom now reside in Adams, and others in Macon County, Illinois. My paternal grandfather, Abraham Lincoln, emigrated from Rockingham County, Virginia, to Kentucky about 1781 or 1782, where, a year or two later, he was killed by Indians—not in battle but by stealth—when he was laboring to open a farm in the forest. His ancestors, who were Quakers, went to Virginia from Berks County, Pennsylvania. An effort to identify them with the New England family of the same name ended in nothing more definite than similarity of Christian names in both families, such as Enoch, Levi, Mordecai, Solomon, Abraham, and the like. My father, at the death of his father, was but six years of age, and he grew up literally without any education. He removed from Kentucky to what is now Spencer County, Indiana, in my eighth year. We reached our new home about the time the State came into the Union. It was a wild region, with many bears and other wild animals still in the woods. There I grew up. There were some schools, so called, but no qualification was ever required of a teacher beyond 'readin', writin' and cipherin' to the rule of three.' If a straggler, supposed to understand Latin, happened to sojourn in the neighborhood, he was looked upon as a wizard. There was absolutely nothing to excite ambition for education. Of course, when I came of age, I did not know much. Still, somehow, I could read, write and cipher to the rule of three, but that was all. I have not been to school since. The little advance I now have upon this store of education I have picked up from time to time under the pressure of necessity. I was raised to farm work, which I continued till I was twenty-two. At twenty-one I came to Illinois, and passed the first year in Macon County. Then I got to New Salem, at that time in Sangamon, now in Menard County, where I remained a year as a sort of clerk in a store. Then came the Black Hawk War, and I was elected a Captain of volunteers—a success which gave me more pleasure than any I have had since. I went into the campaign, was elected; ran for the Legislature the same year (1832) and was beaten—the only time I ever have been beaten by the people. The next and three succeeding biennial elections I was elected to the Legislature. I was not a candidate afterward. During this Legislative period I had studied law and removed to Springfield to practice it. In 1846 I was elected to the lower house of Congress. Was not a candidate for re-election. From 1849 to 1854, both inclusive, practiced law more assiduously than before. Always a Whig in politics, and generally on the Whig electoral ticket, making active canvasses. · I was losing interest in politics, when the repeal of the Missouri Compromise aroused me again. What I have done since then is pretty well known. If any personal description of me is thought desirable, it may be said I am in height six feet, four inches nearly, lean in flesh, weighing, on an average, 180 pounds, dark complexion, with coarse black hair and gray eyes. No other marks or brands recollected.

Yours very truly,
A. Lincoln.

The father of Abraham Lincoln was a thriftless man, undertaking first one kind of work and then another until he finally settled down in a little log cabin on a piece of ground almost barren. Here Abraham was born. He early showed a disposition to study and, without a word of encouragement from his parents, he would travel with his sister, two years his senior, to a wretched little school house, four miles distant, to gain an education. In 1816 his father had some difficulty with a neighbor and, with his family, removed to Perry County, Indiana, where he lost his wife in 1818. The father married a widow of the neighborhood thirteen months afterward. Though she had three children she did all in her power for the two dirty little unfortunates. She became very proud of Abraham who, she said, never gave her a cross word or look and never refused to do any work she requested of him. Young Lincoln reciprocated his mother's love and in after years said, "All that I am or hope to be, I owe to my angel mother." He had but little chance for schooling but improved that little to the fullest extent. He grew in height amazingly and when seventeen he had reached the altitude of six feet, four inches; wiry and strong, with enormous hands and feet, arms and legs far outstretching his proportions; withal, rather a small head and yellow skin somewhat shriveled. His clothes were of coarse homespun material, with trousers usually much too short because of his rapid growth. Imagine all this surmounted by a coon skin cap, and we have the picture of Lincoln at the close of his school days. His remaining life to the time of his discussions with Douglas is the life of all politicians and lawyers who have had to struggle with poverty in their toilsome ascent, and is generally known.

Before this warm contest opened Lincoln and Douglas had been opponents. On December 3, 1839, both men were admitted to practice in the Federal Courts and were frequently thrown on opposite sides, not only in politics but in law as well. Mr. Lincoln was not so prominent as Mr. Douglas in early life because of adverse circumstances. He was repeatedly offered the nomination to represent his district in Congress, but refused to accept after having served a term; he aspired to the office of Commissioner of the general land office, but failed to secure it; he was offered the Governorship of Oregon, but his wife refused to accompany him to that Territory; he also desired to succeed his opponent, James Shields, as United States Senator but Lyman Trumbull carried off the prize, and in the great contest, partaking of such bitter party spirit, between himself and Mr. Douglas, he was again defeated. However, the names of these two men were uppermost in the minds and hearts of the people.

In the search of the Republican party, in 1860, for a Presidential candidate, they found in Lincoln's sentiments their sentiments and believed him to be the man who could carry off the prize. He was accordingly nominated, as was his opponent, Mr. Douglas, and secured the highest office of the nation's trust. So well did he discharge his duties as President that he became his own successor in 1864. [For assassination see Oglesby's first administration.]

Stephen A. Douglas.—The early life of Stephen A. Douglas was somewhat brighter than that of his opponent. He was born at Brandon, Vermont, in 1813. His father, a physician of some notoriety, died when Stephen was but two months old. The mother being left in fair circumstances, moved to a farm, where her son learned to till the soil and think for himself. At the age of fifteen he apprenticed to a cabinet maker, but owing to poor health abandoned his trade after working two years and returned home. He attended Brandon Academy for one year and then moved with his mother to Canandaigua, New York, continuing his education in the academy of that place, where he began fitting for the legal profession. In 1833 he departed for Illinois, but falling short of funds before his arrival, was compelled to walk a part of the way. On arriving at Winchester he opened a school and taught for three months, still pursuing his studies. In 1834 he was admitted to the bar, began a successful practice at once and was appointed Attorney-General one year thereafter. The following positions of trust were tendered him, several of which he resigned for something better: elected to the Legislature, 1835; appointed Registrar of the United States Land Office at Springfield, 1837; nominated for Congress by the Democratic convention in 1837, but failed to be elected; appointed Secretary of State, 1840; elected Judge of the Supreme Court, 1841; elected to Congress, 1843, 1845 and 1847; elected to the United States Senate in 1847, 1853 and 1859, the two latter times becoming his own successor. At the time of the approaching election of 1859 the slavery question had become the main issue. Mr. Lincoln entered the field as his opponent in the canvass and neither being ashamed to express his sentiments or explain the platform upon which he stood, the contest waxed warm. Each becoming the leader of his party, the whole nation turned with interest to their speeches and discussions.

When the war broke out Mr. Douglas, as well as President Lincoln, took strong grounds in favor of maintaining the Union; in fact, there was no man that wielded a stronger influence to aid the President in consolidating the North and preserving the nation than Senator Douglas. When Mr. Lincoln stepped upon the balcony to take the oath of office and deliver his inaugural address he found Mr. Douglas by his side, who kindly offered and held his hat during the ceremony. Thus this great leader showed to his followers his sentiments. They in turn echoed them from State to State and vowed that if the worst must and should come they would stand by the leader who had been successful in securing the chief office of the great Republic; also, when a manifesto had been issued for 75,000 troops, that his position might not be misunderstood, Senator Douglas called on President Lincoln and warmly declared that he would stand by him in this, the great hour of peril. This declaration so delighted the President that he caused a part of the conversation to be published. Seven days after, on arriving in Springfield, he addressed both houses of the Legislature in a long and appropriate speech. In it he said:

"So long as a hope remained of peace, I plead and implored for compromise. Now that all else has failed, there is but one course left and that is to rally as one man under the flag of Washington, Jefferson, Hamilton, Madison and Franklin. * * It is a prodigious crime against the freedom of the world to attempt to blot the United States out of the map of Christendom. * * * Allow me to say to my political enemies, you will not be true to your country if you seek to make political capital out of these disasters; and to my old friends, you will be false and unworthy of your principles if you allow political defeat to convert you into traitors to your national land. * * * Gentlemen, it is our duty to defend our Constitution and protect our flag."

Douglas delivered but one public address after the foregoing. This was in the Republican wigwam in Chicago, in which Lincoln was nominated for President. After retiring to his room in the Tremont House he was taken ill, where he died June 3,

1861. The entire nation felt the loss of this truly great man; party feeling was laid aside in Chicago and all mourned the untimely death of their beloved citizen; the entire city was draped, where he had at one been denied free speech.

YATES'S ADMINISTRATION.—1861–1865.

Governor,	- - - -	Richard Yates.
Lieutenant-Governor,	- - -	Francis A. Hoffman.
Secretary of State,	- - -	O. H. Hatch.
Auditor,	- - - -	Jesse K. Dubois.
Treasurer, { to 1863,	- -	William Butler.
{ from "	- -	Alexander Starne.
Supt. of Public Instruction, { to 1863,		Newton Bateman.
{ from ",		John P. Brooks.
Speaker of { 22d House,	- -	Shelby M. Cullom.
{ 23d "	-	Samuel A. Richardson.
United States Senators, { E.L.,—1861–67,		Lyman Trumbull.
{ { 1859–61,	Stephen A. Douglas.
{ T.L., { 1861–63,	Orvill H. Browning.
{ { 1863–65,	Wm. A. Richardson.

14 Representatives in Congress; Population in 1860, 1,711,955.

The Twenty-second General Assembly convened January 7, 1861, with a Republican majority in both houses, the first time any one party ever held sway over the Democrats of Illinois. Politics ran high until the war broke out, then curses and slander were heaped upon each other, although Illinois to a man was for the preservation of the Union, exclusive of a portion of the Buchanan or Breckinridge Democrats.

Unsettled.—The South having declared its intention to withdraw from the Union upon Lincoln's taking the Presidential chair, war appeared to be brooding though none could foretell the result. Illinois Democrats having met in convention, with the venerable Zadok Casey as chairman, and resolved to preserve the nation's honor, no disturbance within the State was feared except in the matter of war policy. All eyes were turned southward. Our State Legislature early adjourned without the transaction of any business of importance, other than its regular routine of appropriations, etc. The members were scarcely home when Governor Yates issued a summons, April 15, for them to re-assemble. The body convened on the 23d, remaining in session ten days.

To Arms!—April 14 President Lincoln issued a call for 75,000 troops and apportioned six regiments to be raised in Illinois. Beside this number the Legislature provided for the raising of ten additional regiments of infantry, one of cavalry and a battalion of light artillery, to prevent an invasion of the State or rebellion of the residents, to be made up of male citizens between the ages of eighteen and forty-five. An appropriation of $3,550,000 was made for carrying on the war: $1,500,000 for the purchase of weapons, ammunition, clothing, etc.; $2,000,000 for general war purposes and $50,000 to be placed at the disposal of the Governor. Though the war fever was intense the resolution introduced by Aaron Shaw was unimously adopted—" That, while we are ever ready to stand by, and defend, with our fortunes and our lives, the Constitution, the honor and flag of our country, we will frown upon and condemn any effort, on the part of the Federal Government, which looks to the subjugation of the Southern States."

Party Feeling.—On the death of Douglas, June 3, party spirit was aroused in Illinois by the Governor appointing a Republican to succeed him in the United States Senate. From this forward every inch of ground was disputed between the two factions, which, together with the party strife throughout the nation and the bitter epithets hurled at each other by the unreasonable, has kindled a hatred that will only be wiped out as successive generations take their places upon the arena of national government.

————:o:————

1861.

Illinois was one of the most liberal States in her response to President Lincoln's call for troops. The first regiment took for its name the Seventh Illinois because of the first six numbers having been given to the regiments of the Mexican

War. During this year regiments from the Seventh to the
Fifty-second inclusive, also the Fifty-seventh, Fifty-eighth and
Fifty-ninth were enlisted. The cavalry was from the First to
the Thirteenth inclusive. The principal places for mustering
into service were Camp Butler and Camp Douglas. The
former is now nicely fitted up and used as a soldiers' cemetery—
located east of Springfield and two miles southwest of Riverton;
the latter is the resting place of Stephen A. Douglas and is
marked by an elegant monument which stands at the foot of
Thirty-fifth Street, overlooking Lake Michigan, in Chicago.

Guarding the State.—Cairo being in the extreme
southern portion of the State, many soldiers were sent thither
at the first outbreak to protect Illinois from Confederate invasion. Here several boats were captured on their way South
with ammunition and arms.

Arms Seized.—There being but few muskets in the State
wherewith to supply the troops, a petition was sent to Congress
and an order was given on the St. Louis arsenal. This place
was overrun by Confederate spies; besides, troops were scattered
secretly in all parts of the city. The difficult task of securing
this valuable store was put in charge of Captain Stokes, who,
with 700 men from the Seventh Illinois, succeeded in seizing not
only 10,000 muskets, the number ordered, but 20,000, besides
500 carbines and the same number of pistols.

Missouri Campaign.—For the campaign in Missouri
Colonel Mulligan, with the Twenty-third Illinois Infantry,
the First Illinois Cavalry and 1,000 Missouri troops, was sent
into Missouri, but was forced to surrender to Price, Confederate, in the battle of Lexington, September 20. The blame
for this defeat was placed upon Fremont who did not send him
immediate aid. (See U. S. history).

The Sixteenth Illinois, under Colonel R. T. Smith, engaged
the rebel Governor, Harris, at Monroe, Missouri, where it was
besieged by the enemy until the timely arrival of ex-Governor
Wood, of Illinois, with recruits.

October 21, General Ulysses S. Grant, in command of the
southwest district of Missouri with headquarters at Cairo, sent
an expedition to drive the enemy from Fredericktown, which

was accomplished principally by Illinois regiments—17th, 20th, 21st, 23d and 38th. (See U. S. history).

Next occurred the Battle of Belmont, fought exclusively by Illinois troops, save one regiment from Iowa, and the entire command under General Grant. In this contest were Generals John A. McClernand and John A. Logan and Colonel Dougherty; infantries, the 21st, 27th, 30th and 31st, and Fourth Cavalry. The engagement was for the purpose of preventing the Confederates from sending re-inforcements to Price. This was a desperate conflict and without any decisive result.

————:o:————

1862.

During this year seventy-four more Illinois regiments were added to the list of volunteers. Fighting began in earnest and many loyal citizens laid down their lives.

Constitutional Convention.—January 7, 1862, the delegates to the Constitutional Convention, for which the people had voted in November, 1861, assembled at Springfield. This was composed of many distinguished men, but as it was Democratic and the State officers were Republican, harmony did not exist; opposition at once took place between the two factions imbued with ruling power. In the first place the Governor had gone beyond his constitutional authority, having expended about one and one-third million dollars of State money without action of the Legislature; yet it was probably the wishes of the people that he should be liberal: but to kindle opposition and provoke an attack, his agent had purchased a large amount of worthless clothing in Philadelphia, which would have caused a loss to the State of $130,000 had it not afterward been made good. The United States Government saw a tendency to provoke discord in the State and sent an agent to re-imburse the amount expended, but the Governor refused to accept the offer, saying he had the right as authorized by the General Assembly to make such expenditures; yet he had spent over $800,000.

This made capital for the convention which now endeavored to usurp power not allowed them; in short, they went so far as

to inquire into matters that were purely legislative in their character, and voted an appropriation of $500,000 for the support of
destitute families of soldiers, but the Governor paid no attention
to the transaction.

The constitution which they framed was severely criticised
at first, but it was afterward regarded as a great improvement
on the old. The limit it placed upon tampering with State
funds and State sources for revenue is commendable.

Forts Henry and Donelson.—The capture of the
Confederate strongholds in Tennessee, forts Henry and Donelson, to prevent preparation for Northern invasion, was given to
General Grant with his land forces, and Commodore Foote with
his gunboats. Grant's army was separated into two divisions,
commanded by Generals McClernand and C. F. Smith. The
former's division was in two sections, commanded by Oglesby
and Wallace. Oglesby's command contained, of Illinois Infantry, the 8th, 18th, 27th, 29th, 30th and 31st; Wallace's, the
11th, 12th, 45th and 48th, and of cavalry the 4th, with Taylor's
and McAlister's batteries. Fort Henry was easily reduced, February 6, by Commodore Foote without direct aid of land forces,
but at Donelson, ten days later, a severe battle was fought, which
resulted in the capture of the fortification with its extensive store
and 16,000 prisoners. Most of the prisoners were sent to Camp
Butler where they were well treated and not in a semi-barbarous
way as is sometimes pictured by the South. Illinois regiments in
this campaign were the 7th, 8th, 9th, 11th, 12th, 13th, 17th, 18th,
20th, 27th, 28th, 29th, 30th, 31st, 32d, 38th, 41st, 43d, 45th, 46th,
48th, 49th, 50th, 57th and 58th.

At Pea Ridge, Missouri, March 7 and 8, a desperate
battle was fought in which 12,000 Federalists engaged 40,000 of
the enemy. The first of the engagement was fought at Springfield, Missouri, in which the Confederates were routed, but being
re-inforced, they turned upon the Union troops at Pea Ridge,
and after two days' hard fighting were again repulsed. The
Illinois troops in this contest were the 35th, 36th, 37th and 57th
infantries, 3d and a portion of the 15th cavalries. The Federalists were under General Curtis and Confederates under Van
Dorn and McCulloch. The latter was killed in the engagement.

New Madrid.—In the capture of New Madrid, where the Confederates left their entire store—suppers spread, candles burning in their tents—and escaped under cover of a thunderstorm, were engaged the 10th, 16th, 26th, 47th, 51st and 64th infantries and a portion of the Seventh Cavalry.

Island No. 10.—The 12th, 22d, 42d, 51st and 64th infantries, and the 2d and 7th cavalries, all of Illinois, participated in the seizure of Island No. 10, April 7.

Battle of Shiloh.—April 6 and 7 the desperate battle of Shiloh (Pittsburg Landing) was fought. As Grant's army had been somewhat weakened, and as Buell was expected to arrive with re-inforcements, the Confederates determined to strike a blow before the union could be formed. In this two-days' battle Illinois suffered greater loss and maintained a braver resistance than any other State. In the engagement Prentiss and 3,000 soldiers were captured, General W. H. L. Wallace was killed and the Sixty-first Illinois was almost destroyed at the onset. Grant was not present and, as Sherman and Prentiss were at first disabled, being taken by surprise, the brunt of the battle fell upon McClernand and Wallace. Upon Grant's arrival he conducted a retreat to the river brink where, with the aid of gunboats, they maintained this final stand until Buell and his fresh army came rushing upon the bloody field. Grant was now able to pursue the enemy, which retired toward Corinth. The Illinois troops engaged in this contest were the 7th, 8th, 9th, 11th, 12th, 14th, 15th, 17th, 18th, 20th, 28th, 29th, 30th, 31st, 32d, 40th, 41st, 42d, 43d, 45th, 46th, 48th, 49th, 50th, 52d, 55th, 57th, 58th and 61st. After the battle Governor Yates hastened to the scene of action, where he directed, in person, the care of our wounded and dying. He thus earned the admiration of the troops and gained the sobriquet of " The Soldier's Friend."

Railroad Destroyed.—The 19th and 24th infantries from Illinois joined an expedition under General Mitchell, and destroyed the Memphis & Charleston Railroad to prevent supplies and recruits from being transported to Corinth.

Farmington.—In the capture of Farmington, May 3, the 10th, 16th, 22d, 26th, 27th, 42d and 47th, were engaged.

Corinth.—The Illinois regiments brought into action in the siege of Corinth were the 7th, 10th, 11th, 12th, 14th, 15th, 16th, 17th, 18th, 22d, 26th, 27th, 28th, 29th, 30th, 31st, 34th, 35th, 38th, 41st, 42d, 43d, 45th, 46th, 47th, 48th, 51st, 52d, 53d, 55th, 57th, 60th, 64th and 66th. The Federalists were commanded by General Halleck who departed soon after this engagement to assume the office of commander of the Eastern armies, and Grant succeeded to the command of the Western forces. (See U. S. history.)

In the second engagement at Corinth the 7th, 9th, 12th, 28th, 32d, 41st, 50th, 52d, 53d, 56th, and 57th, of Illinois, were brought into action. (See U. S. history.)

Perryville.—The battle of Perryville was fought October 8, the commanding officers being Bragg of the Confederates and Buell of the Federals. The latter was soon afterward succeeded by Rosecrans because he allowed the enemy to escape with plunder gathered in Kentucky. The Illinois troops were the 19th, 21st, 24th, 25th, 35th, 36th, 38th, 39th, 42d, 44th, 58th, 59th, 73d, 74th, 75th, 80th, 85th, 86th, 88th, 123d and 125th. Of the Fifty-ninth Illinois almost one-half were killed, and of the Seventy-fifth one-third lost their lives. (See U. S. history).

Murfreesboro.—In the desperate battle of Murfreesboro, December 31, the 19th, 35th, 44th, 51st, 59th, 73d, 75th, 85th and 88th were among the Illinois troops. The Union troops were commanded by Rosecrans and the Confederates by Bragg. The latter were repulsed with great loss. (See U. S. history.)

First Vicksburg Expedition.—This year an attempt was made by General Grant to capture Vicksburg, but he was repulsed in what was known as the first expedition, through a misunderstanding of orders. In this campaign the Illinois regiments more particularly active were, the 13th, 17th, 18th, 43d, 55th, 77th, 97th, 106th, 108th, 113th, 116th, 118th, 119th, 122d, 126th and 131st of the infantry, and the 2d, 3d, 4th, 11th and 15th of the cavalry. (See U. S. history.)

Unruly Legislature.—The State election of this year gave a Democratic majority of 16,000, and both branches of the Legislature were in their hands. The General Assembly convened January 5, and was from the first a stormy one. Upon the Democratic members rests the blame. Instead of approaching important questions like men of judgment should do and taking legislative action as they believed right, they staved off all business to prevent exorbitant appropriation bills from passing, and by the Republicans getting a steal on them a warm contest followed.   Matters assumed such phases that neither party was willing to concur with the other.

Party Animosities.—After the Legislature adjourned meetings were held in various parts of the State by Douglas Democrats who asserted their disapproval of organizing for a peace convention, and also expressed a willingness to conquer the South since hostilities had begun.   This half-way step, however, was not received in the spirit it was intended.   The bitter feeling already kindled knew no bound and political parties in Illinois could not be reconciled.   Arrests were made for alleged hostile actions toward the Government, that in times of peace would not be noticed.   The Chicago Times was placed under military authority June 1, 1863, no issue being allowed until mob violence was threatened and President Lincoln had revoked the order.   This was done in compliance with a petition from the more thoughtful Republicans of Chicago.

Special Legislative Session assembled in June, when the most important bill that called forth a clamor was that of the army appropriatoin of $100,000 besides a $50,000 appropriation bill.   For the distribution of the former a commission of three was appointed by the House.   When this bill reached the Senate the names of the Governor and Treasurer were added. This change was effected on the 8th, in the absence of three Democrats, one having died, and upon which day they agreed to adjourn.   When the motion for adjournment was sent to the House, it was amended by inserting June 20, but to this the Senate would not agree.   Under the Constitution the Governor had power to name a day for final adjournment, when the two branches disagreed upon a date.   He thus used his power for a political purpose and prevented further legislation.   This was the last Democratic Legislature to date.

Democrats Aroused.—The above proceeding so irritated Democrats throughout the State that a great mass meeting was called, at which over 40,000 persons assembled.   Everything passed off quietly and a set of grievances was passed, the substance of which was for peace, rather than rebellion or tyranny, the arrest of citizens illegally, the banishment of Vallandingham of Ohio; and at the same time denounced fanatic influences that were preying upon the minds of a frenzied people.

————:o:————

1863.

No new regiments were mustered into service from Illinois during this year, but the Fourteenth and Fifteenth cavalries were first thoroughly organized and equipped for service.

Second Vicksburg Expedition.—The first important engagement of this year in which Illinois troops conspicuously performed their part, was the second siege of Vicksburg, May to July 4. Of those present from Illinois were the 8th, 11th, 13th, 14th, 17th, 20th, 23d, 25th, 28th, 29th, 30th, 31st, 32d, 33d, 35th, 38th, 41st, 45th, 46th, 47th, 48th, 51st, 53d, 55th, 57th, 63d, 72d, 75th, 76th, 77th, 81st, 93d, 95th, 97th, 99th, 108th, 113th, 114th, 116th, 118th, 120th, 124th, 126th, 127th and 131st infantries, the 2d, 3d, 6th and 7th cavalries. The capture of this city was one of the most important efforts in the career of General Grant. (See U. S. history.)

The Battle of Chickamauga was fought September 19 and 20, by Rosecrans in command of Union troops, and Bragg in command of Confederates. Rosecrans succeeded in driving his adversary from Chattanooga and, supposing him to be on a long retreat, was in hot pursuit, with his army scattered over a district forty miles in length, when the enemy, with reinforcements and a concentrated army, wheeled about and drove his army from the field; but on the following day the Union forces gained a decided advantage and Bragg withdrew to Chattanooga. Illinois soldiery was represented by the 10th, 16th, 19th, 21st, 22d, 24th, 25th, 27th, 34th, 35th, 36th, 38th, 42d, 44th, 51st, 73d, 74th, 75th, 78th, 79th, 80th, 84th, 85th, 86th, 88th, 89th, 92d, 98th, 100th, 104th, 110th, 116th, 123d, 125th and 127th infantries. (For further information see U. S. history.)

Lookout Mountain and Missionary Ridge.—

Grant now took charge of Rosecrans's army; recruits under Hooker came from the East while Sherman arrived from the South. Two desperate battles were fought: the first, September 24 on Lookout Mountain; the second, on the following day on Missionary Ridge, resulting in a Union victory. The Illinois troops in these engagements were the 12th, 19th, 22d, 26th, 27th, 34th, 35th, 42d, 44th, 48th, 51st, 59th, 60th, 63d, 73d, 75th, 79th, 80th, 84th, 86th, 88th, 89th, 93d, 101st, 104th and 115th. (For general account see U. S. history.)

———:o:———

1864.

At the outset of this year's campaign Grant was placed in command of all the Union forces and in consequence Sherman was placed in charge of the Western forces.

Confederates at Chicago.—A number of Southern leaders had wended their way northward when the war began drawing to a close. At Chicago a deep laid scheme was arranged by which the Confederate prisoners at Camp Douglas were to be freed and then, in consequence, a rebellious army formed. After the plot had been detected stores of arms were found which proved that the design was of no small pretension.

March to the Sea.—General Sherman, seeing the way open, collected an army of about 100,000 able men and started for the Southern Atlantic shores, laying waste the most beautiful of the enemy's country. He broke off from all communications at Nashville, November 16. The Illinois regiments that were with him and played prominent parts in the battles of Rocky Face, Resacca, New Hope Church, Kenesaw Mountain, Atlanta and Jonesboro, were the 9th, 12th, 16th, 26th, 27th, 30th, 31st, 32d, 35th, 38th, 44th, 48th, 51st, 52d, 53d, 55th, 59th, 60th, 64th, 65th, 73d, 74th, 75th, 79th, 80th, 84th, 86th, 88th, 89th, 92d, 98th, 101st, 102d, 104th, 105th, 107th, 111th, 112th, 115th, 127th and 129th. Also the 7th, 10th, 14th, 15th, 20th, 34th, 40th, 41st, 45th, 50th, 56th, 57th, 63d, 66th, 78th, 82d, 85th, 90th, 93d, 103d, 110th, 116th and 125th accompanied the expedition.

Sherman's march to the sea virtually ended the engagements in which Illinois troops took an active part. A few were discharged in 1864, others in 1865 and several regiments retained until in 1866. The limit of this work confines us to a few pages for a description of the Great Rebellion, that would take volumes to tell the story of how the "Noble Sons of Illinois" sacrificed their lives.

Hood's Army Annihilated.—The march to the sea was aided to a great extent by the veteran, General Thomas, who was left to guard the road for supplies and recruits. By skillful managing he succeeded in completely annihilating Hood's army, long the dread of Sherman. This was accomplished in a battle at Nashville, Tennessee, in which the 38th, 42d, 44th, 47th, 48th, 49th, 51st, 59th, 65th, 72d, 73d, 74th, 79th, 80th, 88th, 89th, 107th, 112th, 114th, 115th, 117th, 119th and 122d infantries served and several times bravely withstood a severe encounter, sustaining great loss.

Election.—The Republican State convention met at Springfield, May 25, 1864, and nominated a ticket that corresponds to the head of the following administration. The Democrats did not hold their convention until September 6, when the following ticket was nominated: Governor, John C. Robinson; Lieutenant-Governor, S. Corning Judd; Secretary of State, William A. Turney; Auditor, John Hise; Treasurer, Alexander Starne; Superintendent of Public Instruction, John P. Brooks. The election in November gave the Republican ticket a majority of over 30,000.

BIOGRAPHICAL.

Richard Yates, eleventh Governor of Illinois, was born January 18, 1818, at Warsaw, Kentucky. His father removed to Illinois when Richard was thirteen years old and settled at Island Grove, Sangamon County. Young Yates early took to books, and entered Illinois College, Jacksonville, where he graduated in his nineteenth year at the head of his class. After this he devoted himself to the study of law, and as soon as admitted to the bar his oratory gained him distinction, becoming well known in political circles. He was frequently sent to the Legislature. Although a Whig and in a **Democratic county** (Morgan, his home being Jacksonville) he was usually elected with a respectable majority. In 1850 he was elected to Congress, his opponent being Major T. L. Harris whom he defeated, though a popular candidate; two years later he was elected over John Calhoun, but in 1854 was defeated by Major Harris.

As chief executive he was fearless and daring. In his canvass in 1860 for this office he entered all parts of the State and delivered addresses in opposition to John A. Logan and other Democrats noted for their radical views. In after years Governor Yates became addicted to habtis not in the least befitting man and especially one of his former standing. All the good he ever did as to his life being a fitting example is thus cancelled because of bowing to passion.

Ulysses S. Grant, hero of the Great Rebellion, deserves mention among the prominent people of Illinois. The fame and life of this well-known man are those of a soldier. Lincoln and Douglas furnished powerful reasoning faculties upon theories for settling an important dispute, but a military leader was found necessary to call the nation to order—another Illinois son was accordingly commissioned.

Matthew and Priscilla Grant arrived with a Pilgrim company that settled in Massachusetts in 1630. They chose their home four miles from Boston where the latter died, leaving four children. In 1634 Matthew moved to Windsor, Connecticut. He had a son Noah, and a grandson Noah (Jr.). The latter of these descendants served in the French and English war (1754–63) and lived for a time in Westmoreland County, Pennsylvania, where Jesse Root Grant was born in January, 1784. The father, Noah Grant, Jr., with a large family settled in Columbia County, Ohio, where the mother died. In 1808 Jesse went to live with Judge Todd, at Youngstown, and two years later went to Mayesville, Kentucky, where he learned the tanner's trade. In 1821 he married Hannah Simpson of Point Pleasant, Ohio, where he had opened a tannery on his own responsibility a few years previous. Here Ulysses S. was born, April 27, 1822. The following February the parents moved to Georgetown, the father continuing in his former vocation.

The boyhood of Ulysses was without event worthy of note. He was only ordinarily studious or bright, but early developed an interest in horses, and became a graceful rider. The father was frequently puzzled as to the best means to pursue that his boy might be able to earn a livelihood. He was handy with a team, and after the age of fifteen saw but little of the school-room. When "trade" was named to him he manifested such disgust, and especially for the tanning business, that the father inquired what occupation he would rather follow. He said, " I should like to be a farmer, or a river trader, or have an education." The father had often listened to war stories told by his father (Noah), and believed that he would rather see his son in a military school, and where he could be educated free of expense to himself. The Congressman from his district had no vacancy, but recommended Ulysses to a neighboring Congressman who secured his appointment after a satisfactory examination. The boy having never manifested any extraordinary ability, and being odd in appearance, the neighbors sneered, wondered and commented upon the seemingly mistaken step.

At West Point he made no mark of distinction and ranked twenty-one in a class of thirty-nine. He attracted no attention from his professors save his masterly power over horses, being able to ride those that most other cadets were afraid to approach, and chose one to ride, York, that no others wanted. On military examination day before the board of examiners, he, with this animal made a leap, six feet three inches, over a pole—the best leap on record at West Point Academy. Here he graduated June 31, 1843. On entering this school his name was changed from Hiram Ulysses to Ulysses Simpson through a mistake of the Congressman, and the mistake has never been rectified.

He was stationed at St. Louis as Second-Lieutenant soon after graduating, and when war with Mexico broke out was sent to the front and there promoted to First-Lieutenant.

August 22, 1848, Lieutenant Ulysses S. Grant was married to Miss Julia B. Dent, of St. Louis, with whom he had become acquainted while in that city before the war with Mexico. He remained in the standing army and was stationed at Detroit, where he lived until 1850, when he broke up housekeeping, his wife going to her parents and he soon after to California, where he was promoted to a captaincy. Here he took to drink and, upon hearing the rumor that he was to be discharged, resigned and arrived in New York City penniless, degraded, forsaken and without employment. He wrote to his father at Covington, Kentucky, and his brother Simpson came to his relief. Mr. Dent gave his daughter, Mrs. Grant, a farm near St. Louis, where Captain Grant erected a log cabin and began the career of a farmer. He named the place Hardscrabble, which he soon sold, moved to the city, began the real estate business, did not succeed and again returned to his father as a failure in all he undertook and in governing his passions.

His brothers, Orvill and Simpson, were in the tanning business at Galena, Illinois, where Ulysses, with his family, moved in 1860, and took a position as clerk for the firm, receiving $50 per month. He did not make expenses until his salary was raised to $800 a year.

Politically he was a Democrat, and voted for James Buchanan, the only time he ever cast a vote for President previous to the Rebellion. He had learned something of slavery through his wife, and while on her farm in Missouri kept slaves about him, but his views were suddenly changed upon the subject, probably through the influence of his father and brothers who had united with the Republican party, or possibly the bitter antipathy the South manifested toward Mr. Lincoln induced him to embrace his cause.

When war broke out he presided at the first meeting in Galesburg to raise a company, but another was chosen Captain. Through the influence of Elihu B. Washburn Captain Grant was given a military clerkship in the Governor's office in 1860. Here he was not changed from his position until after a clerk from Galena chanced to be in the office, when he was asked, "What kind of a man is this Captain Grant? He seems anxious to serve, though reluctant to take any high position." The clerk said, "The way to deal with him is to ask no questions, but order him and he will obey." Shortly after the Twenty-first Illinois, from east of Decatur, refused to obey orders of its

Colonel and Governor Yates appointed Grant its commander. From this forward he rose rapidly. He was made a Brigadier-General in July, 1861, and later was made commander of the district of West Tennessee. Advancing his forces up that river, he fought the battle of Shiloh, April 6 and 7. He was second in command to General Halleck during the siege of Corinth, and when the latter was ordered to Washington, Grant was appointed to take command of the department of Tennessee. He captured Vicksburg, July 4, 1863, and after the partial defeat of the Union troops under General Rosecrans, Chattanooga. In March, 1864, President Lincoln appointed him Lieutenant-General and conferred upon him the powers of General-in-Chief of the vast armies in the field, and April 9, 1865, Lee surrendered to him with his entire command at Appomattox Court House, Virginia. July 25, 1866, Congress having created the grade of General of the army, hitherto unknown to the United States armies, he was commissioned General the same day, and Major-General Sherman promoted to be Lieutenant-General. During President Johnson's difficulties, General Grant served for a short time as Secretary of War, August, 1867, to February, 1868.

He was elected President in November, 1868, receiving 214 out of 264 electoral votes, from the twenty-six States then recognized as belonging to the Union. His administration upon the whole was satisfactory, and in 1872 he was elected and served a second term. Dissatisfaction having arisen because of tyrannical treatment of the South, a branch of his party known as Liberal Republicans nominated Horace Greeley for President in 1872, who was also nominated by the Democrats. Grant received 268 electoral votes and Greeley but eighty though his popular majority was only 762,991. Because of financial dissatisfaction during his second term the Greenback party was organized. General Grant lost much honor by accepting the position of President. He had been trained a soldier, not a statesman, and for his success as a General he was loved and esteemed by his country; for such he was honored by nations through which he passed on his tour around the world, upon which he started March 4, 1877, returning in 1880, when he was

again a candidate for re-nomination as was James G. Blaine for
the same position. So determined was each faction that both
men were dropped and the party united on James A. Garfield.

General Ulysses S. Grant retrieved much lost honor during his protracted illness, and upon his death at Mt. McGregor,
July 23, 1885, the Nation bowed reverently, and in full gratitude
for his heroic services. Business was practically suspended in
New York on the day of his funeral, and citizens followed his remains, with the President, Governors, soldiers, officers, and distinguished friends from all parts of the United States, in mighty
procession to their temporary resting place, near which a handsome monument would soon be under course of erection. Illinois
offered to erect a costly monument by President Lincoln's tomb,
Springfield, but the family preferred his burial near their intended future home. Riverside Park, upon the beautiful Hud-
son, was accordingly chosen.

John Pope, General and commander of the Army of the
Potomac, was born at Kaskaskia, March 12, 1823. His father
was the renowned Nathaniel Pope, who took much pleasure in
the education of his son. Young Pope early took an interest in military literature and secured an appointment to West
Point Academy, from which he graduated with honors in 1842.
He was also a hero of the Mexican War.

OGLESBY'S FIRST ADMINISTRATION.—1865–1869.

Governor,	Richard J. Oglesby.
Lieutenant-Governor,	William Bross.
Secretary of State,	Sharon Tyndale.
Auditor,	O. H. Miner.
Treasurer, { to 1867,	James A. Beveridge.
{ from "	George W. Smith.
Supt. of Public Instruction,	Newton Bateman.
Speaker of { 24th House,	Allen C. Fuller.
{ 25th "	Franklin Corwin.
United States Senators, { E.L.,—1861–67,	Lyman Trumbull.
{ T.L.,—1865–71,	Richard Yates.

14 Representatives in Congress; Population in 1865, 2,141,510.

The first session of the Twenty-fourth General Assembly convened January 2, 1865. The first act was the election of a United States Senator, which resulted in the choice of Richard Yates over James C. Robinson by sixty-four to forty-three. Mr. Oglesby was inaugurated January 16.

President Lincoln Assassinated.—April 9, 1865, Lee surrendered, and the war of the Rebellion, in which the State had expended over $11,000,000 and had furnished 200,000 men, was terminated. Troops were returning to their homes when the startling and sad news of that " memorable 15th day of April " reached Illinois announcing the assassination of President Lincoln. This deed was committed by John Wilkes Booth, a noted actor, while the President and his wife were seated in a private box at Ford's theatre, Washington. When the assassin had accomplished his purpose, and as he jumped upon the stage, shouted, " Sic semper tyrannis [thus be it ever with tyrants], the South is avenged." He escaped from the building, but was traced to a barn in Maryland where he was shot by the party in pursuit.

Every pulsation of the wounded President was closely watched by prominent men of a spell-bound nation until the dawn of morning, when the patient expired. The remains were brought to Springfield and laid to rest with imposing ceremonies, within a handsome monument, in Oak Ridge cemetery where now also repose the mortal remains of his wife and three sons.

New State House.—In this administration a bill was introduced in the Legislature for the erection of a new State house. Peoria and Decatur became Springfield's warm contestants for the contemplated new edifice. The entire latter city labored in common. To overcome an argument that hotel accommodations were not good the Leland was built; to outdo other subscriptions a large amount was obligated, and to convince members of the Legislature that the citizens were sociable the city ladies gave parties and balls. Sangamon County agreed to give $200,000 for the old building to use for a court house, while Springfield increased this amount to $450,000. The bill finally passed as the city had desired, and the State agreed to appropriate $3,000,000. In this structure Illinois may justly pride herself, and now that it will soon be completed she can favorably compare it with like structures of the Union.

Election.—The Republican State Convention met at Peoria, May 6, 1868, and a ticket was nominated that corresponds with the head of the following administration.

The Democratic Convention was held at Springfield, April 15, and resulted as follows: Governor, John R. Eden; Lieutenant-Governor, William Van Epps; Secretary of State, Gustavus Van Hoorbecke; Auditor, John R. Shannon; Treasurer, Jesse J. Phillips. The result of this election was strongly in favor of the Republicans.

BIOGRAPHICAL.

Richard J. Oglesby, twelfth Governor of Illinois, was born in Oldham County, Kentucky, July 25, 1824, and was left without parents in 1832. Four years later he arrived with an uncle at Decatur, where he grew to manhood. He early developed an ardent love of sport and spent many hours of his youth in tests of strength, agility or ingenuity with "the boys." He took a fancy to law but did not make much advancement in the profession until he grew older.

When war with Mexico broke out he enlisted and was appointed First Lieutenant of Company C, Fourth Illinois Infantry, distinguishing himself in the battle of Cerro Gordo. After returning home he attended law lectures at Louisville, Kentucky, but in 1852 " took the gold fever " and went to California to seek a fortune. Greatly desiring to see more of the world, he set out, in 1856, to visit Europe and the Holy Land. On returning in 1858 he ran for Congress but was defeated by the same opponent that he in turn defeated in 1864. In 1860 he was elected State Senator, but when war broke out enlisted and was appointed Colonel of the Eighth Illinois Infantry, the second regiment raised in the State. In the battle of Corinth he was dangerously wounded, being shot through the lungs. For his gallantry he was promoted, but because of his wound he was compelled to abandon active service.

His term as Governor was satisfactory, and he was elected to the same honorable position four years later, but a few days subsequent to taking the oath of office was elected United States Senator. He is to-day (1886) filling the Gubernatorial chair, being yet hearty and in the enjoyment of good health.

PALMER'S ADMINISTRATION.—1869-1873.

Governor,	John M. Palmer.
Lieutenant-Governor,	John Dougherty.
Secretary of State,	Edward Rummel.
Auditor,	Chas. E. Lippincott.
Treasurer,	Erastus N. Bates.
Supt. of Public Instruction,	Newton Bateman.
Attorney-General,	Washington Bushnell.
Speaker of { 26th House,	Franklin Corwin.
27th "	William M. Smith.

United States Senators, { E. L.,—1867-73, Lyman Trumbull.
T. L., { 1865-71, Richard Yates.
1871-77, John A. Logan.

19 Representatives in Congress; Population in 1870, 2,539,891.

The Twenty-sixth General Assembly met January 4, and General Palmer was inaugurated January 11.

Innumerable Bills were under preparation to be placed before the Legislature, and on its opening 2,500 were ready. Of this number 1,700 were passed for the Governor's signature. Knowing the efforts monopolists were putting forth to secure legislation in their favor, and with what recklessness bills were being passed, Governor Palmer resolved to scrutinize each. To give him time for this the Legislature took a recess. Whenever a bill of any importance came up the word was, " The Governor has his eyes open and will see the flaw if any can be found."

Constitutional Convention.—On the 13th of December, 1869, delegates from each of the districts met in Convention and framed the Constitution as it now stands.

Chicago in Flames.—On the evening of October 8, 1871 (Sunday), a woman, having to milk at a late hour, took a lamp to the stable with her. By some mishap—the story goes the cow kicked—the lamp was overturned; the hay caught fire, then the stable; the blaze spread to adjoining stables, sheds and houses, kindling one of the greatest conflagrations recorded in any city's history. A gale was blowing from the southwest; there had been a prevalent drouth for some time, and the section from which the fire originated was filled with light frame structures, all of which were favorable for a rapid advance of the flames. The starting point was in the vicinity of Koven and Jefferson streets in the West Division, and in the southwest quarter of the city, the general advance being in a northeasterly direction. They leaped across the river about midnight. The fire fiend then advanced in a majestic column, flanked on the right and on the left by lesser columns a little in the rear.

The Chamber of Commerce was burned about 1 o'clock and the court-house followed shortly after. Prisoners confined in the basement of the latter, having been freed to save their lives, showed their gratitude—or depraved natures—by plundering a jewelry store near by. The great bell in the dome went down, down, sounding its own death knell as it fell, and at about the same hour, 3 o'clock, the large gasometer exploded with terrific violence. The Times and Tribune buildings, Crosby's magnificent opera house, Sherman, Tremont and Palmer hotels, Union Bank, Merchants' Insurance building, office of the Western Union Telegraph, postoffice, McVicker's Theatre and numerous other so-called fire-proof edifices crumbled and succumbed before the furnace heat of advancing flames. Not less than $2,-000,000 worth of treasure was destroyed in the postoffice vaults.

While the people in the North Division were gazing upon the burning dome of the court-house, expressing sympathy for the pitiable condition of the wretched and their homeless friends, they were suddenly awakened to a sense of their own peril—the fire by unaccountable means reached the engine house of the water-works, thus cutting off that means of fighting the conflagration and hemming in a vast region, with fire on the north and fire on the south. The flames swept on till they spent themselves on the north; were stopped by the beach along the lake, and were arrested from going farther southward by blowing up buildings. It is said this work was superintended by General Sheridan. Only two buildings, Lind's block, a brick edifice with iron shutters standing by itself in the South Division, and the residence of Mahlon Ogden in the North Division, were left in all the scourged region.

No language is adequate to describe the horrors and misery of the night of the 8th and the following day. A hundred-thousand people were driven from their homes to escape, if possible, the mad seething fire only to be impeded by the equally mad and frantic throng. In the vicinity of Griswold, Quincy, Jackson and Wells streets, where poverty, misery and vice were heaped together in squalid, rickety houses, the scene was appalling: people rushing half-clad through the streets; curses, prayers, shouts, screams and rude merriment blending weird sounds; stores and saloons thrown open by owners or broken into by desperadoes. Here they fought over spoils until driven onward by approaching fire, then rushed into a swaying crowd crazed with excitement or liquor, only to increase the horror of the surroundings. A little girl with flowing golden hair was noticed running through the streets calling for her parents. Her hair caught fire, when some demented creature threw a glass of liquor upon her, which immediately flashed up enveloping the tiny form in a blue flame.

The lowest figure at which a hack or conveyance could be obtained was $10, and reaching as high as $50. It not unfrequently happened, even at the last price, a driver would start with a load of articles, drive a short distance, then stop and increase the price or demand immediate payment. If the demand was not complied with, off went the goods into the street to be pillaged by " roughs," trampled under foot, or consumed by the flames. Occasionally the owner brought the heartless driver to a sense of his duty by displaying a revolver. E. I. Tinkman, cashier of one of the banks, paid an expressman $1,000 for conveying a box, containing valuables worth $600,000 from its vault to a depot in the West Division. No law, no order, no authority seemed to exist; the police were powerless and terror, destruction, avarice and confusion reigned supreme. One gentleman relates that he saw a man deliberately set fire to a pile of elegant furniture that had been placed in the street.

The bridges were thronged with every variety of vehicle and foot passenger, all bearing stupendous loads. An undertaker, with his employees, was noticed, each carrying a coffin; next an Irish woman trudging along leading a goat by one hand while with the other she clutched a roll of silk. Occasionally an order would be given for a bridge to be turned for the passage of a vessel seeking cooler climes, when a cry of indignation or despair would go up from the anxious multitude.

A narrow stretch of shore, bordering upon a portion of the lake, protected by a break-water, apparently offered a place of refuge. To this many flocked, carrying with them articles of every description saved in their hurried departure from burning homes. Here a frail woman carrying a sewing-machine; there two daughters bearing an invalid and fainting mother; not far beyond a girl jealously guarding her small bundle when a ruffian knocks her down and secures the prize. As the fire approaches nearer the crowd upon this narrow strip of land is forced into the water, where, by constantly drenching themselves, they are enabled to withstand the fierce heat. Many mothers thus stood for hours and supported a child above water.

Along the sandy beach to the northward thousands of rich and poor—or all alike poor—took refuge in a similar manner. Few were drowned by being crowded beyond their depth. The old cemetery, now a part of Lincoln Park, also offered a retreat for at least 30,000 people, who huddled together in this city of the dead. Children were there crying for parents, husband distracted over the loss of a wife, brother hunting for a sister or parents for a child. Here a group of girls weeping for their mother who was too ill to be moved and had to be abandoned; there a lady alone with a bundle of fine dresses thrown over her arm; close by a banker with bowed head sitting on a grave looking into a frying-pan he had unconsciously saved from destruction; a man with an ice pitcher declared it was all he possessed in the world, while scores of men, women and children were carefully shielding the pet canary, parrot or poodle.

The prairie west of the city was also thronged by a homeless multitude while many took shelter with friends in portions not destroyed. At 2 o'clock Tuesday morning came a welcome rain. It added to the misery for the time yet it was hailed with joy.

It is impossible to estimate in reliable figures the loss in the conflagration. The total number of deaths is estimated at 300, but this does not include those resulting from exposure at the time. Several cases of suicide and also of insanity were resultants. About $195,000,000 in property were consumed, on which there was an insurance of $45,000,000.

Many were the questions on the night of the 8th as to whether Chicago would ever recover from such a catastrophe. The response of one old gentleman seemed to be the prevalent opinion: "Our capital is wiped out of existence. You never can get what money is stored up in those vaults. There is not one that can stand this furnace heat. Whatever the fire consumes to-night is utterly consumed. All loss is total, for there will not be an insurance company left to-morrow. The trade of the city must go to St. Louis, to Cincinnati and to New York, and we never can get hold of it again. Yes sir, this town is gone up, and we may as well get out of it at once."

But the energies of this metropolis soon revived. The Mayor telegraphed to neighboring cities for aid, to which they immediately responded by sending bread for the hungry and clothing for those who had lost all. The city authorities at once took measures for the relief of citizens. Many of the business men made arrangements to re-open business at once; some in parts of the city not burned, others in temporary buildings on the site of their old stands, while others immediately contracted for having their places of business re-built.

While many insurance companies were totally ruined and could only pay a few cents on the dollar, others were able to pay the full amount. The State, through the efforts of Governor Palmer, also rendered timely assistance by purchasing the Illinois and Michigan Canal, for which Chicago received about $3,000,000, and the canal passed under the State's control.

Election.—A new national party had sprung up because of dissatisfaction with the Republican policy toward the States lately in rebellion, Missouri becoming the hot-bed of the new contest, which State, though Republican, was about to throw out the clause that disfranchised Confederates. The party was led by Carl Shurz and B. Gratz Brown, in that State, and by

Horace Greeley, of New York. They called themselves Liberal Republicans. This faction grew to such an extent in Illinois that, by a union with the Democrats, success was almost certain. Governor Palmer, Superintendent Bateman, Secretary Rummel, and many other office holders and men of prominence, allied themselves with the new party. A convention was held in Springfield, June 26, 1872, by Democrats and Liberal Republicans jointly, in which the following ticket was nominated: Governor, Gustavus Kœrner, l r; Lieutenant-Governor, John C. Black, d; Secretary of State, Edward Rummel, l r; Auditor, Daniel O'Hara, l r; Treasurer, C. H. Landphier, d: Attorney-General, Lawrence Weldon.

The Republican convention had been held in May and was unanimously successful, the nominees corresponding with names at the head of the following administration.

BIOGRAPHICAL.

John M. Palmer, thirteenth Governor of Illinois and the well-known careful interpreter of law, was born in Scott County, Kentucky, September 13, 1817. His father was a warm Jacksonian, but noted for his anti-slavery views, from whom young Palmer derived his first dislike for the institution.

In 1831 he moved to Illinois with his father and located in Madison County. Until 1834 his education had been neglected, yet he had read much, and on entering college this year at Alton began to display talent for books. In the canvass of 1838 he made the acquaintance of Stephen A. Douglas, from whom he received such inspiration that he resolved to study law, and in the following spring entered a law office at Carlinville, at which place he began the practice of his profession.

He was elected Probate Judge in 1842; a member of the Constitutional Convention, in 1847; State Senator, in 1852; Chairman of the State Republican Convention at Bloomington, in 1856; Republican elector for the State at large, in 1860; Republican member of the Peace Convention, which met at Washington in 1861; Colonel of the Fourteenth Illinois Infantry, in 1861; Major-General, in 1862; Military Governor of Kentucky, in 1865. Thus all through his career important offices have

been opened to him. Though in later years Governor Palmer
has refused the nomination for important positions of trust, he
takes active part in politics and is generally consulted on
leading questions of dispute or doubt. Since the Greenback
movement he has been a firm Democrat. His home is in
Springfield, and he is yet one of the leading law practitioners
of Illinois.

OGLESBY AND BEVERIDGE'S ADMINISTRATION.
—1873-1877.

Governor,	{ to Jan. 23, 1873,	·	Richard J. Oglesby.
	{ from " " "	·	John L. Beveridge.
Lieutenant-Governor,	{ to 1873,	·	John L. Beveridge.
	{ to 1875,	·	- John Early.
	{ from "	·	- A. A. Glenn.
Secretary of State,	· ·	·	George H. Harlow.
Auditor,	· ·	·	Chas. E. Lippincott.
Treasurer,	{ to 1875, ·	· ·	Edward Rutz.
	{ from " ·	· ·	Thomas Ridgeway.
Supt. of Public Instruction,	{ to 1875,		Newton Bateman.
	{ from "		-. S. M. Etter.
Attorney-General,	· ·	·	James K. Edsall.
Speaker of	{ 28th House,	· ·	Shelby M. Cullom.
	{ 29th "	· ·	Elijah M. Haines.
United States Senators,	{ E. L.,—1873-79,		Richard J. Oglesby.
	{ T. L.,—1871-77,		John A. Logan.

19 Representatives in Congress; Population in 1870, 2,539,891.

The Twenty-eighth General Assembly, which convened
January 8, 1874, was composed of 52 Senators and 159 Representatives. Shortly after assembling, Governor Oglesby was
elected United States Senator and Lieutenant-Governor Beveridge became his successor by Constitution.

Statute Revision, to accord with the new Constitution,
was begun in the early part of the administration. The Commissioners appointed for this work were, Henry B. Hurd, of
Evanston; W. E. Nelson, of Decatur, and Michael Shaeffer, of
Salem. The latter two resigned shortly after the work began,

and, as the Legislature made no other appointments, the entire labor was performed by the former, who completed the revision in 1878.

Greenbackers.—The first meeting of this party was held at Bloomington in January, 1873. Having for its object the suppression of monopolies, especially the imposition on the part of railroad companies, it took the name of Anti-Monopolist party; but, upon its beginning to meddle with the money affairs of the country, and hoping to help the poor and indebted out of their difficulties, accepted for its name the Rag Baby party. From the financial policy of issuing greenbacks in place of Government bonds it took the name of the Greenback party.

The pulse of the new party was felt all over Illinois, and in the election of 1874 the independent movement had a marked effect on State politics. The Democrats united with them and the two succeeded in getting a majority over the Republicans in both houses of the Legislature besides electing S. M. Etter, Superintendent of Public Instruction. This party merged into a labor movement, and unfurled its banners under the leadership of Benjamin F. Butler in the campaign of 1884.

A Stormy Legislature.—Although no question of vital issue came before this body, the Twenty-ninth General Assembly became a stormy one with Elijah M. Haines, Speaker, who held the balance of power, as he managed to receive favors from the Republicans on one side and the joint Democrats and Greenbackers on the other. The galleries and aisles were constantly thronged by eager spectators to watch the "circus," as it was usually termed.

Illinois at the Centennial of 1876, at Philadelphia, planned in commemoration of American Independence, made a fairly good display in general, and a grand one in the Agricultural Department by which a medal was awarded to her. The close party vote in the Legislature cut her appropriation to but $10,000. Subscription papers were circulated, and by private contributions the State was fairly represented. Illinois occupied a large handsome building erected for the occasion, and this building was constantly thronged, especially by industry lovers from the Old World.

Election.—In the election of 1876 the same political spirit was manifest that had been in the canvass two years previous, but Democrats and Greenbackers could not unite on any officers except Governor and Auditor. The Greenbackers met at Decatur and nominated for Governor, Lewis Stewart; Lieutenant-Governor, J. H. Pickrell; Secretary of State, M. Hooton; Auditor, John Hise; Treasurer, H. W. Aspern; Attorney-General, W. S. McCoy. The Democrats met at Springfield, July 27, and endorsed the Governor and Auditor nominees of the Greenback party, and nominated for Lieutenant-Governor, A. A. Glenn; Secretary of State, S. Y. Thornton; Treasurer, George Gundlach; Attorney-General, E. Lynch. The Republican convention met at Springfield, May 25, and nominated a ticket that compares with the head of the following administration.

BIOGRAPHICAL.

John L. Beveridge, fourteenth Governor of Illinois, (accidental Governor), was born in Washington County, New York, July 6, 1824, and moved with his parents to Illinois in 1842, settling in De Kalb County upon a farm, where he labored for a number of years. His parents were Scotch Presbyterians, and early took much care of their son that he might not be led astray. These teachings have remained with him through life to the present though he has changed creeds and is now an active member of the Methodist church.

The education of young Beveridge was not collegiate, but academic, attending Granville and Mt. Morris seminaries. He began life for himself in Tennessee, where he gained a livelihood by teaching, at the same time devoting his spare moments to the study of law. By 1854 he had opened a law office in Chicago, the home of his wife, whom he married in 1848. He took an active part in the war of the Rebellion, being promoted from one rank to another until in 1866 he was mustered out as Brigadier-General.

The political career of Governor Beveridge was equally bright. He first became Sheriff of Cook County in 1866, then State Senator, Congressman and Lieutenant-Governor. His Guber-

natorial career was a success throughout, and his fame spread
abroad. He received the appointment of assistant United States
Treasurer at Chicago, in 1881, from President Arthur.

CULLOM'S ADMINISTRATION.—1877-1881.

Governor,	-	•	•	-	Shelby M. Cullom.
Lieutenant-Governor,	-	•	-	Andrew Shuman.
Secretary of State,	-	•	-	George H. Harlow.
Auditor,	-	•	-	Thomas B. Needles.

Treasurer, { to 1879 - - -   Edward Rutz.
{ from " - • -   John C. Smith.

Supt. of Public Instruction, { to 1879, - S. M. Etter.
{ from " - J. P. Slade.

Attorney-General, - • - James K. Edsall.

Speaker of { 30th House, - • - James Shaw.
{ 31st " - Col. W. A. Jones.

United States Senators, { E. L., { 1873-79,   Richard J. Oglesby.
{ 1879-85,   John A. Logan.
{ T. L.,—1877-83,   David Davis.

19 Representatives in Congress; Population in 1880, 3,077,871.

The Thirtieth General Assembly convened January 3, and
the incoming Governor was inaugurated January 9. The joint
Democratic and Greenback vote still held control.

The Senatorial Contest to fill the vacancy of John A.
Logan, whose term was drawing to a close, began almost immediately after the new Assembly had organized. The vote was
close and stubborn. John A. Logan became the Republican
caucus nominee; John M. Palmer, Democratic, and David Davis,
Independent. The first ballot stood, Logan, 99; Palmer, 88;
W. B. Anderson, 7; David Davis, 6; 2 members not voting.
On the twenty-second ballot Palmer's name was withdrawn and
the result stood, Logan, 99; W. B. Anderson, 85, and the remainder scattering. Logan's name was withdrawn on the
twenty-fourth, which ballot stood, Davis, 97; C. B. Lawrence,
86, and the remainder scattering. On the fortieth ballot, January 25, Davis received 101 votes, and was declared elected.

Medical Practice Act.—In 1877 the Legislature passed a law prohibiting all those from prescribing who were not in possession of a physician's diploma or else had been in actual practice ten years before the law took effect. Over 900 so-called doctors closed their pill-cases or moved to other States. The same year a State Board of Health was established.

Labor Difficulties, in 1877, assumed a war-like posture. The United States was going through a season of " hard times;" money was scarce, wages low and work sparing, while confidence in financial abundance began wavering in the minds of the middle class, or operative business men. The laborer, during like seasons, always suffers the penalty. This fact was fully realized by them at the time, and they had already organized, together talked over their grievances and had resolved to act more independent in the future than they had done in the past. A series of strikes were accordingly operated. Business suffered a stand-still, for the wheels of commerce were blocked. To prevent its revival before a compromise could be arranged between capital and labor, mobs were organized. At this time the country, from the pineries of Michigan to the rice fields of the South, from the piers of the East to the fruit orchards of the West, was thronged by a "tramp" element of tradesmen and foreigners who had grown despondent and hoped to see the Union sink rather than float out of the storm into which she had unconsciously drifted. This same element now flocked into cities, and joining hands for mob violence began the destruction of property, the greater loss being in Pennsylvania.

At East St. Louis a mob of 10,000 congregated, and taking charge of the city, defied the civil authorities. Alton and Belleville were also overrun. Governor Cullom visited these localities, and with troops under command of Generals Bates and Pavy restored order.

At Chicago, A. C. Ducat was in command. He also called upon the Governor for troops to suppress, more particularly, the tramp and boy element, which paraded the streets, stopped street cars, closed machine shops, unloaded drays and even took charge of the river bridges. The presence of troops and arrests of several leaders put a stop to further outbreak.

OTHER LOCALITIES, especially railroad centres and mining districts, were kept under guard of State militia. General Ducat was sent to Braidwood soon after completing his work at Chicago, and when within a mile of the town was met by 600 men, mostly miners. He there halted, with his assailants before him. Knowing the Mayor to be in sympathy with the miners, he sent word to him to disperse the mob immediately. His order being obeyed no serious results followed.

EFFECT.—When the strikers saw where the troubles were tending, even the more enthusiastic gradually drifted with the public sentiment, which had soon turned against the cause, where mob violence became the issue. But to suppress its riots and protect property it had cost the State $87,000. The loss by idleness of men and stagnation of trade is untold.

Political.—ELECTION OF 1878.—In the election of 1878 the Democrats and Greenbackers divided, each nominating a separate ticket. The candidates were as follows: Republican, for Treasurer, J. C. Smith; Superintendent of Public Instruction, J. P. Slade; Democrat, E. L. Cronkrite, S. M. Etter; Greenback, E. N. Bates, F. M. Hall. The former were entirely successful and secured a majority in both houses of the Legislature. The vote for Treasurer stood, Smith, 206,458; Cronkrite, 170,085; Bates, 65,689; Jerome A. Gorin, 2,228.

UNITED STATES SENATOR.—The term of Richard J. Oglesby having drawn to a close, the Thirty-first General Assembly proceeded to election. The caucus nominees were, John C. Black, Democrat, and John A. Logan, Republican, the latter being successful.

ELECTION OF 1880.—The Democrats nominated for Governor, Lyman Trumbull; Lieutenant-Governor, L. B. Parsons; Secretary of State, John H. Oberly; Auditor, L. C. Starkel; Treasurer, Thomas Butterworth; Attorney-General, Lawrence Harmon. The Greenback party put the following ticket in the field: Governor, A. J. Streeter; Lieutenant-Governor, A. M. Adair; Secretary of State, J. M. Thompson; Auditor, W. T. Ingram; Treasurer, J. W. Evans; Attorney-General, H. G. Whitlock. A Republican ticket was nominated and became successful. See head of following administration.

BIOGRAPHICAL.

Shelby M. Cullom, fifteenth Governor of Illinois, was born November 22, 1829, in Wayne County, Kentucky. He, as our previous Governor, was the son of a farmer and received his early training upon a farm. When he was but one year old his father moved to Tazewell county where he received suffi-cient education to teach school. In this vocation he saved enough money to enable him to attend Mt. Morris Seminary two years. He began the study of law in Springfield, reading with Stuart & Edwards of that city. In this profession he made marked advancement and was elected City Attorney soon after being admitted to the bar. He first entered the Legislature in 1856, holding to the politics of his father who was a Whig; yet he entertained Republican ideas sufficient to enable him to ride both horses. In 1860 he was returned to the Legislature but was upon the ticket headed by Abraham Lincoln, with whom he often associated, the two becoming warm friends. He was elected to Congress in 1864, 1866 and 1868; in which position he gained much notoriety, and took an active part in the discus-sion of leading questions before that body. In 1872 he was re-turned to the Legislature and was chosen Speaker of the House; also was elected in 1874 and was the Republican caucus nominee for Speaker, but was defeated by E. M. Haines.

As a Governor, he was firm and clear-headed, always prompt in duty and especially in the riots of 1877. A few days after be-ginning his second Gubernatorial term he was elected to the United States Senate, which term will not expire until 1889. In this capacity Senator Cullom is gaining distinction.

CULLOM AND HAMILTON'S ADMINISTRATION.
—1881–1885.

Governor, { to Jan. 1883,	·	·	Shelby M. Cullom.
{ from " "	·	·	John M. Hamilton.
Lieutenant-Governor, {	·	·	John M. Hamilton.
	·	·	W. J. Campbell.

Secretary of State,   -   -   -   Henry D. Dement.
Auditor,   -   -   -   Charles P. Swigert.
Treasurer, { to 1883 -   -   -   Edward Rutz.
{ from " .-   -   -   John C. Smith.
Supt. of Public Instruction, { to 1883,   -   J. P. Slade.
{ from "   -   Henry Raab.
Attorney-General,   -   -   -   James McCartney.
Speaker of { 32d House,   -   -   Horace H. Thomas.
{ 33d "   -   -   Lovin C. Collins, Jr.
United States Senators, { E. L.,—1879–85,   John A. Logan.
{ T. I., { 1877–83,   David Davis.
{ 1885-—— Shelby M. Cullom.
19 Representatives in Congress; Population in 1880, 3,077,871.

The Thirty-second General Assembly convened January 5, 1881, and remained in session until May 5. A special session was called and convened March 23, 1882, the object being to re-district the State according to the census of 1880. This session lasted but forty-four days.

The Election of 1882 did not call out a full vote, it being an " off year." The following was the result on State ticket:

TREASURER.	SUPT. PUBLIC INSTRUCTION.
John C. Smith, r.....250,722	Henry Raab, d.......253,145
Alfred Orendorff, d...244,585	Chas. T. Strattan, r...250,276
Daniel McLaughlin, g. 15,511	Frank H. Hall, g..... 14,306
John G. Irwin, p..... 11,130	Elizabeth B. Brown, p 11,202

Governor Cullom's Resignation.—On expiration of the term of David Davis as United States Senator, Governor Cullom was elected to fill the vacancy. He received 107 votes on the second ballot, and was declared elected. This ballot was taken January 17, 1883, and, February 7, he resigned the Governorship of Illinois, when Lieutenant-Governor John M. Hamilton became Governor.

Collinsville Riots.—The miners of Collinsville and vicinity organized a strike in 1883 that called out the State militia. The proprietor of a mine was imprisoned and threatened even with violence. On arrival of troops an engagement ensued in which one of the mob was killed. Twenty-six were arrested when quiet was again restored.

Election.—The election of 1884 called forth a full vote, and each party did all in its power to insure success. The Democratic State convention convened at Peoria, June 2, and the following ticket was selected: Governor, Carter H. Harrison; Lieutenant-Governor, Henry Seiter; Secretary of State, Michael Dougherty; Auditor, Walter E. Carlin; Treasurer, Alfred Orendorff; Attorney-General, Robert L. McKinley. In the Republican convention a ticket was chosen that corresponds with the head of the following administration. For Presidential vote see appendix.

BIOGRAPHICAL.

John M. Hamilton, sixteenth Governor of Illinois, was born in 1847, in Union County, Ohio, and moved with his father to Marshall County upon a farm, in 1854. In 1864, when he was but seventeen years old, he enlisted and served through the remainder of the Rebellion as a private. Immediately after returning from the war he entered the Ohio Wesleyan University at Delaware, from which he graduated in 1868. He then embarked in the profession of teaching school, and was promoted to the position of professor of language in the Illinois Wesleyan University at Bloomington, at which time he also took a course in law in the same institution. After being admitted to the bar he formed a partnership with Captain Rowell of that city, in which firm he was an active partner when elected Lieutenant-Governor. He now (1886) resides in Chicago.

OGLESBY'S ADMINISTRATION.—1885-1889.
(Third Term.)

Governor,	Richard J. Oglesby.
Lieutenant-Governor,	John C. Smith.
Secretary of State,	Henry D. Dement.
Auditor,	Charles P. Swigert.
Treasurer, { to 1887	Jacob Gross.
{ from "	John R. Tanner.
Supt. of Public Instruction, { to 1887,	Henry Raab.
{ from "	Richard Edwards.

Attorney-General,   •   •   •   George Hunt.
Speaker of { 34th House,   •   •   Elijah M. Haines.
           { 35th   "   •   •   _____
United States Senators, { E. L.,—1885——,   John A. Logan.
                        { T. L.,—1883——, Shelby M. Cullom.
    21 Representatives in Congress; Population in 1880, 3,077,871.

The Thirty-fourth General Assembly convened January 7,
1885, and continued in session until in June. But little business
of importance was transacted, though much time was occupied in
political quibbles. Because of this the House was delayed from
organizing until January 29, and Governor Oglesby was thus
prevented from taking the oath of office until the following day,
when Governor Hamilton retired.

A Legislative Circus was opened upon convening of
the House, which was evenly balanced without the vote of Elijah
M. Haines, who had been elected on the Democratic ticket but
gave indications of willingness to serve either party that would
rally to his desires.

Secretary of State Dement called the House to order at noon,
January 7. Political war manifested itself from the first. In a
ballot for Temporary Speaker the vote stood, for Haines, 76;
Messick, 74; scattering 1. No election was declared and the
House adjourned until the following day when Haines received
a majority of one vote. On taking the chair he declared that he
never before knew of a Temporary Speaker being elected by a
party vote and as he had received support from the opposite
party (Sittig, Republican, of Chicago voted for him) he proposed to act independently from hence forward.

Charles E. Fuller received the Republican Caucus nomination, January 6, for Speaker, and E. L. Cronkrite that of the
Democratic on the same evening. This procedure had left Mr.
Haines out as for being a caucus candidate. January 13 a motion was made to proceed to ballot for Speaker and Clerk. Mr.
Haines declared the motion out of order. The mover appealed
from the decision of the chair. Mr. Haines declared there was
nothing before the House. The Temporary Speaker thus declared himself Speaker of the Thirty-fourth House of Representatives, and from thence forward refused to entertain any

motions on the subject. Warm threats and school-boy broils were the result. Mr. Haines, in person, called upon Secretary Dement and demanded the election returns, saying that he would call in the Senate and in joint session expected to canvass the vote. The papers being refused him, he argued his case, stating that he was Speaker, that the House had adjourned over Sunday without electing a Speaker and if the acting Governor had died during that adjournment he would have become Governor, that the House had ordered him to appoint necessary pages, that he had been given papers by the Secretary himself that none but a Speaker could receive. After consulting leading attorneys Mr. Dement refused him the demanded tally sheets.

Mr. Haines held the chair amid continual turmoil—both parties desiring his vote for United States Senator—until January 21, when he bluntly resigned without allowing a ballot, saying that neither party appeared to have use for him, that he had intended to vote for a man who would support President Cleveland, but thence forward he resolved to act independently. He retired to a private room, when there was a rush for the gavel. It having been secured by Mr. Cronkrite, he was elected Temporary Speaker. To keep Mr. Haines in his party he finally received the Democratic nomination, and with one vote from the Republicans was elected to the office he so much desired.

U. S. Senatorial Contest.—Never before in the history of Illinois have so much time and money been expended in an election of United States Senator, as for a successor to John A. Logan. The Senate stood, Republicans, 26; Democrats, 25. In the House were, Republicans, 76; Democrats, 77. In joint assembly the vote stood, Republicans, 102; Democrats, 102. Necessary to election, 103.

John A. Logan became the Republican candidate, and William R. Morrison the Democratic. The Democrats began balloting first, and both parties mustered a test ballot on February 19, 1885, that stood, Logan, 101; Morrison, 94; Haines, 4; Ward, 1; Lawler, 1; absent, 3.

May 5 Representative J. Henry Shaw, Democrat from the Thirty-fourth District, died. In the election of his successor the Democrats of the district did not believe it necessary to pay much attention to the election, it being strongly Democratic, and after 4 o'clock, P. M., a full Republican vote was polled, when W. A. Weaver, their candidate, was elected. This gave the Republicans in joint assembly 103 members, and the Democrats 101. May 14 Morrison received his full vote (101), and Logan 1. By May 19 Weaver was seated, when the final and 120th ballot was taken, in which Logan's Republican enemies rallied to the cause. This ballot stood, Logan, 103; Judge Lambert Tree, 94; scattering, 5.

Labor Troubles.—EAST ST. LOUIS.—Because of the discharge of an employe of the Southwestern Gould System of Railroads a strike was ordered by the Knights of Labor, in the spring of 1886, that was carried to East St. Louis. The less humane and tramp element believed themselves at liberty to destroy property and lives, and it was not until the Governor's Guards were sent to that city that depredations ceased.

CHICAGO.—For some time May 1, 1886, had been looked to as a time for the various labor organizations to demand eight hours of labor for a day's work, and ten-hours' pay for the time. Upon this day the employes in all freight depots and many manufactories, bricklayers, carpenters, lumbermen and numerous other laborers of the city, quit work. A few employers conceded to the demand, others refused and closed their shops. But few are working on the eight-hour system at present. Riots and a stagnation of trade were the fruits.

Anarchists.—A secret organization has existed for several years, in both the Old World and New, that looks to the destruction of fortune and the sharing of every man alike in property and other possessions. This society, known as Anarchists, also advocates the destruction of law, the burning of police stations, libraries and the Bible, also the overthrow of Christianity, Paganism, Kingdoms, Republics and States.

The organization in America was first led by Johann Most, of New York, whose literature has been spread broadcast throughout the larger cities, where it has been eagerly devoured by vicious foreigners and the cast-offs so common in crowded cities, too lazy to work and very anxious for all the strong drink and tobacco that a toper could imagine. Most's literature advocates revolution and the use of dynamite. In Chicago the organization had a membership of over 300, and many sympathizers. The leaders grew bold and often delivered open-air speeches, generally depicting the grievances and woes of the laboring people. The followers won to their cause were principally Germans, who had refused to become citizens of the United States. It appears that branches, called armed sections, had been under drill with military arms for some time previous to May 1, 1886. At this time labor difficulties were to assume the most serious aspect, when the civilization destroyers were to strike a blow with dynamite bombs. They supposed a bloodier revolution than that of France would follow. The working-men would be their followers—soldiers would lay down their arms and the country would soon be a waste of ruins. The first blow was to be struck in Chicago. Police stations were to be blown up, banking and other large buildings destroyed, and citizens that offered a resisting hand, killed.

On the evening of May 5, a meeting assembled on Haymarket Square, near the centre of town, with intentions of revenge, the participants to come armed. After a course of revolutionary speeches had been made and it being a week of organized strikes, a body of 160 policemen marched upon the square, commanded by Inspector Bonfield. Captain Ward ordered the crowd to disperse in the name of the people of Illinois. Scarcely had he uttered the words when a dynamite bomb, to which was attached a lighted fuse, fell at the officers' feet and exploded. This created havoc among the police for a moment, and firing in quick succession followed immediately thereafter, from the crowd. Orders were given to close up ranks, and with drawn revolvers the police, not killed or wounded, fired upon their adversaries, who rapidly dispersed. Sixty policemen were wounded and one instantly killed. Six of the wounded died.

Wholesale arrests were made, and the Grand Jury brought indictments for murder against eight, who appeared to be leaders. The firm stand of the officers, the prompt action of these, thereafter, and the disapprobation by all classes of the city, made the act very unpopular and the revolution failed to take place. In the trial that followed, twenty-six days were consumed in selecting a Jury; yet, when finally chosen, and upon hearing the testimony, arguments and legal instructions, a verdict was rendered a few minutes after retiring. Those sentenced to be hanged were—August Spies, editor of the Arbiter-Zeitung; Michael Schwab, assistant editor of the Arbiter-Zeitung; A. R. Parsons, editor of the Alarm; Louis Lingg, bomb manufacturer; Samuel Fielden, teamster; George Engel, and Adolph Fischer. Oscar Neebe was sentenced to serve in the penitentiary fifteen years. A motion was made for a new trial, but refused, and December 3, 1886, set for the day of execution. At present writing it is not known whether the Governor or the Supreme Court will interfere or not.

The State House is finally being completed. In the election of 1884, $531,000 were voted for this purpose. Quite a vigorous fight has been waged by other cities of Illinois for the capitol. After $800,000 had already been expended it was found that the wing of the building would extend into the street, and that ground on the south was not sufficiently large to complete the building. Peoria at once raised a tumult for the law-making institution, agreeing to furnish a very handsome piece of ground and pay the expenses already incurred if the capitol would yet be located in that city. Pullman cars were furnished, and the Legislature visited the site. On their return the leading citizens of Sprinfield visited the honorable body and agreed to buy the land, which would cost $40,000, when needed to complete the entrance.

The amount appropriated being expended in 1877, a vote was submitted to the people to appropriate more money for its completion, which was lost, and thus the matter was allowed to go on from year to year until one-half of the forty bondsmen of Springfield have died, and most of those living are in limited circumstances, but the city has agreed to assume the land debt. When completed Illinois can boast of one of the handsomest and costliest State houses of the United States.

APPENDIX.

CIVIL GOVERNMENT.

THE following is a brief summary of the officers of district, township, town, county and State; their principal duties, salaries and terms of office. The Government of the United States is vested in three branches—Executive, Legislative and Judicial. The former is composed of a President and his Cabinet officers; the second, a Congress (composed of a House of Senators and a House of Representatives), and the latter of a Chief Justice and eight Associate Justices. Illinois is similar in her Government to that of the National, while her county ruling powers are but slightly modified, and is likewise separated into divisions, known as political townships or towns, with officers holding certain qualified authority.

TOWN.

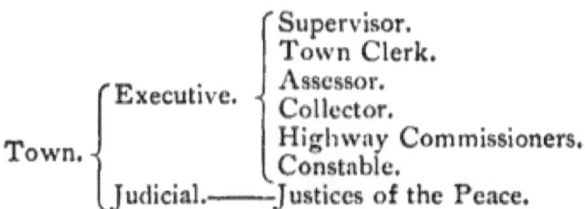

The town government has neither a chief executive nor a legislative government.

EXECUTIVE.

The Supervisor cares for the poor, attends County Board of Supervisors' meetings, acts as treasurer for all town money save school and highway funds and files with Town Clerk an annual statement of his official receipts and expenditures.

NOTE.—In towns of over 4,000 one assistant is allowed with full power at Board meetings; in towns of over 6,500 inhabitants two Supervisors are allowed. Term, one year.

The Clerk takes care of all records, books and papers belonging to the town; records the acts of town meetings and also meetings of the Board of Auditors, and sends to the County Clerk—before the second Tuesday in August—a list of taxes to be levied in the town he represents. Term, one year.

The Assessor makes an estimate of the value of each person's property. Term, one year.

The Collector collects taxes and pays those for school purposes to the School Treasurer; those of the road and bridge fund to the treasurer of the Highway Commissioners, and those for general township purposes to the Supervisor. Term, one year.

Highway Commissioners, three in number, give direction to Overseers of Highway, levy a poll tax and see that it is collected or an equivalent amount in work, lay out new roads and divide the town into suitable number of road districts. Term, three years.

The Constable has power to stop all disorderly conduct he witnesses and execute orders from the Justice of the Peace. Term four years.

JUDICIAL.

Each town is entitled to two or more Justices of the Peace who try criminal cases when the fine is not to exceed $200, those of assault and battery and examine a few cases punishable in penitentiary, holding the accused by bail or in jail until the meeting of the Grand Jury. Term four years.

MISCELLANEOUS.

The township election is held on the first Tuesday of April.

Each officer that handles public money must give a bond of double the amount he is supposed to get in his possession.

The Board of Health consists of the Supervisor, Assessor and Town Clerk.

The Board of Auditors consist of Supervisor, Town Clerk and one or more Justices. This Board examines claims against the town.

The Board of Equalization consists of Assessor, Town Clerk and Supervisor. It meets on the fourth Monday in June and equalizes assessments.

SCHOOL OFFICERS.

The smallest political division outside of village corporation is a school district. No definite law governs its size, but it should contain, outside of cities and villages, four square miles.

School Directors employ teachers (only those bearing certificates from the County Superintendent of Schools), fix salaries and can discharge them for incompetency; visit the school and determine rules for its government; select text books; levy school tax, and make reports to school treasurer. Term, one year.

School Treasurer takes care of the money for a specified number of districts, and cashes teachers' and other school money orders.

School Trustees each serve a term of three years, being elected one each year. This Board has jurisdiction over a township (six miles square).

COUNTY.

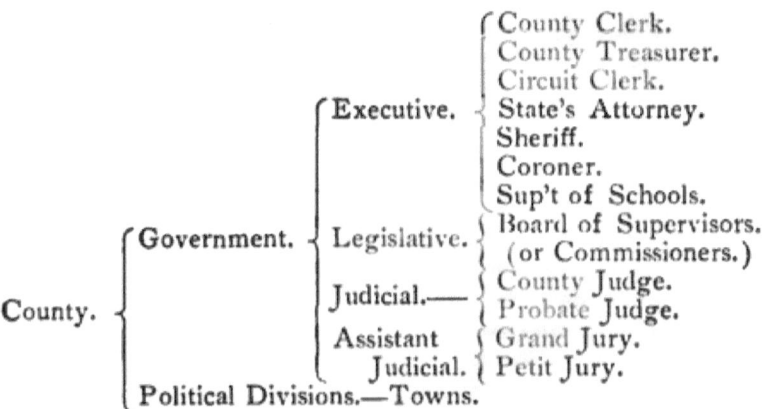

The government of the county, as that of State, consists of three separate branches—Executive, Legislative and Judicial, but the county is void of a chief executive head.

EXECUTIVE.

The executive department of a county is vested in a County Clerk, Sheriff, State's Attorney, Coroner, Circuit Clerk, Treasurer and Superintendent of Schools. The salaries of officers are generally fixed by the County Board (Supervisors or Commissioners), and their terms of office are four years each.

The County Clerk attends the sessions and keeps a record of the proceedings of the county Board and Court; keeps a record of money drawn on the Treasurer; after general elections, with two Justices, canvasses the votes returned to him from the different precincts in the county and forwards them to the Secretary of State; issues marriage license; computes taxes, and presides over Board meetings until a presiding officer is elected.

The Treasurer keeps an accurate account of his receipts and expenditures (for public inspection) of the money belonging to the county. This is usually collected by taxes and is only paid out as directed by law or orders from the Board.

The Circuit Clerk attends the sessions of Circuit Court of his county and keeps records of its proceedings, cost of suits, and receives orders from the court and issues them to the Sheriff. In counties of less than 60,000 inhabitants, he also fills the office of RECORDER OF DEEDS, which office is separate in counties of 60,000 and over.

State's Attorney (is a county officer who) acts for the people against an offender of civil laws. He also acts as attorney for county officers in suits brought against them pertaining to their official duties.

The Sheriff attends the sessions of Circuit Court and preserves order; serves writs and subpœnas; arrests for disorderly conduct wherever, in his county, he discovers it; takes charge of the court-house and jail; conducts condemned prisoners to the State penitentiary, and hangs criminals condemned to death.

The Coroner takes charge of any dead body where the person has met death by accident, murder or an unknown cause; arrests any person suspected of killing the deceased; acts as Sheriff, should that office become vacant or if the incumbent is plaintiff or defendant in any suit.

The Superintendent of Schools visits schools, instructs teachers, looks after the condition of schools; holds institutes and teachers' examinations for certificates; decides disputes in school law, and reports information to State Superintendent.

LEGISLATIVE.

The County Board (Supervisors or Commissioners) constitute the legislative department of a county government. It provides for the erection of buildings and bridges, cares for paupers, etc. Two regular meetings are held each year—second Monday in July and second Tuesday in September. The duty of the chairman is to preside at meetings and appoint committees to look after departments in the Board's jurisdiction.

JUDICIAL.

The county judicial department is vested in a County Judge and a Probate Judge. In counties of less than 50,000 inhabitants these offices are united under one man, and he is called County Judge and his court County Court. They have original jurisdiction over wills, settlements of estates, guardians of minors and conservators of insane; exclusive jurisdiction in sale of property for the collection of taxes and over cases brought before Justices of the Peace, not exceeding $1,000. They have concurrent jurisdiction in a few cases; i. e., the case may be tried before a Justice, County Judge or a Circuit Judge.

ASSISTANT JUDICIARY.

A Grand Jury is made up of twenty-three jurors whose duty is to hear evidence against any person accused of crime, and if advisable to a majority, to report to the Circuit Court an "indictment," in which the case is described. No evidence in defense is heard by them. This body is selected by the County Board, and holds office only a sufficient time to hear criminal cases for the term of court for which it was chosen.

The Petit Jury tries cases under the direction of the Judge, and after hearing the evidence renders a decison, if all agree; otherwise there can be no verdict. Twelve constitute a "selected Jury" to try a case.

STATE.

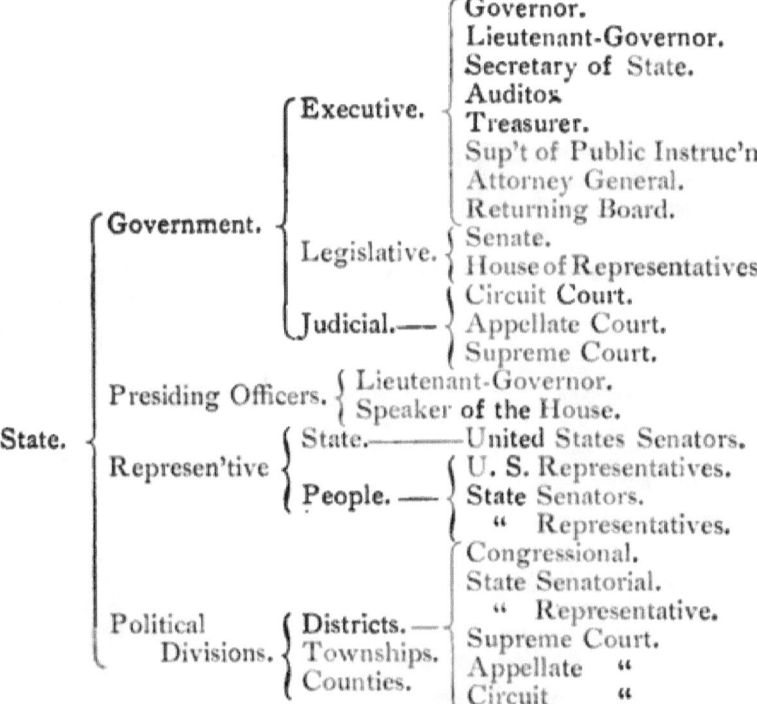

The government of the State (save United States jurisdiction)

is vested in three distinct branches—Executive, Legislative and judicial.

EXECUTIVE.

The executive department consists of a Governor, Lieutenant-Governor, Secretary of State, Auditor of Public Accounts, Treasurer, Superintendent of Public Instruction and Attorney-General, who hold office for a term of four years, save the Treasurer who can hold office but two consecutive years. They are chosen on the first Tuesday after the first Monday in November, on the day of the Presidential election, except the Superintendent of Public Instruction who is elected two years later on the same day, at which time a new Treasurer is also elected.

The Governor executes the laws of the State, sends a message to each Legislature, giving the condition of the State and recommending new laws or the repeal of old ones; has power to veto or sign bills, to reprieve criminals condemned to death, to stay sentences and to pardon those in penitentiary. He is Commander-in-Chief of the State militia while within her jurisdiction, and appoints, by approval of the Senate, certain State officers. Salary, $6,000 a year. NOTE.—A bill may become a law without the Governor's signature by a vote of two-thirds of both houses or by his keeping the bill in his possession over ten days.

The Lieutenant-Governor presides over the Senate and takes the place of Governor should his office become vacant, the President of the Senate pro tem. then takes the place of the Lieutenat-Governor.

The Secretary of State calls the House of Representatives to order and presides until a Speaker pro tem. is chosen; keeps the public laws, cares for the capitol property, State seal, etc. Salary, $3,500 per year.

The Auditor keeps an account of all indebtedness of or to the State, sees that insurance companies abide by the laws, computes the rate of taxation, etc. Salary, $3,500 a year.

The Treasurer receives and safely keeps all money belonging to the State and pays none out without an order from the Auditor. Salary, $3,500 a year.

Superintendent of Public Instruction renders decision on school laws, consults the best educational interests of the State, and properly disposes of all school money coming into his possession. Salary, $3,500 per year.

The Attorney-General acts as attorney for the people or State in suits before the Supreme Court, and for State officials in suits relating to their duties; is also Constitutional adviser.

The Returning Board consists of the Secretary of State, Auditor, Treasurer and Attorney-General who count the votes of general elections as returned to them by County Clerks.

Officers Appointed by the Governor and confirmed by the Senate:

Three Canal Commissioners, to see to navigation of rivers and canals; salary, $5 a day;

Five Commissioners of Public Charities, to see to asylums and homes—no pay save expenses;

Nineteen Justices of the Peace, for Chicago; salary, fees;

Three Penitentiary Commissioners, to see to penitentiaries, appoint wardens, physicians and chaplains; salary, $1,500.

The seven members of the State Board of Health, to prevent the spread of contagious disease if possible, etc. Entire salary for this board must not exceed $5,000 a year.

Three Railway and Warehouse Commissioners, to see that railways and warehouses are conducted in the best interests of the people; salary, $3,500 a year;

One Grain Inspector, for warehouses; salary, $1,500;

Three Trustees, for each of the charitable institutions; no pay;

Two Officers, one at the stock yards at East St. Louis and one at Chicago, to prevent cruelty to animals; salary, $1,500.

Officers appointed by the Governor without being confirmed, are Commissioners of Deeds, Notary Publics, Printer Expert, Public Administrators, Adjutant Generals and all commissioned officers of the State Militia.

LEGISLATIVE.

The Legislature convenes once in two years, unless called in special session by the Governor, on Wednesday after the first Monday in January of years whose numbers are even, and in the capitol at Springfield. It is composed of a Senate and a House of Representatives. It is the duty of this body to levy taxes, make appropriations and enact laws for the welfare of the State; to impeach State officers, and to elect United States Senators.

The Senate is composed of fifty-one Senators, elected from the fifty-one districts, chosen for a term of four years and is presided over by the Lieutenant-Governor, or otherwise by the President pro tempore. Salary, $5 per day and 10 cents mileage; also $50 an assembly for stamps, paper, etc.

The House of Representatives is composed of 153 members (three members from each of the fifty-one Senatorial districts) elected for two years, and is presided over by a Speaker elected from and by their number on convening. Salary, the same as Senators.

JUDICIAL.

The Judicial department of Illinois judges of the Constitutionality of her laws and applies them. It is composed of Circuit, Appellate and Supreme courts.

A Circuit Court is the next higher than a County Court. Illinois is divided into fourteen circuits, each one of which has three Judges elected for a term of four years, and whose salary is $3,500, except in Cook County where it is $7,000. This court has jurisdiction over criminal cases and also tries civil cases between citizens.

An Appellate Court is higher than the Circuit, and is divided into four districts. Each district has three Judges appointed by the Supreme Court from the Circuit Judges, who receive the same salary as the latter. Each district has a Clerk elected for six years. Nearly all cases except criminal may be appealed from a Circuit Court to the Appellate, and its decisions are final on sums less than $1,000.

The Supreme Court has jurisdiction over civil cases involving $1,000 or more, and criminal cases as to appeal. Their decisions are final, save where Illinois law conflicts with that of the United States. Illinois is composed of three districts for holding court, and is presided over by seven Judges, who receive $5,000 a year.

ILLINOIS IN CONGRESS.

United States Senators are chosen by the Legislature, and serve for six years with an annual salary of $5,000 and mileage fee.

Representatives of Illinois in Congress number twenty, and serve a term of two years with a salary the same as Senators. Through these delegates the people of Illinois are on an equality with the people of this entire Republic, and through our Senators Illinois may voice her desired equality with this union of States.

TOWNSHIP.

When the Northwest Territory was surveyed it was laid out in plats six miles square called townships, by which land is located. The township is not used for political purposes save for certain school officers.

The center of population has been gradually making its way Westward since the first census was taken in 1790. It will reach the southern portion of Illinois between 1900 and 1910, where it will probably forever remain.

STATISTICS.

ILLINOIS IN CONGRESS.

The Government of the United States is vested in a President, a Congress and a Judiciary. The former is chosen by the people who vote for electors that cast their ballots for the candidate for which they were chosen. Each State is entitled to as many Electoral votes as there are Representatives and Senators in Congress, Illinois thus being allowed twenty-two. Of the Judiciary there is one Chief Justice and eight Associate Justices, who hold office during good behavior. The Congress is made up of Senators and Representatives.

While Illinois was yet a Territory her wishes were represented by the following

TERRITORIAL DELEGATES:

Shadrach Bond, d Kaskaskia.......................1811–14
Benjamin Stephens, d Edwardsville................. 1817
Nathaniel Pope, d Kaskaskia....................... 1818

SENATORS.

For list of United States Senators see heads of administrations.

REPRESENTATIVES.

When Illinois was admitted into the Union, and until in 1833 (after the census of 1830) it was allowed but one Representative in Congress. Following are the Representatives that have served to date, their place of residence, politics, districts represented and date of service. (For counties that constituted the several districts from time to time see " Table of Counties " following list.)

d Democrat.   † Elected to U. S. Senate.
w Whig.   ‡ Chosen Minister to France.
r Republican.   ‖ Seat contested or del'd vacant.
g Greenbacker.   ¶ Resigned.
* Died in office.   § Joined the army.

1818—1833.

John McLean, d Shawneetown.....................1818–20
Daniel P. Cook, d Kaskaskia....................... 1827
Joseph Duncan, d Jacksonville..................... 1833

1833—1843.

1st dst.—Charles Slade,* d Belleville............. 1833
           John Reynolds, d   "   1837
           Adam W. Snyder, d   "   1839
           John Reynolds, d   "   .... ♦ 1843
2d dst.—Zadok Casey, d Mt. Vernon 1833–43
3d dst.—Joseph Duncan, d Jacksonville............. 1833–34
           W. L. May, d Springfield 1839
           John T. Stuart, w Springfield 1843

1843—1853.

1st dst.—Robert Smith, d Alton.................. 1843–49
           William H. Bissell, d Belleville............ 1853
2d dst.—John A. McClernand, d Shawneetown..... 1843–51
           Willis Allen, d Marion.................. 1853
3d dst.—O. B. Ficklin, d Charleston............. 1843–49
           T. R. Young, d Marion................. 1851
           O. B. Ficklin, d Charleston............. 1853
4th dst.—John Wentworth, d Chicago............ 1843–51
           Richard S. Maloney, d Belvidere 1853
5th dst.—Stephen A. Douglas,† d Quincy......... 1843–47
           William A. Richardson, d Rushville...... 1853
6th dst.—Joseph P. Hoge, d Galena.............. 1843–47
           Thomas J. Turner, d Freeport.......... 1849
           Edward D. Baker, w Springfield........ 1851
           Thompson Campbell, d Galena.......... 1853
7th dst.—John J. Hardin, w Jacksonville......... 1843–45
           Edward D. Baker,† w Springfield........ 1846
           John Henry, w Jacksonville............ 1847
           Abraham Lincoln, w Springfield........ 1849
           Thomas L. Harris, d Petersburg......... 1851
           Richard Yates, w Jacksonville.......... 1853

1853—1863.

1st dst.—Elihue B. Washburne, w Galena......... 1853–63
2d dst.—John Wentworth, d Chicago............ 1853–55
           Jas. H. Woodworth, d   "   1857
           Jno. F. Farnsworth, r   "   1861
           Isaac N. Arnold,   r   "   1863
3d dst.—Jesse O. Norton, r Joliet.............. 1853–57
           Owen Lovejoy, r Princeton............. 1863
4th dst.—James Knox, r Knoxville.............. 1853–57
           William Kellogg, r Canton............. 1863
5th dst.—William A. Richardson, d Rushville...... 1853–56
           Jacob C. Davis, d ———— 1857
           Isaac N. Morris, d Quincy............. 1861
           William A. Richardson,† d Rushville..... 1863

6th dst.—Richard Yates, w Jacksonville........... 1853–55
　　　　Thomas L. Harris,* d Petersburg........ 1859
　　　　Charles D. Hodges, d Carrollton......... 1859
　　　　John A. McClernand, d Springfield....... 1861
　　　　A. L. Knapp, d Jerseyville.............. 1863
7th dst.—James C. Allen, d Palestine............. 1853–57
　　　　Aaron Shaw, d Lawrenceville........... 1859
　　　　James C. Robinson, d Marshall.......... 1863
8th dst.—Lyman Trumbull, d Belleville............. 1853–55
　　　　J. L. D. Morrison, d　　"　........... 1857
　　　　Robert Smith, d Alton.................. 1859
　　　　Philip B. Fouke, d Belleville.......... 1863
9th dst.—Willis Allen, d Marion.................. 1853–55
　　　　Samuel S. Marshall, d McLeanboro....... 1859
　　　　John A. Logan, d Benton.............. 1861
　　　　William J. Allen, d Marion............. 1863

1863—1873.

1st dst.—Isaac N. Arnold, r Chicago............. 1863–65
　　　　John Wentworth, r　　"　........... 1867
　　　　Norman B. Judd, r　　"　........... 1871
　　　　Charles B. Farwell, r　　"　........... 1873
2d dst.—Jno. F. Farnsworth, r　　"　........... 1863–73
3d dst.—Elihue B. Washburne,‡ r Galena......... 1863–69
　　　　Horatio C. Burchard, r Freeport......... 1873
4th dst.—Charles M. Harris, d Oquawka.......... 1863–65
　　　　Abner C. Harding, r Monmouth......... 1869
　　　　John B. Hawley, r Rock Island......... 1873
5th dst.—Owen Lovejoy,* r Princeton............. 1863–64
　　　　Eben C. Ingersoll, r Peoria............. 1871
　　　　B. N. Stewart, d Princeton.............. 1873
6th dst.—Jesse O. Norton, r Joliet................ 1863–65
　　　　Burton C. Cook, r Ottawa.............. 1871
　　　　Henry Stapp, r Joliet.................. 1873
7th dst.—John R. Eden, d Sullivan................ 1863–65
　　　　H. P. H. Bromwell, r Charleston........ 1869
　　　　Jesse H. Moore, r Decatur.............. 1873
8th dst.—John T. Stuart, (?) Springfield.......... 1863–65
　　　　Shelby M. Cullom, r　　"　........... 1871
　　　　James C. Robinson, d　　"　........... 1873
9th dst.—Lewis W. Ross, d Lewiston............. 1863–69
　　　　T. W. McNeely, d Petersburg.......... 1873
10th dst.—A. L. Knapp, d Jerseyville............. 1863–65
　　　　Anthony Thornton, d Shelbyville....... 1867
　　　　Albert G. Burr, d Carrollton.......... 1871
　　　　Edward Y. Rice, d Hillsboro........... 1873

11th dst.—Robert Knapp, d Jerseyville............ 1873-75
   Scott Wike, d Pittsfield................. 1877
   Robert Knapp, d Jerseyville 1879
   James W. Singleton, d Quincy.......... 1883
12th dst.—James Robinson, d Springfield.......... 1873-75
   William M. Springer, d Springfield...... 1883
13th dst.—John McNulta, r Bloomington....... 1873-75
   Adlai E. Stephenson, d " 1877
   John F. Tipton, r   " 1879
   Adlai E. Stephenson, d " 1881
   D. C. Smith, r Pekin................... 1883
14th dst.—Joseph G. Cannon, r Danville.......... 1873-83
15th dst.—John R. Eden, d Sullivan............. 1873-79
   Albert P. Forsythe d, Isabel............. 1881
   Samuel W. Moulton, r Shelbyville....... 1883
16th dst.—James S. Martin, r Salem............... 1873-75
   William A. J. Sparks, d Carlysle......... 1883
17th dst.—William R. Morrison, d Waterloo........ 1873-83
18th dst.—Isaac Clements, r Carbondale........... 1873-75
   William Hartzell, d Chester............ 1879
   John R. Thomas, r Metropolis.......... 1883
19th dst.—Samuel S. Marshall, d McLeansboro..... 1873-75
   William B. Anderson, d Mt. Vernon..... 1877
   R. W. Townsend, d Shawneetown...... 1883

1883—1885.

1st district. R. W. Dunham, r.....................Chicago.
2d " Frank Lawler, d......................Chicago.
3d " James H. Ward, d.....................Chicago.
4th " George E. Adams, r...................Chicago.
5th " Reuben Elwood, r...................Sycamore.
6th " Robert R. Hitt, r...................Mt. Morris.
7th " T. J. Henderson, r...................Princeton.
8th " Ralph Plumb, r......................Streator.
9th " Lewis E. Payson, r...................Pontiac.
10th " N. E. Worthington, d..................Peoria.
11th " Alexander P. Petrie, r.........New Windsor.
12th " James Riggs, d....................Winchester.
13th " William M. Springer, d...........Springfield.
14th " J. H. Rowell, r..................Bloomington.
15th " Joseph G. Cannon, r................Danville.
16th " Silas Z. Landis, d...................Fairfield.
17th " John R. Eden, d.....................Sullivan.
18th " William R. Morrison, d..............Waterloo.
19th " R. W. Townsend, d.............Shawneetown.
20th " John R. Thomas, r...............Metropolis.

TABLE OF COUNTIES.

Counties.	When organized.	Congressional dsts. 1833-43	1843-53	1853-63	1863-73	1873-83	1883-93	Population.
Saint Clair	1809	1	1	8	12	17	18	59,229
Randolph	1809	1	1	8	12	18	20	24,392
Johnson	1812	1	2	9	13	18	20	12,949
Gallatin	1812	1	2	9	13	19	19	12,179
Madison	1812	1	1	8	12	17	18	47,422
Edwards	1814	2	2	9	13	19	16	8,514
White	1815	2	2	9	13	19	19	22,552
Crawford	1816	2	3	7	11	15	16	16,160
Jackson	1816	1	1	9	13	18	20	20,976
Monroe	1816	1	1	8	12	17	18	13,626
Pope	1816	1	2	9	13	18	20	12,652
Bond	1817	1	1	8	10	16	18	14,541
Franklin	1818	1	2	9	11	19	19	16,099
Union	1818	1	1	9	13	18	20	17,830
Washington	1818	1	1	8	12	16	18	20,900
Alexander	1819	1	1	9	13	18	20	10,239
Clarke	1819	2	3	7	11	15	16	21,843
Jefferson	1819	2	2	8	11	19	19	20,590
Wayne	1819	2	2	9	11	19	16	21,275
Fayette	1821	2	3	7	11	16	17	23,201
Green	1821	3	5	6	10	11	12	22,914
Hamilton	1821	2	2	9	11	19	19	16,669
Lawrence	1821	2	3	7	11	15	16	13,344
Montgomery	1821	2	3	6	10	16	17	27,911
Pike	1821	3	5	5	9	11	12	33,450
Sangamon	1821	3	7	6	8	12	13	51,071
Edgar	1823	2	3	7	7	15	15	25,316
Fulton	1823	3	5	4	9	9	10	41,170
Marion	1823	2	2	8	11	16	19	23,384
Morgan	1823	3	7	6	10	12	13	30,578
Clay	1824	2	3	7	11	16	16	16,107
Clinton	1824	1	1	8	12	16	19	18,361
Wabash	1824	2	2	9	13	19	16	9,891
Calhoun	1825	3	5	5	10	11	12	7,466
Hancock	1825	3	6	5	4	10	11	35,175
Henry	1825	3	6	4	5	6	7	36,465
Knox	1825	3	6	4	5	9	10	37,367
Mercer	1825	3	6	4	4	10	11	19,465
Schuyler	1825	3	5	5	9	10	11	16,160

TABLE OF COUNTIES.—Continued.

Counties.	When organized.	Congressional dsts.						Population.
		1833-43	1843-53	1853-63	1863-73	1873-83	1883-93	
Putnam	1825	3	7	3	5	6	7	5,510
Warren	1825	3	6	4	4	10	11	22,642
McDonough	1826	3	6	5	9	10	11	27,825
Vermillion	1826	2	4	3	7	14	15	41,384
Jo Daviess	1827	3	6	1	3	5	6	27,465
Perry	1827	1	1	9	13	18	20	15,230
Shelby	1827	2	3	6	10	15	17	30,194
Tazewell	1827	3	7	4	4	13	13	29,571
Adams	1829	3	5	5	7	11	12	57,247
Macon	1829	3	3	7	8	14	14	30,308
Macoupin	1829	1	5	6	10	17	17	37,258
Peoria	1829	3	5	4	5	9	10	54,831
Coles	1830	2	3	7	7	14	15	26,765
McLean	1830	3	4	3	8	13	14	59,409
Cook	1831	3	4	2	1	*	*	600,362
Effingham	1831	2	3	7	11	15	17	18,895
Jasper	1831	2	3	7	11	15	16	14,467
La Salle	1831	3	4	3	6	7	8	70,309
Rock Island	1831	3	6	2	4	6	11	37,764
Champaign	1833	2	4	3	7	14	15	40,397
Iroquois	1833	2	4	3	7	8	9	35,203
Boone	1835	3	4	1	2	4	5	11,460
Kane	1836	"	4	2	2	4	5	44,387
McHenry	1836	"	4	1	2	4	5	24,857
Ogle	1836	"	6	1	3	5	6	29,829
Whiteside	1836	"	6	2	3	5	7	30,807
Will	1836	"	4	3	6	7	8	52,719
Winnebago	1836	"	6	1	2	4	6	30,351
Bureau	1837	"	4	3	5	6	7	33,016
Cass	1837	"	7	6	9	12	12	14,487
De Kalb	1837	"	4	2	2	4	5	26,675
Livingston	1837	"	4	3	8	8	9	38,150
Stephenson	1837	"	6	1	3	5	6	31,940
Brown	1839	"	5	5	9	11	12	12,982
Carroll	1839	"	6	1	3	5	6	16,950
Christian	1839	"	3	6	10	12	13	28,100
De Witt	1839	"	3	3	8	13	14	16,897
Du Page	1839	"	4	2	6	1	8	19,101
Hardin	1839	1	2	9	13	19	19	5,860

Counties.—Concluded.	When organized.	Congressional dsts.						Popula-tion.
		1833–43	1843–53	1853–63	1863–73	1873–83	1883–93	
Lake.....................	1839	3	4	1	2	3	5	21,215
Lee......................	1839	3	6	2	3	6	7	27,427
Logan	1839	3	7	7	8	13	14	24,681
Jersey...................	1839	3	5	6	10	11	12	15,210
Marshal	1839	3	7	4	5	8	9	15,018
Menard	1839	3	7	6	9	12	13	12,970
Scott....................	1839	3	7	6	10	12	12	10,710
Stark	1839	3	6	4	5	9	10	11,203
Williamson	1839	1	2	9	13	18	20	19,071
Grundy	1841	.	4	3	6	7	8	16,604
Henderson	1841	.	6	5	4	10	11	10,710
Kendall	1841	.	4	3	6	7	8	13,008
Mason	1841	.	7	4	9	13	13	16,018
Piatt....................	1841	.	3	7	7	14	14	15,550
Richland	1841	.	3	7	11	9	16	15,509
Woodford	1841	.	7	4	8	18	9	21,535
Cumberland	1843	.	3	7	7	15	16	13,757
Massac	1843	.	2	9	13	18	20	8,740
Moultrie................	1843	.	3	7	7	15	17	13,679
Pulaski..................	1843	.	1	9	13	18	20	6,237
Saline...................	1847	.	.	9	13	19	19	15,357
Kankakee	1851	.	.	.	6	8	9	24,971
Douglas	1857	.	.	.	7	14	15	15,743
Ford....................	1859	.	.	.	7	8	9	14,989

* 1873–83 Cook contained the 1, 2, 3; 1883, 1, 2, 3, 4.

POPULATION OF LARGEST CITIES.

City.	1880	1870	1860
Chicago	503,185	298,977	112,172
Peoria...................	29,252	22,849	14,045
Quincy	27,268	24,052	13,718
Springfield..............	19,743	17,364	9,320
Bloomington	17,180	14,590	7,675
Rockford	13,193	11,049	6,979
Aurora	11,875	11,152	6,011
Rock Island..............	11,659	7,890	5,130
Joliet....................	11,657	7,263	7,102
Galesburg................	11,437	10,158	4,953
Jacksonville	10,927	9,203	5,528
Belleville	10,683	8,146	7,520
Decatur	9,547	7,161	3,839

ILLINOIS PRESIDENTIAL VOTE.—1836-1884.

1836.
Martin Van Buren, d.. 17,275
William H. Harrison, w 14,292
1840.
William H. Harrison, w 45,537
Martin Van Buren, d.. 47,476
1844.
James K. Polk, d..... 57,920
Henry Clay, w....... 45,528
——— Birney......... 3,570
1848.
Zachary Taylor, w.... 53,047
Lewis Cass, d........ 56,300
Martin Van Buren, f s. 15,774
1852.
Franklin Pierce, d.... 80,597
Winfield Scott, w..... 64,934
——— Hale, f s....... 9,966
1856.
James Buchanan, d.... 105,348
John C. Fremont, r.... 96,189
Millard Filmore, am.. 37,444
1860.
Abraham Lincoln, r...172,161
Stephen A. Douglas, d.160,215

J. C. Breckinridge, d.. 2,404
John Bell, n......... 4,913
1864.
Abraham Lincoln, r...189,496
Geo. B. McClellan, d..158,730
1868.
Ulysses S. Grant, r....250,293
Horatio Seymour, d...199,143
1872.
Ulysses S. Grant, r....241,944
Horace Greeley, l r...184,938
1876.
Rutherford B. Hayes, r 278,232
Sam'l J. Tilden, d.....258,601
Peter Cooper, g...... 17,233
1880.
James A. Garfield, r..308,037
W. S. Hancock, d.....277,321
——— Weaver, g..... 26,358
——— Dow, p........ 443
1884.
Grover Cleveland, d...312,584
James G. Blaine, r....337,411
John P. St. John, p.... 12,005
Benj. F. Butler, i..... 10,849

d, Democrat; w, Whig; f s, Free Soil; r, Republican; am, American; n, National; l r, Liberal Republican; g, Greenbacker; p, Prohibitionist.

TABLE OF POPULATION.

Age.	Males.	Females.	Age.	Males.	Females.
0 to 5 yrs.	211,103	205,211	55 to 60 yrs.	41,175	34,643
5 " 10 "	197,289	194,953	60 " 65 "	33,090	27,592
10 " 15 "	183,610	179,341	65 " 70 "	21,024	18,447
15 " 20 "	163,310	165,827	70 " 75 "	12,915	11,835
20 " 25 "	164,582	156,439	75 " 80 "	6,893	6,625
25 " 30 "	129,832	116,204	80 " 85 "	3,044	3,172
30 " 35 "	108,720	97,327	85 " 90 "	893	1,034
35 " 40 "	97,739	88,233	90 " 95 "	213	263
40 " 45 "	81,039	73,032	95 " 100 "	60	81
45 " 50 "	66,927	60,520	100 & over	20	40
50 " 55 "	63,045	50,529			

PEOPLE PER SQUARE MILE.

Rhode Island	254.81	W. Virginia	25.09
Massachusetts	221.78	Alabama	14.50
New Jersey	151.73	Mississippi	24.42
Connecticut	128.52	Wisconsin	24.16
New York	106.74	Maine	21.71
Pennsylvania	95.21	Louisiana	20.69
Maryland	94.82	Arkansas	15.13
Ohio	75.46	Kansas	12.19
Delaware	74.80	Minnesota	9.86
Indiana	55.09	Texas	6.07
Illinois	54.96	Nebraska	5.94
Kentucky	41.22	California	5.54
N. Hampshire	38.53	Florida	4.97
Virginia	37.70	Colorado	1.87
Tennessee	36.94	Oregon	1.85
Vermont	36.38	Utah T	1.75
S. Carolina	33.00	Washington T	1.12
Missouri	31.55	New Mexico T	0.98
Iowa	29.29	Dakota T	0.92
N. Carolina	28.81	Nevada	0.57
Michigan	28.50	Idaho T	0.39
Georgia	26.15	Arizona T	0.36

SCHOOLS—1884.   COUNTIES.—1820.

Males of school age	532,066	Gallatin (Pop.)	3,155
Females of school age	514,871	White	4,828
Males enrolled	365,512	Edwards	3,444
Females enrolled	351,453	Franklin	1,763
Children of school age	1,046,937	Washington	1,517
Children enrolled	716,935	Bond	2,931
Average daily attendance	459,156	Alexander	626
Number of districts	11,491	Jackson	1,542
Stone school houses	211	Randolph	3,492
Brick school houses	1,295	St. Clair	5,253
Frame school houses	10,091	Madison	13,550
Log school houses	379	Union	2,362
Graded schools	1,166	Wayne	1,114
Ungraded schools	10,814	Jefferson	691
Private schools	731	Monroe	1,537
Male teachers	6,885	Crawford	3,022
Female teachers	12,896	Clark	931
Average salary for males	$49.00	Pope	2,610
Average salary for females	38.99	Johnson	843

NATIVITY STATISTICS.—1880.

Following are statistics showing the greatest influx of population from one State to another in which Illinois is directly interested. Native State in SMALL CAPS; residence State with statistics. (Ex. 102,820 people living in Iowa in 1880 were born in ILLINOIS.)

ILLINOIS.
Iowa 102,820
Kansas ....,...... 106,992
Missouri 103,290

INDIANA.
Illinois.............. 91,388
Kansas 77,096
Missouri 60,094
Iowa 59,278

NEW YORK.
Michigan 229,657
Illinois.............120,199
Pennsylvania 100,490
New Jersey........ 94,692
Wisconsin.......... 86,588
Iowa 82,690
Ohio 64,138

KENTUCKY.
Missouri 102,799
Indiana 73,928
Illinois............. 61,920

PENNSYLVANIA.
Ohio 138,163
Illinois............. 89,467
Iowa 77,357
Kansas 59,236
New York 56,155

OHIO.
Indiana............ 186,391
Illinois.............136,884
Iowa 120,495
Kansas 93,396
Missouri 78,938
Michigan 77,053

The ratio population of Illinois contains 23 foreign-born citizens to 100 native-born. The greatest number of foreigners are in Nevada, where there are 70 to 100; Arizona, 65; Dakota, 62; Minnesota, 52; California, 51, and Missouri, 44. In North Carolina, Georgia, Alabama, South Carolina, Mississippi and Virginia there is less than 1 to 100 native-born.

COMPARATIVE POPULATION.

Year.	Illinois.		United States,	
	Pop.	Gain.	Pop.	Gain.
1820.............	55,162	350.3	9,633,822	33.0
1830.............	157,445	185.4	12,866,020	33.5
1840.............	496,183	215.1	17,069,453	31.8
1850.............	851,470	71.5	23,191,877	35.8
1860.............	1,711,951	100.9	31,443,321	31.1
1870.............	2,539,891	48.3	38,558,371	22.3
1880.............	3,077,871	17.3	50,155,783	55.1

PUBLIC INSTITUTION DIRECTORY.

STATE.

Northern Insane Hospital, at Elgin.
Eastern Insane Hospital, at Kankakee.
Central Insane Hospital, at Jacksonville.
Southern Insane Hospital, at Anna.
Institution for the Deaf and Dumb, at Jacksonville.
Institution for the Blind, at Jacksonville.
Asylum for Feeble-Minded Children, at Lincoln.
Soldiers' Orphans' Home, at Normal.
State Reform School, at Pontiac.
Charitable Eye and Ear Infirmary, at Chicago.
Soldiers' and Sailors' Home, at Quincy.
Illinois Soldiers' College, at Freeport.
Northern State Normal, at Normal.
Southern State Normal, at Carbondale.
Illinois Industrial University, at Champaign.
Northern State Penitentiary, at Joliet.
Southern State Penitentiary, at Chester.

COLLEGES NOT SUPPORTED BY THE STATE.

Shurtleff College, at Alton.
Northwestern University, at Evanston.
Knox College, at Galesburg.
Lombard University, at Galesburg.
Illinois College, at Jacksonville.
Monmouth College, at Monmouth.
University of Chicago, at Chicago.
Wheaton College, at Wheaton.
Lincoln University, at Lincoln.
Mount Carroll Female Seminary, at Mount Carroll.
Monticello Female Seminary, at Godfrey.
Almira Female College, at Greenville.
Illinois Wesleyan University, at Bloomington.
Rockford Female Seminary, at Rockford.
Quincy College, at Quincy.
Peoria County Normal, at Peoria.
Cook County Normal, at Englewood.
McKindree College, at Lebanon.
Blackburn University, at Carlinville.
Methodist Female College, at Jacksonville.
Presbyterian Female College, at Jacksoville.
Hedding College, at Abingdon.
Abingdon College, at Abingdon.
Eureka College, at Eureka.
Westfield College, at Westfield.

FOREIGNERS.	ILLITERACY.
Nativity, number in Illinois and rank with other States.	(Ten years of age and over.)
	Whites 123,624
Germany 235,786 2	Colored............ 9,950
Ireland 117,043 4	Native............. 90,595
Scandinavia 65,414 3	Foreign............ 42,989
England 60,012 3	Total.............. 133,574

CIVIL SERVICE SALARIES FOR ILLINOIS.

PENSION AGENTS.

Chicago $4,000

CUSTOM SERVICE.—CHICAGO.

Collector	$7,000	Clerk	$1,700
Deputy Collector	3,000	Deputy Collector	1,600
Appraiser...........	3,000	Assistant Entry cl'k..	1,600
Auditor	2,200	2 Clerks...........	1,600
2 Deputy Collectors .	2,200	2 "	1,500
Cashier............	2,200	Weigher	1,500
Clerk	2,200	2 Clerks	1,400
Examiner...........	2,000	Assistant Cashier	1,400
"	1,800	5 Clerks	1,200
Deputy Collector	1,800	2 "	1,000
Assistant Auditor	1,800	49 Assistants (day) $2 to $4	
Entry Clerk	1,800	Surgeon—Cairo	800

REVENUE COLLECTORS.

Chicago	$4,500	Champaign	$2,125
Aurora	2,875	Springfield..........	4,500
Sterling	2,500	Cairo	3,250
Quincy	3,500	Deputy Collectors — to	2,000
Peora	4,500	Clerks......... — to	1,800

UNITED STATES SUB-TREASURY.—CHICAGO.

Assistant Treasurer...	$4,500	Bookkeeper	$1,500
Cashier.............	2,500	Assistant Bookkeeper.	1,200
Paying Teller.......	1,800	Clerks.............	1,200
Receiving Teller.....	1,500	Messenger	840
Clerk—coins, etc.....	1,500	3 Watchmen........	720

STEAMBOAT INSPECTORS.

CHICAGO.		GALENA.	
Inspector of Hulls....	$2,000	Inspector of Hulls....	$2,000
" " Boilers ..	2,000	" " Boilers ..	1,600
Clerk	1,000		

CIVIL SERVICE SALARIES.—Continued.

LIGHT-HOUSE KEEPERS.

Calumet	$540	Gross Point	$675
1 Chicago	700	" "	500
2 "	500	" "	400
Waukegan	540		

UNITED STATES CIRCUIT AND DISTRICT COURTS.

Northern District 7th Circuit.		Southern District S. Circuit.	
Circuit Judge	6,000	Circuit Judge	$6,000
District "	4,000	District "	4,000
" Atatorney fees &	200	" Attorney fees &	200
Assistant Dst. Attorney	2,200	Assistant Dst. Attorney	1,500
" " "	1,500	Marshal	fees
Marshal ...... fees &	200	Clerks	fees
Clerks	fees	U. S. Commissioners	fees
U. S. Commissioner	fees		

SALARIED POSTOFFICES.

Chicago	$4,000	Canton	$2,200
Rockford	3,100	Geneseo	2,200
Bloomington	3,000	Lincoln	2,200
Peoria	3,000	Mattoon	2,200
Quincy	3,000	Paris	2,200
Springfield	3,000	Sterling	2,200
Galesburg	2,900	Belleville	2,100
Danville	2,800	Belvidere	2,100
Elgin	2,800	Cairo	2,100
Decatur	2,600	Dixon	2,100
La Salle	2,600	Monmouth	2,100
Streator	2,600	Morrison	2,100
Freeport	2,500	Sycamore	2,100
Jacksonville	2,500	Waukegan	2,100
Joliet	2,500	Carlinville	2,000
Moline	2,500	Galena	2,000
Rock Island	2,500	Morris	2,000
Ottawa	2,400	Pekin	2,000
Aurora	2,300	Princeton	2,000
Alton	2,200	Shelbyville	2,000

(Less than $2,000 a year.)

$1,900.—Batavia, Centralia, Champaign, East St. Louis, Englewood, Evanston, Jerseyville, Kankakee, Mendota, Mount Carroll, Pana.

$1,800.—Amboy, Charleston, Galva, Henry, Kawanee, Litchfield, Petersburg, Polo, Pontiac, Urbana.

POSTOFFICE SALARIES.—CONCLUDED.

$1,700.—Beardstown, Braidwood, Bushnell, **Carrollton,** Carthage, Clinton, Effingham, Fairbury, Hillsborough, Hyde Park, Lanark, Lockport, Normal, Olney, Paxton, Pittsfield, Sandwich, South Chicago, Taylorville, Warsaw, Woodstock.

$1,600.—Arcola, Carbondale, Carmi, De Kalb, **Du Quoin,** Dwight, Greenville, Havana, Marengo, Marshall, Mt. **Vernon,** Oak Park, **Peru,** Rochelle, Tuscola, Vandalia, Watseka, Wilmington.

$1,500.—Aleda, Chester, Delavan, **Edwardsville, El Paso,** Hoopeston, Knoxville, Lena, Macomb, **Marseilles, Mason City,** Minonk, Naperville, National **Stock Yards, Virginia, Wheaton,** White Hall.

$1,400.—Abingdon, Atlanta, Cambridge, Harvard, Lacon, Lewiston, Maywood, Monticello, Mt. Morris, Mt. Pulaski, Murphysborough, Nokomis, Oregon, Rock Falls, Rushville, Sparta, Virden, Warren.

$1,300.—Anna, Bunker Hill, Farmer City, **Flora, Geneva,** Gibson City, Mt. **Sterling,** Nashville, Onarga, Salem, **Washington.**

$1,200,—Auburn, **Carlyle,** Chatsworth, **Chenoa, Earlville,** Elm Hurst, Elmwood, **Fairfield,** Farmington, Fulton, Griggsville, Lemont, Metropolis City, Plano, Pullman, Sawanna, Shawneetown, Waverly, Wenona, Winchester. Barry, $1,150.

$1,100.—Collinsville, Eureka, Gilman, Girard, **Highland Lake, Forest,** Melford, Newton, Odell, Pocatonica, Sheldon, **Sullivan, Toulon,** Wyoming. Forreston, $1,050.

$1,000.—Albion, Bement, Braceville, Graville, Havelock, Highland Park, Kirkwood, Lebanon, Leroy, Lexington, McLeansborough, Maroa, Momence, Morgan Park, Mt. Carmel, Palatine, Port Byron, Princeville, Robinson, Roodhouse, Rossville, St. Charles, Saybrook, South Evanston, Staunton, Upper Alton, Waterloo, Wright's **Grove.**

POSTOFFICE CLERKS (Salary, $600 to $3,400).—Chicago, 357: Quincy, 6; Peoria, 5; Springfield, 5; Bloomington, 4; Cairo, 2; Decatur, 2. Alton, Aurora, Elgin, Galena, Galesburg, Jacksonville, Joliet, Kankakee, Monmouth, Morris, Ottawa and Rock Island, each 1.

LETTER CARRIERS in cities of over 50,000 inhabitants, first year receive $600; second year, $800; third year and after, $1,000. In other cities, $600 to $850.

SUMMARY OF EVENTS.